Praise For
GOLD FEVER
Part One

"GOLD FEVER is a deftly written historical novel ... in which the author, Ken Salter, pays close attention to getting the background details right. The result is a riveting, entertaining novel from first page to last. Very highly recommended reading."
— THE MIDWEST BOOK REVIEW

"... a well-researched novel about the California Gold Rush. The author blends into his narrative the gold mining challenges faced by the men who searched for the precious mineral. ... If you are interested in understanding the history of the California Gold Rush ... you [will] enjoy this book."
— HISTORICAL NOVEL SOCIETY

"GOLD FEVER depicts in vivid detail the plight of new immigrants, women and scoundrels in the Gold Rush."
—ANNICK FOUCRIER
Professor of North American History
at the University of Paris, the Sorbonne,
and Director of the Center for
North American Research

GOLD FEVER

PART TWO

"SAN FRANCISCO" circa 1852, an engraving in
Meyer's *Universum*, 1852 *(author's collection).*

GOLD FEVER

PART TWO

SAN FRANCISCO

1851–1852

Ken Salter

REGENT PRESS
Berkeley, California
2015

[Paperback]
ISBN 13: 978-1-58790-300-7
ISBN 10: 1-58790-300-8

[E-book]
ISBN 13: 978-1-58790-301-4
ISBN 10: 1-58790-301-6

Library of Congress Control Number: 2014955491

Cover Design: Paul Veres

First Edtion

First Printing

To Order Books or for Further Information contact
REGENT PRESS
regentpress@mindspring.com

Manufactured in the U.S.A.
REGENT PRESS
www.regentpress.net

California Gold Rush Journal
∽ PART 2 ∽
TABLE OF CONTENTS

California Gold Rush Journal
∽ PART 2 ∾

LIST OF ILLUSTRATIONS

From the Author's private collection, some of which were donated to
Le Musée du Nouveau Monde in La Rochelle, France.

17. "CARRIAGE FROM THE PIROGUE AND MULE TRANSPORT IN FROM LAKE NICARAGUA," 1851.
18. "STEAMER TAKING ON COAL ON THE PACIFIC COAST," 1851.
19. "CITY OF STOCKTON," 1851.
20. "MAP OF THE SOUTHERN PLACERS," 1851.
21. "STREET SCENES IN SAN FRANCISCO — WIND AND MUD," 1850-51.
22. "DIGGER INDIANS IN NATIVE TO WESTERN ATTIRE," 1851.

California Gold Rush Journal
∞ PART 2 ∞

INTRODUCTION

Berkeley, California — January 2015

The first half of 1851 proved to be traumatic for merchants and miners alike as told in *Gold Fever Part I*. San Francisco had been torched twice in six weeks, once in May and again in June. Wood-framed, redwood houses, shops, stores, saloons, theatres, many wharves and most warehouses and gambling palaces burned quickly and thoroughly given the density of buildings cramped together on small lots. Most brick buildings were gutted as well when their wooden porticos, balconies and roofs fueled the firestorm. Lack of water and poorly-equipped and inadequately-placed fire fighting companies could not contain the infernos. San Francisco's downtown commercial center was effectively destroyed. Even City Hall, police stations, and jails were not spared.

San Francisco was at a crossroads. Merchants with gold reserves could and did rebuild immediately. Many others, without means, folded and were forced to sell their lots for tickets home. With considerable gold still arriving daily from the mines, surviving merchants made windfall profits. But the fires and lack of prosecution of arsonists, looters and robbers by corrupt and inept civil authorities left the survivors angry and determined to root out the perpetrators who had sought to destroy commerce for short term gain. While most fingers pointed to the complicity of the notorious "Sydney Ducks," former and escaped felons from Australia's penal colonies, there was little concrete proof to support allegations.

Fear that chaos would rule and rebuilding would spark even more attacks on uninsurable premises persuaded most citizens and merchants to support the Committee of Vigilance and take the lawless city into their own hands. Thus, the scene was set for a protracted conflict between feeble and often compromised civil authorities and members of the Committee of Vigilance to impose order and bring to justice the arsonists and looters who had effectively sacked the city.

With legions of new immigrants — gold seekers, women seeking rich husbands, gold-diggers, political refugees and opportunists arriving monthly, the city was poorly equipped to house them, feed them and provide non-skilled work. After the fires, the city was once again a tent city in the areas decimated by the June fire. Fortunately, most businesses destroyed in the May fire and rebuilt, were spared.

Our story begins with Pierre and Manon now married and expecting a child in these uncertain times. Fortunately, their brig, "The Eliza," docked on the Long Wharf was spared the wrath of both fires. Manon's wharf-side canteen, serving hearty soups, pâté sandwiches on fresh baguettes with a glass of wine from their wine bar, is doing a roaring business thanks to the elimination of so many competitors and the increased number of travelers taking the paddle-boat ferries from their wharf to Sacramento, Stockton and the mines.

Still, they face serious challenges in these uncertain and

dangerous times. Can Manon realize her dream to be the first woman to own and operate a quality French restaurant given male domination of all the fine eating establishments in the city? Will anti-foreign immigrant sentiment affect and limit Pierre's ability to mount successful business enterprises? Will the dearth of easy to mine placer gold along the river banks and continued influx of unskilled immigrants, political undesirables, hoodlums and prostitutes limit Pierre and Manon's ability to achieve their goals? And so their story resumes in these turbulent times.

— *Ken Salter*
Berkeley, California

California Gold Rush Journal
∽ PART 2 ∽

CHAPTER ONE

San Francisco — July 1851

A
s with the disastrous fire of May 3-4, the newly burned area of the June 22nd arson fire was now a scene of frenetic rebuilding. Though the City's administrative center was still sooty rubble, the rest of the burned area from Montgomery Street to Broadway was rife with the sound of carpenters' hammers on redwood framing and the slapping of masons' mortar on bricks as the affected commercial and residential areas quickly were resurrected anew.

Manon's catering business and accompanying wine bar were booming on the Long Wharf where our British brig, "The Eliza," was berthed. Manon's newly liberated partners, Teri and Giselle, who ran our food and liquor tables on the wharf, were largely responsible for the increase in male patronage at their stands. Both now eschewed "respectable" married woman's traditional mode of dress—high-necked dresses with petticoats and a fash-ionable bonnet to discreetly hide one's hair. Teri, whose Chil-ean boyfriend had dumped her and stolen her earnings after his liquor store burned in May, now wore her long, blond tresses loose down the back of her form-fitting Chilean peasant's dress with low-cut bodice. Giselle, more reserved, now wore a minimum of petticoats under form-fitting dresses that no longer covered her dainty shoes and boots which now gave an alluring glimpse of well-turned ankles as she served Manon's hearty soups and thick slices of home-made pâtés on freshly baked baguettes to an ever increasing male clientele. Each women now wore a flower in their loose flowing hair to signify they were no longer married or bound to an unappreciative male.

After the fire, my assistant, Georges, took the first paddle-steamer leaving for Panama and was on his way to escort his American fiancé, Nelly Swanson, to San Francisco to thwart her father's plans to marry her off to an eligible New York bachelor who could help promote the father's many business interests. He'd received a tear-stained letter from Nelly attesting to her desperate plight. Their shipboard romance on the trip to New York on the Clipper, "Flying Cloud," and Georges' departure meant I now had to find another assistant to help in my newly established private detective and notary business serving the legions of French arriving weekly and those already trying their luck in the gold fields.

I decided to head for town, scour the newspapers for the latest efforts of the Committee of Vigilance to apprehend the villains responsible for torching half the city less than six weeks after the last arson that destroyed the main commercial area and most warehouses. I also wanted to seek the advice of our friend, Pierre-Louis, proprietor of *Les Bons Amis* restaurant on Dupont Street.

The papers teemed with caustic accusations against the Sydney Ducks, who were generally blamed for the fire. The city was now effectively without police or judicial protection. City Hall, the courts and police headquarters all burned in the fire. The Committee of Vigilance was the only organized group that had the backing of the business and professional communities and the capability to arrest, incarcerate, try and execute arsonists and criminals. They were currently detaining 30-40 suspects at their armed headquarters, which had escaped the fire's wrath.

Judge Campbell sought to thwart the Committee of Vigilance by appointing a new grand jury to investigate the fire and charge criminals. The grand jury was the sole judicial body that was difficult to corrupt or bribe as its members were not randomly selected but appointed from the city's leading citizens — bankers, merchants and professionals who owned property. Ironically, several members of the new grand jury were also Committee members.

The papers were screaming for the neck of a Sydney Duck, named James Stuart, also known as "English Jim," who claimed he was Thomas Berdue. He'd been recognized by a Committee member on the street and arrested. He was wanted for the murder of Sheriff Charles Moore in Auburn, California during a robbery attempt in October, 1850. Stuart had been convicted of murder and sentenced to hang in Marysville. He escaped and fled when the rope around his neck broke. Berdue protested adamantly not to be Stuart, but the Committee sent him to Marysville to be quickly retried and hung.

"What do you think of the Stuart affair?" I asked Pierre-Louis when he joined me for an aperitif. "Do they have the right man?"

"Even if they don't, the guy's a Duck and in with the gang that torched the city and nearly got my restaurant this time. I say hang 'em all or deport 'em; enough's enough," Pierre-Louis replied with vehemence.

I explained my dilemma at the loss of my assistant, Georges. "Any ideas how I might find a replacement?" I asked.

"You could always put a help wanted ad in the French sections of the newspapers, but you'd be flooded with unqualified and desperate job seekers. Better to ask people you know and trust," he replied.

"You're right as usual. I'll try to be patient and ask around. I can't afford to make a mistake." I was thinking of the latest delivery of several sacks of mail from the French Consulate. I needed someone who could read and sort through the piles of letters addressed to the thousands of French gold seekers who couldn't read or write or were constantly on the move in search of richer diggings. Most of the letters were addressed to someone "at San Francisco" or simply "in the gold fields."

My agreement with the consulate required me to match names of emigrants with ship's manifests provided by the consulate and forward the letters to the groups of French miners working either the northern or southern placers where the consul general had sent the mostly impoverished arrivals. Georges and I had delivered letters to the northern mining camps along the north and south forks of the Yuba River. I would now need to take a similar trip to the southern placers and seek out French miners there.

Hundreds of new immigrants arrived weekly and brought even more letters from mothers, wives, fiancées and other family members desperate to know their loved one was safe and sound and hopefully getting rich. By visiting French mining camps and delivering letters, I made contacts and solicited business for my newly established notary enterprise. For those I couldn't locate, I sent a letter back to France informing the anxious relative that their loved one arrived safely in San Francisco and had been dispatched by the consulate to join other French miners. For a fee, I promised to try to locate the loved one and deliver the letter and mail a reply. Fortunately, the cost of mailing letters from California to France was only a few cents. The consulate paid me $1.00 for each letter the overwhelmed post office couldn't deliver or decipher the name of the sender or addressee.

While there was little profit in this activity, it made important contacts I hoped would translate into increased business. I calculated that my offer to locate miners and others who'd not made contact would promote my detective service with those who could afford my daily fee of $64.00 (four ounces of gold) plus expenses. I was reminded of how John Sutter abandoned his wife and kids in Switzerland in order to try his luck first in the Sandwich Islands and then the fertile lands of the Sacramento Valley. I was sure he wasn't the only scoundrel to seek his fortune in the gold fields while leaving a family and debts behind. Time would tell if my gamble paid off.

I was curious to see how the Italians in the "Little Italy" part of town that burned were making do. Manon had been impressed with the quality of the Italian *salumi* we had sampled in the *trattoria Bella Toscana* before the fire. She was considering adding Italian cold cuts and spicy sausage *panini* and pasta with cheese from Parma to her lunch menu if we could secure a reliable supply at a reasonable price. As the proprietor, Luigi Salterini, spoke French, I was determined to find him and sound him out on the idea.

As I made my way down the burned part of Dupont Street toward Broadway, I had to dodge tenacious carters hauling lumber, bricks and building supplies through the bog the street had become. Reluctant horses bellowed their displeasure at the slippery slog along the once elegant street while their carters whipped, yelled and cursed at their reticent animals. One cart full of barrels of nails and metal doors had broken an axel in a deep pot hole and now blocked half the street with its spilled load and frenzied horses. The gridlock and resulting chaos would be funny if the two carters seeking to pass the accident in opposite directions were not threatening to shoot each other for the right to pass first.

When I reached Pacific Street and the start of "Little Italy," I was surprised to see that while very little new construction was underway, lots had been cleared of burned structures and debris and were now occupied by Italian merchants selling goods from makeshift stalls — rough-planed lumber supported by barrels to make a stand for merchandise, the bed of a lumber cart, or a tent with makeshift tables and goods stacked on barrels. Each merchant had a tent to stow goods and a shotgun to defend against thieves and squatters during the night.

As I approached Broadway and the area where Luigi Salterini's trattoria once stood, I hailed a merchant selling olive oil and pasta. "*Donde posso trovare Luigi Salterini?*" I muttered in halting Italian. The merchant, a bright-eyed, bushy-haired, olive-skinned man in his forties, laughed and waved his arm to indicate down the street somewhere.

I turned left on Broadway, as I remembered when Manon and I first sought out his restaurant after visiting "Little China," with Manon disguised as an American sailor boy the day the Committee of Vigilance hanged the Sydney Duck, Jenkins, in Portsmouth Square for armed robbery. I strolled along the street pleased to hear the sing-song lyricism and beauty of the Italian language as buyers with colorful baskets haggled the price of the wares for sale.

Salterini was clapping his hands together to ward off the chill breeze now blowing down the street while he chatted animatedly with customers for his *panini*, sausages, salamis, cheeses and Italian red wines on a makeshift counter inside a large tent. I admired his friendly, sociable selling manner as his customers selected his appetizing foods and their favorite wines. For some customers he knew, he marked their purchases in a ledger for payment later, while others paid in gold dust or coin.

Once the transactions were completed and the little store emptied of customers, I made my presence known.

"I'm pleased to see you survived the fire and are still in business," I said in French and thrust out my hand to him. "Bravo!"

I added as he pumped my hand with gusto. Despite his losses, this small, full-fleshed man with rosy cheeks and bulbous nose the color of the wine he sold looked cheerful and upbeat.

"We Italians are used to hard times. That's why we left Italy for California. The Ducks aren't going to drive us out. We'll rebuild and let the Committee of Vigilance stretch their necks at the end of a rope," he said with conviction.

"I'm glad you and the rest of the community feel that way. The French merchants are of the same opinion. Will it take long to rebuild your *trattoria*?"

"Hopefully, not too long. I have two nephews who managed to strike some good gold in Mariposa. With what I've saved and their help, I can build again. The problem is we are last on the list to get materials and skilled carpenters. We are merchants, not artisans, so we must wait our turn until the Yankee gambling houses and stores are rebuilt and back in business. Until then, we sell out of our lots and keep the bad guys out."

"I'm surprised to see so much good merchandise for sale. I would have thought it would have burned with the businesses," I said pointing to his *panini* sandwiches and the heaps of sausages, salamis and other goods.

He laughed and rubbed his ample belly. "When you live and work so close to crooks and robbers, you don't leave all your eggs in one basket. We learned our lesson after the first fire and knew there would be more. We hired a ship to store our goods. My nephews and others live on the ship and guard it where it's anchored in the bay. We take off what we need or can sell each day and nothing more."

"Smart," I beamed. "That's what my wife and her associates do as well. We have our ship docked at the Long Wharf and pull up the gang plank each evening. She sells breakfast and lunch to the dock workers and travelers going to and from Sacramento on the paddle steamers that leave from the wharf.

She'd like to supplement her French offerings with some Italian dishes as well. She would like to offer Italian sausage and salami sandwiches and pasta with a marinara sauce and cheese from Parma. Is it possible to get a steady supply of these items?"

Salterini pointed to a rough stool and motioned me to sit down. From behind the counter he pulled out a half-full, corked bottle of Chianti and swiftly filled two glasses. "We're not gonna discuss business without a glass of wine and some of my best smoked sausage." From behind the counter, he pulled out a wooden cutting board and large butcher's knife and began to slice one of the sausages on his counter. That done, he popped a large slice in his mouth and washed it down with a healthy slug of wine.

"*Ah bellisimo. Que combinazione—salciccia e vino rosso, che divino, no?* Sorry, I got carried away. Please try some sausage with the wine; it's almost as good as red wine with Italian cheeses. Sadly, so many of our cheeses don't keep during the voyage through the tropics. Only the hard parmesan cheeses come through okay." He hacked off a big sliver of parmesan from a huge round and thrust it at me. "Try this with the wine," he said with big grin as he shoveled another slice of sausage into his mouth.

After sampling both the sausage and cheese with a refilled glass of wine, I beamed my appreciation. "Divine it is as you say. It's almost as good as a glass of *Gigondas* with a slice of *saucisson sec de l'Ardèche* or an aged *fromage de Salers*." I said tongue-in-cheek.

Salterini guffawed so hard he spit out his mouth full of wine and sausage despite an effort to control it. "My friend, you must be kidding. You French have very good wines and cheeses but not better than the best from Italy," he said seriously as if Italian honor was at stake.

"Let's agree that the French and Italian wines and cheeses are the best in the world," I said in a spirit of compromise. "We can drink to that, non?"

Salterini quickly topped up our glasses and we toasted both countries' wines and cheeses. "I know my wife would agree. I'd like to buy one of each you sell along with a hunk of parmesan so she can sample them for herself. Do you think you could supply the ones she prefers on a regular basis?" I asked.

"But of course, my friend. She's that cute little sailor girl you bring to my *trattoria*, yes?" I nodded yes. He took a white crayon and marked a figure on the skin of several different sausages and salamis. "I mark a special price for your *principessa*. We maybe can trade food if she has good meat and seafood for me when my restaurant is rebuilt, eh?"

I nodded my assent. "We get a weekly delivery of deer and boar meat from French hunters along with duck, quail, partridge and other game birds." I paused to let him salivate while I contemplated the effects of the red wine on his bulbous nose. "And of course she has regular deliveries of fresh shellfish for her fish stews—shrimp, oysters, clams, mussels, scallops and often tasty salmon and trout, and of course, fresh baby squid and crab when in season." Salterini's rapt attention to each item I mentioned indicated that he was clearly hooked on the prospect of fresh *calamari fritti* and pasta dishes loaded with shellfish.

While he savored the prospect of preparing Italian cuisine with our products, I opened a new subject. "You said your nephews were miners in the Mariposa area. Would they know someone familiar with that area who speaks and reads French? My assistant left for New York and I'm looking for someone who can help me in my legal business and my contract to deliver mail to French mining camps in the southern placers."

Salterini opened a new bottle of Italian red wine from Tuscany as he pondered my question, then poured more wine. "My nephew, Gino Lamberti, might be very interested. He speaks French and Spanish as well as the English he picked up here. He worked in Genoa as a shipping clerk and is good with figures.

He went often to *Nizza* where they speak Italian and French. He's not too excited to work on the ship or in my restaurant. He knows the mining camps in Calaveras, Tuolumne and Mariposa counties. He and his cousin worked with both Chilean and French miners. He might just be your man. Would you like to meet him?"

"I'd love to meet him. How soon do you think you could arrange it?"

"I can send a message to the ship this evening. Where can he meet you?"

"See if he can join me for lunch tomorrow at 1 p.m. at the French restaurant, *Les Bons Amis*; it's on Dupont Street past the plaza on the right hand side."

"He'll be there. He loves eating in restaurants and with almost all Italian restaurants destroyed, he'll jump at the chance to meet you in a restaurant." Salterini hurriedly packaged the salamis, sausages and cheese and added a couple of bottles Italian red wine and thrust it at me while motioning newly arrived clients to sample the few pieces of sausage he had not polished off with the wine. He waved off my attempt to pay. "We'll settle when your *principessa* decides what to order. Make her sample my food with our Italian red wine only," he said with a wicked grin.

The satchel he'd packed was heavy but my heart light as I headed back to our ship on the wharf. Manon would be delighted to sample Salterini's wares and know he could supply her needs. I was looking forward to our sampling session together and the lunch meeting the next day.

California Gold Rush Journal
∽ PART 2 ∾

CHAPTER TWO
San Francisco — July 1851

anon was finishing preparing a hearty fish soup loaded with chunks of local bass, mussels, clams and oysters in our ship's galley when I returned in late afternoon. "What took you so long, Big Boy? Your Manon slaves away in the kitchen while you eat Italian goodies and drink lots of red wine, yes?" She said, waving her big wooden spoon at my blushed nose and rosy cheeks and gave me that "naughty boy" look of hers. I hid Salterini's bag of salamis and other foods behind my back and threw her my best "boys will be boys" sheepish look. We both laughed.

"What are you hiding behind your back, eh? Better be something special for Manon." She said as she slowly and seductively loosened and discarded her cook's apron and released the pins in her hair. She gave me a wistful smile as she let her lustrous black tresses tumble down her shoulders and back, then crooked her finger for me to approach. As I reached out to take her in my arms, she raised her finger to say "wait." Then she pointed to her belly which now showed the presence of our child. She did a pirouette so I could embrace her from behind. I massaged her belly and whispered in her ear, "*Je t'aime.*"

"And what about your baby?" She said nuzzling my cheek with her head.

"I'll love him too, when he gets here," I whispered.

"And what if your baby is a girl, huh?"

"I'll be a jealous Papa. If she's as beautiful as you, I'll have to keep all her suitors at bay even while she's a kid. She'll be our pride and joy."

"You promise?" She said turning to kiss me.

"Yes. And if she's got your character and spunk, she'll probably be able to handle the boys on her own. So we'll just have to wait and see what we get, won't we?"

"The doctor said maybe we gonna get two babies. Lots of twins in my family. So what do you say to that, Big Boy?"

I gave her a long, lingering kiss before replying. "You really are full of surprises. How could he know so early?"

"He doesn't know. He just said it's a big possibility because of my family history," she said looking me in the eye.

"You know what the Americans say, 'two for the price of one is a better deal,' so we should consider ourselves lucky if blessed with twins."

"Our kid or kids were made with love and passion in Valparaiso and they have loving parents, and that's probably more than most kids could hope for."

Manon looked at me with tears in her eyes. "Since you gonna be such a good papa, maybe we should have triplets, non?" We both laughed.

"We can try to add another tonight, if Manon is not too tired, non?" I said mimicking her, tongue-in-cheek.

"Well let's see what's in that bag you been hiding. If Manon likes what you bring her, then maybe Big Boy earns a reward with his pregnant wife, non?"

I handed her the satchel full of Italian goodies and the two bottles of Tuscan red wine and recounted my meeting with Luigi Salterini.

"So, he wants to trade for shellfish and other food, yes?"

"I am sure he does. His eyes got bigger than yours at the mention of fresh clams, baby squid, mussels, scallops and shrimps. He was licking his lips at the thought of *calamari fritti, pasta con frutti di mare* and all the other dishes he could prepare with shellfish. He's obviously tired of eating and preparing dishes with oysters which every cook can obtain easily. He can get some shellfish with Italian fishermen, but they'll be quite expensive. So, I think he'll be pleased to work with us on a wholesale trade basis."

I told her of my plan to meet and interview Salterini's nephew for a position as my assistant. With Georges gone for several months I needed help with the letter concession and someone who could be my guide to the French mining camps in the southern placers.

Manon gave me her most devilish look. "So you gonna abandon your very pregnant wife again and gallivant around the mining camps with a young Italian Lothario, yes?"

"Your Pierre will have no time to chase the *señoritas*. He has a family to feed and if Manon's doctor is right, he'll soon have a nursery full of hungry mouths hollering for food. Let's try the salami with a glass of Italian red wine and see if your Pierre has earned his reward."

After helping Giselle and Teri set up our stands to sell Manon's soup, slices of fresh brioche, pâté of wild venison and duck sandwiches and our wines and spirits by the glass, I headed to my makeshift office at the back of a pharmacy to pick up my messages. As the morning fog over the city had not yet dissipated and had left everything clingy-damp, I bought all the daily newspapers and headed through the Clay Street side of Portsmouth Square to take refuge in Pierre-Louis' restaurant, *Les Bons Amis*. I could always count on Pierre-Louis for the latest tidbits of gossip he picked up from early morning clients, police, firemen, and merchants, some of whom were members of the notorious Committee of Vigilance.

As usual, I took a rear table where I could see all who entered. Pierre-Louis brought me a strong coffee during a lull in business.

"So, what's the latest with the Committee?" I asked.

He sat down, added water to his *pastis* and took a sip of the cloudy colored mixture before replying. "Well, one of the Committee members had coffee this morning and said there's conflicting evidence in the trial in Marysville whether the guy calling himself "Berdue" is really James Stuart. Evidently, two of the members of the court testified the Berdue character was not Stuart. They claimed he was two inches shorter and eyes were a different color."

"Does that mean he'll walk free?"

"Dunno. The prosecution claims it's got to be Stuart based on physical evidence. They say Stuart had a finger tattoo, a stiff middle finger and a scar on the right side of the jaw. All of which this "Berdue" character has. So it's pretty sure they'll convict and hang him."

"So, they think they got the right guy who killed the sheriff?"

"Dunno for sure." Pierre-Louis took a long slug from his glass before replying. "The guy's a Duck and that's enough for me to see him hang given what they've done to our town. Hanging a bunch of 'em quickly is the only message they understand. They didn't pull up stakes when they hung Jenkins, so maybe if the Committee hangs enough of them fast this time, they'll clear out for good."

While I didn't like the idea of vigilante justice, I understood Pierre-Louis' position and hatred of the Sydney Ducks and all the other hooligans that preyed the city's citizens and merchants. Manon and I were with him during both the recent arson fires and saw how close he had come both times to losing his business and life's savings. I told Pierre-Louis that I was meeting a potential employee for lunch and asked him to prepare a special shellfish lunch for us. I ordered a carafe of white wine and settled in to read the papers and enjoy a good cigar.

All the newspapers featured the sensational story about the hanging of a Mexican beauty in Downieville, a rough mining town high up on the north fork of the Yuba River in the northern placers. According to the papers, the young Mexican señorita was twenty-three, slender, with striking black hair worn in two braids and was "well set-up," according to one journalist who claimed to be present at her trial. According to all accounts, though she was vivacious and quick-tempered, she was not a whore. She lived in a cabin with her beau, a Mexican gambler.

A Scotsman named Cannon (nick-named "Loose Cannon" by one wag) got drunk and gambled at Juanita's boyfriend's table and lost. Angry, he went to the gambler's house, intruded and made a drunken scene. According to the Scotsman's confidants, he returned to the gambler's cabin the next day "to apologize" for is drunken behavior of the previous evening. According to Juanita and the boyfriend, Cannon used the word *puta* referring to Juanita and she grabbed a knife, stabbed him in the heart, killing him.

After the stabbing, she and her boyfriend both fled to a saloon in town seeking refuge. On hearing of the stabbing, an angry mob of miners seized both of them, hauled them to the town plaza to try them for murder while screaming "hang her!"

Juanita verbally defended her actions, but the mob was hell bent on hanging her. The miner who attempted to defend her was knocked off the barrel he was standing on pleading her case and beaten up. The mob chanted, "hang her, she's guilty." A local doctor, Cyrus Aiken, declared to the "trial court," made up of members of the mob, that Juanita was three months pregnant and thus by law, couldn't be hanged. The mob ordered Dr. Aiken to leave town "or else."

According to eyewitnesses, Juanita calmly accepted her fate and even put the noose over her own head, let them tie her hands and said "*adios señores*" as her executioners cut the rope and she dropped to her death. She died proud and unrepentant to the end. Her paramour was acquitted and beat it out of town as fast as his horse would carry him.

I was touched by the story of this beautiful, defiant woman. I had heard stories of miners' juries hastily trying and hanging claim jumpers, thieves and murderers at the diggings, but this case gave me cause to worry about more travel to miners' camps. If the Yankee hatred of foreigners could be quickly coalesced and focused on a beautiful, pregnant *Mexicana*, then any foreigner could suffer the same fate if the object of mob hatred in this lawless land. The journalists now referred to Downieville as "Hangtown." My musings were interrupted by the appearance of a handsome young man with a lady-killer smile.

One look confirmed Manon's claim of an Italian "Lothario." Gino Lamberti was a tall, sinewy, olive-skinned Adonis. His deceptive "baby face" with dimples and a patrician nose was encased in long black, curly hair tied in a pony tail that had a raven's glossy sheen. Unlike most Italians, Gino's eyes were dark blue. He looked to be in his late twenties or early thirties and was dressed casually in tight trousers, open-necked shirt, suede vest and Italian moccasins. Around his neck hung a gold chain and icon of his patron saint. After a brief question to the waiter, he strode confidently back to my table, threw me a charming smile and jutted out his hand. "Monsieur Dubois,

I am pleased to meet you. I'm Gino Lamberti, Luigi Salterini's nephew," he said in French with a pleasing accent.

I grasped his hand and was surprised at his steely grip. His hands were tough and hardened by physical labor which I deemed a good sign. "Pleased to meet you Gino. Call me Pierre. Have a seat. Your uncle recommended you to me as I'm in need of an assistant who speaks and writes French and English, can gather information from all sorts of people from snooty bankers to rough speaking miners of all nationalities, and has a good knowledge of the French mining camps in the southern placers."

Gino nodded his head in agreement. "I can do all of that except write English. But I can speak Spanish as well as French and that could help getting information as well. In the southern diggings, many of the French work with and alongside Mexicans, Chileans, Peruvians and other groups from South America. I'm an experienced and successful miner and I can easily navigate the trouble spots in the southern mines. I've been to most of the foreign mining camps and know the lay of the land. I'd be pleased to be your guide."

I was pleased that he'd listened carefully to what I'd relayed to his uncle and seemed to want the job. He spoke easily without exaggeration or conceit and maintained good eye contact at all times. "As you are a successful miner, I'm surprised you'd want to work as an assistant to a *notaire* and private detective, especially as I can pay only $16.00 a day."

I was surprised he didn't blink or show surprise at my proposed compensation. "Some days in the placers, we made nothing and some weeks we only made enough to buy American beans, flour and coffee. Most miners I saw never made a dollar's profit after a season of back-breaking work and many ruined their health. In the end, you either make a lucky strike or you fail and go home with your tail between your legs to face your family who counted on you to buy them out of poverty. It's not a job with a possibility to use your brain and learn new things or a trade. In Genoa, I worked as a shipping clerk for a firm that exported wine, olives and oil. It was interesting at first, but became routine and boring with no chance for advancement even though I had a better education than my boss, so my cousin and I decided to try to make our fortune in the New World."

I poured him a glass of white wine which he accepted gratefully. "Since you were one of the lucky ones to hit pay dirt, how come you don't use the money to start your own business and be your own boss?" I asked as we both emptied our shallow bistro glasses in a go.

"My uncle financed our trip and we paid him back. The only other way we could have come was as indentured servants on a contract to rich masters. When he lost his *trattoria*, which was the love of his life, we were honor bound to invest our gold to rebuild his restaurant. I could work in his restaurant, but it's not what I want to do. I like to travel, meet new people, and learn new things. When uncle mentioned I might be able to work for you, I jumped at the chance. My cousin, Antonio, is happy to work in the restaurant, but I'm not. So, I'd be happy to work for $16.00 day and try my hardest to help your businesses grow profitable."

"Some of the work, for instance replying to letters and dealing with the mail, may prove to be tiresome and boring," I said refilling our glasses.

"Of course, probably for you as well. But my uncle said you were an entrepreneur and seeking to establish many businesses. That's what I like. I want to stay in America where there is so much opportunity. I hope to learn what I can do working for you," he said seriously.

I was really starting to like this young man who was only a few years younger than me. He had Georges' good looks and charm, but there was a serious side and hunger in him to make something of himself. I signaled to Pierre-Louis that we were ready to start lunch. I decided to hire him on a trial basis that would last through our trip to the southern placers and we could reevaluate our relationship at that time.

I made sure Gino got his fill of shellfish which Pierre-Louis incorporated in a tomato-based soup. I wanted him to be able to report to his uncle how the French could cook a tasty fish dish. For our main course, we ate braised venison served with a savory brown hunter's sauce with cream and chanterelle mushrooms. We parted with a friendly handshake and agreement that he could start work in three days once he'd completed a plan for visiting the French diggings in the southern placers and an invitation for him and his uncle to join us for dinner on our brig two nights hence.

California Gold Rush Journal
ᗯ PART 2 ᗣ

CHAPTER THREE

San Francisco — July 1851

C onsul Dillon at the French Consulate recommended an American attorney he had recent dealings with and whose work he found satisfactory. The young man was trying, like me, to establish a new practice in the nearly lawless city and Dillon assured me that he was not a hired gun for the mayor and his cronies.

I had flirted with the idea of trying to practice law in the city's civil courts on my own, but on reflection thought it better to associate with an experienced lawyer given the destruction of the court house in the recent fire. I had been fortunate to secure an order to seize the replacement Chilean wine Teri's ex-beau had ordered after the fire using her savings. I couldn't count on another American judge accepting my pleadings as I had no legal degree or experience pleading cases in court. Many French lawyers had come to California to seek their fortune in gold, but none were qualified to practice law after going bust in the placers. American civil law was based on English common law principles and case law precedent, while French civil law was based on an outdated Napoleonic Code. Further, no legal education was available in the city other than to become apprentice to an American lawyer. As most French did not speak fluent English, even that option was out.

Thomas Hawthorne's office was a cubby-hole off the second floor stairs of a newly rebuilt brick and mortar building on Commercial Street.

He answered my knock himself and proffered a well-manicured hand to shake. His hand was soft but his grip firm. He signaled me to take a seat on a well-used captain's chair in front of his neat but nicked-up walnut desk that had seen better days. The only source of light other than a plain whale oil lamp on his desk was a window at his back.

Hawthorne was tall, suavely-dressed, sported a prominent Adam's apple, an aristocratic nose and looked to be in his early thirties. He wore his dark hair fashionably long. His New York tailored suit seemed oddly out of place in this Spartan setting.

"How can I help you, Mr. Dubois," he said after perusing my business card in French.

I explained how I would need a lawyer to effect the seizure of Chilean wine on behalf of my wife's associate, Teri, whose ex-boyfriend had stolen her savings to restart his wine merchant's business after the fire of May 3rd. He raised his heavy black eyebrows in surprise when I handed him Judge Roberts' order to confiscate the wine when it arrived until the merits of the matter could be resolved in court.

"How did you get the order of attachment," he asked with a frown.

"I sweet talked the judge's clerk to sign it and affix the judge's seal," I replied honestly.

"With a bribe?" He asked carefully gauging my demeanor.

I laughed to break the building tension. "The only inducement needed was to assure the lustful clerk he would get to meet the hot-blooded, vivacious and spurned *señorita*. While there, I arranged a date for the judge to marry me and my fiancé and assured him the *señorita* would be present as a witness and dressed to the nines."

Hawthorne gave a visible sigh of relief at my explanation. "You need to know that I refuse to conduct business or trade favors for bribes."

"I hoped as much. Consul Dillon assured me that you are honest and not part of the widespread corruption that has led the Committee of Vigilance to intercede in the detention and prosecution of the city's criminal class."

"Yes, and that sometimes presents problems in resolving cases. Biased judges and bribed jurors can skew just outcomes. That's why I refuse to practice criminal law. I don't admire either the judges or prosecutors who run the criminal courts or the extra-legal approach of the Committee."

"Can a lawyer make a living just handling civil cases and avoiding the widespread corruption?" I asked.

"I hope so. If not, I'll have to pack my bags and return to Connecticut. I can always practice with my father's firm, but I've always wanted to make my own way in life. My father and I don't get along all that well to tell the truth."

"Is that what brought you to California?"

"Yes, I figured from what I read that there'd be a lot of newly rich men and successful merchants who'd need a competent lawyer to do contracts, probate and civil litigation. I wanted to escape the stuffy, "Old Boy" dog-eat-dog East Coast lawyer cliques where you have to coddle clients, join the right clubs and be socially acceptable to get and maintain clients."

His explanation reminded me of my former boss in Paris and why I'd agreed to come to California to escape a similar legal environment. "Like your father's practice?"

"Yes," he sighed. "But I didn't realize what a challenge San

Francisco would be. Most of the legal work is defending criminals and con-men and most merchants do their own contracting and can't afford to play Russian roulette with the notoriously
unreliable and unpredictable court system. In Connecticut, you
can move your case before an experienced judge of your choice
and challenge a biased or self-interested judge, but not here."

I explained my arrangement with the French Consulate to
locate and deliver mail to French miners in the placers as I did
recently to camps in the north along the forks of the Yuba River
and my planned trip to the southern mines with my new assistant, Gino Lamberti. I outlined my business plan that included
detective services to find missing persons, notarization and
translation of legal documents from French to English for use in
contracts, litigation, immigration, citizenship, inheritance, and
dissolution of marriage cases. "When matters are contested or
need legal intervention, I will need an American lawyer to assist
me. Would association in these enterprises interest you?"

"Of course, I like the variety of situations you will be handling. I like new challenges," he said without hesitation,

"Good. How's your French?"

He choked briefly before muttering, "Well, ugh, of course I
studied French in high school, but that was a long time ago and
I've had no occasion to speak it. Is that going to be a problem?"
He said nervously. It was apparent he wanted the work and it
was time to set the terms of any association. "What do you usually charge clients? Do you work by the hour or the job?"

He hesitated before answering. "That depends on the case
and the amount of time it will take. Like all practitioners, I
request a retainer from new clients which guarantees at least
partial payment. Once you commit to litigation, it's not easy to
withdraw even if you're not being paid."

I understood the desired retainer system where the client
pays up front to secure the lawyer's services and a commitment

to handle the client's legal needs. My boss in Paris worked that way. He paid me only a fraction of the hourly rate he demanded in his retainer to do his legal work. He was free to glad-hand, hobnob and dine with his clients and woo his mistress while I did the grunt work and ran his practice.

"I'm afraid I'm not in a position to pay retainers on cases. Like you, I'm trying to build a new practice from the ground up. What I have in mind is for us to work as associates or partners. We each record our time on the cases we work together and when we're paid, we divide the proceeds proportionally based on the time each has put into the case."

"As equals?" He squinted, giving me a dubious look.

"Yes. I worked as the chief clerk for a prominent *notaire* in Paris for several years. I prepared all the contracts for marriage, drafted all the property conveyances and petitions for succession by heirs in probate matters and a host of other civil matters. A French notary acts like your civil attorney in America. The only difference is he doesn't litigate cases. If necessary, the *notaire* associates an *avocat* to try the matter before a magistrate. That's the relationship I'm proposing for us."

I paused in my spiel to gauge his reaction. While he sought to mask his reaction to my proposal, the uncontrolled bobbing of his Adam's apple betrayed his unease.

"Let me give you an example how such an association would work. My wife's business partner, Giselle, decided not to return to France with her husband after his wine business burned in the May 3rd fire. I negotiated the terms of their separation and grounds for divorce. I prepared notarized declarations in English and French for submission to American and French courts. I persuaded the husband to declare he was abandoning his wife in California to facilitate her divorce here and gave him her notarized statement that she had refused him her bed because she no longer wanted kids. Thus, he would have grounds for a

Church annulment of the marriage and be able to remarry if he chose." I paused to let him grasp my ability to negotiate a settlement between warring parties.

He nodded his acquiescence and I continued. "As you can see, I have laid the groundwork for you to prepare a petition for an uncontested divorce here and to obtain a divorce decree. I will be paid for my time settling the case at the rate of $16 an hour and you will be paid the same amount for your time in preparing the petition and the court appearance before the court. The same is true for the time it takes to execute the attachment order on the shipment of Chilean wine in the other matter I mentioned."

I watched him suck in his breath while he pondered my offer. I knew from Consul Dillon that he had demanded $25.00 an hour but settled for $20.00 in the hope of repeat business. As my rate was $16.00 an hour I was insisting on parity for payment of our work together. I hadn't charged either of Manon's partners for my legal work but that was my business. "Well?" I asked to force a response.

"I suppose I could do it for $16.00 an hour. I'm used to a much higher rate but I have the time," he said reluctantly.

"Good. Let's do these two cases together on a trial basis. If we're both satisfied with the arrangement then we can tackle new ventures together. My wife runs a French food business on the long wharf where our brig, "The Eliza," is docked. Why don't you join us for dinner one evening this week. You'll be able to meet both your new clients and enjoy a meal with us."

The prospect of a home cooked meal and a chance to socialize with two new single women clients brought a smile to his previously dour visage. We shook hands on our agreement and made a date for dinner.

California Gold Rush Journal
◦⃝ PART 2 ◦⃝

CHAPTER FOUR

San Francisco — July 1851

I made my way up Commercial Street to check my bank balance with Adams Express Co. and then moseyed up to Dupont Street to take a coffee and hear the latest gossip from Pierre-Louis at his restaurant before checking on my partnership to fabricate and sell Bear's Grease Pomade. All the morning newspapers screamed headlines about the James Stuart affair. As usual, Pierre-Louis waited for a lull in business so he could join me for coffee and shoot the breeze.

"So my friend, any success in partnering with a local lawyer?" Pierre-Louis said as he served me a dark coffee and poured water into his glass of anise-flavored drink.

I chuckled. "I think I hooked one despite his grumbling at working for my hourly rate and condescending to share fees with a lowly *clerc de notaire*. I hope he he's not like my former boss who let me do all the work and paid me a pittance."

"How did you get him?"

"He dropped his fee for a small job he did for the French Consulate, so I knew he's desperate for paying work. He'll change his tune quick enough when he meets his two beautiful clients. Let's hope Teri doesn't eat him alive and scare him off with her glaring stare. She's still mad as a hatter at men the way Raoul treated her."

Pierre-Louis struggled not to choke on his drink. "So you're gonna snare him with your two vixens. What if he falls for one?"

My turn to guffaw. "If he does, he'll have the hardest case of his life. A once spurned woman will put a ring in this one's nose and lead him to the trough. What's the latest on the James Stuart affair? The papers are screaming about a new arrest."

"A member of the Committee recognized a man calling himself "Stephens" as the real James Stuart and they took him into custody to interrogate him. The Committee sent a relay of fast riders to Marysville to try to stop the execution of the man named Berdue that they sent to be hanged."

"They're sure they got the right man this time?"

"They're sure, but all hell's gonna break out if the Sheriff in Marysville hangs an innocent man railroaded by the Committee to the gallows. It plays into the hands of the Governor and his cronies who've been dragging their heels at reigning them in. According to what I heard this morning, the Committee has decided to try "Stephens" here for murder and a whole series of other crimes so they can hang him straight away. They even let him choose his own lawyer to defend him."

"Who would risk the wrath of the Committee to defend a sheriff killer?" I asked incredulous thinking of my recent interview with Thomas Hawthorne.

"Well in light of the recent hanging of the Mexican woman, Juanita, by the crazed mob in Downieville, the Committee has decided to grant the accused the same rights he would have in a criminal court. Stuart asked to be defended by an attorney named Frank Pixley who defended him at his first trial. Pixley applied to a judge he knows for a writ of habeas corpus to compel the Committee to release Stuart to the corrupt civil authorities where he could get him off on a technicality by bribery. The Committee member I spoke to said Pixley was rotten to the core. They have heard testimony that Stuart paid Pixley $730.00 to arrange his escape from the hangman's noose."

"Oh La La," I chimed in. "The plot thickens like a 5 Cent novel the street hawkers sell. No wonder the town's atwitter."

"The plot gets even more sleazy. Stuart arranged with his mistress, a "Mrs. Hogan," to store goods stolen by the Sydney Ducks at her crib for stolen property. They were planning to escape together to Los Angeles and take a boat with the loot to Mexico before he was caught. When they arrested her, she was wearing a tintype photo of Stuart on a chain around her neck. The Committee thinks he'll confess his crimes if they agree to let her go."

Pierre-Louis had to attend to newly arrived clients, so I decided to continue my stroll along Dupont Street to visit the French Pharmacy on Broadway owned by Bernard and Françoise Lefèbvre. I had supplied them with bear's fat and oil and they'd agreed to prepare and market a bear's grease pomade for slicking the hair of the local dandies and card sharks and a scented bear's oil sold as both a hair product and a cure-all remedy for hair. Mme. Lefèbvre threw me a friendly smile with her milky-blue eyes, then nodded in the direction of her husband at his rear counter where he was mixing remedies.

"I think you will be very pleased with Bernard's results." She proudly handed me a medium sized porcelain pot with paper labeled top that read "LEFÈBVRE'S CALIFORNIA BEAR'S GREASE/ Made With The Fat of California Bears According To A New, Secret Formula/ Guaranteed Superior To Any Imported Competitor." The text formed an oval around the lithographed image of a California Black Bear sitting on his haunches and growling to show his ferocious teeth and massive front claws.

"Go ahead, open the top and smell it," she prompted as her

husband joined us at the sales counter.

The thick, greasy concoction smelled of lavender and rosemary. "What do you think?" Bernard Lefèbvre said with a twinkle in his eyes while tugging on his superbly waxed mustache.

"I like the label and the price of $3.25 a pot. I trust your judgment as to the product. I've never used it myself."

He laughed and put his arm around his pleasantly plump wife who beamed with pride at her husband's accomplishment. "I had to play with it quite awhile to get the right mix of scent and viscosity. It's lighter and easier to apply than most of the imported bear's grease and our price will undercut the imports by 30%, but we'll need to advertise to attract clients for our new product."

"I agree. If you give me the stencil for the paper label, I'll order a small classified advertisement in all the local newspapers and have my assistant distribute small flyers and broadsheets to all the gambling establishments and saloons. I'll have the printing bills sent to your store and you can pay them out our profits. I expect our margin of profit will be substantial, right?"

Mme. Lefèbvre gave the game away in her anxious glance to her husband. We hadn't discussed the selling price of the product or what it would cost to make it when we agreed to fabricate and sell it on a 50/50 basis. As I supplied the bear's grease, there had to be a substantial profit as porcelain pots, paper labels, scents and advertising in this expensive town could not be more than $1.00 a pot, if that. I had seen ads in the Eastern newspapers for highly scented bear's grease at 75 cents for a large pot.

Bernard Lefèbvre hesitated just a second too long before replying, "Yes, we'll have a nice profit eventually. But the start up costs are substantial." He began ticking off the elements before I interrupted him.

"My research indicates our finished product shouldn't cost more than 50 cents a pot as I provide the bear's grease and you developed the formula. Right?"

Lefèbvre's normally confident demeanor cracked. Still dressed as dapper as ever, he now looked stooped and his voice had become more shrill. "Well, we might get our costs down low as you suggest when we have clientele and can sell lots of pots. But the advertising you suggest will be costly, won't it?" He said in a whiny voice.

"Initially, it may be costly. But, if you expect to corner a lucrative market, you have to promote your product. I'll have my assistant return your stencil and a list of advertisements and the costs I negotiate. I'll take this pot to show prospective buyers. Of course, if you feel the start up costs will be more than you can afford, I'm sure I could secure a silent partner to cover these costs for a percentage of the profits."

"Oh no," Lefèbvre blurted out. "We can handle the costs."

After Mme. Lefèbvre handed me the stencil, I put it and the bear grease pot in my satchel and wished them a pleasant day.

My next stop was my cubby hole of an office at the back of a wholesale pharmaceutical store. Sophie Benson, the saleswoman for the shop, smiled sweetly and informed me that my new assistant had dropped by and would return shortly. I showed Sophie the bear's grease pot with the paper label. She opened the top and extracted a small sample on her finger and teased it between two fingers, then smelled the sample. "It's very nice. As good or better than the imported ones. The label's nice, but not nearly as attractive as the blue and white transfers on the French pots. But, the low price should assure it will sell well."

While waiting for Gino, I added text for the ad bills and broadsheets to the bear's grease stencil and drew a list of newspapers to place the ad in the classified section where most merchants advertised. When Gino arrived, I sent him off to the printer and charged him with placing the ads and arranging for the distribution of the ad bills and broadsheets once we had printed copies. That would keep him busy for a couple of days while I prepared instructions for how to sort and distribute the bags of French miners' mail starting to fill up my small office. I worked on this unpleasant task until Gino returned from the printer. I showed him how to match letters to the passenger lists of French ships provided by the consulate.

I left Gino to work alone while I returned to our ship. Gino and his uncle would dine with us this evening and I wanted to give Manon a helping hand in the preparation. Teri and Giselle were packing up their stands after another successful day selling Manon's food and our wines and spirits. Giselle's dog, Fido, a piebald terrier and excellent rat killer, eyed me suspiciously from behind Giselle's skirts. He was prepared to die in battle to protect his mistress and he constantly growled lowly and bared his teeth when male clients got too close to Giselle. Her cat, Gamelle Boy, eyed me absently from the top of the gangway. He waited on his daily perch for Giselle to fill his bowl with scraps from the food trays.

Manon was delighted to see me return early and without the smell of wine or liquor on my breath and the telltale signs of having dined in someone else's restaurant while she labored in our kitchen preparing meals for tomorrow's clients and guests tonight.

"So *Chéri*, did you remember to chill the white wine for dinner?"

"Not yet. But the buckets are ready to be lowered into the bay." Everything will be ready for our *apéro*." I picked up a wooden spoon and tried to sample the delicious concoction bubbling in a large casserole.

"Ah, no sneak preview for the naughty waiter," as she grabbed my spoon and shook it to scold me. "Big boy has a lot of work to do before he samples any of Manon's wares," she said with a pixyish look full of innuendo that suggested a special treat might be in store after our dinner party if all went well.

"*Oui, oui, mon capitaine,* I shall follow your orders to the letter right into bed," I gave her a smart-alecky salute, then scooted out of the galley before she could shoo me out with her spoon.

Manon's menu for the soirée was a secret, but my short foray in the galley tipped her hand that she was preparing a special New Orleans gumbo for the main course. Giselle's selection of white wines and champagnes from her ex-husband's stock guaranteed it would be a memorable evening as Manon sought to impress her potential Italian associate.

With the table set, the wine chilled and dining table arranged with little name tags on plates for seating, Teri and Giselle disappeared to their cabins to dress for dinner. I almost dropped my jaw when they returned. Giselle had eschewed a traditional matron's dress billowed out with petticoats or hoops in favor of a slinky, form-fitting, long-sleeved satin dress that emphasized her ample curves and whose bodice gave brief, but tantalizing glimpses of her ample bosom when she leaned forward. She'd done her deep auburn hair with red highlights in a lose chignon that allowed curly tendrils to escape to both sides of her face. She looked stunning. She would have outshone even Empress Joséphine at a royal ball.

Not to be outdone, Teri appeared in her high-neck, fiery-red Argentine dress with slits on both sides that hugged her body and showcased her delectable coppery legs and thighs when she walked or crossed her legs. She wore her golden tresses loose to her back and sported a white carnation behind her left ear. My, oh my, what a treat for the Italians. I was relieved that we dined aboard and not in town where these two ladies would cause a riot even in a respectable restaurant.

Our guests were right on time. Salterini carried two bottles—one of Italian sparkling wine and the other a vintage Barolo. His nephew's arms were full of red roses for Manon. Manon introduced her two associates to her guests. Salterini's eyes glowed large with surprise and satisfaction as he kissed first Giselle's and then Teri's hand. *"Che Belle Donne,"* he muttered to himself. Gino Lamberti coolly assessed the charms of the two single women and following his uncle's lead, bowed and brought each woman's hand to his lips. After holding Teri's hand just a tad too long, he snatched a single red rose from Manon's bouquet, clipped the stem with his Bowie knife and replaced Teri's white carnation with the rose. It was clear Gino was making a statement of interest, but given Teri's recent castigation of all would-be admirers, I was surprised to see her reward him with a gracious smile and little curtsey.

The scene was not lost on Manon, who quickly reshuffled the seating chart to allow Gino and Teri to sit face-to-face at the dinner table. She placed Giselle at one end of the table between me and Salterini and she sat next to Teri on the side nearest the galley. While both Italians spoke conversational French, Gino realized that Teri spoke haltingly and immediately switched to Spanish when addressing her.

For starters, Manon served savory crab cakes made with fresh, local Dungeness crab which we washed down with a vintage Chablis wine. The main course was Manon's surprise New Orleans Creole gumbo that she was preparing when I intruded in her kitchen.

"Mama mia" exulted Salterini after a couple of mouthfuls. "I can taste the parsley, pepper, bay leaf and thyme, but there's something else I never taste before. So good. What is it?"

Manon laughed. "It's the secret of a real New Orleans gumbo. It's called "file." The Choctaw Indians in Louisiana grind leaves from the sassafras tree and make this special spice that flavors the gumbo. The French Canadian Creoles who settled the mouth of the Mississippi River learned the secret of the spice from the Choctaws. As there are lots of shrimp, crayfish and other shellfish in the warm waters of the Gulf of Mexico, they devised special ways to prepare gumbos as they called their shellfish dishes and stews."

"How can we get some of this secret "file" for our cooking?" Salterini asked hastily.

"Manon shook her finger at him as if he were a naughty boy. "You only get secrets if we work together, non?" She replied with a twinkle in her eye.

"How can an Italian gentleman resist the charms of *la futura mamma*. Especially, when she's such a good cook. Your *bambini* are going to grow up in *paradiso*." Looking at me, Salterini uncorked his bottle of Italian sparkling wine, filled our glasses and proposed a toast. "To the future of our Franco-Italiano alliance. May we prosper as associates and enjoy the fruits of our labors together as friends."

We clinked glasses and attacked the scrumptious gumbo in earnest. During the toast, Gino's eyes never left Teri's, who reacted with raised eyebrows and an enigmatic smile that suggested she would not be adverse to courtship, but would be no easy conquest. Based on my knowledge of her treatment by her ex-Chilean boyfriend, he would have to take it slow and prove that he was not just another good looking Latin Romeo on the make. By working for me, he'd have a chance to prove himself.

We concluded our celebratory meal with a selection French cheeses— a Salers, a bleu d'Auvergne, and a tasty goat cheese made by a Frenchman and supplier to Pierre-Louis who had gone bust in the placers, but managed to buy a herd of goats on credit and returned to making cheese as he'd done in France. Delectable cheeses smeared on fresh baguettes and washed down with two bottles of 1840 Chateau Haut Brion cabernet sauvignon from Giselle's stock topped off our wonderful dinner party. Manon was pleased with her successful soirée and saved my special "dessert" for our boudoir.

Photos of French Bear's Grease Pot and
B. Lefevre Pharmacy Pots dug in San Francisco
(museum donation).

California Gold Rush Journal
☜ PART 2 ☞

CHAPTER FIVE
San Francisco — July 1851

I met Gino the next day to review the bear's grease advertising. He tendered me a hand-written note from his uncle for Manon praising her cooking and beauty and thanking her profusely for the wonderful evening. Though Salterini's written French was full of grammatical and spelling errors, Manon would be pleased to soak up the praise and recognition from a fellow restaurateur and charming associate.

Gino surprised me by asking permission to woo Teri. He explained that he had discussed the matter with his uncle on their way home last evening and his uncle suggested he court her patiently and respectfully in the old-fashioned, Italian courtly tradition of a troubadour.

"You don't need my permission to court Teri, but I do agree with Luigi that you should go slow. She's had a bad experience with her last boyfriend who violated her trust, betrayed her, and left her with a bitter taste in her mouth. But, I'll tell her that you asked my permission. She may take kindly to your approach." I said.

"I have learned there will be a special French Ball later this month. I thought to ask Teri to go with me to dance and have fun. What do you think?"

I had heard talk from the French Consulate that a group of French merchants planned to rent the Cairo Saloon for an evening of dancing and light refreshments to include wine. It was to be a private ball by invitation only. "Why a French ball?"

"I thought maybe you, Manon and Giselle would like to come too. I think Teri might feel more comfortable with me on a first date if she had her friends around her."

"How were you planning to get an invitation? I've heard it's a private affair," I replied.

"Well, since we do the consulate's work, I figured we could secure an invite," he said with a strait face.

I laughed. "You mean you expect me to wrangle an invitation for two non-French to attend their ball?" I said with mock reproach.

Gino shrugged sheepishly, then grinned broadly. "I knew I could count on you," he said as if it was a done deal.

I could see that he'd planned his moves shrewdly. I hoped his romantic aspirations and machinations were a sign he would turn into a good investigator for my detective business. Time would tell. "I'll talk to Manon and her partners and see if they are interested in the ball. Let's get to work promoting our bear's grease." I handed him a directory of businesses in the city so he could plan his route to hand out the flyers and broadsheets from the printer.

"By the way," he said as I was about to leave my office, "There was a lot of buzz on the street on my way here about the Committee. Most folks think the vigilantes will hang Stuart straight away before the governor, city officials or the Sydney Ducks can rescue him. Be careful where you go. You don't want to run into a mob of angry Ducks."

I gave Gino a friendly salute of thanks for the warning and

headed straight for *Les Bons Amis* restaurant to see what information Pierre-Louis could add to Gino's.

Pierre-Louis brought me a strong, black coffee and one of his best cigars and joined me for a chat.

"My new assistant warned me that the streets might be full of Ducks seeking revenge and an opportunity to free Stuart," I said striking a Lucifer to fire up my cigar.

"It's not only angry Ducks on the war path, but also Sheriff Hays with a posse of armed police who intend to seize custody of Stuart. That's what my client told me this morning."

"How so? Are they planning on shooting their way into the Committee's heavily fortified quarters? It would lead to civil insurrection. We'd be involved in a war." I exclaimed nervously.

"Apparently, Sheriff Hays secured writs of *habeas corpus* from judges who are his cronies to take Stuart and his lover, Mrs. Hogan, into custody. They're both being held and interrogated by the Committee. They say it was Stuart's corrupt attorney, Frank Pixley, who bought off the judges. They're afraid of the growing power of the Committee. When the sheriff showed up at the Committee's headquarters early this morning, several prominent members told the sheriff that Stuart was not in their "personal custody."

"How can that be?"

"Evidently, they knew about the plan to serve the writs and spirited Stuart to a secret location. According to my informant, Stuart confessed to a whole series of crimes including horse stealing, robbery and organizing gangs of Ducks to set fires so they could steal from merchants during the chaos and stash their loot at Mrs. Hogan's crib. He also fingered a host of accomplices including many Ducks, two policemen, a couple of sheriffs and attorney Pixley."

I blew a couple of smoke rings. "Oh boy! Now everybody has a motive to see Stuart swing. What he said under interrogation is mostly hearsay and wouldn't be admissible in court without corroboration. Stuart surely signed his death warrant. Why would he do it?"

"He probably knows the game is up and wants to settle some scores. He can't count on being rescued. He saw how neither the police nor the Ducks could save Jenkins from the noose. He may have bargained to save his best friends and Mrs. Hogan by not implicating them and giving the Committee enough rabid dogs to pursue to satisfy their anger over the fires."

We both jumped at the frantic clanging of the bell on the Plaza and the sounds of other bells adding to the intense clangor throughout the city. We rushed to the door. No smoke anywhere in the sunny morning air freshened by a mild sea breeze. The angry clanging could only mean the Committee was calling its members to assemble for a hanging.

The streets were soon clogged with pedestrians dodging carts, horses, teamsters and the usual loafers about town.

Pierre-Louis called out to a well-dressed merchant he knew was a member of the Committee of Vigilance, "where is the meeting to be?" as the merchant rushed past the restaurant.

"We're to assemble in front of the Committee's headquarters on Battery Street," he replied over his shoulder as he raced toward the waterfront.

"I want to see the bastard hang. You were here when they torched the city last month. They nearly got me that time. They'll need help keeping the sheriff and the Ducks at bay to get the job done. We need to join them."

I was torn. I don't like violence and had no desire to witness a frenzied mob string up an individual, even if he proved to be guilty as charged. Our business had not been threatened the way Pierre-Louis' had been. Had the wind not died, he surely would have lost his restaurant which was his life's investment and his pride and joy. He arranged with his staff to close the restaurant until he returned. He pulled two Colt revolvers from behind the bar and handed one to me.

"Let's go," he commanded. I tucked the loaded firearm in my belt beneath my waist coat and took a last puff on my cigar on my way out the door behind my friend.

We muscled our way through the Plaza which was clogged with citizens streaming towards the waterfront. The bell on the Plaza continued to sound like a metal war drum in its call to arms. As the Committee's headquarters were not far from my small office, we took the smaller, narrow side alleys to circumvent the mob and arrived at the bay side of Battery Street, which was not yet overcrowded.

A group of about four to five hundred men with pistols drawn sealed both sides of Battery Street in front of the Committee's headquarters. We took a position on the loading dock of a warehouse opposite the headquarters where we could look down on the scene as it played out. On the side of Battery Street nearest the Plaza, a mob of at least three thousand were jostling for position in anticipation that Stuart would be hung from a yardarm run out of the Committee's upper windows where their prisoners were held and interrogated. The men sealing both sides of the street with their revolvers kept the mob from surging forward. Many in the crowd were chanting, "Hang the bastard now!"

"The men restraining the mob are Committee members," Pierre-Louis whispered over the noise of stamping feet and hooting calls for action now and demands of "bring him out now." After several minutes a Committee member, calling himself "Colonel Stevenson," emerged from the barricaded headquarters. He waved for the crowd to be silent.

"I am here to inform you good people who seek justice in the matter of the recent incendiary and criminal acts against the law abiding citizens and businesses of San Francisco that James Stuart, also known as 'English Jim,' has been fairly tried before a jury of the Committee of Vigilance and has freely admitted to his crimes to wit: he was one of the robbers who viciously assaulted and robbed the hardware store owner, Jansen; that on his escape from the gallows at Marysville, he stole a horse to make his getaway and later sold it for profit; that he organized a gang of criminals who preyed on citizens and businesses alike; that he and his accomplices, who were named and will be arrested and interrogated by the Committee of Vigilance, planned and were prepared to set fire to the city again. As a consequence, the trial jury has convicted him of those crimes and sentenced him to hang..." At this point, the crowd interrupted him with cries of "hang him now!"

Col. Stevenson motioned the crowd to be quiet. "The Executive Committee has summoned you good people of San Francisco to serve as a court of review before any sentence is carried out. Do you agree to convict Stuart? What is your verdict?" The mob howled, "Yes."

"Shall he hang for his crimes?" An immediate and almost unanimous roar of approval erupted from the mob. "Hang him."

With that, the armed members of the Committee formed in columns of two to thwart any rescue attempt and Stuart, with hands tied behind him, was marched out of the Committee's headquarters, placed in the middle of the armed phalanx of Committee men and marched past us south down Battery Street towards the Market Street pier.

The throng following behind was boisterous and ugly as members jostled and trampled others to get to the scene of the execution. Pierre-Louis and I waited patiently for the last stragglers to leave the scene before heading back to the restaurant. Neither of us had a stomach for the last act. Pierre-Louis opened a bottle of red wine to go with a platter of hard cheeses and sausage slices. The distant roar of the mob told us that the execution had taken place.

"HANGING OF JAMES STUART," 1851.

California Gold Rush Journal
◌ PART 2 ◌

CHAPTER SIX
San Francisco — July 1851

Ichecked with the consulate and was assured I could have tickets to the upcoming French Ball at the Cairo Saloon. I broached the subject with Manon before discussing it with Teri and Giselle.

"So Daddy-to-be wants to check out all the pretty French ladies in town while Manon lugs his progeny around in her bigger and bigger belly, yes?"

"That's only partially true," I said tongue-in-cheek. "I look at all the pretty ladies every day, but none compares to you, Mommy-to-be."

"Hah. So you admit your roving eye can't be trusted, Heh!"

I laughed at her attempt to say "Gotcha." "But of course not, *ma Chérie.* We are being invited to chaperone Teri and Giselle if they want to go. Gino wants to invite Teri and he's afraid she won't go with him unless we tag along. We both thought it would be good for Giselle as well to meet other Frenchmen and have some fun. There will lots of successful French businessmen and merchants in attendance. I thought it would be a safe outing for all of us."

"Yes, and there will be all the French dance hall girls and barmaids and *pouffiasses* who work in the bars and gambling palaces and make their real money on their backs who will be there to snare respectable French ladies' husbands, Non?"

"I am not afraid. You can come in your sailor boy outfit with a carving knife in your boot and your marine pistol in your belt. No conniving wench will be able to get near me with you to protect me."

It was Manon's turn to laugh. "So you gonna just dance with your pregnant wife dressed as a pot-bellied sailor boy all night?"

"Maybe I'll get to dance with Teri and Giselle as well if my favorite wife gets tired?"

"Ha, you make goo-goo eyes at any other woman, and mother-to-be will cut you up in little pieces and feed you to the seagulls on the wharf," she retorted ignoring my reference to her partners.

"So, you're willing to go?"

"We go only if Teri and Giselle go," she stated emphatically. "And you don't go unless I go, so there, Big Boy."

I let it go at that. I opened the subject at our next communal dinner. All three women were surprised when I related that Gino asked my permission to date Teri. Teri agreed she'd go if we all went as a group. Giselle was unsure and hesitant, but Manon prodded her to tag along with us. Manon even offered to have me dance with her if she didn't want to dance with any of the men present. Manon gave me a devilish tit-for-tat look.

Later she informed me that the lawyer, Thomas Hawthorne, had been ordering his lunch "take out" the last few days from Giselle's stand on the wharf and had been finding excuses to hang around, sip a glass of wine and engage Giselle in conversation in his limited French. She suggested I get a ticket for him as well, but not tell Giselle.

"So we are now conniving and running a matrimonial agency?"

"Maybe," she said coyly. "I sneaked a look at him and he is tall and not unattractive. You don't expect me to dance only with you when we have other men seeking favors, do you, Big Boy," she said flirtatiously.

I laughed. "Do you think Giselle will welcome him as part of our group?"

"Well, you are going to do business with him, so we'll find out. Maybe a chance encounter will break the ice. Giselle is still shy and fearful of men and the lawyer is too timid to ask her for a date. So, we just help the matter along, non?"

"My, my, Manon has become quite the little intriguer, hasn't she?"

Manon puckered her pouty lips and fluttered her long, black eyelashes for full effect. "If you are going to forsake mother-to-be and go gallivanting around the mining camps with Gino, then who better than a lawyer in love to protect three abandoned women?"

As usual, I was being out maneuvered and chastised at the same time by my clever wife. "It looks like I better get that extra invitation soon so you can finish your theatrical plotting. Just tell me the role you want me to play in your scheme."

Manon threw me a victory smile. I promised to secure the invitations and headed for my office. I picked up the day's papers which all featured yesterday's events culminating in the hanging of Stuart.

The Committee marched Stuart to the Market Street wharf, blocked the entrance to prevent rescue, and hanged him from a cargo derrick. The mayor angrily responded to the hanging declaring in a proclamation that he "would not shirk his duties to curb the power of the Committee of Vigilance." Judge Alexander Campbell vented his outrage by declaring the hanging an "abomination," and vowed that "those who aided and abetted the hanging are murderers and would be brought to justice before his grand jury."

One wag gleefully responded to Judge Campbell's threats by reminding readers that eight members of the grand jury were members of the Committee of Vigilance. Despite the posturing of the officials, the editorials pointed out the reality that the only civic group with the power to arrest, try, convict and punish criminals effectively in San Francisco was in the hands of the Committee.

The Committee's response was to release Thomas Berdue with an apology and a sack of gold coins to appease him for his close call with a noose at Marysville and announce that they would be boarding all incoming vessels to ferret out criminals and troublemakers. They promised to investigate and try all of Stuart's accomplices named in his "confession."

I made enquiries to locate Etienne Derbec. He was working for a bilingual newspaper in the City. I had been impressed with his candor and uncompromising assessment of the fraud committed by mining societies when I was still in France. He evaluated the situation on arrival in California and wrote in 1850 to warn off French emigrants desiring to come to the placers. His letters, published in *Journal des Débats*, in Paris had a simple message. Don't come to California unless you can afford expensive supplies and provisions and have lots of money. His candid assessment of how hard it was to find gold fell mostly on deaf ears given the gushing, frenzied accounts of success in the popular press in France in 1850 and 1851.

I learned that many of his conclusions about the harsh conditions emigrants would face in the mines were based on a trip he'd made to the southern placers. I wanted to meet him to pick his brain as I prepared to visit the same areas he'd traveled to the year before. I had Gino deliver him an invitation to join me for an aperitif when he finished work. I alerted Pierre-Louis and asked him to prepare a plate of cold cuts, cheese and pâté for my meeting.

Derbec arrived promptly at 6 p.m. He was easily recognizable in his baggy corduroy pants, long-sleeved cotton shirt and ink-stained apron slung over his arm. He was short in stature but barrel-chested and muscular. His tawny, penetrating eyes sparkled with energy. He wore his long, black hair in a pony tail. Pierre-Louis directed him to my table at the rear.

"Monsieur Dubois?"

I nodded yes and offered my hand. His no nonsense grip was firm and powerful. His stubby fingers were stained with ink but bore the marks of one who was used to manual as well as intellectual labor. I introduced myself as a private investigator and explained my purpose in visiting the southern placer mines he'd written about in his dispatches to Paris newspapers, most of which had been published while I was at sea. I motioned to Pierre-Louis to bring two carafes of wine—one red and the other white.

"White or red?" I asked.

"I only drink red wine," he replied. I poured him a large glass of red and one of white wine for me. "How can I help you?" He asked as we clinked glasses.

I explained in general terms what I had seen in the French mining camps along the Yuba River and its tributaries in the northern placers. I also detailed my assignment to gather evidence of promoter fraud against the Californienne Mining Co.

"What can you tell me about the French mining in the southern placers from your experience last year?"

He laughed heartily. "I can probably tell you a lot of things you'd rather not hear," he said seriously. "Have you read my dispatches to the *Journal des Débats?*"

"I've read only a few as many were published while my wife

and I were en route from France to San Francisco via New York. Hopefully, someone will establish a reading library for French newspapers and books."

"But you know how I have urged the French not to come for mining or expect help from fraudulent mining associations."

"Yes, of course. It's why I wanted to meet you and learn whether your experiences in the south were markedly different from mine in the north. I heard that there were altercations between the French and other miners at *Les Fourcades,* which the Americans call Mokelumne Hill."

"Ah yes, Moke Hill. The French were the first to strike gold in the area, but they caused a lot of resentment. The first big group there was *Les Gardes Mobiles*, a paramilitary group sent by the government. They were organized as a militia, wore military uniforms, were commanded by officers and marched in formation to the beat of drummers. They even flew the French tricolor. They made a big strike at Moke Hill and stirred up a lot of animosity with nearby American and Irish miners."

"Because they were flying the French flag?" I asked and refilled his glass and mine.

"That was part of it. They were mostly angry because they were working poor gravel deposits and only earning enough to pay their food and living expenses while the "Frenchies," as they called us, were living high off the hog and getting rich. So, the Irish confronted the French and demanded they abandon the Moke Hill diggings or prepare to fight them and the Americans."

"Was part of it related to the Miner's Tax?" I motioned Pierre-Louis to bring more wine and the plate of cold cuts now that we were getting to the nitty-gritty.

"The Miner's Tax caused resentment among the non-American speaking miners including the French. For the Americans and Irish, it validated their belief that the gold in the ground belonged to them and not cheeky foreigners. The Irish had left harsh conditions in their own country, and like the Americans, felt entitled to the most profitable claims and thus, the challenge to give them up or fight."

I chuckled to myself. Most Irish I'd seen in San Francisco seemed ready to fight over a lot less, even a schooner of beer. I'd even seen one Irishman drop a large pack across the entrance to a saloon, then order drink from the bar and wait. The first person to kick the pack aside was challenged to a bare-knuckled fight for injuring precious property.

"So the Irish actually attacked?"

Derbec shoveled several slices of sausage and a hunk of cheese down his craw and washed it all down with big slugs of red wine before replying. "Yes, they led the attack with pistols and shotguns, but the French had had time to construct a fortified perimeter. The Irish managed to wound several French miners and lost one dead in the initial assault, but couldn't breach the French positions which were at the top of the hill."

"Is that when Consul Dillon intervened?"

"Yes, it was basically a standoff with the French holding the high ground and the Irish and Yankees not wanting to risk more serious casualties in storming the French positions. Dillon got the Irish and Americans to agree to a truce and the French were allowed to stay and work their hill, but it created bad blood and ill will that still exists today. The Yankees were ticked off that the Governor didn't send troops to chase the French out of their redoubt."

"Did this animosity spill over into other diggings?"

"Yes, but after the Moke Hill confrontation, each group stayed apart. The Yankees, Irish and English speaking miners worked together, often effectively in large companies, while the French worked alongside and camped with Chilean, Mexican and other Spanish speaking miners. Essentially, the two opposing camps tried to avoid each other as all were armed to the teeth and prepared to defend their claims."

"Were other groups of French able to make major strikes like *Les Gardes Mobiles?*"

Derbec laughed, then stuffed his mouth with a big gob of pâté on a slice of baguette and filled his empty glass again. "One reason the Gardes were so successful was their organization. They worked and lived as a mining company and shared the profits of their labor equally according to rank. The French were arriving in large numbers when I was there, but they did not work in organized groups. By then, the easy, close to surface gold was gone. Unlike the Americans, who worked in large companies and were able to divert rivers and tributaries to expose the bedrock where the best concentrations of gold lay, the French worked in small groups or solely with a relative. So, they were relegated to the accessible but poor paying river banks or mining claims that had been abandoned because they paid poorly."

"Couldn't they see that the American system brought better results?" I asked incredulously.

"Hah. You know our race. Every Frenchman is an individualist; he believes he'll be successful on his own, and tomorrow he'll make the lucky strike that will make him rich and he doesn't want to share it with anyone else. Many new arrivals believed the myth that there was gold to pick by walking the river bank or wading in shallow water. I saw one bunch of French arriving with rakes believing they could just rake the gold out of shallow water. One paunchy Frenchman arrived with his well-fed wife and daughter who carried embroidered stools to sit by the river and pick up gold nuggets with tongs. *Incroyable!*" Derbec took a gulp of wine, but sputtered and choked as it went down the wrong channel.

I decided to change subjects as his face had gone bright carmine and a neck vein was throbbing uncontrollably. "Was there an organized system for French miners to get their mail regularly?

Derbec refilled his glass and made a half-hearted effort to dab the splotches on his shirt and trousers made by the red wine he'd sprayed about. "Miners around Mariposa, Moke Hill, and Sonora had to walk to town to get or send mail from the post office when they came for provisions or to gamble. Mail only arrived once a month, if at all, in the most remote areas the French mined."

"Did anyone bring mail to the camps?"

"No, it was too expensive. It cost $2.00 to $3.00 a letter to get mail delivered and most didn't have it. There were 6,000 to 8,000 French miners working in the south and most were just eking out that much a day to pay for food and shelter."

Derbec had finished the plate of cold cuts and the second carafe of red wine. I decided to terminate the interview. I had a good sense of what to expect on my trip south and how to prepare and to provision. I invited him to stay and eat dinner at the restaurant as my guest, but made my excuses to leave, pleading a need to help my pregnant wife prepare our meal. Thank goodness Manon did not hear my ignoble excuse. She would have sent me packing with a portion of stale bread and pitcher of water for the evening.

California Gold Rush Journal
◌ PART 2 ◌

CHAPTER SEVEN

San Francisco – July 1851

The City was abuzz with fallout from the hanging of Stuart. All daily newspapers applauded the result while state and local government officials cried foul and vowed to bring the Committee of Vigilance to its knees. The Committee's supporters responded to the officials' braggadocio that there had been an average of two murders a day as well as a plethora of instances of theft, robbery, assault, arson and other crimes in the months preceding the hanging and not one criminal had been executed by the authorities.

The newspapers published the names of the numerous, fancy-named dens of inequity frequented by the Ducks and their cronies where criminals could plot their crimes openly and were immune from government interference. The "Magpie," the "Bobby Burns," the "O'Shanter," and "The Bird-In-The Hand" had been established by the Ducks and still carried on their tawdry trade where one could purchase a harlot for a few pinches of gold dust. One principal attraction was at the "Boar's Head," where a naked woman and a live boar put on a lascivious show and another at the "Fierce Grizzly," where a live female bear was chained beside the entrance.

The Committee added fuel to the blaze of indignation by asserting that various members of the Ducks had boasted openly to destroy San Francisco by fire and a known habitué of Sydney Town had been seen running from the paint store on the Plaza just before it burst into flames in May and ignited the fire that consumed the downtown business district. Other fires started almost on signal moments after the paint store, fueled by oils and highly combustible materials, which exploded, sending incendiary missiles arcing to the roofs of neighboring buildings.

The Committee responded to Governor McDougal's threats by fingering Beckler Kay as a key conspirator with Stuart. Kay, an escapee from Van Dieman's Land in Australia, who arrived in San Francisco in 1849, was appointed Port Warden for San Francisco by McDougal. As Port Warden, he was privy to inside information on ship movements and cargoes which he passed on to his confederate Stuart and his gang so they could plan their robberies based on knowledge where valuable cargo was stored and how it was protected.

Kay skipped out of San Francisco the moment he learned of Stuart's arrest and evaded capture by the Committee in Sacramento by disguising himself as an old woman and fleeing back to San Francisco to allow the police to arrest him in order to avoid the Committee's hangman's noose. The Committee alleged that Kay was relying on the governor and his corrupt appointees to protect him from the vigilantes.

Despite the public's fascination with the power struggle between the Committee and the authorities to seek and arrest members of Stuart's gang, most San Franciscans sought to steer clear of both warring factions. That included us. There was a high level of anticipation and excitement aboard our ship at the prospect of our first big social outing to attend the French Ball at the Cairo Saloon. All the women anxiously awaited the eve of July 21st and their debut at the gala.

Gino Lamberti was the first to arrive to claim his date for the ball. Gino struck a dashing pose as he tendered a dozen red roses to Teri. Gino looked as if he had just stepped out of a Venetian palazzo attired as an Italian troubadour—baggy silk Venetian trousers and ruffled shirt open at the collar, suede vest and short coat, soft, pointy Italian shoes and a Venetian cap posed rakishly over his long, dark curly hair secured with a silk tie. Teri regarded this very handsome, romantic young suitor with an amused smile as he dropped to one knee and brought Teri's hand to his lips.

Teri had eschewed her stunningly sexy Argentine dress for a more practical Spanish Flamenco dress that molded her full bust, narrow waist and then flared with short petticoats into an A-line that would allow her to swirl and whirl her petticoats on the dance floor. To show her appreciation for the roses and Gino's courtly manners, she did a little pirouette on her ballerina shoes that gave the still kneeling Gino a dramatic glimpse of delectable legs, calves and ankles and long blond tresses in motion.

Manon whispered to me, "Oh la la! Gino's gonna have to fight off all the other Romeos when she starts showing off her legs to all the single males, non?"

I laughed. "Probably the married ones as well. Maybe Gino should've worn an Italian sword with his costume. But no, I don't think so. Teri likes Gino so far and she's a tough cookie. She'll keep the Lotharios at bay if she stays interested in Gino. Hopefully, they'll make all the men surrender their weapons at the door. Teri won't be the only hot señorita or sexy mademoiselle at the ball. Should be lots to choose from," I replied.

"Hah! Father-to-be plans to ogle all the pretty ladies, yes?"

"As the English say, 'you can look, but not touch.' Isn't that the purpose of a fancy dress ball? You'll size up all the men and they'll ogle you as well. The loose fitting dress you're wearing hides your growing tummy. So, you may have to fight off Romeos as well."

"Hah. That's what dutiful husbands are for," she pointed to my large gold wedding band she insisted I wear and laughed. Then she motioned me closer as if to whisper in my ear and gave a hard tug on my ear with her teeth to let me know worse would come if I stepped out of line.

Thomas Hawthorne arrived next. He carried a bouquet of summer flowers as he walked up the gangway. He was dressed in a well-tailored summer suit unsuitable for the cold, ocean breeze that chilled the city despite a lingering, veiled sun that had lost its warmth. He looked quite out of place alongside Gino, Teri, and Manon. Giselle greeted him with a welcoming smile and graciously accepted the bouquet and helped him fasten a corsage on her wrist. She was dressed in a flowing mauve, high-topped, linen gown that molded her mature figure and flared with petticoats to allow her to move freely on the dance floor. She wore her reddish-auburn hair up in an attractive chignon held in place by a tiara of small, sparkling diamonds. Hawthorne blushed as she demurely held out her hand for him to shake or kiss.

I had chilled a bottle of champagne in our frigid bay waters which Manon opened and served to loosen everyone up before we set off for the gala. Manon chatted up Thomas Hawthorne and Giselle in an effort to reduce their shyness with each other. I puffed up Gino's importance as my assistant to ease Teri's concerns about his intentions. The bottle finished, we donned our winter cloaks, chained the gangway and set off on foot for the Cairo Saloon, which was a ten minute walk from our wharf and near the French Consulate.

The doorman checked our invitations carefully and informed us that no weapons were allowed inside and must be checked with our cloaks. As we were all unarmed, we were invited to serve ourselves to wine and hors d'oeuvres set out on the spacious bar. A throng of inquisitive merrymakers appraised each new arrival. I ushered our group to a table for six at the far corner of the saloon away from the small group of musicians on a raised balcony who were practicing arpeggios and tuning their instruments. It would give us a good view of the entire dance floor and afford a bit more privacy than other tables aligned against the walls to allow maximum room for dancing. I asked Gino to bring us tray of drinks and hors d'oeuvres and order us a bottle of champagne while we waited for the musicians to play.

The saloon was decorated in red, white and blue bunting in honor of the French tricolor flag and party favors in the same colors adorned each table. The paintings of nude, immodestly posed women hanging on the wall behind the bar had not been covered and appeared to set the tone for the evening as I surveyed the men and women present. Hatless card sharks and dandies in their striped trousers, ruffled shirts with ostentatious cravats held in place by gold stick pins and pomaded hair nursed their drinks at the bar and ogled the women as they arrived.

Most of the unmarried younger women wore their hair loose down their backs like Teri and all were stuffed into dresses with tight fitting bodices or daring necklines, billowing petticoats and bloomers which allowed one to assess well-turned ankles and shapely feet. Each dress sought to emphasize the woman's *appas,* her feminine charms to advantage. A few wore Venetian carnival masks to add intrigue to their identities and to attract attention. The few married matrons present wore turbaned hats and clung to the arms of their husbands as if their lives depended upon it.

"So *Chérie,* Manon was right, yes? Papa-to-be enjoys ogling all the *pouffiasses* on the make, yes?" She said pinching my cheek hard.

"*Mais oui, madame. C'est du spectacle!* Where else can one see so many sharks circling their prey and each other. Look at the one in the green velvet vest. He's making his move on his target." We watched as he made a beeline for a fulsome young woman with dark, curly locks and a daring décolletage.

"Ha, that one is going to cost him a bundle. She probably has her hours and rates tacked on her door," Manon whispered while giving me a good poke in the ribs.

Fortunately for me, the orchestra announced an opening waltz and began to play. I guided Manon on to the dance floor and took her in my arms to dance. Other couples joined us, while most of the dandies at the bar watched to size up the most vulnerable and available women. As we glided around the floor, I noticed Teri and Gino moving gracefully together and she appeared to be enjoying herself as she laughed at something Gino said. Giselle and Thomas Hawthorne were still seated stiffly at our table eyeing the swirling couples.

"I think we need to break the ice before one of the sharks moves in. You dance with Giselle while I talk to Thomas," Manon said as she dragged me back to the table.

I took Giselle for a spin while Manon took charge of Hawthorne. Giselle was light on her feet and followed my every lead as the waltz was followed by a rousing polka. We were both gasping for breath and Giselle was giggling as I delivered her back our table. Hawthorne rose stiffly and offered his hand to Giselle, who masked her surprise and accepted to be led back to the dance floor.

"So, your scheming is working, eh?"

"Manon knows more about shy men than you do. Look at them dancing and you understand the problem," she said pointing to Hawthorne, who was struggling to lead Giselle in a fast-paced waltz. "He was embarrassed to ask Giselle to dance because he's how they say it, 'all left feet, yes?'"

I chuckled. Hawthorne was looking at his feet rather than at Giselle as he struggled to lead and Giselle strived to keep him from stepping on her toes. "So he was embarrassed because he's a poor dancer, huh?"

"Yes, once he saw us dancing, he became very nervous and self-conscious. He was afraid Giselle would be unhappy with him and he'd spoil her evening once she saw he danced poorly. I told him if he really liked Giselle, he needed to dance with her before some audacious male tried to steal her away."

"So, he must really like her if he was afraid to lose her, eh? I hope he's not so shy when he has to argue our cases in court."

Manon gave me a sly look and pointed. Giselle was now leading Hawthorne and he was dutifully following as the waltz gave way to a fast-paced polka. "See the goose now leads the gander. Some men just need to follow a woman's advice for a change, yes? Maybe that should be the way of the New World, eh?"

I laughed. "Hah! Just because you can wrap Hawthorne around your little finger, is no reason to change the order of things. How about we settle for equality between the sexes rather than one sex lording it over the other?"

"Hah. Men still run the show here and you know it. Look at all those fickle parasites lounging at the bar and scheming to get nice girls in their beds to get what they want and then it's bye-bye baby and on to seduce the next poor girl, yes? Try to tell me it's not true," she said wagging her finger at me.

I was saved from replying to the argument I was losing badly by the *chef d'orchestre's* announcement that the noted singer, Frank Ball, would favor us with some special songs from his repertoire. We all watched as Ball, who was comically dressed in costume for the occasion, mounted the steps to the balcony and waved to us. He wore a knee length skirt and bloomers and his face was blackened like the minstrel singers who performed at various comic theatres and clubs. All the dancers returned to their tables including our Teri and Giselle to view Ball's antics. No sooner had we a full glass of champagne in hand than he started singing minstrel songs in a high falsetto. We gave him a rousing hand of applause when he finished, waved and bowed to his appreciative audience, then descended to the dance floor as the orchestra retuned their instruments to resume playing.

Ball was halfway across the dance floor when suddenly he stopped dead in his tracks at a commotion at the door to the saloon. A huge, hulk of a man lumbered onto the floor to confront Hall. I overheard a woman in the next table cry out, "My God, it's Dutch Charlie!"

He had been in the news frequently and was known as a brute, a bully and the "enforcer" for the democratic political machine. He towered over Frank Ball, put his fist in Ball's face and said in a drunken slur, "I want to kill you."

Ball looked him square in the eyes and replied, "Easily done, I am unarmed." Ball turned to leave and Dutch Charlie sucker punched him with a tremendous open-handed stroke to the head. As Ball struggled to get up, Dutch Charlie kicked him hard in the chest near the heart. Ball collapsed back to the floor unconscious. Everyone in the saloon was stunned by the violence of the unprovoked attack. I came to my senses and said to our group, "Let's get out of here before things get worse." I hustled our women ahead, grabbed our cloaks and made a beeline for the safety of our ship. Gino and Thomas followed. As all the papers had gone to press, we'd have to wait until the next day to learn what transpired after we left.

"FANCY FRENCH BALL, 1851.

California Gold Rush Journal

∽ PART 2 ∾

CHAPTER EIGHT

San Francisco — July-August 1851

I learned the next day that "Dutch Charlie's" real name was Charles Duane. Apparently, Frank Ball had been on a jury that failed to convict Duane of beating and stomping a man, then shooting him in the back. Duane held a grudge because Ball had voted for conviction. Ball was also a member of the Committee of Vigilance and Duane was convinced they were out to get him because the Committee alleged that Duane's lawyer bribed a juror to keep Duane from being convicted.

I also read in the French sections of the morning papers that the French community was incensed at the attack and its aftermath which ruined the gala evening for us all. The Executive Committee of the Committee of Vigilance voted to arrest Duane but was too late. He was in police custody where his cronies would protect him from the Committee.

Members of the Committee were divided on how to proceed as a Duck named Lewis was being tried in the courts for arson. Conservative members of the Committee felt the Committee's work was done as robbery and arson were less of a threat and many of the troublemakers were on the run.

More radical members voted to intensify activities against the Ducks and announced they would hang Lewis when convicted. They were angered that the Executive Committee had voted to hand over to the civil courts three principal associates of Stuart held by the Committee—James Burns, T. Ainsworth and George Adams. The radical wing called an assembly of Committee members and refused to give the three up.

The next day the grand jury indicted James Burns for serious felonies and ordered his immediate trial. The grand jury also declared that the actions of the Committee in trying and hanging Stuart were "in the best interests of the whole" community and refused to indict any Committee member. The action of the grand jury mollified enough Committee members to allow Burns to be turned over for civil trial on a close vote.

Meanwhile, Frank Ball died of his wounds inflicted in the vicious assault by Charles Duane. Judge Campbell presided over Duane's trial and made sure there were no Committee Members on the jury. Duane's lawyer successfully argued there was no intent to kill because Duane used no weapon despite his threat to kill. An intimidated jury voted to convict Duane of manslaughter but recommended leniency. Judge Campbell dutifully sentenced Duane to one year in prison which everyone knew would not be served given his political connections.

Governor McDougal issued his pardon on August 17th. His cronies rejoiced declaring Duane was "a useful wheel of the democratic political machine," while the Committee of Vigilance denounced the pardon as a double-cross intended "to take care of one of the boys," when they learned of it later and vowed to retain and try prisoners in its custody.

I was anxious to take a trip to the southern placers, but didn't want to leave our women unprotected until the tug of war between the civil authorities and the Committee of Vigilance was settled and the Ducks reined in for good. From the look of things, it looked to be a long struggle.

Manon was now uncomfortable with her pregnancy and the doctor confirmed she was carrying twins. I didn't want to leave her until she gave birth which wouldn't be until late November or early December. I hoped that Georges would be back with his Nelly by then and could help Manon in the kitchen. I determined to contact all senders of the letters we possessed and put Gino to work on the task.

I drafted a form letter for the printer that asserted my authority and commission by the French Consulate to track down and deliver letters to miners in the northern and southern placers for a fee of five francs per letter which was to be paid by return mail. I explained that mail delivery was spotty at best outside San Francisco and letters to French miners were routinely returned as "undeliverable" by postal clerks who could not read French and dumped them to rot in a dead-letter storage at the city's postal facility. I asserted my intention to take their letters to the mining camps, collect replies, and forward them to those who had sent their 5 francs.

Fortunately, the postage rate from San Francisco to New York and on to Europe was modified by the Postal Act of March 3, 1851. It lowered the postage rate to 3 cents prepaid and 5 cents collect per ½ ounce for a distance of less than 3,000 miles and to 6 cents prepaid and 10 cents collect for over 3,000 miles effective June 30, 1851. The Act also provided a special rate of 5 cents for unsealed circulars traveling over 3,500 miles. I planned to frank our letters with a 5 cent stamp bearing the likeness of Benjamin Franklin which had been in use since 1847 and was still available at our post office.

As the Act of 1851 declared the use of the 1847 5 and 10 cents stamps invalid after June 30, 1851 and provided for printing of a new series in 1, 3 and 12 cent denominations, I had a hand stamp made to say "5 cents paid" which we would stamp next to the 5 cent stamp. As it would be months before the new stamp issue arrived in San Francisco, our contacts at the post office assured me that the use of the 5 cents stamps would pose no problems coming from California. France might demand some additional postage upon delivery, but the recipient would be sure to pay it to learn the whereabouts of a loved one.

I instructed our printer to use heavy paper that could be folded and to print a small vignette of a view of San Francisco on the fold to contain the addressee and 5 cent stamp and to print larger views of miners panning gold and working the "Long Tom" on the inside of the circular above the text. I thought the circular with attractive views would motivate those with the means to send the requested 5 franc note by return mail. Time would tell.

Since my trip to the southern placers was on hold, I debated how to best keep Gino busy and earning his keep. The answer came from an unexpected source. While Gino addressed and stamped our circular for France, I took a break and decided to visit Pierre-Louis to learn the latest inside info on the struggle between the judicial authorities and the Committee of Vigilance. I was stunned to see *Les Bons Amis* restaurant chained shut with no note of explanation on the door. I hurried to the French bakery that supplied Pierre-Louis' restaurant and our wharf-side stands daily with fresh baguettes and other goodies. The baker, Emile, was cleaning his ovens and prep tables when I hailed him.

"Emile, what's happening at Pierre-Louis' bistro? I just passed there and the place is shuttered."

"Ah, I guess you haven't heard. Pierre-Louis fell coming down the stairs from the apartment over the restaurant and hurt himself badly."

"When did this happen?"

"Two days ago. The cook came by to say his boss was in the hospital and the restaurant would be closed until further notice.

The cook was really upset to be out of a job just like that."

"Did he say which hospital?"

"Yeah, since he couldn't walk, the ambulance wagon took him to the American hospital over by the entrance to the harbor."

"I'm going to hire a cab and see how he's doing."

"See if you can find out when he plans to reopen the restaurant so I can restart bread deliveries."

"Will do. Thanks for the information. I'll be in touch."

I rushed over to the Plaza to the taxi stand where a paunch-bellied, irate business man in a suit and top hat haggled for a lower rate for a ride to an address on the steep slope of Broadway. I brushed past the man and hopped into the cabriolet.

"I'll pay double the rate to get to the American Hospital as soon as you can," I said.

The cabbie untied the reins of his horse from the hitching post and hopped onto the driver's seat in a flash.

"Hey. You can't do that. That's my cab. I was here first," the now livid business man yelled. I just waved goodbye and the cabbie roared with laughter as he deftly maneuvered his nag around the corner of Clay Street and avoided a dray cart loaded with lumber and a matronly woman trying to protect her layers of petticoats as she herded a young boy in knickerbockers, school coat and cap across the street and around piles of horse dung.

The cabbie must have thought it was a matter of life and death as we whipped down Kearny Street on the way to North Beach. I just held fast to the grips beside my seat and marveled at the cabbie's skill in avoiding obstacles and near misses as he honked a horn by his seat and yelled to make way. When we arrived at the entrance to the hospital, I tipped my hat in appreciation of his skill and arranged for him to wait for me to return.

The duty nurse passed me off to a gangly, acne-faced orderly in his twenties who led me down a long hallway and pointed to a door on the right. "You'll find him in there with the rest of the patients with broken bones who can't walk," he said and retreated back the way we'd come.

The large room looked like a school dormitory with metal beds lined against both walls at three feet intervals with a center isle wide enough that two wheelchairs could pass. Most beds had a metal A-frame attachment with ropes and pulleys to elevate broken limbs. Pierre-Louis spotted me before I saw him. "Thank god you've found me Pierre," he shouted from a bed near the far wall.

Both his legs were bound in casts to his hip and slightly elevated on the iron triangle over his bed. I scrounged a beat-up wooden chair nearby and dragged it alongside his bed. "Thank God you're alive," I said softly with my back to his nosy neighbor who had craned his neck like an alert, big-eared jack rabbit at my approach.

"Just barely," replied Pierre-Louis. "If I understand the bloody doctors, my legs are broken in several places and it's going to be a bitch to heal them. They're not even sure I'll be able to walk with a cane for several months. Thank God for the laudanum. The pain's been a killer. But the worst thing is being trussed up like a living mummy in this infernal room with a bunch of noisy, obnoxious buffoons. Snoring, wheezing, coughing and yelling all night. You've got to get me out of here pronto, *mon ami*. They'll kill me with their lousy food, weak coffee and ignorance. If I'm going to be trussed up like this, I need good food, alcohol, the newspapers and good cigars," he pleaded.

I laughed, looked around me to assure no attendants could see and poured a large measure of cognac from my pocket flask into Pierre-Louis' empty water glass. Pierre-Louis seized the glass, put his nose to savor the aroma and quaffed it in a go. "Ah, *mon dieu*, but that's good. I've been dreaming of good wines, our cheeses and cigars in that order. It's incredible what the Americans serve you to eat here. I ate better as a poor private in military service in France," he said holding his glass out for a refill.

I shook my head, no. "Not all at once, my friend. I'll leave you the flask, but you'll have to go slow. I've been told that laudanum and alcohol don't mix. It's dangerous to take too much of either; together they could kill you if the dose is too much." He took the flask greedily and stuffed it inside his blanket.

"How did it happen?"

"Stupidly, of course. I was late for an appointment, rushing down the stairs, not looking at the steps and missed the bottom ones. I fell hard on both legs at a bad angle trying to avoid hitting my head. Just like that I become a cripple in this infirmary. Worse than a prison where you can buy liquor and cigars and newspapers to read. You must get me out of here, Pierre."

"Where do you want to go? You need full-time nursing care and medical supervision. You're going to be trussed up like this for a long time according to what you've been told."

"Find me a French nurse and a ground level apartment. I've money to pay whatever is necessary. My legs are in plaster of Paris casts, so I can't move and no doctor can help until it's time to remove them."

"We can do that, but what about the restaurant and your employees? The baker said your cook was distraught."

"I've had nothing else to think about since they parked me here. I've been contemplating a change for some time. You know I've groused about how I hate to provide a cheap fixed-price meal for the miserly new arrivals, who are too cheap to order a carafe of wine to wash it down. It sends the wrong message to my regular customers. The place needs a new look and better clientele. Obviously I can't do it, especially in my condition. Do you think Manon would take it on?"

"Wow, that's a big order. She's always wanted to run a restaurant of her own. I'm not sure she'd want to run one that wasn't hers. Plus she's five months pregnant with twins due near the end of the year. What sort of arrangement did you have in mind? I'll ask her, of course."

"I thought you and Manon could buy the restaurant. We could arrange favorable terms so you make payments from profits. I think the Americans call the arrangement a lease with option to buy."

"How would it work and what would be your role in the business?" My interest was now peaked.

"We could do a long-term lease and agree on a monthly lease payment that would be credited to the purchase price. I have enough savings to live comfortably and frankly, it's time I eased up. That's what the doctor told me. Said I've also got a problem with my ticker. Said if I'm not careful and don't cut back on my drinking, I'm at risk to stroke out any time. So, you see, I need to make arrangements now while I'm not incapacitated. If I don't, I'll return to premises full of squatters and have to start from scratch. I'm too old for that."

"So, we'd buy the restaurant business and the entire building including the apartment, right?"

"Yes, with these crippled legs I'm not going to risk those treacherous stairs again. I need to be at ground level both for my legs and heart. That's what the doctor said."

My mind was racing at the possibilities. Manon would have her cherished restaurant and I could use the large room at the top of the stairs as my office. We could use the apartment as a residence. We'd both be close to the business and not have to traverse dangerous streets at night when we closed the restaurant.

"How soon would we need to reopen the restaurant?" He really had my interest now.

"As soon as you possibly can so we don't lose our suppliers or regular customers. I'm sure my cook, Henri Royat, would be happy to work for Manon. He loves his job and the restaurant."

"But, he's never worked for a boss who's a woman. Manon's very independent and will insist to run the restaurant her way; that's why she came to San Francisco."

"It's true French chefs are all male. Henri's a good cook, but he has always taken orders from me and I determine the menus. I think he'd like to see a more lively operation and the kind of glamour only a woman can bring, especially in this town starved for women."

"Well, I have to talk it over with Manon. It's going to be difficult to run two businesses with her pregnancy."

"I've worked up some figures for how I think it could work," he said and handed me some sheaves of notebook paper filled with figures and the address of his cook. "And *mon ami*, next time you come, bring me a refill for the flask and a couple of dry sausages from my cellar. I'm dying for some real food."

I laughed. "I'll have Manon prepare a basket of her best goodies. I'll try to get back to see you tomorrow; if not then, the next day."

I took my leave of the depressing premises and ordered my cabbie to take me to the Long Wharf and home to the Eliza. My head was so full of ideas and possibilities that I hardly noticed my cabbie's skill in evading the myriad obstacles in our way that could have sent us both back to the hospital as patients.

California Gold Rush Journal
∽ PART 2 ∽

CHAPTER NINE
San Francisco — July-August 1851

I dropped a bottle of champagne in a bucket into the bay to chill and sought out Manon, who was cleaning her galley.

"So, *Chéri*, you've been gallivanting around town enjoying yourself while your doubly pregnant wife is hard at work paying the rent and carrying your progeny, yes?

"Suppose your loving husband has spent a long and arduous day negotiating the purchase of a restaurant for his favorite wife, eh? What would she say to that?

"*Chéri*, don't joke about such a thing. You know we can't afford to buy a business."

"What if we could, would you want to take it on now if we had to open in a week with the twins only months away?"

Manon gave me a quizzical look. "*Chéri*, are you serious? What has happened? Don't keep me in suspense," her dark eyes pleaded and her hands waved in excited anticipation.

"Answer my question first. If we had to open a restaurant in town by the end of the week, would you be able to do it?"

Manon threw her arms around me and hugged me tightly.

"Oh, yes, yes. It's my big chance. Of course, I can do it. Tell me. Tell me, *vite*. What are you up to?" She stuck her tongue in my ear, then pulled out of my arms and gave me that "you've been up to no good" look as she wagged her finger at me.

I laughed. She had used the same technique on me when she made me declare I would marry her before she dropped the bomb that she was pregnant. I motioned her to take a seat and related what had happened to Pierre-Louis and his offer to sell to us.

"Oh my god, it's too good to be true. He really would let us buy the restaurant and the building out of profits over time?" She shrieked.

"That's what he said. The doctors say he can't work for months and he doesn't want to see the business folding or squatters breaking into his building."

"Oh la, la! What a chance. And I get to run the restaurant the way I want, yes?"

"Yes, you're the boss, though he did mention his cook, Henri Royat, was upset at the closure and loss of his job. Pierre-Louis may insist you employ him."

"Won't be a problem. I have to have a cook staff who can cook what I tell them. We'll be cooking for the restaurant and the wharf. I can train him to cook my recipes and we have time to get all the pieces in place before you are happy papa, yes?"

I nodded yes and suggested getting the bottle of bay-chilled champagne to celebrate our new opportunity. Manon shook her finger "no." "Not so fast, Big Boy. We have much to discuss and do, before we pop a cork," she said as she bussed my lips tenderly. "Papa-to-be has given his Manon another precious gift to go with the others," she said patting her belly and then her wedding ring. "Papa has earned a big reward. Come."

She led me by the hand to our cabin and locked the door. She undressed me slowly and led me to our big doublebed. Once I was propped on a pillow to watch, she unpinned her lush mop of dark curls and shook them out, so they fell across her ample breasts; then, she slowly and teasingly removed her own garments in her best pantomime of a bawdy stripper. When she got to her chemise, she let it drop slowly so that her unruly curls framed her engorged nipples. She cupped her belly in one hand and a breast in the other as she did a slow pirouette. "Like what you see, Big Boy, yes?" We both cracked up with laughter.

I crooked my finger for her to come to me. Our loving was tender and imaginative. Discussion of the details of our new venture was deferred for pillow talk after sating our hunger for each other and celebrating the unforeseen opportunity that had dropped in our laps.

Gino's first task next day was to search for Pierre-Louis' cook, Henri Royat, and have him meet me at the restaurant, then to find a rooming house where Pierre-Louis could rent a ground floor room not too far from *Les Bons Amis* restaurant. Manon prepared a picnic basket of special foods for Pierre-Louis. Manon wanted him close enough that we could easily visit and deliver him restaurant meals each day.

I sought out my lawyer-associate Thomas Hawthorne who was shaking his head over something he was reading in a large tome of "Blackstone's Torts."

"What's up?" He said with a pleased expression. "I can use a break from the confusing rules of trespass English judges compiled through trial and error and case by case." He was dressed in the same well-worn tweed suit and bow tie he wore on my first trip to his cubby-hole office over a bank. It was probably the only one he owned or which was presentable.

I filled him in on my conversation with Pierre-Louis and handed him the sheet of figures Pierre-Louis had scribbled on a piece of note paper.

"He mentioned that we could do a 'lease-option to buy.' How would that work?"

"There are several possibilities. The most common is to lease the premises for a fixed period of time at the end of which the lessee can exercise a right to purchase the property outright for a fixed sum."

"Does the fixed sum have to be paid in full or can it be paid in installments?"

"It can be either way."

"Must installments bear interest?"

Hawthorne paused before answering. "An interesting question. I don't know. I've never read about or seen an installment sale contract that didn't bear interest. It would be most unusual," he said with a puzzled look.

"Just because it's not the normal way of contracting, would it still be legally enforceable if challenged?"

Hawthorne rubbed his chin while he pondered my question. "I don't honestly know. If both parties wanted it that way and there was no undue influence on the seller, I don't see why it would be against public policy even though the bankers would hate the idea. Is that what is contemplated in this case?"

"Yes. It's what Pierre-Louis himself suggested. He's going to be laid up in a nursing home for several months with broken legs and wants Manon to run the restaurant and own it eventually. He proposes that we lease the premises for 5 years and 50% of the restaurant's monthly profits be paid towards the purchase price of $20,000.00. We would have the right to pay more at the end of the year to pay down the mortgage if we were able and wanted to."

"I don't see any mention of interest in his notes. Did you discuss interest on the mortgage?"

"Yes, it was agreed the sale including the mortgage would be interest free. Can you draft a contract of sale and the mortgage note on those terms?"

"Well, it's highly unusual. Normally, there is mortgage

interest which is the consideration for the sale."

"Well, how about we add that the seller shall be entitled to a free daily meal with a liter of wine so long as we own the restaurant."

"You mean even after the purchase price is fully paid?"

"Yes, it may not be monetary consideration like interest, but it's something of value that the seller wants and needs. He's trussed-up like a plaster mummy in a hospital dormitory and forced to eat food that's worse fare than miners get."

"Well, it's certainly unusual consideration, but as you say, it does have a value, especially if it continues after the mortgage is paid."

"Good. I need you to draft the contract of sale and mortgage agreement today so that we can sign tomorrow morning. Every day the restaurant is shuttered risks losing its steady clientele and tempts squatters and vagabonds to break in."

Hawthorne sucked in his breath. "I'm not sure I can do it that quickly. I'll have to find the legal description and with the recent fire, who knows where the recorded deed might be."

"Do the contract first. I'll have the legal description delivered to your office early this afternoon." I was hoping I could sweet talk Pierre-Louis' cook into giving me access to the apartment over the restaurant so I could search for Pierre-Louis' copy of the deed. Worst case scenario, I could send Gino with Manon's basket of home cooked foods to Pierre-Louis and learn where he kept the needed documents. I dropped three $20 gold coins on Hawthorne's desk, which made him smile.

"Will Giselle work in the restaurant?" He asked sheepishly as he eyed the gold coins.

"Don't know yet. I'll ask Manon. Get to work on the paperwork. Time is of the essence as they taught you in law school." When I arrived at the restaurant, the door was unchained and Henri Royat was furiously attempting to corral the accumulated dust with a worn and inadequate broom. When he spotted me, he stopped his futile task and exclaimed, "*Enfin!*" Henri knew me as a regular client and friend of his *patron*. Henri was short and stocky. Pierre-Louis often joked about his cook's ample belly, which kept growing the more he sampled the food he cooked in Pierre-Louis' kitchen. His bald pate glistened from his recent efforts. I suggested he fetch us a bottle of red wine from the bar's cellar. He returned with an opened bottle, two glasses, a wooden platter with a large *saucisson sec,* and a bowl of black olives from his native south of France.

I motioned him to take a seat and poured us each an ample glass of red wine while he deftly sliced the dry sausage.

"How have you been?" I asked.

"Miserable. I'm so worried about what's going to happen," he said in this thick Toulon accent. His cheeks and chin were encased in two-day-old black and white stubble and his large, bug-like eyes were bloodshot. He truly looked miserable.

"I've been to see your boss and he has sold the restaurant to me and Manon." I paused to let this unexpected and potentially unpleasant news sink in. He was poised to pop a large slice of sausage into his craw when he froze open-mouthed. "Qua?" was all he could mutter as the slice of sausage slipped to the table.

"Sold? It's not possible. He just went to the hospital. How could he sell the restaurant? Is he out of his mind? What about me?" His big eyes now looked ready to pop out of their sockets and his hand shook so violently that he could only spill red wine from the glass he sought to drink. I let him stew in agony until his hand stopped shaking and he could gulp a mouthful of wine.

"That's why I wanted to meet with you. Manon will be deciding the menus and greeting clients. It will be her restaurant and she plans to reopen in two days. Pierre-Louis asked me as a favor to offer you a job in the kitchen. Manon said she would consider it," I bluffed as I had discussed the situation with Manon, but not Pierre-Louis. We weren't sure Henri Roy-at would be able or want to take orders from a woman, so I approached the situation offhandedly. We were short-handed and needed Royat badly, but I didn't want him to realize he could barter conditions of his employ. He knew French women couldn't be chefs or own restaurants in France. But this was San Francisco and he needed a job, knew the suppliers, how to run the kitchen, and prepare Pierre-Louis' hearty stews and simple but nourishing fare. He'd have to be willing to learn Manon's more sophisticated dishes and accept taking orders from a woman which he didn't have to do in France.

"Manon has a cook staff for her catering business, but with the restaurant and wharf-side operation to run, food for both locations will be cooked in the restaurant's kitchen. We thought you might want to continue to work in the restaurant's kitchen."

Royat paused to contemplate. "Will I be the chief chef?" He said petulantly.

"Pierre-Louis said you were his cook, not a chef. Isn't that so?" I bluffed.

"Well I was in charge of the kitchen and prepared the menu. There was no one over me," he said peevishly.

"Well, that would different with us. You would be the number one cook, but my wife is a chef and owner. She decides the menu and you work for her. Once you are familiar with her recipes and menus, she'll let you do the cooking and wear a chef's toque. What was Pierre-Louis paying you?" I asked before he had time to react or reply to what his role in the kitchen would be.

He hesitated before replying. "Pierre-Louis paid me $20.00 a day."

"We would be willing to pay you $25.00 a day as there will be more work. You will have to cook for both locations. The soups and meals for the Central Wharf stands have to be prepared the day before as the stands open early. We will no longer serve breakfast at the restaurant except on special occasions. We will open the restaurant for lunch and dinner only. That will allow you time to prepare the hearty soups and other dishes like cold platters and pâtés for both locations in the morning. Can you handle the additional work?" Ball in his court.

"I'm sure I could," he replied uncertainly.

"Good, how soon can you start," I tendered my hand to seal the deal.

"Umm, I guess right away," he said staring at my out-stretched hand. Sheepishly, he gave it a weak shake.

"Good. Now before you get a shave and make yourself presentable for our suppliers, show me where the keys are kept. Pierre-Louis asked me to find some important papers he needs urgently and which he thinks he left in his apartment."

Royat led me behind the bar and indicated two key rings on pegs—a set for the apartment and another for the restaurant. I instructed him to finish cleaning the premises, draw lists of supplies we would need to purchase and inventory the wines and other non-perishable foods in the cellar.

California Gold Rush Journal
∽ PART 2 ∾

CHAPTER TEN
San Francisco — July-August 1851

A s soon as the cook left to clean-up, I relocked the restaurant and unlocked the door on the street to the apartment above. It, too, was covered in a film of dust from the street. The rooms were large but poorly lit. Only the entryway and adjacent parlor room had light from windows overlooking the street. The building shared walls with other commercial establishments on both sides. I lit a hurricane lamp and did a quick perusal of the premises.

One passed from the entry room at the top of the stairs to a large parlor room with fire place and wood stove. From there a hallway running along the side of the apartment led first to a poorly stocked kitchen with cooking stove, then doors to a WC and vanity and to two large bedrooms at the rear in that order. Pierre-Louis used the first bedroom as an office and the other to sleep.

His large oak desk had a roll-top closure and all the cubby holes were jammed with papers and receipts. After sorting papers for a half hour, I hit pay dirt. A leather document pouch contained a copy of his deed along with other important personal papers including his French passport. I glanced through his account ledgers for the restaurant before rolling the top closed. He was barely covering operating expenses and his profit was minimal for the last three months compared to what Manon made in her wharf-side stands. I verified that Henri Royat was earning $20 a day.

When I returned to the restaurant, the cook was cleaning the kitchen. Most of the dry sausage had disappeared along with all the olives and only a half glass of wine remained in the bottle. As Gino had not yet returned, I decided to deliver the legal description to Attorney Hawthorne and take my lunch with Manon so we could plot our next moves.

Manon had thought to bay-chill a bottle of Chilean sauvignon blanc wine which complemented her delicious fish stew she'd saved for us. How nice to have a "working lunch."

"So *Chéri,* when do I get my restaurant?" Manon asked sweetly.

I filled her in on my negotiations with the cook and instructions to Attorney Hawthorne.

"If all goes well, Pierre-Louis will sign the sale papers tomorrow and we can legally take possession immediately." I dangled the restaurant keys past her nose and wrenched them back when she tried to snatch them. "Not so fast madam. You'll get the keys when we have a legal right to enter the restaurant."

"Ah, but papa-to-be has the right to eat and drink in the restaurant and sneak around the apartment snooping into a friend's business ledgers without permission, but his poor, working wife cannot even inspect the premises she is going to have to open for business in a few days, yes? It's not fair and you know it Big Boy."

"Yes, life is not fair, my love. That's why I am a private detective who snoops and you are a fabulous cook, wife and mother-to-be. I don't want you to spook the cook too soon as we are short-handed and need him. He's not used to working for a woman. He knows you by sight as a feisty, independent woman, so you need to charm and cajole him. Make him feel important in our enterprise. Promise him a toque when he masters your fabulous recipes. Charm him like you did with Sammy on the ship. You know the restaurant, its bar, kitchen and cellar. Let's do the prep work to assemble our team, put together a dazzling menu and wine list and figure out who we are going to invite to your gala opening of *Chez Manon.*"

"Hah. Now who is cajoling whom?" Manon said with puckered lips, then laughed. "You know me too well. I won't tolerate a cook with haughty airs just because he cooked for Pierre-Louis and resents a woman boss. My first command will be to sack that two-tongued food preparer, Ah Fong," she said with satisfaction and a devilish smile.

I chuckled. A payback for crossing Manon on our trip through Little China and trying to keep her from seeing its more sordid venues. "So, who do we use to prepare the vegetables and wash the dishes?"

"What about Gino's cousin, Antonio?—the one who wants to work in Luigi's *trattoria* when it's rebuilt. Maybe he could help in the kitchen until Georges gets here with his Nelly, yes? If he's not interested, there must be lots of former restaurant workers like me who need a job, no?"

"I'll have Gino ask him. What do we do for a waiter or waitress? Use Giselle? Hawthorne would love that. We'd have him as a client every evening. He'd be afraid another Lothario would catch her eye and she'd surely get better offers than on the wharf," I said with a grin.

"No, I think we use Gino for the evening service. I greet the clients and take their orders; Gino serves the meal, opens wine and clears tables. He can also tend the bar."

I laughed. "Poor Gino, he agreed to be my assistant so he could learn about business and not work in his uncle's restaurant. I hope he will do it and not quit."

"Hah. You men don't know men as well as women do. We can't leave Giselle and Teri alone on the ship at night. They also need help to set up the tents and stands in the morning. We have Gino sleep in Georges' cabin until he gets here with his Nelly and Georges can help them. Since he wants to court Teri, he'll jump at the chance to be the man on the ship and close to Teri. You'll get him back when Georges and Nellie get here. You will be barman as well and help run the restaurant," Manon gave me her "This is my baby" look.

Suddenly, our priorities had shifted. All our efforts had to focus on making the debut of *Chez Manon* a success and my business activities had to wait. She was right, of course. Pierre-Louis was not making a real profit with his business plan. We would have high and immediate increased overhead. Henri Royat, Gino and his cousin would cost us $50-60 dollars a day in addition to food and supplies.

"Pierre-Louis always claimed that an attractive bilingual waitress would bring a more diverse clientele—well-heeled Americans, bankers, and entrepreneurs in addition to the French."

"No, this is my baby and I'll attract the new clients. Giselle and Teri are making money for us all on the wharf. We may need some of that profit to invest in the restaurant, but we use our profit only. We cook in the restaurant for both locations and Giselle and Teri can eat dinner in the restaurant if they want or cook on the ship. But the staff eats in the kitchen or the banquet room. Too many attractive, single women eating in the dining room every evening will create a distraction and with so many horny men roaming the streets at night, we'll fill our tables with unruly, single men wanting to drink and hustle them. They want that kind of action, they can buy their drinks at Raoul's new woman's whorehouse," Manon said giving me her "tough girl, that's the way it's gonna be" look.

"You're right as usual. We'd have nothing but trouble. Gino and Hawthorne would be forced to defend the honor of our women and it would chase away the kind of clientele we want to attract."

"Yes, and papa-to-be will be here to defend his wife if needed."

"I've thought about that. I'll make my office in the entry room to the upstairs apartment. That way, I'll be around most of the time to either help out or protect the mother of our twins if necessary. I thought we could live in the upstairs apartment while we establish our clientele. That way, when we close the restaurant for the night, we don't have to traverse the Plaza and evade the ruffians and cutthroats lurking along the route to our ship."

"So, since Manon can't inspect her restaurant before tomorrow, maybe she should see her new living quarters, no? I'm sure it's a mess and will need cleaning and decorating, yes?" Manon gave me her "better not say no" look and threw her hooded coat over her shoulders and crooked her finger for me to follow into the chilly, windy afternoon air.

When we reached the restaurant, I accompanied Manon up the stairs to Pierre-Louis' living quarters. After lighting lamps and doing a cursory inspection with Manon, I left her to figure out how to make it livable for us and twins down the road.

Gino was downstairs helping Henri inventory crockery while he waited for me

"Any luck finding an apartment for Pierre-Louis?"

"I looked at everything available in the neighborhood. Most of the buildings rebuilt after the May fire are for commercial use. There's a rooming house on California Street that might do. The street's steep, but if he's in casts, it probably won't make any difference. The landlady says she has a room next to the downstairs parlor that she could rent to a convalescent. But it's expensive."

"How much?"

"She wants $250 a month for room and board."

"How big is it?"

"It's quite roomy and light. There's a big bay window look-ing onto the street. The owner said she had been using it for her own sitting room but needs additional rent, so she'll rent it only to a very respectable gentleman."

I laughed. With two broken legs and unable to walk, Pierre-Louis would be the ideal renter. He couldn't get into much mis-chief trussed-up in a bed. I took down the address and tasked Gino get a cab on the Plaza and take Manon's basket full of eat-able goodies and the day's newspapers to the hospital. I instructed him to tell Pierre-Louis I would see him next morning with the purchase agreement and a plan to extract him from the hospital.

I told Henri to leave the inventory and lists of suppliers on the bar when he locked up. I told Manon I would fetch her as soon as I checked out the possible rental for Pierre-Louis.

I was huffing and puffing by the time I got to Mrs. Hale's room-ing house. It was a two storey wooden structure built originally as a residence for a wealthy merchant. Mrs. Hale, a stout Scots wom-an in her fifties, fixed her gray-blue eyes on me and appraised me from top to bottom before regarding my business card.

"What is a *notaire* if I may ask? Never heard of such a call-ing before," she said in her high country brogue.

"It's like a Scottish solicitor — a French civil lawyer who handles real property and probate estate matters but doesn't plead in court."

"Frenchie, huh?" She said rolling the 'r', "An' that young man you sent around was Italian weren't he?"

"Yes, he's my assistant. However, I'm here on behalf of my client, Pierre-Louis Lerouge who owns *Les Bons Amis* restau-rant on Dupont Street not far from here. I'm sure you've seen it. He's had a bad fall and needs a comfortable, quiet, private room to recuperate during his convalescence."

"On crutches is he?" Mrs. Hale said now showing some interest.

"Not yet I'm afraid. Both legs are still in casts. He'll be bedridden for a while yet. He has a private nurse to call on him daily and take care of his needs during the day," I bluffed. "So, he won't cause you any trouble. He's quiet and reads a lot. You'll hardly know he's here. Doctor has him on a special diet which is cooked in his restaurant and will be brought round for him daily. So, other than coffee and tea from your kitchen, he won't be taking board here, just a room. My assistant said you have a room next to this parlor to let."

Before she could object, I made for the door to the left of her parlor. I had seen the bay window from the street. She let out a little wheezing sound of surprise and followed me into the room which was furnished with a desk, a table and three chairs. As Gino said, it was spacious and well lit from the large curved window overlooking the street. It even had its own small WC. It would be perfect for Pierre Louis.

"This will do nicely. You quoted my assistant $250 a month with board. I noted on your tariff sheet that non-residents could take monthly board for $75 a month, thus the room without board is $175 a month."

"Well I dunno," she stammered. I pulled out my money pouch and slowly counted out eight $20 gold coins onto the fruitwood desk and added a $10 and $5 coin to the pile. Her eyes were transfixed by the glimmering coins. While she greedily eyed the coins, I inked a quill pen and wrote a receipt for a month's rent in the name of Pierre- Louis.

"Just sign here," I said handing her the pen.

"Well now," she sputtered. "I run a respectable house. No women allowed in rooms and all doors locked by 10 P.M. No shouting or rowdy behavior. No chewing tobacco or spitting…"

"He's a gentleman with impeccable manners and behavior. You will hardly know he is here," I said cutting her off. "Just sign here please," I said pointing to the receipt.

She hesitated, then scooped up the gold. The pen shook in her hand as she hesitated. "Just put your mark here," as I guided her hand to make a cross. I realized she couldn't write her name.

Manon was hard at work trying sort out items Pierre-Louis would need when he escaped the hospital when I returned. The cook had locked the restaurant and left for the day. I noted that the roll-up cover of Pierre Louis' desk I had left down was now open.

"Would you like to celebrate our good fortune with a glass of Champagne, madam?

Manon gave me a quizzical look, then threw me a tantalizing smile. "*Mais oui mon cher.* You don't expect Manon to work in this dark bachelor's apartment and not get a little reward, do you?"

"Of course not." We closed up the apartment and I unlocked the restaurant. While Manon checked the kitchen, I scrambled down the ladder to the cellar and selected the coldest half bottle of Veuve Cliquot I could find. Manon had two champagne glasses ready.

"So, what do you think of your new domain?"

"It will do," she said coquettishly as we clinked our glasses of the cool, but not cold bubbly and she handed me a long list of things to do.

I gave it a quick perusal. At the top of the list was to hire a sign painter to rename the restaurant *CHEZ MANON.* The rest of the list would take Gino and me at least three days to accomplish. "When do you want to have your grand opening?"

"As soon as you can get the invitations printed and distributed to these people," she said with a big grin as she pulled out another long, folded list from her soft leather gloves.

"My, oh my! Manon has been very busy while I was renting Pierre Louis' living quarters. Time to draw these lists and sneak a look at the Pierre Louis' account ledgers." I said with a "caught ya" look.

"Yes, Manon has to plan how to make money with *her* restaurant and not make the same mistakes as Pierre-Louis. Women understand that you have to go after the right men for clients to have a successful restaurant and you have to do it from the start. You approve?" She said referring to the list of inaugural invitees and daring me to object.

"I think your idea of an opening by invitation only is very clever. It sends a signal that your restaurant hosts exclusive events and is not just for everyone. Those left off the grand opening will want to see what they missed when the restaurant is open to the general public. Your list of invitees guarantees that the grand opening gets a lot of free press. The French will be jealous and curious as they were not invited."

"Manon will have a second evening by invitation only where the consul general and the most important members of the French and Italian communities are invited. Friday opening for the Americans and Sunday opening for the French and Italians," she said with a devilish smile. "I plan to divide and conquer," she added with a flourish and more champagne. "I'm even thinking of inviting the famous Chinese courtesan, Ah Toy, to the first gala opening. Imagine what an impression it will make on the wives of the leading merchants to see in person the beautiful and infamous courtesan their husbands' patronage has made into a legend."

"Oh la, la. How the plot thickens. The newspapers and gossips will have a field day," I said and poured the last of the champagne.

"Hah. That's the whole point. What do you think of the list for the first night?" She said giving me a sly look.

"It's a stroke of genius to invite Sam Brannan and the most important and influential members of the Committee of Vigilance. It sends a signal to all San Franciscans that they are the group to be courted and that they alone have the power to curb lawlessness in the city. It guarantees immediate and positive publicity for your restaurant and will make members of the civil government jealous to be snubbed, but eager to come see for themselves what they missed. I hadn't realized you followed the doings of the Committee so thoroughly," I added.

"You should thank Pierre-Louis. It was his list of the most influential members I culled from the desk while you just looked at figures," she said with a look that said "touché."

The next few days were going be quite busy but very interesting.

·

"SAM BRANNAN," in 1851.

California Gold Rush Journal
⤬ PART 2 ⤬

CHAPTER ELEVEN

San Francisco — July-August 1851

I ducked into my office on the way to Hawthorne's cubby hole to check for mail. There were two more sacks of French mail from the consulate to process. Sophie Benson handed me a letter. To my surprise it was postmarked from New York with Georges' distinctive scrawl. He'd managed to secure his Nelly and they were on their way to San Francisco via the newer and closer overland route through Nicaragua. If there was a steamer ready to sail when they reached the Pacific coast, they could be in San Francisco as early as September.

Manon would be reassured to have much needed help with her restaurant before and after the birth of our babes. Thomas Hawthorne greeted me with a smile and tendered me a dossier to read. He'd followed my instructions to the letter.

"If I notarize the agreement, will you be able to file it with the Recorder's Office?" I asked.

"No, the agreement does not need to be notarized, but the mortgage will have to be notarized by an American notary once the option to buy is executed so it can be recorded. As you are a principal in the transaction, it would be a conflict of interest for you to notarize a deed in which you are self-interested."

"Good. I'm sure you know an honest notary when we need one."

"Of course. Did you get a chance to speak with Manon about whether Giselle will work in the restaurant or still sell on the wharf?"

"As you can imagine, a lot of things are up in the air at the moment. From what I know so far, Giselle and Teri will continue to run the wine bar and canteen on the wharf as it's a profitable business. Manon may have to call on Giselle from time to time to help in the restaurant when she hosts a gala event." Hawthorne's muddled, worried expression betrayed his concern that Giselle might slip away from him if she mingled with the movers and shakers in the City. If he knew of Manon's plan to use Giselle as a waitress in her opening galas, he'd have real cause to worry as we didn't plan to invite work associates.

I bought all the day's newspapers and revues with French language sections from a stand in the Plaza and stuffed them in Manon's charity food basket for Pierre-Louis. The cabbie who'd driven me to the hospital hailed me before I saw him. We were soon bouncing along the rutted streets of North Beach towards the hospital.

Pierre-Louis greeted me with a big smile. "*Mon ami,* you are a life-saver. The taste of real food your Gino brought has revived my spirits.

What news? Can you get me out of here?" He said eyeing Manon's second food basket and the pile of newspapers hungrily.

I brought him up to date on my efforts to find him suitable accommodations and described the room in Mrs. Hale's rooming house I'd rented. "I bluffed about having a daytime nurse for you, so we still have to find one before they'll let you out of here. Gino is checking the merchants who sell hospital beds and convalescent supplies. The room is currently furnished with a large desk and comfortable armchairs with side tables."

"I've been thinking about how to get out of this damned, infernal place. There's a French doctor, Dr. François Benoit, who has a medical practice over a shop on Dupont Street. He often takes his midday meal at the restaurant and we're friendly. I'll offer to pay him to take over supervision of my recovery, especially as my new room is only a short walk from the restaurant. I'm sure he'll know of a nurse looking for employment."

"I'll have Gino locate him and make an appointment for me. I'll ask him to write a letter requesting your release from here into his care. I'll see it's done today." With that pressing matter settled, I handed him the lease with option to buy agreement for the fixed sum of $20,000 to be paid out of monthly restaurant profits as he had suggested. He smiled broadly when he got to the stipulation in the agreement that he would be entitled to eat his meals free at the restaurant so long as we owned the business.

"What about the money for the room rental? I don't have a sou on me here and if I did, the orderlies would steal it. One tried to snatch food from Manon's basket yesterday. All my money is locked up in my safe in the restaurant."

"Not to worry, my friend, we will apply what we expend to the down payment of our lease/purchase agreement. We'll get your safe moved to your rented room whenever you want. Is the agreement okay?"

"Yes, it solves a lot of problems for me. I hope Manon won't mind if I take my meals at the restaurant once I'm up and about. I'll promise to keep out of her hair."

"I'm sure it won't be a problem and Manon insists on it. She'll probably make you show her how you make your chocolate soufflé to perfection. By the way, your cook, Henri, will stay in the kitchen. I hope he's able to work with a woman owner."

"As long as he gets to sample what he cooks and wash it

down with a glass of wine from time to time, he'll adjust." We both laughed at the thought of the portly Henri stuffing his face and tossing back wine as he cooked.

"When she opens the restaurant, we plan to use the apartment upstairs as a residence. Is it okay to store your personal belongings?"

"Of course. It makes sense to stay there after closing the restaurant, especially when the babies come."

"What about the provisions and equipment in the restaurant?"

"Since you'll cook for me, I have no further need for anything in the restaurant. I'll need only my safe, clothes and personal possessions from the apartment eventually."

"Manon will be pleased she can use the restaurant stock. It'll allow her to open sooner. Gino will bring your food and newspapers daily and we'll get you out of here quickly."

Pierre Louis signed the original and two copies of the agreement and we sealed our deal with a swig of cognac each from my pocket flask.

I delivered one signed copy of the lease to attorney Hawthorne and sought out Manon who was barking orders to her new cook, Henri. "So, *Chéri*, does Manon now own her restaurant?" She said with a pouty smile and dancing eyes.

"Of course, my love. You only have to sign the agreement," which I waved past her pert nose and hid behind my back before she could snatch it. "We get to have everything in the restaurant and live in the apartment. He wants only his safe, personal effects, and, of course, your delicious cooking."

"So come here Big Boy and get your reward," she said crooking her finger and beckoning me with a teasing look. She took the agreement, glanced through it quickly and signed it with a flourish. She tucked her copy in the pocket of her cook's smock and put her arms around my neck.

"You get your reward upstairs tonight, my love," she whispered in my ear and nipped it gently. "But now there is still much more work to do," and handed me a sheaf of papers from her pocket.

She'd prepared the text of her invitations and announcements—both in French and in "franglais," her charming mixture of French and English. "Don't laugh," she scolded. "You better put them in good American or you get reduced reward tonight," she warned giving me her "you better not be a naughty boy" look.

I laughed. "When do they need to be printed?"

"I think we invite the Americans first for Friday and the French for Sunday. So, we need them printed tomorrow so Gino can deliver by hand, non? That way they have only two days to reserve and must make a decision quick or be left out since we have only sixteen tables plus the private dining room. Also, we put an announcement in all the papers that CHEZ MANON's grand opening is this Friday and Sunday by invitation only. Announcement also says we open for business Wednesday through Sunday only for lunch and by reservation only for dinner. No drop-in rowdies or curious bachelors to stand at the bar and nurse a drink to wait for pretty women to ogle."

"Won't we miss clients that way?" I asked perplexed.

"Hah, Big Boy. You don't know the restaurant business. Leave it to Manon. Manon doesn't want a restaurant like Henry Bruen."

I was surprised Manon knew about Henry Bruen's restaurant. He installed *cabinets particuliers*—small, private, well-upholstered dining rooms upstairs where men could entertain their mistresses or others with champagne and a turn on the sofa. Waiters were instructed to knock and wait discreetly for the turn of the lock latch before entering. They were already the source of many salacious scandals and a number of divorces. As one wag commented, "No woman ever went upstairs in a French restaurant to say her prayers."

Manon was amused by my surprised reaction. "Manon doesn't want those kinds of clients. She wants only people who appreciate fine cuisine and expensive wines and spirits. You don't want men ogling and propositioning Teri, Giselle or your Manon now, do you?" She said with a self-satisfied smile and raised eyebrows.

"Teri and Giselle?" I stammered. "Are they going to be partners in your restaurant?" I asked, taken by surprise.

"No, but they agree to work in the restaurant for pay and tips while we get started. After closing the wine bar and canteen in the afternoon, they will join us for an early dinner in the restaurant. Teri will run the bar and Giselle will serve food with Gino and you, too, if necessary. Gino will escort them back to our ship when we close," Manon stated matter of factly.

"What about lunch?" I asked.

"Gino will run the bar and serve the tables until Georges gets here. And maybe we can use Nelly when she is not taking care of our twins. No pretty women to hustle at lunchtime and a more simple and limited menu. We make our money and reputation with our dinner menu and by requiring reservations," Manon said smugly. "Here is a list of the wines and liquors we need for the bar," Manon added as she shooed me out the door and stormed back into the kitchen to supervise the cook.

Gino arrived and gave me a hang-dog look. He, like Henri, the cook, was not used to being given marching orders by a determined drill sergeant. We went upstairs to Pierre Louis' former office which was now empty of his effects. After re-writing Manon's invitations and the ad announcing our opening, I sent Gino off to the printer and newspapers to meet the afternoon deadlines.

I decided to seek out and enlist Dr. Benoit in Pierre-Louis' cause. As the boy in the newspaper kiosk on the Plaza was shouting new developments in the tug of war between the Committee of Vigilance and the Sheriff, I bought the latest paper on the way to the doctor's office.

Dr. Benoit's waiting and consultation rooms were at the top of the stairs over a millinery shop on Dupont Street. One entered into a small, friendly but dimly lit waiting room that was fortunately empty. A sign tacked to the consulting room door stated the doctor was occupied with a patient and requested new arrivals to take the highest remaining card from a deck of cards on a small table and be seated.

The newspaper headline screamed in bold type that the Committee of Vigilance had the infamous Sydney Duck, Sam Whittaker, in custody. Whittaker had been fingered in James Stuart's confession as the ring leader who had organized numerous robberies and planned the torching of the commercial district. According to the paper, Whittaker had fled San Francisco for Sacramento after Stuart was hanged. Despite his attempt at disguise and flight, he was recognized and arrested by Sheriff Hearn in Santa Barbara. Whittaker sought to join his mistress, Mrs. Hogan, in San Diego where they planned to flee to Mexico and escape the wrath of the vigilantes.

Sheriff Hearn arrived in San Francisco with Whittaker by boat and left him in the custody of the captain while he tried to locate Sheriff Hays in San Francisco to hand over the prisoner. Two members of the Committee of Vigilance learned from the boat's crew that Whittaker was held shackled on the boat and demanded that the captain release him to their custody, which he did before Sheriff Hearn returned. The Committee now had both Whittaker and Mrs. Hogan, who had helped fence the Ducks' stolen property, in custody and under interrogation. Sheriff Hays, the mayor, and the rest of the police establishment were furious at the unexpected turn of events. According to the report, wagers were already being taken as to whether Sheriff Hays would try to rescue the prisoner and if so, whether he would succeed.

The door to Doctor Benoit's consulting room opened suddenly and an attractive young woman rushed out with petticoats flying and tears streaming down her over-rouged face. She raced past me and swept recklessly down the stairs at full speed. She was followed by a kindly looking, balding, middle-aged man in a white smock over suit and tie whom I took to be the doctor. I introduced myself and apprised him of Pierre-Louis' condition and request for assistance.

"Of course, I'll be glad to supervise M. Lerouge's recovery. It's a wonder my last patient didn't meet the same fate."

"Why was she so upset?" I asked

"It's never welcome news to learn you are pregnant with no husband and no interest in becoming a mother," he said sadly. "She became hysterical when I informed her that I would not assist in aborting her baby. You witnessed the rest. Unfortunately for her and the life she is carrying, she'll probably risk both lives at the hands of an abortionist in a dirty, back alley shanty."

I had to suppress my anger at his self-righteous position. If he abhorred the young woman's only option which risked her life, why not refer her to someone who could help her if his convictions precluded his assistance. Instead of venting my anger, I gave Dr. Benoit the particulars of Pierre-Louis' confinement and his new lodgings along with an invitation to continue his lunches at our new restaurant. He assured me he would get Pierre Louis released to his care next day.

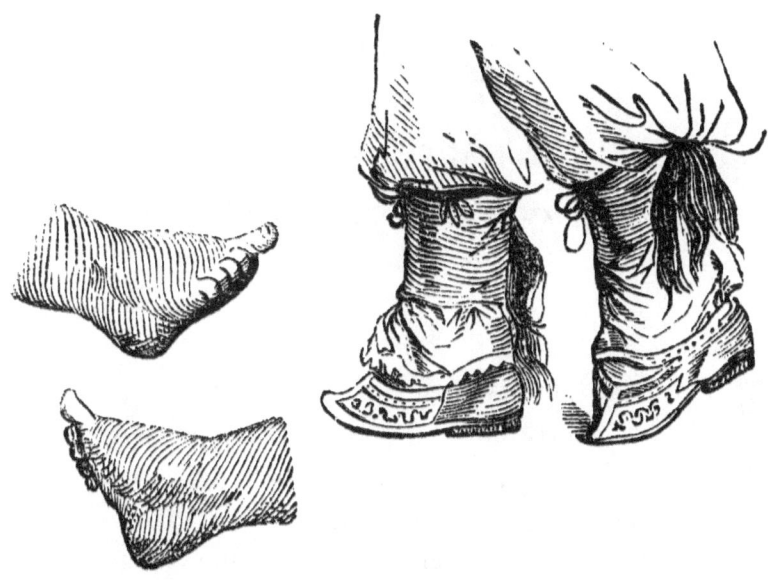

"AH TOY'S LILLY-BOUND FEET AND SHOES," litho c. 1850.

California Gold Rush Journal
∽ PART 2 ∾

CHAPTER TWELVE

San Francisco — July-August 1851

The next few days saw flurries of hectic activity on all fronts. Pierre-Louis moved to his new room at Mrs. Hale's rooming house and Dr. Benoit found him a charming day nurse who fussed over and pampered him much to his delight. We set up house in the apartment over the restaurant. Manon provided long lists for all of us to accomplish daily and on time or else. She issued orders like a major general organizing her troops into battle for the sole purpose of conquest.

San Francisco already had several very good, expensive and popular French restaurants—*La Maison Riche, La Maison Dorée* and others including Henry Bruen's restaurant with its *cabinets particuliers.* Manon intended to leave them all in her wake. All had male chefs and owners and she was determined to show discriminating diners and the social elite of our town that a woman could do it as well or better. She counted on her two gala openings to make her reputation and provide the cuisine and ambiance that would silence critics of the fair sex.

I was entrusted with the menus for both gala openings and instructed to ensure the printed menus for each table were not leaked to the press or curious competitors. Gino delivered invitations to our first gala opening by hand. Manon was like a cat dancing on a hot stove as she awaited the responses. The first to reserve was Sam Brannan who requested a table for eight. Manon let out an excited shriek and ran to throw her arms around me shouting in my ear, "I knew it. *Ça va aller! Tu verras.* It will be a success." I hugged her tight saying, "which tables shall we give his party?"

"That depends on who else from his faction reserves. We can't put the radical members of the Committee of Vigilance near the more conservative ones or they will ruin the evening with their political animosity and suspicion of each other."

Sam Brannan's reservation was extremely important; he was one of the founders of the Committee of Vigilance. He had successfully orchestrated the trial, conviction and hanging of the thief, Jenkins. While still a leader and member of the executive committee, he opposed turning captured Sydney Ducks over to the police or sheriff. He had no confidence in the corrupt civil authorities to convict and execute arsonists, murderers or the thugs their ringleaders employed. He wanted to see Whittaker and his gang interrogated, tried and executed to end once and for all the criminal activities and influence of the Sydney Ducks.

Brannan was always a controversial figure. Brigham Young sent him with a small band of Latter Day Saints to San Francisco before the discovery of gold when it was still a sandy tent outpost, called Yerba Buena, catering to ships that took on cargos of hides and tallow. Brannan had been ordered to find a route through the Sierra Nevada that the Mormon faithful could use as an alternate to the overland route to their new settlement in Utah. Brannan defied Brigham Young and decided to stay at Yerba Buena where he founded San Francisco's first newspaper and engaged in land speculation which made him a rich man after gold was discovered.

The more moderate wing of the Committee argued that given the gravity of the charges and effects of the two recent incendiaries, the civil authorities had no choice but to convict and impose maximum penalties. They also worried that the governor might carry out his threat to declare martial law in San Francisco and send in troops to storm the Committee's fortified headquarters to rescue prisoners held there and deliver them to the civil authorities for trial.

Manon was convinced that once the conservative wing of the Committee learned Brannan and his top lieutenants were attending our gala opening, they would be compelled to match their presence. If so, she would be serving dinner to the most important business and political movers and shakers in the city. Their attendance would guarantee maximum publicity of our opening in all the city's newspapers as she also invited the town's leading reporters whom she planned to seat at the same table to gossip, observe and scribble their columns.

While we hoped some of the important members of the business community would bring their wives, we couldn't be sure. To ensure more notoriety and grist for the scribblers, Manon invited the legendary Chinese courtesan, Ah Toy. She was one of the first two Chinese women to arrive in San Francisco in 1848 and the first to ply her trade. Unlike the many short and pubescent Chinese slave girls with large peasant feet Manon and I had seen in our tours of Little China, Ah Toy was a tall, beautiful, mature Chinese woman with aristocratic "lily-bound" feet and no master or pimp to control her activities or steal her money.

She set up her first residence in a small shanty in an alley off Clay Street above Kearny. At the time of her arrival, there were over 780 womanless Chinese men in the city as well as thousands of men of other nationalities. She soon had lines of men waiting as long as a block at times. As her reputation spread by 1850, successful miners arriving from the placers scurried to her door. An individual claiming to be her "husband" sued her in court in an effort to access her growing fortune. She denied being married and the judge ruled in her favor.

While the *Alta* in May 1850 did report the marriage of one Henry Conrad to a China woman named Achoi from Hong Kong, there was no further mention of him. By this time she had become the madam of her own large parlor house off Clay Street in an alley known as Pike Street with a stable of newly arrived Chinese girls.

In 1850, this remarkable woman actually sued several non-paying clients in Judge George Baker's Recorder's Court. According to newspaper accounts, she arrived in court dressed in an apricot-colored satin jacket with willow-green pantaloons and colorful tabis on her small, tightly bound feet. She wore her hair in an elegant chignon.

The judge asked her what the non-paying men came for.

"They came to gaze upon the countenance of the charming Ah Toy," she replied in broken but colorful English. The packed courtroom audience roared in appreciation of her guile. She went on to testify that she charged each customer one ounce of gold, worth $16.00, which she weighed on her own scale for the right to gaze upon her countenance. She claimed several miners whom she pointed out in court had tried to cheat her by mixing brass filings with their gold. When the judge asked for proof, she produced a basin full of brass filings. The amused judge, ruled tongue-in-cheek that she had not proved that the specific men named in her complaint did the actual cheating.

Concurrent with the Committee of Vigilance's investigation of the crimes committed by the gangs of Sydney Ducks, the Committee launched an investigation of prostitution in the city in 1851. Several rival parlor house madams singled out

Ah Toy as one who should be arrested and deported. John A. Clark, a member of the Committee's prostitution investigation patrol discovered Ah Toy, fell in love and became her lover and protector. Manon specifically invited them both to her opening gala. If they accepted, it would guarantee a journalistic coup, especially with so many of her former clients having to meet her on socially equal terms.

As Manon predicted, other members of the Committee of Vigilance quickly accepted Manon's invitation including Stephen Payran, President of the Executive Committee, Issac Bluxowe, Secretary of the Committee and G. W. Ryckman, who it was rumored was the chief interrogator of Sam Whittaker and other Sydney Ducks currently held by the Committee. The newspapers were clamoring for Whittaker's neck in a noose and the Governor, mayor and Sheriff Hays were threatening members of the Committee with retribution if Whittaker were to hang.

Many political analysts warned that should the civil authorities attempt to storm the Committee's fortress to retake Whittaker, the result would be civil war. Manon's grand opening was shaping up to showcase the major players in the struggle over who would be the force of law and order in the city. Manon was immensely pleased with her strategy. All the major players in the Committee as well as Ah Toy and other notables had reserved for her gala opening for Friday, August 15, 1851.

Once all our tables were reserved, our focus returned to food preparation. Henri already complained he was overworked, but Manon was having none of it. The success of the menu would establish or ruin her reputation as a top restaurant. Manon was pushing our suppliers hard to provide the fresh ingredients she needed to make a tour de force impact. Once the menus were printed, she was committed to produce the goods.

We were all nervous when the inaugural evening finally arrived. Manon set candles and a bouquet of roses on each table. She asked Giselle and Teri to wear high neck satin dresses that showed little skin but molded their mature figures. Gino looked good in a snappy waiter's uniform in black and white with bow tie and Giselle wore an embroidered apron over her mauve satin dress with few petticoats. Both women wore their hair up in attractive chignons. Manon wore a pale blue tunic to mask her now large belly over a dress of royal blue muslin. She wore her dark, curly tresses loose down her back held in place by clasps fashioned from gold nuggets embedded in quartz crystals. The effect was stunning. With each bob of her head the facets of crystal caught the light of the whale oil lamps and shimmered like a halo.

The first guests to arrive were in the party headed by Sam Brannan and George Schenck, the two leaders of the more radical, minority faction of the Committee clamoring for Whittaker to hang. Brannan, as always, was richly dressed in a costume with long coat, tie secured by a ruby stick pin tucked in a vest from which hung a gold fob and chain. He was broadshouldered, barrel-chested, and dapper. He grabbed Manon's hand and bussed it lightly with his lips.

"Madam, I am delighted to make your acquaintance and share this inaugural evening in your charming establishment," he said in a booming voice and with a familiar manner.

"We were delighted to receive your reservation. Please meet my husband, Pierre Dubois," she said indicating me. We shook hands and I said, "*enchanté monsieur.*" George Schenck proffered Manon a dozen red roses, bowed stiffly and also kissed Manon's extended hand.

"Thank you Mr. Schenck for the lovely roses on our special evening; it's very thoughtful of you," Manon said while favoring him with a gracious smile.

Schenck appeared ill at ease under Manon's penetrating gaze and quizzical smile. "It's from all of us," he managed to sputter. Manon motioned to Giselle to lead him and the rest of his group to their table and serve a welcoming glass of champagne while the other guests arrived. Manon had prepared a seating chart to ensure we kept the warring factions apart. The table with the four journalists buzzed with muted chatter and finger pointing to identify all present. The complimentary champagne produced the desired effect. The level of excited conversation continued to mount so loud it was hard to hear across any table clearly. Only one table lacked occupants. Manon hesitated whether to serve the first course of the fixed menu or wait.

Ah Toy chose that moment to make her grand entrance. She complimented Manon on her dress and dazzling hair clasps, shook her hand and shuffle-stepped across the dining room to the only unoccupied table on her tiny bound feet with her lover following sheepishly. Ah Toy wore a traditional Chinese *qichao*, a form-hugging silk dress with high, embroidered collar and a long slit from her thigh that revealed a tantalizing glimpse of delectable leg and well-turned ankles down to her tiny red and green shoes with a miniature cork heel. Her entrance and well-practiced shuffle in her stunning red silk dress cut conversation in the room to a stunned silence as all heads turned to watch the spectacle.

Once Ah Toy and her companion, John Clark, were seated, Manon signaled Giselle and Gino to serve the first course. Manon's *terrine de canard truffée maison* was one of the few dishes she could prepare in advance. It was served on bed of mixed salad leaves and with small French *cornichons*. Teri served a chilled Saint Amour wine from the Beaujolais region to complement the dish. Manon and I watched our diners load their terrine on chunks of fresh baguette and scarf the lot with big swigs of wine. The only dainty eater in the house was Ah Toy who alternated small bits of the pâté with tiny sips of wine.

Teri and Giselle generated considerable attention as they served second helpings and refilled wine glasses. Several members of each political faction attempted to make sustained eye contact with the two women and one undisciplined member tried to pinch Teri's bottom only to have his hand swatted away while the other members of his party laughed nervously.

Manon let her guests clean their plates before serving the second course, a *salade des écrevisses à la nage*. It had taken lots of cajoling to secure a supply of the fresh water crayfish to serve a full restaurant. They were served in a mixed salad with a vinaigrette sauce Manon concocted specially for the dish. She was sure her American diners had rarely, if ever, tasted these delicious critters with crab-like claws and lobster-like tails. She would have liked to serve abalone, but our Chinese suppliers couldn't guarantee a large enough supply. She could stretch the crayfish in a salad. Teri served a well-chilled Cheverny white wine to complement the delicate, nutty taste of the crayfish's tail.

The main course entrée, *La Côte de Cerf Rôtie*, was greeted with acclaim from several tables once they poured Manon's *sauce béarnaise* over the meat and took their first bite. The sauce was such a hit that they poured it over the *pommes soufflées* and *les asperges à la Fontenelle* as well. Manon had to order a grumpy Henri to make more sauce in a hurry. Teri served a well-aged Chateauneuf-du-Pape red wine to go with the rich elk meat and sauce.

While the *sauce béarnaise* is typically a rich, creamy sauce married to the best quality cuts of beef, Manon decided to offer it with the more gamey, red meat of the stag deer rather than a traditional deer meat sauce. She was sure her guests would find the combination irresistible and she hit the nail on the head.

When the last of the *sauce béarnaise* was sponged off the

plates with bits of baguette, Manon personally served her *Baba au Rhum* dessert while Teri served champagne to our now pleasantly sated guests. Manon made a point to chit-chat with all her guests who were rewarded with dazzling smiles in exchange for their compliments on her cuisine and personal charm.

All in all, the evening was a roaring success. Even members of the opposing cliques were now talking loudly to each other and on seemingly friendly terms. Ah Toy had made discrete eye contact with several womanless guests, who would undoubtedly pay her parlor house a visit before calling it a night. Our four journalists scribbled furiously in between courses and were the first to scramble to their respective night editors as soon as they'd gobbled their dessert. Teri, Giselle and Gino all received generous tips for their service and Manon presented our cook, Henri, with his toque and led him from table to table at the end of the soirée to receive his congratulations which Manon had to translate as he spoke no English.

We'd all be curious to read the reviews in tomorrow's papers, but for now it was all Manon and I could do to bank the kitchen fires, lock up and flop exhausted into our cold bed upstairs.

California Gold Rush Journal
⚭ PART 2 ⚭

CHAPTER THIRTEEN
San Francisco — August 1851

A fter delivering food to our ship, Gino brought the morning papers and joined us for coffee and croissants at the restaurant while we scanned the reviews. Our scribblers had done their job. The *Herald's* headline screamed "Committee of Vigilance Mends Fences At New Restaurant." The journalist went on to describe how by the time fabulous *sauce béarnaise* arrived, the Brannon-Schenck faction and the moderates led by Payran and Bluxowe were actually toasting each other and sharing confidences as their glasses "were topped up with a fabulous red wine served by a buxom blonde with fiery blue eyes and coppery skin."

It was kinder praise than most Chilenas received. Hopefully, Teri would take it in stride. The article went on to speculate about the inner workings of the Committee and whether their interrogators had broken Whittaker or McKenzie, their chief prisoners, denounced by Stuart in his confession. The journalist claimed Whittaker had confessed to crimes but offered only speculation and no proof. His theory was Whittaker would crack in order to safeguard his lover, Mrs. Hogan.

The review in the *Alta California* also speculated on the political machinations of the Committee and announced its next meeting for Tuesday evening August 19th, but had more to say about the restaurant. Their journalist cited the Brannan party's gift of roses, the delightful ambiance of the restaurant, the attractive serving staff, the charming owner, and the fabulous food, concluding "Chez Manon has the promise of establishing itself as a top eatery in San Francisco—a place where even political opposites could meet on friendly terms and partake of the finest food and wine the city could offer." Needless to say, the *Alta's* review brought cheers from all of us. Neither review mentioned the presence of Ah Toy and her protector on the Committee.

We'd have to wait for the other two reviews which would appear in afternoon editions. Meanwhile, we had one day to recoup and prepare for our second gala opening on Sunday. We had invited Consul Dillon and his wife and other notables in the French community as well as Gino's uncle and other important members of the French, Italian, Mexican and Chilean communities. Henri arrived late to work but in better humor after his accolades from our first gala. He immediately donned his toque and a clean apron and went to work under Manon's critical eye.

The other two reviews of our soirée with the Committee of Vigilance concentrated more on the personages present than the politics of the Committee. One journalist not only described Ah Toy's presence and eye-stopping saunter to her table but also listed her former clients present at the gala. The last journalist must have had a bone to pick with the Committee because he waited in secret near Ah Toy's parlor house so he could identify in print which members of the Committee sought the services of her girls after leaving the restaurant.

Manon wanted to serve California lobsters or abalone steaks as her main entrée, but couldn't secure a large enough supply of either. She opted instead to serve a *Bisque de Langouste* soup as her first course accompanied by a vintage Sancerre white wine.

We were both more at ease after passing the test with the Americans. It was soothing to hear our pleased guests chattering away in melodic Spanish, Italian and French. Consul Dillon presented his wife, Pauline, to Manon, whom she complimented on her stunning hair clasps and attire and asked politely when her baby was due.

"Our twins are due in three months," Manon replied sweetly.

"My goodness, you are courageous to undertake a new restaurant with twins on the way," the Consul's wife said in an aristocratic accent.

"Women must seize once in a lifetime opportunities when they present themselves. Better to be a pregnant owner here than an under-chef in Paris, don't you think?" Manon said pointedly.

"Yes, I see what you mean. It's true there are no other restaurants even here with women chefs or owners," the Consul's wife admitted as Teri handed her a glass of champagne and Giselle led them to the head of the table they had ordered for their group.

Gino was delighted to serve his uncle, Luigi Salterini, and the coterie of Italian merchants and notables, who shared a table for eight. Their group was the most animated of our guests. Gino reported they relished the opportunity to be together and to celebrate Manon's successful debut, especially after most had lost their business premises to the fire of June 22nd. Gino had, of course, fully briefed them on Manon's success with the Committee, so they were primed to be a part of a successful opening. Many, like Salterini, were hoping for a similar success in reestablishing their own businesses.

Manon signaled Giselle and Gino to serve the second course, *Terrine de Faisan Truffée Maison*. To complement the pheasant terrine with truffles, Teri served a red Sancerre wine. Like the Americans, our mostly European diners heaped gobs of terrine on pieces of fresh baguette and washed it down with gulps of the delicious Loire valley wine served chilled. The convivial chatter during the soup course now escalated to an animated roar of mixed Latin tongues. Manon was smiling as she moved from table to table with Giselle behind her offering second helpings to those with empty plates while Teri refilled empty glasses.

Manon offered for her main course *Cailles dans une Sauce de Morilles à la Crème*. Teri poured a vintage Saint-Joseph red wine from the rich Rhone wine country south of Lyon that is best known for its big, hearty red wines like Gigondas and Chateauneuf-du-Pape. Manon calculated that her lesser known Saint-Joseph of equal quality would be a pleasant surprise even to the French and would complement her quail entrée with morel mushrooms in a cream sauce perfectly. She had brought her dried morel mushrooms from France around Cape Horn for just such an occasion.

Manon sent Gino and Giselle to ladle more sauce to the table headed by Consul Dillon and Teri to top off the glasses of the Spanish speaking group while she moseyed over to the Italian table headed by Salterini.

"So, Luigi, what's your verdict? Do you need to take a vote?" Manon asked tongue-in-cheek as he pushed another gob into his mouth.

"Ah my dear hostess. How could you know how much we Italians miss our morel mushrooms? Your sauce is divine and the little quails are delicious." Salterini paused to address members of his group in Italian. Their response was a united "*Brava!*" They then raised mostly empty glasses which they clinked and demanded "*Piu Vino Rosso e Salsa Per Favore.*"

Manon laughed and pointed to Salterini's napkin he'd tucked into his shirt like a bib. "Dribble less sauce down your front and you wouldn't have to ask for more," she chided him playfully. Members of his party who understood French roared their approval at Manon's antics. Two Italians started to sing a drinking song as they waved their empty glasses. Manon motioned for Teri and Gino to bring more wine, sauce and bread to soak up the sauce.

By the time the dessert was ready to be served, the lively Italians were singing popular songs and arias from their favorite comedies and operas. The more stuffy French tried in vain to ignore the unrestrained gaiety of their Latin neighbors. Pierre-Louis would be laughing in his beard if he had one. The singing was interrupted by the arrival of the first batch of Henri's crêpes flambées which Gino served first to the Italians while Teri served champagne and tots of cognac.

Once everyone's champagne glass was full, Consul Dillon rose to give a toast to Manon and her new restaurant. "This is a happy occasion for all of us to welcome Manon and her superb French cuisine to our fair city. As we can all attest from tonight's fare, *Chez Manon* will be a culinary landmark every important visitor or resident in San Francisco will want to experience." Gino and his uncle translated Dillon's remarks to the Italians and Teri to the Spanish speakers. At a signal from Dillon our guests shouted "Hurrah," in several languages.

We had not invited any journalists to this more intimate second opening gala as they were not needed. The Latin language communities in the city would hear testimonials by word of mouth from those present. *Chez Manon* would be known as a friendly venue for a special meal where non-English speaking patrons would be welcome.

The French and Latin Americans left shortly after the desert and coffee service. The Italians stayed to order after-dinner drinks from Teri's bar and congratulate Gino on his association with the successful new enterprise. We had stocked the bar with *grappa* and *acquavite* for the Italians, just as we had laid in a supply of cognac and Armagnac for the French and Bourbon and Scotch whiskey for the Americans.

As we felt very comfortable with the Italian contingent, we ordered after dinner drinks on the house and invited our cook, Henri to join us. Now that we'd made our mark with our future clientele, it was time to relax and let the tension of the two openings drain away in friendly company.

"So, Luigi what do you think of our French cooking and wines now?" I asked playfully.

Salterini laughed. "You're not going to get me on that one like you did on your ship. Let's ask my friend here, who had the best Italian restaurant in North Beach before the Ducks wiped him out," he said pointing to a tall, square-faced man in his fifties with a big, bushy moustache, prominent nose, and ruddy complexion sitting at the end of the table. Salterini posed the question in Italian.

His friend, Salvatore Benetti smiled graciously at Manon, who was now seated nursing a glass of champagne. Benetti lifted his thick, black brows and sheepishly uttered, *"Bene, molto bene la cucina e el vino rosso e la salsa sono si saporita."*

Manon and I laughed. "Spoken like a true Italian gentleman," Manon replied and Benetti, looking at Salterini for confirmation, stood and gave an elegant bow to Manon, who offered him her hand to kiss.

"We won't let you off the hook so easily, Luigi. When Benetti reopens his restaurant, we expect to be invited to the grand opening." Salterini translated to Benetti, who nodded his agreement vigorously.

"Let's just leave it at that. We enjoy your excellent French food and wines and you'll get to do the same with our Italian specialties. We learn from you and you learn from us. But, to-night you win the big prize with those morel mushrooms and the sauce." Salterini said proudly.

Manon gave Luigi a big nod of appreciation for the compliments. I could see Manon was tired and starting to fade. I asked Gino to serve his uncle and friends as long as they liked to stay and then lock up and take Teri and Giselle back to our ship.

Gino seemed to be making some headway in his efforts to court Teri. We were all beat and decided not to open our wharf-side canteen and wine bar the next day. We would wait for reservations and not open the restaurant for dinner again until next Friday which was four days hence. Teri had been making considerable eye contact with Gino during their long weekend serving tables and they were whispering to each other when they could during our two galas. With a day off from food preparation tomorrow it was a good time for a romance to jell, if it was to be. I noted that Gino shared a glass of champagne with Manon, but declined to join his uncle and friends in after dinner drinks.

We bade good night to everyone and wearily trudged up the flight of stairs to our cold bed, snuggled up for warmth and were soon sawing logs.

California Gold Rush Journal
ᖣ PART 2 ᖣ

CHAPTER FOURTEEN
San Francisco — August 1851

As Gino had a day off, I decided to take Pierre-Louis' basket of leftovers from our second gala to him myself to see how he was getting on with his nurse and recovery. A stern-faced Mrs. Hale met me at the door of her rooming house.

"Ah, you'se the one I wants t'a see. That woman what's waiting on Mr. Lerouge doan speak no English. She's a comin' an' goin' all hours of the day and night. You got'a tell 'er this 'ere house doan tolerate no funny business. She needs ta keep proper hours like a real nurse an' no flitting around or hanky-panky's gonna be tolerated," Mrs. Hale proclaimed in her staccato basso like a Scotch drill sergeant.

I smothered my inclination to laugh. The thought of any hanky-panky with his legs in casts and trussed-up in a hospital bed was risible. "I'll be sure to advise them both of your concerns," I dead-panned. I knocked before entering the room just in case.

"Come in," Pierre-Louis yelled.

Before I could open the door, it was swept open and I was

face to face with the new nurse. "And who might you be?" The woman demanded.

"For god's sake woman, stop the interrogation. Pierre's a good friend."

"My name is not 'woman'; I'm Mrs. Gemmer to your friends and everyone else," the nurse said in a chiding tone.

Oh boy, I thought. There's nothing like being physically helpless and pushed around by someone you must depend on. Mrs. Gemmer moved in front of a table by a window and struck a pose holding a short whisking broom and long-handled broom between crossed hands over her bodice as if she were leaning on the tip of the broom handle. She was dressed in a maid's uniform—a full length black dress that while practical, showcased her still small waist, full bosom, and mature figure. She'd rolled the ruffled sleeves up to her elbows to show sturdy arms and hands that were still delicate and unadorned by a ring. To complete her image, she'd tucked a large, white apron into the narrow belt at her waist, draped a small, cotton shawl over her shoulders and wore a maid's bonnet over her still dark black hair parted down the middle and worn in a bun under her bonnet.

She was above average height and looked to be in her late forties. I forgot about Mrs. Hale's desired pep talk about no hanky-panky. Mrs. Gemmer looked to be the type of widow angling to snatch a well-to-do husband. Her cocked head and suspicious look at me suggested she'd settle for no less than marriage. I hoped Pierre-Louis realized he was in deep trouble if he viewed Mrs. Gemmer as a temporary nurse only.

"Matilde, would you take Mr. Dubois' basket and prepare our meal, please," Pierre-Louis said to my surprise. I hadn't anticipated that she would partake of the food we delivered daily or that they would already be on a first name basis. She'd have to prepare his plate and he always did like company when he ate. I wondered if she'd let him have his tots of cognac in the evening. Probably not. The doctor would have apprised her of his heart condition and prescription for less alcohol. No point having him pop off before she had a gold band on her finger. Matilde took the basket and set about preparing two plates.

"Have a seat Pierre. I want to hear all about your opening day successes. I read the reviews in the papers, of course, about the first opening. Whose brilliant idea was it to invite both factions of the Committee?"

"It was Manon's, but she gives you an assist for the idea. She relied on the lists you made while cleaning out your desk for storage. They all had a good time, drank a lot and gobbled up the food like it was their last meal on earth."

"And whose idea was it to invite Ah Toy? I would love to have seen the startled looks when the city's top madam made her dramatic entry." Mrs. Gemmer's back was turned to us as she arranged their midday meal, but at the mention 'top madam,' she turned and gave us a sharp, disapproving look.

"The Ah Toy invite was strictly Manon's idea. She rightly figured she'd come and it guaranteed publicity by the tattle-tale gossips for both Manon's restaurant and Ah Toy's parlor house." The mention of "parlor house" brought an under the breath snicker from Mrs. Gemmer's corner. I could sense that she and Manon would not get along well. I wondered if she expected us to cook for her once Pierre-Louis' casts are off and he was able to get around on his own.

"It's nigh on 12:30. The doctor wants you to eat at regular times, you know," Mrs. Gemmer announced in a sing-song voice that made it clear I was expected to terminate my visit and unwelcome gossip. I could see that she'd prepared a tray with plates that held small slices of Manon's pheasant terrine, and the morel mushrooms that accompanied the quails lacked most of the rich cream sauce that we knew Pierre-Louis loved. There was a very small carafe of red wine and two glasses. My friend was getting wartime rations at best.

"Come back again soon," Pierre-Louis acquiesced, much to Mrs. Gemmer's satisfaction. Had Pierre-Louis not been looking, I'm sure she would have shooed me out the door with her broom. Instead, she gave me a sweet but disingenuous little smile and curtsey to let me know she could play the game but held the high cards.

Manon would not be pleased with my report, but Pierre-Louis was infirm, lonely, and needy. He was also a big boy and would have to handle his Mrs. Gemmer on his own. I was doubly glad we had a firm, enforceable lease and option to buy the restaurant that she couldn't force him to disavow.

Manon's decision to open her restaurant for dinner only Friday through Sunday was due to a number of factors. We still had the profitable wharf-side concessions to cook for. We only had one cook in addition to Manon. Teri and Giselle needed time off if they were to sell on the wharf and work in the restaurant. We might try to alternate Teri and Giselle for the dinner service, but they preferred to work together and were both happy to serve our nouveau riche clientele who were above making crude propositions and trying to pinch bottoms or cop a feel. Both were very attractive single women looking for the right man, who wouldn't be found on the wharf in all likelihood, but might be found dining in our restaurant.

So, we all decided to open our canteen and wine bar only Monday through Friday from early morning to 2 P.M. Gino would do the wine bar on Mondays to give Teri a day off and take Giselle's place on Tuesdays to give her a free day. Both women were glad to work six days a week as they were earning very good money in wages, profits and tips.

Manon decided after her success in our opening soirées that she would do a fixed but different menu each week. We couldn't afford to include fabulous wines with a set menu, though we'd suggest them for each dish. Clients would have to order from the wine list, which would include good French table wines at reasonable prices. We were trying to stretch Giselle's superior wines inherited from her ex, but we needed to add to it soon. We wouldn't serve Chilean wine with our French cuisine even though we had a large stock in the hold of our ship.

After a quick bite with Manon at the restaurant, I made my way to my makeshift office I maintained in the back of Jonathan Delay's pharmacy near the Long Wharf. His salesclerk and companion, Sophie Benson, greeted me with a rueful smile and pointed to the two big sacks of mail just delivered from the French Consulate. With Gino working in our food enterprises full time, we'd neglected our contract to process miners' mail for delivery and apprise their senders their letters were received but undeliverable. The little back office I shared with Sophie was already full of sacks of unattended letters.

"Did the delivery man ask how we were getting along with so much mail?" I asked with a frown.

"No, he was just happy to be rid of the burdensome sacks. Fortunately, he didn't see what's stashed there," she said pointing to our now very cramped office space.

"I'm at a loss as to what to do. With Manon's advanced pregnancy and the new restaurant, neither I nor Gino has time to work on this tedious project. Do you think Jonathan knows someone reliable who could work on this enterprise? I'm afraid when the consulate finds out I'm shirking my duties in our agreement, there'll be all hell to pay, especially since I took an advance on time and expenses."

"What about me? There are often slow periods without customers like now. I don't think Jon would mind if I helped out, especially as it will clear up the clutter in the office," she said in her lilting French-Canadian accent while batting her doe-brown eyes playfully.

"Your help would be a godsend, Sophie." As there were no clients in the store, I explained the arrangement with the consulate. I showed her the passenger lists with which to match arrivals in San Francisco with addressees of letters and instructed her how to respond to the sender when there was a return address using my printed handbill offering my finder services for a 5 franc note, which roughly equaled one dollar.

Sophie chuckled as she grasped my money making scheme. "Really, you're almost as bad as those barkers hustling clients for the gambling palaces on the Plaza. Aren't you ashamed to take advantage of worried parents and loved ones fearful for lack of news of a relation sent off to wilds of El Dorado to be eaten by wolves or scalped by Indians? And you want me to be a part of it too?" Sophie put one hand on her narrow waist above her hooped skirts and stays and shook the finger of her other hand at me just like Manon to signify "naughty boy. "

"I am no more ashamed than you and Jonathan should be for selling patent medicines and cures you know don't work, are mostly flavored drinking alcohol, and often dangerous," I replied tongue-in-cheek. To make my point in our tit-for-tat competition, I picked up a small, oblong bottle embossed "Mrs. Winslow's Soothing Syrup" and waved it her.

"Actually, that's one remedy that works, especially when babies are teething or have the colic. It eases pain and calms them to sleep," she replied throwing me a "gotcha" look with raised eyebrows.

"Is that why doctors call it the 'Baby Killer?' I am sure you're aware it contains the opiate, laudanum, that when given to infants in too strong or repetitive doses, puts them to sleep for good," I retorted.

"Yes, of course, it has a potential for harm if misused, just like the wine and alcohol you sell. Men and women have killed themselves by drinking themselves to death. Too much alcohol in the blood at one time is a poison that can kill. Just wait until your twins are both yelling and screaming at the same time and driving you both crazy. I'll bet you'll come crying for a bottle of 'Mrs. Winslow's Soothing Syrup' to sooth your little ones when they are teething or in pain."

Sophie, like Manon, is used to winning her arguments. We both like to spar and even wager on topics of interest to us both. Sophie is a petite, energetic woman in her early thirties with a quick wit and wonderful sense of humor. She's fun to work with.

"Now Mr. Dubois, what do I get paid to work in sin on your predatory scheme?" She said eyeing me narrowly, suppressing a grin.

"Ah, the moment of truth is finally arrived. The wages of sin must be paid. The consulate agreed quite reluctantly to pay me seventy-five cents per reply sent to France," I fibbed. "That sum includes pre-paid postage, alas."

"Well, since you have done nothing and are in danger of losing both your contract and your already suspect reputation, it seems only fair to pay me the full amount you receive from the consulate, less postage of course, if I'm to work by the piece. Agreed?"

"Since you can't work full-time on this project and there's a huge backlog to deal with, I surely need a margin to add another part-time worker, won't I? So, let's say I pay you fifty cents for each letter you actually post to France. Agreed?"

Just then two fashionably dressed ladies entered the shop and looked at me quizzically, then at Sophie. Sophie nodded to me that she agreed to my offer and moved to attend her clients. Saved by the bell. Sophie would ring my neck if she found out the consulate agreed to pay me one dollar for each letter posted to France. I removed my consulate dossier from my desk in the back office, doffed my hat to the ladies, and scooted out the door for the Long Wharf to inspect wine supplies still stored in the hold of our ship.

"LIKENESS OF MRS. GEMMER," litho c. 1851.

A trade card for
"MRS. WINSLOW'S SOOTHING SYRUP," c. 1880.

California Gold Rush Journal
❧ PART 2 ❧

CHAPTER FIFTEEN
San Francisco — August 1851

I spent the next two days marshaling supplies for our restaurant and haggling for wholesale rates for the better French wines we'd need to build a sustainable wine list. I also watched the shipping news hoping for an auction of good French wines on newly arrived ships. There was still so little warehousing available after the last fire, that cargos continued to be auctioned aboard arriving ships to buyers with storage space who had to take immediate possession and pay custom fees on the spot.

We needed both good French table wines and a stock of high-end French wines such as we served with our openings. We would need a stock of both before we could print a wine list. Manon wanted a variety of good wines to complement the variety of dishes she planned for her menus. She was determined to be the top French restauranteur in town. Her ability creating a new set of gourmet offerings each week was a must. She was prepared to work hard to eventually surpass her male competitors, some with reputations earned in Paris or New Orleans.

But, we'd need an excellent wine list to appease connoisseurs.

Manon was sparring with Henri about how to prepare desserts and pastry when I arrived with newspapers reporting the shipping news. Henri was unused to preparing pastries as Pierre-Louis made them or purchased them from a *pâtisserie*. I planned to look for new arrivals carrying French wine. Manon left the kitchen and motioned me to sit with her at a table farthest from the kitchen. She brought a small carafe of red wine, two glasses and a wooden platter with slices of *saucisson sec* to nibble on while we chatted. She handed me a piece of note paper.

"So, *Chéri*, what do you think?"

"Won't this cause a big problem?" I said in a low tone motioning to the kitchen. Manon's note was an ungrammatical draft of an ad to hire an apprentice cook.

"Maybe, but we're short-handed in the kitchen. I need someone young, who is eager to learn what I can teach. Since our two successes, he thinks he's now a top chef and should decide menus and ingredients. He has a big fat head now. If he doesn't get his way, he'll quit and slink off to one of our competitors and take my recipes with him. He's complaining all the time he's underpaid for a top chef and shouldn't have to work so much."

"Do we need to pay him more or just coddle him and his big fat ego?"

"*Non*, if we pay him more, he'll want a raise every time we have a full restaurant. He knows we make good money already in the restaurant and on the wharf. He'll probably stay until I birth our twins.

"He's learning how to really cook from me, so I think he'll stay to learn more. When the babies come, he'll try to blackmail us when we need him most. He gets his demands or quits."

"Oh boy, I can see why we need an apprentice cook tomorrow, but won't he get even more pushed out of shape if we hire a woman?"

"I don't think so. He'll get to boss her around just like they did me in Paris. The secret is to find someone like me, who has already worked in a restaurant under a domineering male. I teach her how to cook what I want and when she's good enough, we let him go and hire another apprentice. We make it clear from the start, that if she works hard and does the prep work for fat head without complaining, we'll promote her." Manon had that gleam in her eyes.

I could see a storm brewing. She was conspiring to sack Henri on her terms, like she did Wah Fong, and have a top restaurant with a woman owner and chef. I forgot about the carafe of red wine and set to work drafting her ad in good French. When I'd finished the ad, I took it and our announcement of our second week's menus to the newspapers to be printed in English and French.

I could tell something was up even before I arrived at the door to the *Herald*. The raised voices of the overexcited clerks and staff could be heard from the street. The scene inside was bedlam. Various reporters dashed to and fro in and out of the editor's office, all trying to shout over one another and jockeying to catch the editor's ear.

"What's happening?" I asked a well-dressed chap who, like me, had ads to place at the publicity desk which was unattended.

"From what I can gather, the Governor slipped into town last night and with the mayor's and sheriff's help, they managed to spirit away two prisoners held by the Committee of Vigilance."

"Good God. The sheriff rescued Whittaker and McKenzie?" I asked in disbelief.

"Apparently so, I heard tell that they've got them holed up in jail with a small army of marshals and police guarding the place."

"Did the Committee offer resistance? Was anyone killed?" I asked fearing the answer. I couldn't imagine that the Committee would let the corrupt civil authorities keep the prisoners without a fight.

"Don't know the details. I guess that's what the ruckus here is all about. Figuring what to write about the incident and whose side to take."

We were soon joined by others with ads to place before the deadline for the morning edition. It took us ten minutes of pounding on the empty desk and lots of verbal abuse before a clerk deigned to serve us and place our ads.

I rushed out early the next day to buy the morning papers. I was concerned whether the enmity of the Committee for the Governor and the city's authorities over the fate of the two prisoners would affect dinner reservations for the weekend.

According to the papers, Governor McDougal secretly traveled from Benicia, the State Capitol, by boat on Tuesday, August 19th and arrived in San Francisco around 11 P.M. He went directly to the Union Saloon near the Long Wharf where he met with two members of the Committee, who served as informants. He learned that Whittaker and McKenzie were still being held by the Committee at their headquarters on Battery Street, but they were to be moved to a more secret, secure place next day. He was told that the mayor and sheriff wanted to storm the Committee's headquarters by force before the Committee could either move the prisoners or hang them.

The Governor summoned the mayor and Sheriff Hays, who had to be rousted out of bed. Together they proceeded to the house of Judge Myron Norton, who they awakened by repeated pounding on his door. The judge signed a warrant for Sheriff Hays to arrest Whittaker and McKenzie. It was now 3 A.M., Wednesday, August 20th. The Governor, the mayor, Sheriff Hays and his chief deputy, John Caperton, proceeded by carriage to the Committee's headquarters and parked nearby out of view. Sheriff Hays could have taken an armed contingent to storm the Committee's bastion, but chose not to. His advantage was stealth and surprise in the wee hours of the morning. A large posse might make noise and alert the armed guards inside the headquarters. It would take only one "loose cannon" to spoil the caper and risk a shoot out.

According to the papers, the Committee members assigned to guard the two Sydney Ducks were sleeping and drowsy when the Sheriff knocked on the door with his warrant in hand. The two prisoners were in the same room as their guards and they were not fettered or shackled to benches, as usual, as they were to be transported in early morning to where they were to be hanged. The prisoners had been tipped off by an informant that they were to be rescued.

A sleepy guard opened the door thinking it was another Committee member and Sheriff Hays barged his way into the room waving his warrant and demanding the two prisoners in the name of the law and authority of Judge Norton's writ. His deputy, Caperton, kept the door open while the Sheriff fetched the two prisoners, who willingly scooted out the door, down the stairs, and into the waiting carriage with hands still bound. The lightning-fast raid and rescue was over in a jiffy.

Before the slumbering members of the guard could react and organize, the prisoners and their rescuers barreled down still empty streets to the jail house without pursuit. Fortunately, no shots were fired or needed during the daring rescue.

While the newspaper accounts varied slightly in the reported details, all were agreed that the Sheriff's custody of the two prisoners risked civil insurrection and possibly civil war. As news of the raid spread through the city, large, angry crowds gathered in front of the Committee's headquarters demanding the Committee storm the jail and retrieve the two prisoners who had confessed their crimes, been tried by the Committee and were sentenced to hang. It was now Thursday, the day before we hoped to serve dinner in our nearly fully booked restaurant.

Pierre-Louis told me that his Mrs. Gemmer usually did her shopping and personal business in late afternoon. I decided to pay him a call to seek advice on what we should do, if anything, during the impending crisis and see if he'd learned more than the journalists published in the morning papers from a former client and member of the Committee who still visited him regularly.

As luck would have it, the imperious Mrs. Gemmer was out and the nosy Mrs. Hale was not lurking by the door. Pierre-Louis hollered, "Come in. The door's not locked," as I knocked and announced my presence.

"What do you think of the Sheriff's coup? Do you think there'll be war between the two sides as the papers intimate?" I asked offering Pierre-Louis a nip of cognac from my pocket flask.

After taking a long swig and cooing his pleasure, he replied, "Tough questions to answer and especially to predict what the Committee's response will be. My friend Cyrus, who's a Committee member, says there's a lot of internal dissension among members. Everyone is furious that security was so poor that thirty guards assigned duty that night were unprepared for the Sheriff's rescue. He says the Committee has called an urgent meeting of its Executive Committee to investigate their failure and plot their response. Cyrus thinks they will sack Van Bokkelen, who was in charge of security, and may go so far as to dismiss Payran and Bluxowe as heads of the Committee."

"So, will that take some time? I've been concerned that events might affect our restaurant business this weekend," I said anxiously.

"It should take time, as long as the hotheads don't prevail immediately or give in to the mob outside their headquarters urging them to storm the jail. Cyrus said the most logical course of action is to assess Committee security, find out where it broke down and fix it before facing off against the civil authorities."

I hoped Cyrus' assessment would rule the day. We'd been

scrambling to assure adequate supplies of large and small game from our hunter suppliers in Marin County and shellfish from our Chinese fishermen to feed our customers for the three nights we'd be open starting next day. Wholesale cancellations or a significant number of no shows would leave us with meat and shellfish that would spoil as the August weather had turned hot and humid and the bay fog we relied on to cool things down was absent. While we did have ice delivered every day, our dinner provisions would spoil before the next week. Manon's credo for a top restaurant was to use only fresh, seasonal foods in her menus and not to doctor old meat and fish with sauces. I shared these concerns with Pierre-Louis.

"That's the restaurant business, my friend. It's why I stuck with a simpler fare like soups, stews and charcuterie plates that would keep longer. Most of my desserts came from pastry shops, as you know. I rarely had a full restaurant to prepare for and if I ran out of stew, I made omelets and crepes and offered after dinner drinks on the house. Manon's ambitious entry into high cuisine with a fixed menu is risky given the times. A scared public is going watch civil insurrection from behind a curtain on the second floor and not from a seat in an expensive restaurant."

Food for thought. Maybe Manon should have a more flexible *à la carte* menu to go with a fixed menu like most French restaurants in the city. On the other hand, we were the new restaurant in town everybody was talking about. We were almost fully booked for the next three nights and couldn't meet our patrons' expectations if we didn't have the variety of fresh foods and exciting offerings that would make her cuisine standout. Worst case scenario, we could make additional soups and stews for sale at our canteen on the wharf or even open the restaurant all week for lunch if we had to.

Since Mrs. Gemmer had not yet returned, I took the bull by the horns. "So how is it working out with your nurse?"

Pierre-Louis chuckled. "You saw her. She works hard, keeps the room orderly and tends to all my needs, which in my present condition is what I need," he said rather nonchalantly.

"What brought her to San Francisco?"

"She lost her husband to cancer and his lingering illness and inability to work forced them to mortgage their home to pay his care and treatments. She had to nurse him until he died; then, in order to pay the mortgage lien, she had to sell the house and work as a nurse to others. She used the last of her house money to travel from her native Strasbourg to Le Havre and passage to San Francisco."

"Can a nurse really make more here than in Strasbourg where she is known and has contacts?"

Pierre-Louis gave me an understanding look and motioned for my flask before responding. "She, like me, left France to start a new life after losing a loved one. When I lost my wife I became depressed and started to drink heavily. I couldn't stand the too familiar faces, old haunts or the conniving of family and friends to marry me off to widows of their choice. Instead of serving the same clients the same meals everyday and listening to the same old stories I'd heard a thousand times, I decided to sell my restaurant and get a fresh start somewhere interesting. I considered New Orleans, but I didn't want to have to cook just for Creole tastes. So, I settled on San Francisco once I learned lots of French were emigrating here and there was a distinct French community in an exciting boom town." Pierre-Louis motioned for the flask again and I signaled "no."

This was the first time Pierre Louis discussed his personal life before coming to San Francisco. He'd had two good swigs of cognac and I didn't want to chain myself forever in Mrs. Gemmer's dog house for breaking the rules. "Sounds like you and your nurse have a lot in common," I said with sympathy. "Does she want to remarry?"

Pierre-Louis gave me a knowing look. "Yes. She wants to find a respectable man her age she can love and share the rest of her days with."

"Do you think she would consider you such a man?"

"Yes. We've talked about it. I have the means to support us both. Neither of us has children nor will have to work once I'm out of these damned casts."

Mrs. Gemmer hadn't wasted her time. She had a nice, eligible widower captive under her exclusive care who would need looking after even once the casts were off. I understood better her possessiveness and initial animosity to me and the restaurant business. She was sheltering my friend from his bad habits—drinking, overeating and smoking. Undoubtedly, he had recounted to her my sneaking a flask of cognac into the hospital in violation of doctors' orders. And I'd done it again today while she was out. Given it was likely he'd marry her eventually, I needed to mend my bridges with her.

"I'm very happy for you, my friend. She's still a very handsome woman and from the care she gives you, I'm sure she'll make an excellent wife. Please give her my congratulations when the matter is decided. We'll look forward to seeing lots of you both when you can walk again. Please tell her your little tot of cognac was solely to celebrate our pleasure that you are considering marriage."

My words brought tears of joy to Pierre-Louis' eyes. I was glad to see him so happy. I might even get out of the dog house on a tether when he recounted my comments, which he was sure to do. There would be no way of masking his breath, so I, at least, gave him a good excuse. I told him I'd check in with him again soon and report first-hand our second weekend in the restaurant.

"THE LINE AT THE POST OFFICE ON
PORTSMOUTH SQUARE," 1851.

California Gold Rush Journal
⌘ PART 2 ⌘

CHAPTER SIXTEEN

San Francisco — August 1851

Our restaurant was full and profitable all weekend long despite the tension in the city over the standoff between the Committee and the civil authorities. The Committee announced the suspension of Van Bokkelen for his failure to secure the two prisoners. Apparently, he had left the guard room to use an outside privy and was absent when the Sheriff sprung his surprise raid. The Executive Committee appointed Samuel Brannan to investigate why security had failed and learn who had betrayed them to the authorities. Brannan's appointment signaled that the radical wing of the Committee was back in power and appeased the mob calling for the necks of Whittaker and McKenzie. They had faith Brannan would get the prisoners back and hang them.

We thought Brannan's task to investigate the Committee's security lapses would probably take some time, so we'd set about preparing for our second weekend sure that the political standoff would not affect our business in the near term. Any plan to the retrieve the prisoners would fail, if informers in the Committee alerted the authorities of its timing and tactics. Brannan surprised everyone by demanding the Governor appear before his investigative committee. Even more surprising, the Governor agreed; this was after the Governor had just issued a proclamation in the form of a handbill plastered all over the city warning the Committee. The proclamation alleged there could be civil war if the Committee tried to rescue the two prisoners and cited the penal code punishments for fomenting insurrection. According to the newspapers, the Sheriff also agreed to be questioned by Brannan's committee.

We worked to secure several cooking ingredients in short supply. Many of Manon's recipes called for fresh mushrooms, shallots and *crème fraîche*. American cuisine called for lots of garlic and onions, but seldom used shallots or fresh mushrooms. Manon's supply of dried mushrooms would soon be exhausted and there were few quality mushrooms in the markets. I knew from my travels through the placers that chanterelle and several types of savory boletus mushrooms grew in the countryside. I sent Gino to inquire of his uncle, who in the Italian community scoured the forests for mushrooms. We'd need a supplier after the first rains teased them to pop to the surface. Manon was negotiating with some French farmers in the Santa Clara Valley to grow shallots year round and with a dairy to guarantee a continual supply of fresh cream and butter.

There was a good response to Manon's ad for an apprentice cook. She was just finishing interviewing the last of the applicants Sunday afternoon, August 24th when the fire station bells started clanging furiously. The ruckus brought residents out of houses and shops. After a quick look for dreaded smoke, most men set out on a run for either the jail or the Committee's headquarters. The next act of confrontation had begun. I sent Gino to find out what was happening. Manon and I stayed at the restaurant preparing to close it securely in case rioting broke out, concerned about whether to open our fully booked restaurant that evening. Our cook and staff were due to arrive at any moment. Shortly after the bells stopped clanging, we heard a huge roar in the direction of the Committee's headquarters on Battery Street.

A short time later Gino returned at a trot, huffing and puffing and out of breath. "They've hung the two Ducks," he managed to spit out as he gulped trying to catch his breath. After he calmed down, he recounted what happened.

"It was incredible. The people hanging around the Committee's headquarters saw it all. A carriage roared up just after 2:30 P.M. just after the bells started clanging. Members of the Committee jumped out of the carriage with pistols drawn and hustled the two prisoners up the stairs into the building. Other Committee members poured out of the building and circled it with guns ready. Members inside ran two beams out the upper windows to serve as gallows already prepared with ropes. The two Ducks were shoved out the windows with nooses around their neck and tied to the beams. Seconds later they were swinging from the beams."

"Were any police there?" I asked, stunned at the speed of events. It had only been three days since the Sheriff's stunning raid and not a hint that the Committee planned to respond in kind.

"No, the Sheriff's men weren't there. It wouldn't have mattered if they came. There were thousands of people jamming the street in both directions, so they couldn't have rescued the Ducks if they wanted to. There was a huge roar of approval when the Ducks dropped off the beams. It was what they've been waiting for."

Just then Henri arrived to fire up our stoves and ovens in preparation for our evening dinner guests. He was flustered and argued we should close the restaurant until the dust settled. We decided hanging or not, we'd prepare our dinner service. We gave Gino our two pistols to hide in his cloak to escort Teri and Giselle to the restaurant as soon as possible. There was a happy mob on the streets, but things could and probably would turn ugly once the mob got tanked up at the saloons. Hopefully, any counterattack from the Sheriff's posse wouldn't come tonight with so many loose cannons on the streets. If it were to materialize, in all probability it wouldn't be in the French quarter.

We were pleasantly surprised that almost all of our reserved dinner guests arrived. Some were members of the Committee, two with their wives, the rest a mix of French and other foreigners. The members of the Committee ordered a round of champagne for all present to celebrate the afternoon event. They also ordered our most expensive wines to complement Manon's courses. They were an ecstatic group. They ate with gusto Manon's *terrine de foie de canard* on toast which they washed down with a Chablis premier cru. Their gaiety was contagious. Soon all our guests were celebrating, ordering our best wines and sharing toasts with each other.

Manon offered for her main course loin of antelope with a cream sauce similar to her opening night with other members of the Committee. The Committee members ordered a vintage *Romanée-Conti,* a top red wine from the Burgundy region. For their dessert Manon served a chocolate mousse according to Pierre-Louis' recipe; we offered our guests a vintage sauterne dessert wine from Bordeaux on the house. They ordered more champagne and finished off the wonderful evening with snifters of cognac and Armagnac. The streets were quiet when our guests stumbled out our doors and made their way home. We'd have to wait until the morrow to learn how the Committee had pulled off their counter coup. Even our guests from the Committee didn't know how Brannan brought it off. But, they were joyously happy with it.

The morning newspapers had all evening to gather their accounts and the headlines screamed "DUCKS HANG—JUSTICE DONE!" Apparently, once Brannan learned the names of the Governor's informants, James L. Malony and V. Turner, he reasoned that there might be others as well. He shared his plans only with a select few members he'd worked with to hang Jenkins, the first Duck to swing by order of the Committee after trial by them.

Brannan sent his colleague, Ryckman, who interrogated Whittaker and got his confession, to visit Whittaker in jail and assess how it was defended. He managed to inform Whittaker that there was no escape from the Committee and he would hang despite his rescue. The Committee with its new president, James B. Hule, one of the first members along with Brannan, learned that the Governor had secretly pardoned the infamous "Dutch Charlie," the same day he planned the rescue of Whittaker and McKenzie. They considered it a double-cross and were even more determined to rescue the two prisoners.

Ryckman observed that the old flintlock rifles sent from the fort at the Presidio were nearly useless. Most lacked flints and weren't serviceable. He learned that the best time would be on Sunday during a church service when most of the guards would be distracted and the prisoners freed from their cells to attend the service in an open enclosure used for prisoner exercise and more accessible to the Committee's plan of attack.

Brannan organized two small teams of six to assault the two entries to the enclosure. He had 30 other members ask to attend the services as well to create a diversion at the moment the teams attacked the entry doors. Brannan was concerned about Sheriff Hays and wanted him out of the way. He had Schenck, who was on good terms with the Sheriff, invite him to a bullfight to divert him from the jail. He was afraid the Sheriff would smell a rat when he saw so many Committee members attending church services in the prison. The two rescue squads stationed themselves at both front and back doors armed with sledge hammers, weapons and crowbars and awaited a signal that Reverend Williams had finished his sermon.

At the signal, the squads pounded on the doors startling the guards, then bashed the lock and stormed the compound. They grabbed the prisoners and hustled them to a waiting carriage. The carriage raced up Broadway, swung left on Stockton just as the bells clanged to summon Committee members and the public to their headquarters. The carriage slid to a stop at the Battery Street headquarters and the prisoners were swinging from the makeshift gallows within thirty minutes from the time the Committee took them back in their custody.

Monday, the *Alta's* headline soberly announced "QUIET." The editor's commentary reflected the emotional exhaustion that had settled on the city due to Sunday's events and hangings. It was time to wait and see. The Committee's only action was a resolution directed at Charles Duane: "That said Charley Duane have notice to leave the City of San Francisco and not return under penalty of death and that this act of the Governor meets with our unqualified disapprobation." The Committee still held eight prisoners as well as three married couples from Sydney they had taken off ships on arrival. They released Mrs. Hogan, perhaps as part of a deal to secure Whittaker's confession.

As it was Teri's day off, I decided to visit our ship and see how Gino was getting along with Giselle and Teri. I arrived just as Gino and Giselle were dismantling the canteen and wine bar after another profitable day selling. I was surprised to see Thomas Hawthorne pacing back and forth waiting for Giselle and trying to avoid being nipped by Giselle's dog Fido. After the tents and gear were stowed and the unhappy, barking dog attached to his leash at the top of the gangway, I invited Gino to join me for a glass of wine and a cigar on the poop deck, which was bathed in soft, afternoon sun instead of the more typical light fog and cool ocean breezes.

"So, what's up with those two?" I said pointing to Giselle and Hawthorne who were strolling along the wharf toward town.

"He wants to marry her when her divorce is final, but she won't make the commitment."

"Is there someone else?"

"I don't think so. She thinks he's a nice guy and very attentive to her, but she's not ready to settle down. She's making more money than he and that upsets him. I don't think he could afford to marry and set up a household on what he earns despite his good education and being a lawyer. I've only seen him wear two different suits."

I chuckled. "Giselle's already gone that route. Another male who wants her to settle down to domesticity when she's just had her first taste of freedom and independence. Doesn't he see that?"

"I think he's blinded by jealousy. He's aware that both she and Teri get notes slipped to them along with their tips at the restaurant. Some men offer marriage; others, especially the married ones, want a mistress and are willing to provide a residence and large monthly allowance."

I laughed. "They made the same offers to Manon when I was away visiting the northern mines. Some men think if they've got sacks of gold, they can buy anything they want. They obviously don't understand our women anymore than Hawthorne does. They didn't come here and decide to stay to be any man's plaything or a second fiddle." I paused to take a drag on my cigar and watch Gino's reaction. "How are you getting along with Teri?" I asked pouring us glasses of Chilean red wine from a carafe.

"How do you French say it, *'comme-ci, comme-ça?'* She knows I like her a lot and would like her to be my woman, but she won't commit anymore than Giselle," he said with a sigh.

"I thought with all the looks and whispering going on in the restaurant that romance was brewing. What happened?"

Gino sighed deeply. "I thought so too. She let me take her to my cabin to make love, but she wouldn't stay the night. She said it was nice fun on that special occasion, but it wasn't going to be a regular thing. Then she went to her cabin while I stewed the rest of the night. Next day she was friendly, but acted as if our love making never happened."

Oh boy, I thought, Teri and Giselle are going to break a lot of hearts before they agree to settle down with a man again, if at all.

"Welcome to the New World, Gino. Giselle refused to return to France with her husband and Teri was cheated and dumped by her macho boyfriend. California offers them what no other country offers its women—the right to own a business and earn a living without the control of a husband or father as in France, Italy and Chile. Why do you think so many ships are arriving each month from the Old World with so many women eager to work and escape the social and class restrictions Europe places on women? Giselle and Teri may not want to marry until they want to start a family, like Manon and me."

Gino took a deep breath and a gulp of wine. "My uncle says the women are coming to snag a rich merchant or miner and marry him. So, if they're coming to get married, why is it so different with Teri and Giselle?"

"Well, some may be coming to make a good marriage because California law also allows them to inherit their husband's estate instead of it going to male survivors or to a woman to be controlled by a father or elder male relative as is often the case in Europe. But not all women are coming to seek an inheritance. Many like Giselle, Manon and Teri came to make something of themselves by their own labor and escape the yoke that paternalistic legal codes imposed on them. Once a woman realizes here that she has needed skills and can earn her keep and pay her way, it's hard for her to give up that newly won power and liberty..."

"Yes, but Manon agreed to be your woman and live with you before you learned she was pregnant," Gino said cutting me off, exasperated.

"Not all cases are the same. We were lovers in Paris and we came to the New World together to be equals in business and our private life. Giselle came as a married woman under her husband's control and refused to accept that role here when she learned she had more choices."

"What about Teri? She worked with and lived with her Chilean boyfriend. So, why must it be different with me?"

"Teri was not an equal partner in her relationship with Raoul. He had the capital, owned the business, employed her to sell his wine and warm his bed. He held all the power and could have thrown her out at his leisure. She was even convinced once he made his pile, he'd return to Chile, marry into the moneyed class and dump her along the way or offer to keep her as a mistress. As it turned out, he stole her money and dumped her here. So, she's telling you in so many ways that she doesn't have to tolerate an unequal relationship again. She's an independent woman and wants to remain that way."

Gino frowned. "So you're saying it's hopeless."

"No, I'm not saying it's hopeless at all. She likes you and she'll come to your bed as she's already shown you, but on her terms, not yours. If you really want her to be your woman, you'll have to continue to woo her, accept that she may want to see other men as well before she finally decides who she wants to live with or marry. As your uncle said, you've got to woo her, the old-fashioned, Italian, romantic way."

Gino flicked his cigar into the bay and grimaced. "It's so damned hard. It's so different here from Italy or even France when I worked there…"

I cut him off. "Forget about the old countries and their ways where men still call all the shots. If you really want a woman as spirited as Teri, you'll have to wait her out and accept her on her own terms. If you want an easy conquest or a wife like in Italy or France, hundreds of attractive women are arriving each month. Many would be satisfied to marry a handsome, young Italian with a financial interest in a San Francisco *trattoria* and a job working for us."

I left Gino to ponder his relationship with Teri and finish the carafe of wine, while I made my way back to our restaurant.

"THE HANGING OF WHITTAKER and MCKENZIE, 1851."

California Gold Rush Journal
⟨ PART 2 ⟩

CHAPTER SEVENTEEN
San Francisco — August 1851

anon winnowed her applicant list for an apprentice down to two young women and decided to interview them both again. Many of the applicants were unsuitable because they could not read and write sufficiently well to keep a detailed journal of what they learned or read recipes and calculate and measure ingredients accurately. Manon asked me to sit in on her interviews of the two finalists.

The first young woman, Joséphine Arras, accompanied her mother to San Francisco after her father's untimely death. Joséphine was a petite twenty-two year old with a youthful, trim figure, lively brown eyes and honey-brown hair she wore in a bun for her interview. She was modestly dressed in a summer muslin dress with embroidery on the bodice.

"Tell me again why you came to San Francisco so my husband understands why you want to become a cook," Manon asked.

"It was mother's idea after father died unexpectedly. Mother read about how women in California could keep what they earned or inherited. My older sisters were married, but there was no dowry for me. Mother thought with all the single miners in California wanting wives and to settle down after striking it rich, that we'd be able to make good matches even though neither of us had a dowry," she said circumspectly.

"You're young and pretty and could certainly attract a husband with means to support you. So, why would you want to learn to be a cook?"

"I read the reviews of your opening weekend. I was amazed. I've never heard of a woman owning a restaurant, let alone being a top chef. I knew immediately when I saw your classified ad that I wanted to work for you. I want to become an accomplished cook."

"It's not an easy job. You have to rise at dawn to shop the markets at the other end of town near the Spanish Mission for the freshest fruits and legumes. You'll have to haggle for the best prices. There's lots of competition. We can only use what's fresh and in season. Then you have to peel potatoes, chop onions that make your eyes burn and work in the scullery room cleaning and arranging pots and pans, dishes and cutlery. The hours are long and the work hard. Your dainty hands will become chaffed and your back, sore. Why would you want to commit to a year or more of hard work when you could cook for a husband and raise a family?" Manon stated soberly.

Joséphine didn't hesitate to reply. "I don't want to get married and be a housewife like my mother. Raising kids and doing all the housework—changing diapers, preparing meals purchased from the markets you describe, scrubbing floors and being lorded over by a husband who married me because I'm pretty and will warm his bed on his terms is just as hard or harder than working for you," she said adamantly.

"Yes, but you'll be supervised by a male head cook who isn't sympathetic to female underlings. How will you respond to his criticisms and nit-picking of your efforts?"

"I'll just have to grin and bear it. It won't be as bad as being married to a husband who'll criticize and nit-pick as well. Being married is a 24 hour job and the work just as hard or harder for women of my station. As an apprentice, I'll be learning a trade that will allow me to become independent and not subservient to anyone. If and when I marry, I'll be a good cook with the prospect of running a business and being treated as an equal," she said defiantly. I suppressed a chuckle at this young woman's spunk. No wonder she made Manon's final cut.

"Isn't this going to cause friction with your mother? She arranged your transport to San Francisco to find a good match for a dowerless daughter. Won't she be furious?"

"Yes, of course. She was furious when I said I was going to apply for the position. We fought the whole way over on that cursed ship where we both near died of the bad food, water and unsanitary conditions. I don't want to be a housewife for sale for the highest bidder. I saw all the drudgery that goes with being a subservient wife and mother. My sisters had to take the first guy with an annual income that would have them. I may be poor, but I'm a fast learner, want to be a cook and I'll work my fingers to the bone if necessary to succeed. I'm almost twenty-three and like it or not, my mother can't dictate my fate here in California like she threatened to do in France," she stated defiantly as color kept rising on her cheeks. Oh boy, I thought. Henri's in for big trouble if Manon hires this one.

The last interviewee, Rose Boucher, was a dark-skinned young woman in her mid-twenties with Bohemian looks—long, glossy, raven-black hair worn in a braid, a strong nose, blazing black eyes and a fierce intensity to her visage. She was dressed in a brightly colored and embroidered peasant dress from Eastern Europe. She had worked as an under-cook apprentice in Bergerac. She'd jumped at the chance to join her brother, a carpenter, to come to California.

"Why would you leave France just to take a similar apprenticeship here in San Francisco?" Manon demanded.

"I don't think it's the same opportunity at all. I worked in three different restaurants and cafés before becoming an apprentice cook. I waited tables, did vegetable prep, washed dishes, fended off groping hands and indecent propositions from patrons and was hounded to sleep with my boss at each job if I wanted any advancement. I read about your opening successes and I jumped at the chance to learn to cook from a woman," Rose said confidently.

"Did you leave the positions in Bergerac because of the sexual harassment or where there other reasons?"

Rose laughed then nodded her head affirmatively. "The harassment would've been the same wherever I worked in Bergerac and I can deal with it. It was the same on the ship getting here for most women, but I had my older brother who stood up for me. I've always liked to cook and hoped one day to have my own restaurant or bistro. In France, the only way I could have it would be to marry the owner of a small restaurant or café who'd let me do the cooking. That's not a likely scenario for a woman apprentice in Bergerac despite its reputation for the fine food and wines. When my brother said he'd pay my passage if I wanted to join him on the trip to San Francisco, I jumped at the chance to leave a future of dead-end jobs."

"If I train you to cook my special recipes, what's to stop you from marrying a successful miner or merchant who'd stake you to your own restaurant?" Manon said locking her black eyes on those of Rose.

"If I'm given the chance to become a top chef in your restaurant based on merit, I'd never have a reason to leave. It's what I've always dreamed of and no man would give me that opportunity even here in San Francisco. From what I've seen here and on the ship, the only women who get rich have to sell sexual services or marry the men with the money. It's not my cup of tea," Rose stated with emotion.

"I am considering hiring two apprentices. As you can see, I'm carrying twins and will be able to do less and less as their birthing approaches. Would you be willing to work with a less experienced apprentice? Even wait tables in a pinch, if necessary until I'm through this period?"

Rose responded without hesitation. "Of course, I'm flexible. I'll do whatever is necessary to help the restaurant run smoothly."

"Even take orders from a bossy, sexist male chef and not complain during my difficult period?"

Rose smirked. "Of course, I know it's part of the job. I know how to keep my lips buttoned and take criticism. I just want the opportunity to learn to cook like you. I'll do whatever it takes if given the opportunity. You can count on me."

"Can you survive on $150.00 a month to start? It's all we can afford to pay at the moment. We're the new kid on the block and must compete with well-established competitors until we have a regular clientele. That will take some time." Manon and I both watched carefully for Rose's verbal and non-verbal reactions. $5.00 a day was a very minimal wage.

"I'll be happy to start at $150.00 a month as an apprentice cook. I live with my brother in a flat near the Mission. He has steady work with all the rebuilding and earns $12.00 a day and I cook and do the housework. He'll be happy I can start contributing my share and have a good job. It's why we came to San Francisco," she stated proudly.

"Good, you're hired. You start tomorrow. Since you live near the fruit and vegetable markets, let me know who is selling the freshest and best quality produce when you report tomorrow at 9 A.M." Manon handed Rose a bound notebook. "I want you to take note of everything you learn on the job. I'll read your journal once a month and we'll discuss what you've learned and your progress as an apprentice."

Rose's dark eyes flashed contentedly and her big grin slowly developed into a broad smile. "Thank you so much. It's what I've always wanted. I'll make you proud of me," she said as she donned her shawl and bonnet and skipped out the door.

"I see why you wanted them both, but can we really afford them both?" I said mentally calculating the wages we were committed to pay— $600 a month to Henri, now $300 to two apprentices, $450 to Gino and $15 a shift to Giselle and Teri for serving in the restaurant. In addition we had to pay for meat, fish and cooking ingredients. I wondered whether we'd have any profit to apply to our purchase agreement. My income was minimal at the moment as most of my time was spent helping get the restaurant up and running smoothly at the expense of hustling clients. It would take time to see a return on my postal concession with the consulate and other ventures.

"I see my husband's got big money worries, yes?" Manon said crooking her finger for me to embrace her. When I enfolded my arms around her now significant belly, she whispered in my ear, "Husband thinks mother-to-be is extravagant and spendthrift, yes? Won't be money to raise father-to-be's children or pay off the mortgage, yes?" Then she nipped my ear and laughed. "You leave money worries to Manon. She knows how to make a restaurant profitable. What aspect of restaurant business is most profitable do you think?"

"I suppose it's getting 75% or more of the tables reserved the three nights a week we're open," I replied calculating that we have tables to accommodate 32 diners in the restaurant plus 16 more in the private room at the rear. We'd had 48 diners each gala opening for a fixed price menu at $25 per person including wine. Our gross was $1,200 each evening. Without the wine, we now priced our gourmet menu at $15 per person which amounted to just less than an ounce of gold, and which only the newly rich or well-heeled could afford. A full house would bring in $720 and 75% occupancy $540 a night. As we were open for dinner only 12 nights a month, our gross take would be $6,480 a month. I thought, however, it was unrealistic to expect we could fill 75% of our tables month-in and month-out. Manon knew the figures as well as I.

"Papa-to-be is only partially right. The biggest area for profit is not the food; it's the wine and liquor we sell with the meal. If the meal is delicious and the occasion special, our clients are not going to order a *vin ordinaire*. They're going to order the most expensive wines we suggest complement each dish. Businessmen entertaining clients can't afford to look cheap. Many of our diners come in groups. You saw what happened our second weekend. Our diners ordered the most expensive wines. By buying frugally from distressed wine merchants or ships that must auction their wine, we can make four times what we paid on each bottle, just like we did with the gourmet tins and bottles of food we brought with us from France."

I shook my head in disagreement. "I've been round to the wine merchants with the best wines and they'll only give me a wholesale discount of 35% off their selling price. I have to bid against them on the lots auctioned aboard ship."

"Yes, but you have something they need and can't get anywhere for several more months, if at all," Manon said with a big pouty smile.

"We have storage space on our ship. Is that what you mean? They want to sell me wine in their store, not stock more wine."

"We need to make a deal with wine merchants who want to get a better share of the retail market. The profit lies in being able to corner the market for the best red wines which need to age in a cellar. We're a steady wholesale customer and we're able to store wines in our ship's hold. Most houses and wine merchants don't have real wine cellars. San Francisco's soil is sandy and most commercial buildings don't even have a basement. The hold of our ship's as good as a real wine cellar in France as the wines are stored in a dark, cool place."

"But how do we convince the wine merchants to store wines in our ship?"

"We build bins in the hold of our ship to stock wines for merchants and to list on our menus with an agreement that when the wine is featured on our menu, we inform our diners the wine can be purchased through us at a special price. Like our reservation system, we can provide exclusive access to top wines."

Oh boy, I thought. Manon's going to have us in the wine business too. "So, how does it work? What's the incentive for the wine merchants other than cellar-like storage of wines that need aging?"

"We are providing both a recommendation for the wine and the opportunity for buyers to taste it with a delicious meal. The wine merchant can't afford to open a bottle of very expensive wine just to let a potential client taste it before buying it. If they did, all the idlers, moochers and dandies would ask to taste the most expensive wines in the merchant's store with no intention of buying. Our diners have tasted and paid for the wine, and now want to buy it. We split the profit with the wine merchant for bottles sold out of our ship to our clients and when the wine is featured on our dinner menu, we get it at cost."

I was starting to really appreciate the ingenuity of Manon's proposal. "And we could even have exclusive wine tastings on the deck of the Eliza for special clients wanting to stock up or start their own cellars," I added.

Manon's broad grin was contagious. "So what I tell you, Big Boy. You leave the restaurant business to Manon, yes?"

"I think this discussion now calls for a bottle of champagne, don't you Chérie? I'm starting to see lots of possibilities for your scheme. Once we have clients who want to start private wine cellars, we have monthly wine tastings and offer to cellar their purchases in private wine bins in the hold of Eliza. My, my, what a clever cookie I married."

"LIKENESS OF JOSÉPHINE ARRAS," 1851.

California Gold Rush Journal
∞ PART 2 ∞

CHAPTER EIGHTEEN
San Francisco — August-September 1851

Manon confided to me she was going to groom Rose Boucher to serve dinners in place of Gino. She'd need her waiting tables once she was ready to birth our twins. That meant I could use Gino more on the postal contract with the consulate and my other business ventures. Gino wouldn't be happy about the change, but I needed him to work for me. With Sophie Benson's help, we had several hundred letters to mail to France.

I secured an appointment with Consul Dillon to present him with a copy of our mailing list and my bill for the work. This time I waited only ten minutes to be ushered into his lushly appointed office. No doubt Manon's gala played a role in my ability to gain access to the busy consul.

Dillon was impeccably dressed as always in a fashionable suit and vest. Dillon greeted me warmly and offered me a cigar from a small glass humidor on his desk. "Lovely dinner party at your restaurant. You're blessed to have such an accomplished and charming wife."

I smiled my appreciation for his compliments and handed him the list of French addressees we had replied to. He scanned them quickly, and put the list aside.

"I'm sure you've read of our government's plans to conduct a national lottery to raise funds to send 5,000 more poor and destitute citizens to California?" Consul Dillon said unsympathetically. "As you know from the French ships arriving here weekly, we're already overworked and understaffed to handle the deluge of requests from new arrivals. It will mean even more letters for you to process."

"No problem," I replied. "I've hired more staff to process the present backlog," I exaggerated. "But why 5,000 emigrants more when there're already too many job seekers for too few unskilled jobs? Surely, they're not foolish enough to send more inexperienced gold seekers who can't hope to earn their keep. Manon advertised for an apprentice cook and had 25 applicants. She'd have had twice the number if she hadn't specified the position was for a woman."

The Consul sighed. "I'm afraid it's a done deal. The Lottery of the Golden Ingots is already underway. We received notification in June from our Minister for Home Affairs that the lottery of the golden ingots was approved by the government and tickets are already on sale."

"How is it supposed to work?" I asked.

"Tickets will be sold nationally for one franc each. There will be 214 prizes, each consisting of a bar of solid gold. The gold ingots will range in value from a 400,000 franc bar to be given to the ticket holder whose name is drawn first. The values of the gold bars will decrease on a sliding scale down to two hundred 1,000 franc bars on subsequent drawings. The total value of all the prizes has been set at one and one-half million francs." Dillon paused to relight his cigar. "The profits are to be used to pay transport to California for 5,000 unemployed workers. The latest dispatch stated that millions of tickets are being sold and thousands of unemployed laborers are signing up for the chance to emigrate to California," the Consul stated soberly.

Oh boy, I thought. What a clever scheme to take advantage of France's gold fever and the glowing reports of French miners striking it rich that were still peddling French newspapers. Even the poorest of the poor would find a way to buy a lottery ticket for one franc, which was worth about twenty American cents. I had no faith in lotteries. It was a sucker's game for dreamers. Economic conditions in France were so bad, that millions of desperate poor folk would undoubtedly risk what few coins they had to try to win a gold bar.

"How can we be sure that the drawing won't be rigged?" I asked.

Consul Dillon paused before replying. "The Ministry for Home Affairs informed us that the drawing of tickets scheduled for November 16th will be strictly and personally monitored by the Paris Police Prefect. They plan to have young boys from good families draw the tickets in front of a live audience to assure there can be no fraud."

I took a long puff on my cigar. The reports I've been reading about the political and economic situation in France were that the republicans, who had overthrown King Louis Philippe, elected Napoleon Bonaparte's nephew, Louis Napoleon, to be President. The leftist press warned he's a chameleon, who secretly seeks to restore the monarchy and install himself as Emperor. They also pointed out that government coffers were near empty. To the political cynics, the lottery of the golden ingots provides a means for Louis Napoleon to rid himself of his political foes and other undesirables by rounding them up and shipping them to California. If Napoleon and his cronies could rig the lottery to their benefit, they'd be rich as well.

"You said the proceeds of the lottery would be used to send

5,000 unemployed workers to California. Are they going to let the thousands of workers and the poor draw lots for a berth on a ship, or will there be some realistic criteria for the selection based on need here?"

"Your question is troubling. However, we've been assured that those selected and shipped to us will have employable skills. I have informed the Ministry that California needs more skilled construction workers—masons, carpenters, mechanics, cabinet makers, tool smiths and others. We also need more agriculturists to farm the rich valleys on both sides of the bay to feed an ever growing population," the Consul said unconvincingly.

Pierre-Louis learned from his contact in the Committee of Vigilance that the American Consul in Marseille, France sent a letter of warning to San Francisco Customs Collector, T. Butler King, who forwarded it to the Committee. The consul indicated their informants believed the lottery scheme was designed to enrich the promoters, like the selling of worthless shares in gold mining ventures in California, and provide the means to round up and deport criminals, prostitutes, pimps and "some of the worst desperadoes of Europe" to California. The Committee members were so alarmed that they immediately sent an emissary to France to get assurances the consul's information was incorrect. I wasn't sure Consul Dillon was aware of the Committee's concern or involvement. I decided to keep mum on what I'd heard.

"Are you charged with finding accommodation and employment for the lottery emigrants when they arrive?"

"Alas, they're sure to come empty-handed as with most of the fortune seekers. We have no choice but to aid them. I've requested that they arrive only in summer and early fall and not the dead of winter when lodging and opportunities are minimal. I keep demanding more staff and funds and the Foreign Office keeps stalling. I expect they're skimping on funds. We're so far away that we've next to no influence despite being responsible for more than 25,000 French currently in California," he said in an exasperated tone.

"Well, let me know what I can do to help when the time arrives. Meanwhile, we're making a gallant effort to process the backlog of correspondence the post office can't handle. I need you to authorize a payment draft for that lot," I said pointing to the list I'd presented which he'd put aside.

He winced, but penned the draft with a flourish. He undoubtedly realized that our agreement was going to be more costly than anticipated and his budget would be strained with another 5,000 coming soon to San Francisco.

I deposited the draft with my bank and headed for "Little Italy" to see what progress our Italian friends were making to rebuild. Our new apprentice, Anne Boucher's brother, Jacques, worked for the Italians and I wanted him to implement Manon's wine club and storage plan. As I moseyed down Dupont Street toward Broadway, I was surprised to see so many new stands with French bootblacks. Most were dressed in the costume of failed miners—baggy trousers tucked in worn-out high boots, red flannel or wool shirts now rolled up for work, a bandana tied around the neck, and a slouch hat perched jauntily over both ears.

As the streets were still coated with a mix of horse manure and night soil that seeped through the planks lining the street, I kept to the raised cedar planks which served as sidewalks. I warily avoided the splashes of carters and carriages. I watched a dandy ahead of me carefully negotiate an intersection so as not to foul his shiny black boots and striped trousers. All of sudden, a dog dripping mud, dashed across his path and splashed his boots. The dandy let out a cry of anguish at his soiled shoes and quickly repaired to a bootblack's stand. I laughed.

I was surprised to see the same dog repeat the same trick a block later on the opposite side of the street. The dog was obviously trained to splash gentlemen's boots to provide customers for its master's blacking stand. The dog eyed me warily and I popped into a café until the dog moved on to find another mark.

As I approached the end of Dupont Street and the Italian quarter, the cries of workmen and ringing of hammers on nails reverberated through the haze of a light fog creeping over the Broadway hills heading for the bay. A string of lumber wagons loaded with roughly planed redwood floor joists, beams and planks lined the street making for one way traffic jams and angry carters, carriage and cab drivers. I was pleased to see Luigi Salterini's lot was a beehive of activity. The flooring and framing for his new *trattoria* was well advanced. Gino's cousin, Antonio, supervised the workers while Luigi sold his Italian sausages, cold cuts and wine from his tent store now located on a corner of his large lot.

"Hola, Antonio, how goes it?" I asked.

Antonio paused to wipe his sweaty brow with the handkerchief around his neck. "It's hard work, but more fun than peeling potatoes for your cook, Henri. I'm glad Manon found an apprentice."

"Two, actually. Both are serious young women who want to be chefs."

"Hah, that's gonna make old Henri jealous. Two more ambitious women with knives and cleavers tucked into their aprons. He'd better watch his back. Are they pretty?"

I laughed. Antonio, like his cousin, had a slim, athletic figure, dark curly hair, worn fashionably long, a patrician nose and a roaming eye for pretty damsels, of which there were few available. "Depends on your taste and whether you like hardworking, serious young women who are more interested in learning a trade and making something of themselves than being wooed by young men trying to bed them. I thought you Italians liked to woo innocent young maidens with music, song and protestations of undying love."

"Oh boy, not two more like Teri! What's with these women anyway? Why can't they act like women in the old country?" Antonio said with a perplexed expression. He'd obviously been following Gino's trials and tribulations with Teri.

"The young women arriving today have more options. They don't have to be dependent on men if they can earn their own keep. Why don't you utilize your charms on nice young Italian girls?" I said baiting him.

He guffawed. "There aren't many here and they're watched like hawks by chaperones; they're available for marriage only. They're not like the French girls, who flirt and tease, but expect you to pay them."

I laughed. "What do you expect? Many of the girls and women who've come to San Francisco are working girls. They can't mine the rivers in long skirts and it's illegal for them to wear trousers or appear in a man's costume. Many are hard-scrabble girls who could be had in Paris for ten francs or less depending on the time of the month. Here they're "ladies" capable of earning $16.00 an evening as hostesses in a gambling palace and $100-$200 more a night if they sell themselves. With so many unmarried, goatish young men vying for women, your choice is to marry or pay. Maybe you'll get lucky when you work for your uncle." I said letting him stew on his problem. From what I'd seen of our two new apprentices, Antonio might get a curious look but wouldn't get far in trying to romance them.

During a lull in sales, Luigi invited me to share a glass of red wine and shoot the bull.

"So, how long before you're back in business?" I asked as Luigi poured big glasses of red wine and offered me a platter of salami sliced very thin.

Luigi sighed and popped a couple of slices of salami in his mouth. "Not too long I hope. The masons will build the ovens in a day or so," he pointed to a large stack of bricks and sacks of mortar. Antonio wants us to make a special dish they do in Na-poli. They make a kind of flat pie topped with sausage, salami, chorizo, mushrooms, black olives, eggs and other ingredients and they call it 'pizza.'"

"Why does he want to make a dish from Napoli when you have such good *salumi* and make *panini* with it?"

"He says we need to attract a younger crowd. He says Sal-vatore Benetti and others will corner the traditional Italian res-taurant and luncheon business. We need something new and tasty to appeal to young workers who greatly outnumber older diners and who can't afford an expensive meal. He wants to make a variety of pasta dishes which are easy to make and not expensive and served with a half liter of wine. The pizza cooks quickly in a hot bread oven and with so many different ingre-dients for toppings, the diner can get a fast, nutritious and tasty meal with wine for $1.50."

I pondered Antonio's formula. "You know I think he's right. Manon uses hearty soups and pâté sandwiches which are tasty, inexpensive and served with wine. Clients on the wharf are mostly young men who work as stevedores or carters. They buy a tasty nutritious meal, eat it quickly and come back the next day for more. It's the same with the Chinese. They have carts and stands in their quarter that serve hot noodles with fish, meat bits and dumplings, and it's hot, filling, tasty and cheap. There are lots more clients for a quick, cheap, appetizing dish than for the traditional three course meal that only the well-heeled can afford."

"I hope he's right, my friend. He's part owner now, and full of ideas to make the new venture successful."

"It won't hurt to try. It's worked well for Manon. The wharf stands are very profitable and now have a steady clientele that's growing. How about security? Is there still tension with the Ducks nearby?"

Salterini paused to refill our glasses and slice some more salami. "You know, it's really strange. Since the two hangings, we haven't heard a peep out of the rowdies or the Ducks. We think they got the message. We've seen some loading carts with belongings and merchandise. Hopefully, they're booking passage home or moving to another state."

If true, it was good news and not a lull before the storm. I'd check the situation out with Pierre-Louis. I wished Luigi godspeed on completing his restaurant and good luck with Antonio's new business plan and set out to locate Rose's brother, Jacques Boucher, who was working in the area.

"LOTTERY OF THE GOLDEN INGOTS," 1851.
(museum collection)

California Gold Rush Journal
∞ PART 2 ∞

CHAPTER NINETEEN
San Francisco — August-September 1851

I got amused chuckles for my efforts to locate Jacques Boucher with my halting Italian and heavy French accent. As several French carpenters were at work for the Italians, it took a few misses to find my man as the Italians referred to all the "Frenchies" as *i franchesci*. Jacques Boucher was nailing roofing tiles when I caught up with him. He was tall, good-looking and dark-featured like his sister. He readily agreed to build wine bins aboard our ship as soon as he finished work on the nearly completed store where I found him. We made an appointment to meet Sunday morning at the ship to inspect the job and calculate the materials needed.

From "Little Italy" I made my way back along Dupont Street past our closed restaurant and up California Street to see how Pierre-Louis was getting along and eat some humble pie if nurse Gemmer was there.

Mrs. Hale was in her chair monitoring the door to her rooming house when I opened it. "So an' dinya tell that there nurse t'was to be no monkey business or foolin' around like I told ya? She's a been stayin' later an' later. Doan see no need for late hours from that woman. When her nursin's done for the evening, she should go home an' stay there. This here house has male boarders and women are not allowed. What's she up to anyhow?" Mrs. Hale said giving me a hard, disapproving look.

"I assure you she's a very proper and respectable nurse. Due to Mr. Lerouge's condition in two leg casts, his doctor insists that he be moved into various sitting and lying positions at regular intervals to avoid developing bed sores. As he's not able to do it on his own, he requires help from his nurse to shift positions; thus, the longer he's in the leg casts, the later she needs to stay to see it's done. I assure you she is only following the doctor's orders." As my assistant Georges would say, "An that's as big a pack of blarney as I've heard all day an' then some."

Mrs. Hale gave me a nasty, disbelieving look and muttered, "Hrrump, Bloody Frenchies," under her breath. I ignored her and knocked on Pierre-Louis' door, which was quickly opened by Mrs. Gemmer. She ushered me in and slammed the door shut.

"What's that horrible woman complaining about now? She's forever spying on me and seeking reasons for barging in here. I now keep the door locked and that infuriates her even more; the lord only knows what she's yammering about because I don't understand a word she says," Mrs. Gemmer stammered irately.

I chuckled and Pierre-Louis looked worried. "I think it's a bad case of jealousy, quite frankly. She's a mean-spirited, sour and unhappy widow who lords her rules over her boarders like a drill sergeant; she's angry that the two of you are getting along famously and enjoy being with each other. She's frustrated that she can't find some improper behavior to condemn that would justify her annulling the rental agreement. She can't stand the thought that others around her might in fact be happy." Pierre-Louis gave a sigh of relief and Mrs. Gemmer gave me a favorable look and smiled.

"You may call me Mathilde, Mr. Dubois. Pierre-Louis told me about your last conversation and you are forgiven for breaking the doctor's rules by sharing the contents of your cognac flask so long as it doesn't happen again. Pierre-Louis has asked me to marry him and I have accepted," she stated proudly and stuck out her ring finger to show her diamond-studded engagement ring.

"I'm thoroughly delighted and I'm sure my wife will be as well. We'll look forward to hosting a champagne reception after the wedding. Have you set a date?" I was surprised at the ring because we hadn't yet moved Pierre-Louis' safe to this location and I knew he had no money available to give her to buy it. She'd undoubtedly spent her own money to clinch the deal.

"No, we'll wait until Pierre-Louis' casts are removed and he can walk. I'm looking for a small house or lower floor apartment we can rent now, so we can get away from the horrible woman who runs this place. Pierre-Louis said you could advance some money to pay on a lease," she said coolly with a faint smile.

My, oh my, I thought, things have progressed rapidly. Mrs. Gemmer is wasting no time setting the matrimonial ball in motion. "Pierre-Louis' money is in his safe, I can have it delivered here if it's needed," I said gauging Pierre-Louis' facial response. He couldn't bend down to open it, so he either trusted her to open it or would have me open it and parcel money to her. Ball in his court.

"I'll give you the combination," he said addressing me. "Please take out $500.00. Give Mathilde $150.00 and hold the rest for deposit on new lodgings. I don't feel comfortable bringing my safe here with the landlady and her boarders lurking about. As soon as Mathilde finds a suitable rental, we'll move the safe and my belongings there." I watched his Mathilde out of the corner of my eyes for her reaction. She was very careful to let her face not betray whatever she thought of the arrangement.

"Very well, I'll send Gino with money for Mathilde later today with your evening supper. I'll take out the rest when you need it. It'll be secure with us in the restaurant."

"Have you heard anything new about whether Sheriff Hays or the Governor will attempt to retaliate for the hangings?" I asked to change the subject. Mrs. Gemmer took a seat by the bay window and perused the want ads in the afternoon papers I brought. I couldn't blame her for wanting to move away from Mrs. Hale's evil eye. Pierre-Louis' casts were due to be removed in about two weeks. She'd need time to set up their household. Her relaxed manner led me to believe I was out of her dog house and would be useful in her plans to move and marry.

"Cyrus doesn't think they dare retaliate against the Committee given the overwhelming popular and press support for the hangings. In a way, the hangings solved problems for the civil authorities in light of the disclosure that the Governor secretly pardoned Charlie Duane."

"Will the Committee try to arrest Duane?"

Pierre-Louis chortled. "Too late. He slipped out of town on the steamer 'Pacific' heading for Panama as soon as he heard the Committee issued an arrest warrant for him. He's a marked man with noose waiting if he stays."

"It's a good sign the brute got the message that his bosses couldn't save him from swinging once they caught him. I visited Luigi Salterini in North Beach where he's rebuilding his restaurant. He says he's seen signs that many Ducks are packing up and scuttling out of town as fast as they can go."

"Yes, Cyrus reports the same. They're closely monitoring movements in Sydney Town. He, as well as many Committee members, believes the Ducks know they are finished in San Francisco and will pull up stakes and skedaddle with their loot before their identities and crimes become fully known. Apparently, the Committee's remaining prisoners are scared and naming names to save their skins to earn a free passage back to Australia."

"Isn't there a danger they'll torch their dens of iniquity and hovels rather than let others have them?"

"There's always a danger of arson with those desperadoes. But they appear more interested in getting moveable property and loot out of San Francisco before the Committee can confiscate it. They also know the Committee organized and endorsed an independent slate of candidates for the upcoming elections. They're afraid the candidates supported by the Committee will hold the balance of power and clean out the corrupt judges and law enforcement officials. If so, they're between a rock and a hard place with both the Committee and reformers on their tails. Cyrus thinks the Committee will hand over all its remaining prisoners to the civil authorities for trial or deportation."

"Is the Committee planning to disband?" I asked with mounting concern.

"No, not actually disband. Just reduce itself in size to an Executive Committee that serves as a watchdog over the civil authorities. Apparently, Schenck has resigned as have many others. They see their job as done for the time being."

"Let's hope so," I added. "I'm sure if they rang the tocsin bells out of need, their supporters would rally to their cause."

I was wrong about Henri's reaction to our hiring two apprentice cooks. He saw it as recognition that he was overworked and needed underlings to do the basic food prep, drudge work and take orders from him. We were both pleased that Rose Boucher took Joséphine Arras under her wing and counseled her how to deal with our "chef" and his bossy ways. Henri didn't have a clue he was a marked man in their eyes and they'd work together to topple him.

Manon and I were pleased that dinner reservations were exceeding 80% capacity and we were doing a brisk business the days we opened for lunch. I related Antonio's innovative plan to serve quick lunches and something he called "pizza" to the younger working crowd with a small carafe of wine for $1.50.

"I don't think the formula would work for us even on the wharf. We've got attractive ladies to serve food and sell drinks at a wine bar. Luigi and Antonio don't have our advantage. We make more money with the wine bar than the food menu. They have to find a niche market and we don't. But Antonio's right, they can't compete with top Italian restaurants, especially so far away from the commercial district. So, maybe they can make money with the new approach. They've got a lot of competition and the Italian community is much smaller than the French who live here."

I chuckled to myself. Not only was the French community growing larger weekly with emigrant arrivals, but the French wouldn't eat in Italian restaurants or drink their excellent wine. Pierre-Louis proved the point when he counseled us to avoid offering a cheap menu to the miserly newcomers. As he pointed out, the penny-pinchers would order a carafe of water, which was free, rather than splurge on a carafe of cheap house wine.

Manon interrupted my reverie. "By the way, *Chéri*, we have a reservation this weekend from another lady and her beau who's almost as famous as Ah Toy," she said with a whimsical and flirty look.

"Oh, really? I can't imagine anyone topping Ah Toy for beauty, grace and notoriety. Who is she?" I asked intrigued.

"Maybe papa-to-be should have to wait and see. Sometimes it's hard to tell the parlor house madams from the Jezebels looking to snatch successful miners and businessmen, non?"

"Actually, I thought the madams dress better and wear more real jewelry the fortune seekers can't afford," I said tongue-in-cheek.

"Hah, papa-to-be claims to know all about the ladies for hire despite his many denials that he visited bawdy houses in his travels to Sacramento and the gold placers. Manon will give you a big hint. This madam runs her parlor house in Sacramento and maybe you even know the name now, eh Big Boy."

I racked my brain for a name to no avail. I'd heard about a top madam in Sacramento, but despite Manon's suspicions Georges and I did not seek the company of women on our travels and we'd arrived late and left early the only day we'd been in Sacramento. Even if I knew the name, I wouldn't tell Manon, who was getting sensitive about her now enormous belly and starting to tire easily.

"No, I'm afraid you've got me stumped. I'll just have to wait and watch our diners. Do I get a prize if I guess correctly?"

"Hah, Big Boy doesn't earn a prize. Clue number two—the bawdy lady is the mistress of Charles Cora."

Cora's name rang a bell. I'd heard about him in Marysville. He was a professional gambler who owned an interest in a Marysville gambling house called "The New World." The owner of the hotel we stayed in Marysville, Maurice Ricard, spoke of Cora and his voluptuous "wife," Belle. They had stayed in his hotel. Cora was Italian born and came to America as a young boy and by his early twenties was making a reputation as a serious gambler in New Orleans before moving on to San Francisco in 1849 with a group of gamblers and their molls.

According to Ricard, Cora was good-looking in a rugged way and made his reputation in Sacramento by losing $60,000.00. It was rumored that his mistress, Belle, had staked him to $20,000.00 three times from the earnings of her bagnio and he'd lost it all; they'd headed north to the rough and ready mining towns and camps to recoup their losses with less sophisticated gamblers. Apparently, Cora was addicted to high stakes games. Ricard mentioned Cora won a $10,000.00 bet in Marysville.

Ricard described Cora's woman as in her mid-twenties, and dressed real fancy to showcase a voluptuous figure. From what he knew, she seemed quite dedicated to Cora and they eventually left Marysville in 1851 for the southern mining town of Sonora where he gambled and she was the madam of a high-price parlor house. While Sonora was a town of only 3,000 residents, the number swelled to 8,000 when the miners came for the weekend to gamble, drink and buy the most expensive woman their poke would allow before they lost it all again on monte, faro and other games of chance.

"I heard about Cora, the gambler, in Marysville from our hotel keeper. He said Cora's mistress was quite a looker and his faithful companion. I don't recall anything about her running a parlor house," I fibbed.

"Hah, we gonna see, aren't we, Big Boy?"

"When are they coming to dinner?"

"Sunday."

California Gold Rush Journal
∽ PART 2 ∾

CHAPTER TWENTY
San Francisco — September-October 1851

Jacques Boucher strode up the gangplank of the Eliza as the church bells struck 10 A.M. calling the faithful to the city's various churches. Boucher was dressed in a blue French artisan's combination. His long, coal-black hair was neatly secured by a velvet ribbon and his carpenter's tools and measures hung from a specially made belt. He greeted me with a big smile and a handshake that could crush bones if not quickly released. "Nice ship," he said, not flinching from Fido's menacing yaps as he surveyed its construction and rigging.

We clambered down the rope ladder to the hold and I lit the wall lanterns. I led Boucher through the main hold still full of barrels of Chilean wine and casks of rum to the smaller, curved hold below the forecastle at the bow of the ship. "I thought we'd start here with the wine bins and expand back through the larger holds as needed. What do you think?"

Boucher regarded the curvature of the ship's hull carefully as he paced off distances in meter strides and marked results on a small slate.

"I agree with you, that this is the best place to store wine. It's cool and dark and not too humid. It's a challenge and more work to build bins due to the curvature of the ribbing, but I learned how to do it in France. Many of the larger houses and manors supported their roofs with an upside down version of a boat's ribbing we called *charpente à bateau*. I would build the bins in redwood."

"Why redwood and not oak, like the ribbing?"

"Oak is hard, heavy, inflexible and expensive. Redwood is easier to work with, abundant and cheaper. It's also more flexible. We can bend thinner planks to the curvature of the ship's spine. We can use nails instead of the wooden oak pegs which will be cheaper and much faster. Also, in an environment where worms and other parasites may penetrate oak resting in salt water, redwood is acidic and impervious to worms," Boucher stated matter-of-factly.

"I'm sold on all the points. When can you start?"

"I'll calculate the materials I'll need today, so they can be delivered Tuesday. I can probably start Wednesday. Do you want bins the size of the ones we saw holding empty bottles by the ladder or a larger size?"

"I think we should make bins in different sizes where possible. The smallest should hold 24 liter bottles or 12 magnums."

"What about a table to decant and do wine tasting?"

"I thought we could do the tastings in the forecastle as we don't use it for living quarters. We could even build some bins there to hold the wines we taste. You're right, we should build a table to decant wines and serve hors d'oeuvres. Let's have a look."

We made our way back through the belly of the ship and were temporarily blinded by the bright sun as we got to the top of the ladder to the main deck. I couldn't help but think of the poor emigrants who could only afford steerage passage and had lived, suffered and died in small cubbyholes two decks below the main deck. While Boucher was measuring the forecastle for our modifications, Teri appeared on deck to enjoy the sun.

"What's going on?" She asked. She was barefoot and wearing a brightly colored Andean peasant's dress with lots of embroidery and a scoop neck. She'd pulled the dress's shoulders down even with the bodice to let the sun warm her shoulders and back. She'd pinned her blond tresses in a high bob that glinted in the sun and exposed the lovely lines of her neck. She seated herself on the steps of the poop deck for maximum exposure to her face, shoulders, and legs. She radiated a sensual, wholesome glow with sun on her creamy, coppery skin.

"Rose's brother is measuring the forecastle to transform it into a wine tasting salon. Another of Manon's creative ideas."

"Oh, is her brother a woodworker?" At that moment Jacques Boucher emerged from the entrance of the forecastle with his list of calculations and stopped dead in his tracks. His inquisitive black eyes locked like magnets with those of Teri. After holding their mutual regard and wonderment for several electrifying seconds, each broke into a broad smile. Boucher approached Teri, as she leaned casually back on the rail of the poop deck stairs, and gently lifted her hand and he bussed it gently while never breaking eye contact.

"How marvelous to see a real sun goddess being caressed by the sun's rays. I'm envious," he said without releasing her hand. Teri turned his hand over, regarded the palm, then lightly kissed the tips of his fingers one by one.

"I just met your lovely sister. Why don't you join me? It's so rare to enjoy the sun on my day off," she indicated he should sit next to her.

Boucher looked at me for approval, which I gave with a nod. "Enjoy it while it lasts. Drop the materials estimate by the restaurant tomorrow, if you can, and I'll prepare a bank draft," I said waving goodbye.

Manon arranged for Rose to wait tables Sunday evening and gave Teri and Giselle the day off. She tasked me with running the bar and serving wine and Gino to assist Rose. Joséphine assisted Henri in the kitchen. I noted on Gino's arrival that he was in a melancholy mood. During our communal dinner before the arrival of our guests, I tried to sound out what ailed him. "I don't want to talk about it," was all he'd say.

Charles Cora had reserved a table for four. Most of our clientele were seated and busy smearing gobs of Manon's *terrine de foie gras* on fresh baguettes when the Cora party arrived. Cora strode confidently to a vacant table set for four without asking to be seated. He was dressed in an expensive linen summer suit with vest and wore black, shiny half-boots. He was above average height with coal black hair he'd teased with pomade, had a low forehead, luminous dark eyes and dusky complexion. He sported a large, droopy mustache that hung over his lips. He was debonair and oozed confidence.

His companion, Belle Cora, was dressed in a gauzy, green muslin dress with deep décolletage that underscored her voluptuous figure. She was very fair-skinned and wore her long, brunette tresses loose down her back, held in place by gold clips that matched her gold-hooped earrings. Her hazel eyes turned greenish as she gave her fur stole to Cora and let him seat her. Every male eye in the restaurant was riveted to the swell of her bosom as she gracefully obliged their curiosity by leaning forward in a practiced, coquettish move to study her menu.

The couple sharing their table appeared quite vulgar in contrast to their classy hosts. The man was a swarthy dandy in his forties and inelegantly dressed in the costume of a card shark—striped trousers, ruffled shirt, pink foulard, vest stuffed with a gold watch fob and pink silk handkerchief. His companion was a quite pretty woman in her late twenties, but over-rouged and garishly dressed as a tart to expose all but the nipples of her abundant bosom. The couple reminded me of Jacques Vincent and his "wife", Odile, who used her ample, exposed bosom to lure marks to Vincent's gambling table in order to signal to Vincent the player's cards as she brushed her swelling globes over the mark's arm and dipped her daring décolletage on the playing table to entertain and distract the game's players and observers.

Cora waived to me at the bar and hollered, "Bring us the best champagne you have to go with the first course."

Belle Cora gave me a curious, once-over look as I poured chilled Veuve Cliquot champagne from a vintage year. "Don't I know you from somewhere?" She asked inquisitively.

Good lord, I thought. I hope she hasn't confused me with someone else. Fortunately, Manon was occupied with guests in the back dining room and couldn't hear the question. She'd have me tarred and feathered in short order as I'd never convince her I hadn't visited Belle's parlor house on my trip to the mines. "I'm sorry, *madame*. I only wish I had. I would never forget meeting a woman as beautiful and elegant as you. It's *our* pleasure to welcome you and your companions to our restaurant this evening. My wife has prepared a special menu and I'm delighted to serve you, your husband and friends." I bowed to Belle and extended my hand to Cora, which he dutifully shook.

Belle seemed to accept my explanation and pointed to the menu. "What are the *coquilles de fruits de mer?*"

"It's our fish course. They're fresh sea scallops served with bay shrimps in a light cream and gruyère sauce in the shell of the scallops. It's delicious."

"I was hoping your menu offered fresh abalone. I've heard it's the best sea food delicacy in California, even better than the local crab. I've never been able to find a restaurant that serves it. How disappointing. I'm dying to taste it," she pleaded with her luminous hazel-green eyes.

I was fully aware that Manon's eyes were drilling a hole in

my back. "Yes, it's sad we can't get a sufficient supply to offer it on our menu. It's as you say, one of the best delicacies along with the local lobster and crab which are both out of season."

"I'll pay an extra $30.00 per person and order your most expensive white wine if your cook can find four abalone steaks for my wife and guests. It's a special occasion and we want to celebrate in style."

Oh boy, I thought. He wants to buy special treatment and show off for his woman and guests. How's this going to play with our other guests? Will it jeopardize Manon's fixed menu concept if we accede in his request? I knew for a fact we did have several fresh abalones which we planned to eat ourselves, but not enough to serve the entire restaurant.

"I'm not sure it's possible. I don't know if we have any abalone at present," I fibbed. "I'll have to ask my wife whether anything can be done."

"So, *Chéri*, I see you're making fast talk with the gamblers and their *pouffiasses*. Those four dancing titties seem to have mesmerized your brain. We have other guests waiting for wine, you know," she said pinching my cheek hard.

I quickly explained Cora's request and offer. "Let me handle this," Manon said now patting tenderly the red pinch mark she'd made. She pointed to the tables I should serve and instructed Rose to serve the Cora party large helpings of her terrine and put another bottle of champagne in an ice bucket.

When Rose finished serving, Manon sauntered over to Cora's table. "My husband informs me you are having a very special celebration this evening and inquired about the availability of abalone, yes?"

"Yes, it's a special celebration for my wife. It's the only local delicacy that's eluded her since we arrived in 1849 from New Orleans. Can you indulge us? I'll pay whatever it takes."

"We do, in fact, have a few abalones on ice, but not enough

to serve to all the guests. Some diners would take offense if we served your table abalone steaks while they had only our seafood offering on the menu. It would cause a big problem and affect our reputation. I would be happy to accommodate your request if we had enough abalone to go around," Manon said sweetly.

Cora was emboldened by the knowledge there were abalones on hand. "Surely, madam, there must be a solution. Name your price. I promised my princess she would taste abalone before we returned to Sacramento," he said squeezing Belle's hand.

Manon put her hand to her forehead as if deep in thought. "Hmmm," she murmured while all eight eyes at the table watched her intently. "Maybe there's a solution, but it would be very expensive."

"Tell me what you can do. You've got the abalones and we have the money," Cora said overeagerly as if it was a done deal.

"You'll have to go along with my story to the rest of diners. I'll tell them that you had arranged for the purchase of several abalones for a celebratory occasion tonight. I'll have to cook all seven abalones. Four for your table and the other three you will generously offer to share samples with the rest of the guests. The abalones will cost $35.00 a piece in addition to the regular menu. They were purchased for another group for a private party and I'll have to make amends. We'll offer free after diner drinks to all diners in honor of your generosity. Is it a deal?" Manon extended her hand.

Cora didn't blink an eye. He seized her hand. "It's a deal." Belle's now green eyes flashed triumphantly.

Manon headed for the kitchen to apprise Henri and Joséphine of the menu change. I had to admire my wife's business acumen. The Cora party would be paying $305.00 instead of $60.00 for their meal and ordering more expensive wine. The free samples for the rest of our guests would make the papers and only heighten our reputation and attract customers.

Needless to say, our gullible guests bought Manon's white

lie told sweetly from table to table about the abalones. I had to show Joséphine how to open the strong shells and slice the abalone steaks. Henri cooked the steaks to perfection—30 seconds on each side in a very hot, buttered pan. Rose served the Cora party their abalone steaks in abalone half shells with sides of little cups of hot, drawn butter to dip each tasty morsel. The "oohs" and "ahs" from Cora's table were soon echoed throughout the restaurant as the other diners were served their samples along with the shellfish course.

One grateful guest ordered a bottle of champagne be sent to the Cora table and proposed a toast of thanks for the memorable tasting. A rousing roar of approval followed. The jovial mood carried through to the next course — *Le Tournedos Rossini.* For this classic dish, we had been able to secure some excellent grade tenderloin of beef from a rancher in Santa Clara and fresh goose liver from the farm supplying Manon's eggs and chickens. The tender rounds of beef were briefly pan-fried in butter and served rare with strips of goose liver also pan-fried in butter to which is added a truffle sauce with Madeira wine. We had recommended a rich, aged Gigondas wine to complement the dish.

The follow-up to the abalone was so well received that Cora asked us to send the cook to his table for his compliments. Henri's face beamed as we translated Cora's words of praise for the two delicious dishes. After Henri bowed deeply, and muttered, "*Merci beaucoup!*" several times, Cora reached in his vest pocket and slipped a pair of gold coins in the chef's hands. The rest of our dinner guests clapped roundly and hooted their pleasure. The dessert course, *Le Biscuit à la Reyne*, served as an anti-climax, but the perfect touch to a special meal. The dessert was invented by Louis XIV's *pâtissier* to honor the queen of France. The cake is delicately perfumed with anise.

Manon winked her pleasure to me. We saved our dessert for our big double bed upstairs.

California Gold Rush Journal
∽ PART 2 ∾

CHAPTER TWENTY-ONE
San Francisco — September-October 1851

anon's abalone evening highlighted all the newspaper
gossip columns thanks to Charles Cora who bragged
to one and all that Chez Manon was the best and only
restaurant in San Francisco that could produce an abalone dish
cooked to perfection on demand. He was wrong of course. He'd
just never eaten in the better Chinese restaurants in the "Little
China" area of town, where all the shellfish specialties including
abalone could be had any night of the week. Given the Yankees'
prevailing view that Celestials, their derogatory name for
Chinese, were an inferior race and not entitled to share in the
gold or other riches of California, there was little chance that
the Coras or other "superior" folks would ever learn our little
secret—the San Francisco Chinese fishermen supplied all our
shellfish delicacies.

Many others shared my concern that as soon as the Ducks
and other criminals learned the Committee had turned its remaining prisoners over to civil authorities for trial, the undesirables would slip back into the city as they did following the first

hangings of Jenkins and Stuart a little more than 100 days ago. My fears were addressed on October 8th in an article published in the *Alta California*. A resident, Andrew Goodwin, presented a petition to the Committee's Executive Committee alleging that his ten-year old niece, Mary Lye, had been taken from him by Ernest Kohle and his wife and spirited to Marysville and held there in a house of prostitution.

Sam Brannan, along with other Committee members, traveled to Marysville where they consulted with the Marysville branch of the Committee. The Marysville contingent confronted the Kohles at their bagnio and retrieved the girl and restored her to her uncle's custody. The Committee's actions were taken as a sign they were prepared to act and intervene quickly upon demand. The newspapers also noted the noticeable reduction of criminal activity since the double hanging of Whittaker and McKenzie. The newspapers reported that many of the Chilean pimps closed their sleazy bagnios and fled San Francisco with the women they had tricked into servitude contracts and prostitution with promises of gainful employment.

Manon was now in her eighth month of pregnancy and concerned for what would happen to her restaurant once she went into labor. We were deliberating the problem over a late breakfast at the restaurant, when Gino arrived out of breath, a worried expression on his face.

"What's the matter?" I asked. I figured it was to do with his deteriorating relationship with Teri. Rose informed me that her brother and Teri spent Monday together and Jacques stayed the night in Teri's cabin. Apparently, Gino saw Jacques leave Teri's cabin Tuesday morning, which explained his glum mood. Manon laughed it off by suggesting Gino should pay court to Rose to avoid a family feud.

"Your employee, Georges, and his wife arrived this morning and claimed my cabin. What am I supposed to do?"

Manon and I looked at each other. She raised her brows in amusement and shrugged. Ball in my court. "Remember, I said you could stay in Georges' cabin until he returned from New York with his woman. You'll have to arrange to lodge elsewhere. Return to the ship and clear out your cabin, so Georges can settle in. You can stow your gear in the forecastle until you get settled elsewhere. Tell Georges and Nellie to join us here at the restaurant for a late breakfast or early lunch. Then, go see your uncle. His restaurant should be finished. You can probably stay with your cousin, Antonio."

Gino gave me a hang-dog look and shook his head in disbelief at the double misfortune in the same week. The girl he's courting takes a new lover and now he's out of his digs. When he left, Manon commented, "It's for the best that Gino leaves our ship and lives elsewhere. He's going to get even more upset with Teri and it will provoke a fight eventually. Teri has to be free to see whomever she wants without having Gino spying on her comings and goings or confronting her male companions."

"Yes. I agree we need to keep them separated. Gino's very prideful and he feels he's lost face. He'll get over it, but it'll take time. I will assign him to work on the post office correspondence for the consulate with Sophie Benson at my office. Can you do without him at the restaurant?"

"Yes, Georges can run the bar and escort Teri, Giselle and Nelly to the ship at night."

"Nelly?"

"Yes, we train her to wait tables and when our babies are born, she can care for them while I run the restaurant. They both need a job and we're short-handed. Georges can work for you when we don't need him as barman. He loves bars, doesn't he?" Manon said with a big grin.

I ignored her jibe. "What about Giselle and Teri?"

"Now they can work full-time running the business on the

wharf. We make good profits there. Georges and Nelly will be happy to have good jobs with us. They have free room on the ship, eat with us, and they'll make good tips in the restaurant, yes?"

"I see what you mean. They'll make more with us than working elsewhere. Nelly's English is perfect. She'll wait on the Americans and Rose on the French and other Europeans."

"Yes, 'an no more horny males slipping offers for sex, marriage and money bribes to the serving staff."

"Hah, you may know the restaurant business, but male behavior won't change. They'll just focus on Rose and still go for Nelly even though she wears a wedding band."

"But there'll be a big difference. Rose and Nelly will dress more conservatively and wear their hair up, not loose and flowing like single girls. Men on the make think they can buy all single women like the ones in the gambling palaces, yes?"

I laughed. "If they've had enough to drink or a big sack of nuggets, they believe they can buy any woman married or not."

"Yes, that's why respectable married women have to watch their husbands like a hawk. Husbands think when they travel with a handsome single assistant and leave wife home, it's okay to have little roll in the hay, yes? What the little wife doesn't know can't hurt, non?"

"Some nice married ladies think the same way when their hard-working husbands have to travel on business to make money, non?" I said mimicking Manon's accent.

"An' maybe that's why some husbands keep their wives knocked-up with big bellies full of kids and others in the nursery when they travel, yes?"

Manon was not about to lose this little argument. Better to give in gracefully. "Except when wife is a noted cook and has a selection of sharp knives and cleavers ready nip off a nose or an ear when the husband is a bad boy, yes?"

"Glad some husbands understand woman's intentions so clearly." We both laughed, I hugged her now enormous belly and felt the kicking she was receiving. I was nuzzling her neck and whispering sweet nothings in her ear, when Georges arrived.

"Gar, now ain't that somethin' to see after all these months. Looks like you two are gonna have three or four kids in a go."

Manon laughed and pointed to Georges' shiny new wedding ring. "Just wait 'til it's your turn," she pointed to the now blushing Nelly Swanson, who lowered her head and fingered her matching gold band.

"Welcome home to both of you. Pierre get us a bottle of champagne and some nibbles, please; we've a lot of catching up to do."

When I returned with the champagne and a platter of sliced Italian salami, parmesan cheese and a bowl of olives, Manon was explaining how we came to acquire the restaurant from Pierre-Louis. When Manon proposed they both work in the restaurant, Georges beamed satisfaction at the thought of running a bar and Nelly bobbed her head excitedly at the prospect to work as a waitress and help care for our twins.

"It's so wonderful to arrive here and know we have jobs, can work together and have your support. For me it's a dream come true, I've been worried silly not knowing what opportunities we'd have on arrival. It's all so new and exciting," Nelly said with emotion while twisting a strand of her light auburn hair.

After toasting our new workers and sampling the platter of hors d'oeuvres, Manon and I wanted to hear highlights of their trip. Georges had opted for the recently opened route through Nicaragua. On the map it was closer, faster and appeared to offer more boat travel than the Panama route.

"What convinced you to take passage through Nicaragua?" I asked.

Nelly replied in English. "Once I knew for sure Georges was

coming to get me, I made inquiries at all the navigation companies that offer transport by the various routes. The company booking passage through Nicaragua advertised rates from New York to San Francisco that were cheaper and faster than their competitors. They provided a map of the trip which indicated we'd sail by paddle steamer from New York down the Atlantic coast and take provisions again in Florida and one of the Caribbean islands before getting to the coast of Nicaragua. From there the map claimed we'd travel 95% via large river launches and small steamers across Nicaragua to the other side where a large paddle-wheeled steamer would take us up the Pacific Coast to San Francisco."

"Did you believe their guarantees?" Manon asked.

"Oh no, it sounded like pie in the sky, too good to be true. I asked for the names of New York merchants who'd returned via this route. Surprisingly, they gave me three names of persons with New York business addresses who'd booked with them. They confirmed the trip was easier, safer and faster than the Panama route they'd taken to San Francisco."

Georges added proudly, "An' she had the tickets for us to depart four days after my arrival."

"Did the trip live up to your expectations and the company's representations?" I asked. This would be important if any of my French clients wanted to travel here from New York or New Orleans.

"You know how I hate to travel by sea. I managed to keep my stomach settled for the first couple of days out of New York, then we hit a storm and I was sick like on our ship to New York. They did stop in Santo Domingo to refuel and take on fresh provisions," Nelly stated.

"What was the trip like once you started to cross Nicaragua? Was it really 95% by boat as they advertised?" I asked.

"Well, our ship docked at Grey Town on the coast. It was

really pretty primitive—a few frame houses with shingles, native huts thatched with mimosa leaves and straw, a couple of hotels with American hotel keepers and one poorly stocked grocery store that contained mostly fruits and stale crackers. Fortunately, Georges had the foresight to buy lots of provisions in New York and Santo Domingo. The shipping company didn't warn us that no provisions would be provided during the trip across Nicaragua." Nelly looked to Georges.

"I learned from fellow travelers on the way to New York that the run through Nicaragua could be short of opportunities to buy good food and at some stops they'd only have fruit and eggs to sell. We stocked up on crackers, cookies, and nuts that wouldn't spoil. I also bought a big, cured ham and $10.00 worth of dimes 'cuz they're worth twelve and a half cents in Nicaragua. I also bought a Colt pistol and two boxes of bullets as well as hammocks to sleep in," Georges said refilling his glass.

"It was good thing Georges knew to bring hammocks and mosquito netting. The river boat up the San Juan River could not sleep all the passengers on deck. They let us women stay on board and sleep in hammocks at the stern, but Georges had to sleep on shore in a shanty which cost 50 cents. He was able to avoid the fleas and bedbugs by sleeping in his hammock and we both had mosquito netting rigged with our hammocks."

"What were the boatmen like?" Manon inquired.

"They were a ragtag bunch from all nations," Georges said. "There was local Indians what they called Mosquito Indians. They wore small little breech cloth patches over their privates. There were Negroes and mixes of Indians, Negroes an' whites what they called mulattos. They paddled and the ones up front had rifles to shoot alligators what got in our way. There was all kinds of colorful birds and monkeys swingin' from vines from tree to tree an' raisin' a hell of a racket the whole time—screeching an' howling at us the whole way. Some even tried to spit on us when we got close to shore."

"The Indians looked fearsome with their tattoos and scars, but they were actually kind and respectful. Most of the passengers were men, some with wives, from New York. They were woefully unprepared for the heat and humidity. Some had to buy food from Georges at Castillo Rapids where we had to leave the boat and walk around the falls and rapids to a small paddle-wheel steamer for the next leg of the journey," Nelly added.

Georges drained the last of the champagne into his glass which prompted my next thought. "As it was hot and muggy, did the boats offer fresh water or other beverages?"

"They had some barrels of water on board what they claimed was rain water, but it didn't look or smell good. We was able to buy bottles of beer at most of the evening stops. Some make-shift bars offered local rum and other spirits. We was afraid to drink the water after some who drank it got sick." I laughed at George's characterization. I couldn't imagine him without a glass in his hand for long. He'd drink any kind of alcohol rather than water.

"We could also buy various fruits and drink the juice," Nelly added. "Natives would approach the boat from little dugout canoes they called "bungoes" with offers to sell whatever they were trying to market—bananas, lemons, oranges, coconuts, coffee beans, plantains, tobacco leaves, native corn, peppers, even small monkeys."

"Monkeys?" Manon asked in a surprised voice.

Nelly flushed anew and replied, "Some were on leashes and sold as pets along with parrots and parakeets in wicker cages. Others were to eat. Our boatmen would make a stew ashore in a big iron cauldron when we stopped for the night. Sometimes they used monkey meat or whatever else was fresh and available— snake meat, birds and an animal that looked like a small beaver with webbed feet and a long hairless tail; they called it a 'nutria.'

It's some kind of rodent that lives in the banks of the rivers."

"It were more like a big rat if you ask me. Ugly bugger with a rat's tail, but the natives swore it was a delicacy," Georges snickered.

"So, did you try it?" I asked tongue-in-cheek. Nelly grimaced and Georges laughed, then his shoulders shivered.

"No way I'm gonna eat a rat 'less I'm starvin' in a prison cell," Georges stated adamantly.

Manon and I laughed. "What did you eat when the ham ran out? Just drank rum?" Manon asked cheekily.

"When we got to the settlement of San Carlos on Lake Nicaragua, there were 50 to 60 native huts and about 25 canvas huts selling provisions. Georges did buy several bottles of rum, but there was also a fresh, sugary bread, cooked chicken, dried beef jerky and cans of beans and a large selection of fruits and nuts. So, we had food and juice across the large lake. The hard part came after we arrived to Virgin Bay and had to leave our ship," Nelly said.

"Har, it were sight," piped in Georges. "They anchored the ship about 300 meters from shore and transferred baggage and passengers to a large dugout boat about 20 meters long and 3 meters wide. They tossed the women from the arms of one burly native on the steamer to another one on the 'bungoe.' You should've seen the petticoats flyin' and women shriekin' and flailin' their arms in the air. They pulled the dugout to shore with a long line. Some of the women had to ride the last 5 meters on a native's back to keep their skirts from gettin' wet. Nelly here just raised her skirts, carried her shoes and hopped into the water."

Nelly's cheeks flushed a beet red. "I wasn't about to climb on a native's back and have his hands under my skirts," she said defiantly. "It was so hot that what little got wet, dried quickly. The worst part was at the end. We had to get over some hills to the Pacific coast on mules. The track was muddy and slippery.

The men had to walk in the mire and lead the mules charged with women and baggage. I preferred to walk in the muck barefoot rather than sit on smelly, sweaty mules. I washed my feet and legs when we got to the coastal town of Del Sud. There was a large hotel built from dismantled vessels and quite a few canvas huts selling provisions for the trip up the Pacific coast to San Francisco. We finally had a hot meal of sea bass in a civilized setting."

"We had a stroke of luck at the coast. A coal-burning steamer was waiting for us and it sailed the next day. We stopped in a coastal town in Guatemala for more coal and went ashore for more provisions. We made similar stops in Acapulco, Mexico and San Diego, California. It was a lot slower than when we came up the coast in the Clipper "Flying Cloud," but we're here," Georges stated proudly with chest puffed out.

"And where did you get married?" Manon asked cheekily with raised eyebrows and mischievous smile.

Georges' chest deflated and Nelly replied, "I told Georges that if we were going to make a new life together in California, it would be as man and wife. I bought the rings in New York and the captain of the ship taking us to Nicaragua married us as we sailed off the coast of Charleston. I insisted our marriage be performed in American waters by an American ship captain, so Georges could get a United States passport when we arrived in San Francisco and any children we might have would be American," Nelly stated with a confidence and assurance we had not seen while on the clipper from Le Havre to New York.

Manon suggested we take a break and lunch on the hearty venison stew she'd prepared for the wharf canteen.

"FRENCH BOOT-BLACKS," 1851.

"DEPARTURE OF A STEAMSHIP," 1851.

"SAN CARLOS FORT, LAKE NICARAGUA," 1851.

"HARBOR AT SAN JUAN, NICARAGUA," 1851.

"CARRIGE FROM THE PIROGUE AND MULE
TRANSPORT IN FROM LAKE NICARAGUA," 1851.

"STEAMER TAKING ON COAL ON THE
PACIFIC COAST," 1851.

California Gold Rush Journal
∽ PART 2 ∾

CHAPTER TWENTY-TWO

San Francisco — October-November, 1851

ith Gino full-time and Georges and Sophie Benson working part-time on the stacks of correspondence from the consulate, we finally made significant progress catching up. I managed to squeeze another expense check out of Consul Dillon, who clamored for me to take mail to the miners. I assigned Gino the task of organizing letters we should take on our trip to the southern mines as he knew the mining camps and could plan the route. I hoped to make the trip shortly after our twins were born if the rains held off. Manon wouldn't like me going then, or frankly any other time, so I planned to do the trip while everyone would be fussing over our new babes.

Manon and I were pleased at the change in both Georges and his Nelly. Georges loved running the bar where he was in his natural element. Nelly applied herself admirably to her new situation. No longer the shy, introverted young woman who kept to her cabin or promenaded on Georges' arm on our clipper trip from Le Havre to New York, she blossomed into a confident, self-assured young matron and restaurant worker. She and Rose got along well and shared tips earned serving food to our patrons. She volunteered to teach both Rose and Joséphine English in her spare time. When things got chaotic in the kitchen, she pitched in to help without being asked.

She helped Manon set up a nursery in the spare bedroom in the apartment and knitted baby booties and other items in spare moments. She taught Rose how to dress demurely when waiting tables. Rose taught her how to put off would-be Lotharios in a nice, but firm manner. Georges' friendly, easy manner and ability to chat up our patrons kept the bar busy, the wine and liquor flowing and provided the latest gossip and doings about town. Pierre-Louis was busy setting up house with his new wife, so Georges kept us abreast of the latest political and social trials and tribulations in the city.

Georges learned from a member of the Committee of Vigilance that the mayor, ironically, had to call on the Committee to resolve a dispute between sailors and their ship's officers. When the sloop "Challenge" arrived in San Francisco on October 31st, its sailors claimed on coming ashore, that the captain and other officers subjected them to brutal treatment at sea. Their claims inflamed local stevedores and other sailors on the wharf. The outraged crowd soon became a mob chanting for hanging the "Challenge's" officers.

The mayor ordered the fire stations' bells rung to summon members of the Committee. The immediate presence and show of force by responding Committee members quieted the mob. The captain was arrested and stood trial for his harsh treatment and was fined. We took it as a sign that with peace and cooperation between the civil authorities and the Committee, the legal system could function equitably. The Committee became a de facto court of appeal.

Manon broke her water and went into labor in the early

morning on a cool foggy day in the second week of November. Dr. Benoit arranged a midwife for the birthing and he assisted with the deliveries in our apartment over the restaurant. Fortunately, the restaurant was closed for dinner service and Georges and I could fret, pace and worry downstairs while the labor ran its course.

Georges was heating soup and stew for our dinner when a beaming Dr. Benoit strode into the restaurant.

"Two more healthy, bawling, hungry Americans to populate our fair city," the doctor announced, his face beaming with contentment.

"What about my wife? Is she okay?" I asked nervously.

Dr. Benoit chuckled. "Rest assured, she's tired but fine. The births were only four minutes apart. She's young and healthy and will be up and about in no time. The hardest part is going to be feeding the two rascals at the same time."

"Speaking of rascals, are they both boys?" Georges piped in.

"No, Mrs. Dubois birthed a boy and a girl, but it's hard to tell them apart when they're hollerin' to be fed. Lung capacity is extraordinary on both of them. Guaranteed to be a handful," the doctor said, a twinkle in his eye, while Georges produced three brandy snifters from the bar and poured stiff doses of cognac.

"Congratulations," the doctor said as we clinked glasses and downed our tots of fire water.

"When can I see my wife and kids?" I asked.

"Best give the ladies some more time to clean up and your wife to nourish the rascals. You'll not have any peace and quiet until they've had their fill."

Oh boy, I thought, just like that your life changes. We were now going to be at the beck and call of our two babes. Dr. Benoit interrupted my reverie.

"Whatever's on the stove sure smells good. I wouldn't mind a taste or two with a glass of wine," he angled.

"Sure, of course. Join us for a bite to eat. Georges get the doctor a plate and open a good bottle of wine. We have an event to celebrate. I imagine everyone upstairs will be hungry after the ordeal. I'll just pop upstairs and see how they're coming along."

Before the doctor could object, I bounded up the stairs to our apartment. Nelly met me with a big smile. "I was just coming to get you. Manon's asking for you. What beautiful babies you've got," she said beaming with excitement and possibly envy.

Nelly led me to our bedroom. The midwife was just on the way out. I invited her to join Dr. Benoit for a plate of stew and a glass of wine if she was in the mood. Manon's face was still drained from her ordeal, but broke into a big, roundhouse grin when she saw me. Our two babes were wrapped in swaddling clothes and busy clenching and unclenching miniature fists in rhythm with their mouths sucking milk at each breast.

"So, Papa, what do you have to say for yourself, huh? Just like in the kitchen, Manon had to do all the hard work to get your kids born," she said in her "You're a naughty boy" voice and laughed.

"You're all so beautiful. Look at you. I should be envious of our tots getting their fill, but I'm not. I'm just happy the ordeal is over and our babes will grow up in this land of opportunity. We're heating up a meal downstairs. The doctor and midwife are already gobbling venison stew and tossing down wine. Shall I bring up a plate of stew or bowl of soup?"

"No, once they've gorged themselves, they'll want to sleep. I'm tired, but too excited to sleep. Have Nelly take a bite with the doctor. She can put them to bed and watch over them while I join you for a glass of champagne and some *terrine de canard truffé*. Manon earned a little celebration, non?"

"Manon has earned more than a little celebration. But are you sure you want to deal with going up and down the stairs? I can bring a bottle of champagne and your terrine up here."

"Hah, you don't know us strong French women. Husbands think their wives are weak little things good for cooking, housework and tumbling into bed, yes? We fought on the barricades beside our men during the revolution and peasant women often birth their babes in the fields where they do a man's heavy labor and continue working after they've suckled their newborn. So, send Nelly up in about twenty minutes. We have to discuss what to name our baby boy and his sister."

I informed Nelly of Manon's wishes and she beamed her acceptance. Georges better watch out, I thought. Nelly's sure to want a babe of her own after caring for our twins. As the doctor was still soaking up venison sauce with a piece of baguette, I asked, "Which baby was born first?"

"Your daughter arrived first and your son shortly after. They're a healthy pair just like their mother; they're all healthy as a horse," he said tendering his empty glass to Georges for a refill. The midwife ate a hasty bite and had excused herself to attend another woman's birthing. No point asking the doctor's opinion whether Manon should descend the steep stairs to celebrate the successful birthing with champagne and goodies. She'd need plenty of nourishment to feed her young colt and filly.

As Dr. Benoit was taking his leave, Teri and Giselle arrived all flushed and out of breath accompanied by Gino who was still moody and glum. They'd just learned of the births and couldn't wait to see Manon and the twins. I ushered them up the stairs and returned to organize festivities with Georges. After selecting several bottles of vintage champagne for our ice buckets, Georges suggested we light up cigars while we awaited the women folk.

"No cigar smoke allowed," I cautioned. "Manon finds it disagreeable and we don't want to ruin her celebration. Let's pass out one of our best cigars to the doctor and others to smoke after Manon retires." Georges nodded his acquiescence and handed Cuban cigars to Dr. Benoit and Gino.

I took Gino aside and revealed my plan to make a quick for-ay to the southern placers to distribute as much mail as possible and give notice in the major supply centers that we held sacks of French miners' mail consigned to us by the French Consul-ate which could be picked up at my office for a small fee. I'd instructed him to draw lists of names of addressees and senders we'd deciphered from the letters and have them printed.

"How soon do you think we could be ready to leave?" I asked.

Gino looked surprised. "You mean to leave during the rainy season? We could get stuck there if the tracks all turn too mud-dy for mules. The terrain is difficult to travel even when it's dry."

"I know we can't visit the small, remote mining camps in rainy weather. Many miners will winter in towns near their diggings; others will winter in place to be the first to work the new gravels for gold that flows with the rains. I want to try to visit the larger towns and supply centers where there are French merchants and a sizable French presence—hotels, restaurants, merchants who supply the French workings. What towns do you suggest from your experience?"

Gino paused to think. "I'd say the major town central to the French mining camps is Sonora. It's a big settlement with lots of merchants and facilities and supplies mining camps work-ing the south fork of the Stanislaus River and the creeks that feed into it such as Mormon Creek just north of Sonora and the creeks that flow south of Sonora that feed the Tuolumne River— Wood's Creek and Sullivan's Creek. Most of the French, Chilean and Mexican miners work in a radius around Sonora. The Mexicans got there first and they're friendly with all min-ers who speak Latin tongues."

"Good, that's what I want. We can contact all the French businesses there and have them post our printed lists. How long will it take to get to Sonora?"

"It depends on how much rain is falling. We'll have to cross the Stanislaus River at Knight's Ferry to get to the southern mines. If the river's too high and flooding, we may not get over and back."

"We'll have to take that chance. It's only mid-November.

Manon arrived escorted by Giselle and Nelly. "Teri's looking after the twins first while Nelly eats. Giselle will relieve her in turn. I'm thirsty and starved. Bring on the champagne," Manon announced.

Georges popped a cork and the celebration was on. Our festivities ended three empty bottles later and when the stew and terrine pots were scraped clean. I escorted my exhausted, tipsy wife up the stairs to grab some shuteye before our progeny demanded their next feeding.

California Gold Rush Journal
➣ PART 2 ➢

CHAPTER TWENTY-THREE

San Francisco – November-December, 1851

M anon was not happy with my decision to make a quick trip to Sonora to deliver mail. I argued that Consul Dillon would cancel my concession if I didn't go, and I needed it continued to gain benefit from all the flyers we'd posted to France.

"Papa's wasting no time abandoning his wife and poor little Fanny and Jules, is he? And what do I tell them when their Daddy gets washed away by a flooding river or shot by a drunken miner or angry Yankees or Indians, huh?" Manon emphasized with a pout.

We were both aware of the animosity between the Yankee miners and the Chilean, French and other foreigners. Most of the trouble occurred in the southern area I planned to visit. An area named Chile Gulch was the site of the so-called "Chilean War." The three gold camps in this area were worked primarily by Chilean miners in 1848. An enterprising Chilean named Dr. Concha worked his mine using peon workers under indenture to him. He had the audacity to stake claims in the names of his menial workers to expand his control of valuable terrain. When he drove a party of American miners off a rich, hilly area near Mokelumne Hill, the so-called "Chilean War" exploded like a bomb in the winter of 1848-49.

The Americans were furious and retaliated by meeting on the disputed "hill" and passing a resolution banning the Chileans from the diggings. Dr. Concha went to Stockton and secured a warrant to arrest the Americans. Armed with the warrant, a group of about sixty armed Chileans marched to the "hill" they referred to as "Mok Hill," and killed two American miners who resisted and took thirteen others prisoner. This action incited Americans in the area to take up arms. They appealed for help from a company of government rangers in Stockton.

Before the rangers arrived, the American prisoners escaped and turned the tables on the Chileans. They marched the Chileans at gun point into the tent settlement at Mokelumne for trial. Three Chileans were hanged and several others received harsh punishments. This marked the beginning of the bad blood between the American and foreign miners. Legislative passage of the discriminatory miner's tax of $20.00 a month championed by the Americans added fuel to the growing tensions between the groups. The American miners claimed the tax established their priority to harvest the gold and push foreigners, especially the Chinese, off the better paying gravels.

I learned from Etienne Derbec that the Mokelumne River gravels were very rich in gold and easy to work. The largest chunk of gold found during the Gold Rush was spotted by a soldier mining in the area when he went to the river to get a pail of drinking water; it weighed 161 pounds. The find and other large chunks of gold from the river gravels sparked intense competition for access to the richest and easiest gravel bars.

The second "ethnic war" over the Mokelumne River placers occurred between the French and Americans with their allies, the Irish, during the late summer of 1851 while Georges and I were touring the northern mines along the south fork of the Yuba River. The town of Mokelumne Hill is overlooked by the so-called "French Hill," and an organized group of French miners working the hill's gravels hit rich pockets of gold. American and Irish miners working less profitable diggings nearby became jealous and decided to try to run the French off the hill and take their claims.

The French responded by hoisting their tri-color French flag to signal they were not intimidated. Some hot-headed Irish responded by charging the hill and wounding some French before being repulsed and taking casualties. The French built a barricade at the top of the hill and refused to surrender their workings. From their now fortified position the French could effectively repel any further attack. Realizing they would take heavy casualties if they attempted to fight an uphill battle, the Americans and Irish appealed to the government to evict the French.

The governor ordered the militia to restore order and asked the French Consul, Patrice Dillon, to negotiate a settlement. Dillon's efforts led to an agreement that the French would continue to mine their hilltop concessions without interference from Irish or American claim jumpers. Dillon's settlement created more bad blood and ill will between the hostile groups. The French were furious their attackers were not subjected to miners' justice at the end of a noose; the Americans and Irish were resentful the French could continue to mine their rich claims while they were relegated to inferior diggings.

As word of the incident spread throughout the gold fields, foreign miners grouped themselves together for protection and all miners worked their claims heavily armed and prepared to shoot first and ask questions later. Manon learned all about the French "Moke" hill war from me and Consul Dillon's wife, so her concerns for my safety were justified. In addition to the volatile situation between the competing groups of miners, they all occupied local Miwok and Yokut Indians' traditional sites for gathering acorns and hunting game for meat and skins below the snow line, which they needed to survive the harsh winter season in the Sierras.

The encroachment by hoards of miners seeking the rich placers in the streambeds of the area led to the Mariposa Indian War of 1850. While the Indians couldn't stop the miners' take-over of their traditional foraging areas, they could steal animals, tools and food and kill isolated or drunk miners when they had the chance. This was a matter great concern in my trip to the northern placers when a band of Maidu Indian hunters stalked us and planned to rob or kill us if we gave them an opportunity. Fortunately, our trapper guides recognized the danger and we avoided a confrontation. I regretted now that Georges and I had embellished the incident with Manon and the others. I had given Manon another legitimate cause for concern.

"I agree it's not a good time to travel to the placers, but I feel compelled to show good faith to the consulate to keep our mail concession. I promise not to travel to outlying mining camps or take risks with the weather. My plan is to get to and from the two major towns of Sonora and Mariposa where French merchants supply French miners. I've had Gino print the names of writers and recipients which I can leave with the merchants to share with their clients. Hopefully, miners will deputize individuals to come to San Francisco to collect letters. Where miners are known to the merchants, we'll leave the letters with the merchants for their clients. From what we've learned, there's no post office in either town. Derbec mentioned a French merchant in Sonora who sends a man to San Francisco to collect letters for his clients every two weeks. I'll start with him. His man can collect from us for the other merchants in Sonora until they establish a post office. So, you see, I'll spend time in the two towns meeting contact persons, drop off what mail I can and be back at my wife's side quickly, ready to bounce our babes on my knee and listen to them coo."

I tried to lay out my case in a cogent manner, but Manon's energetic foot tapping signaled she was having none of it. "Hah, derelict-duty papa plans to spend time eating, drinking, hob-nobbing and carousing with French merchants and shady ladies in Sonora and Mariposa, yes?"

"There won't be time or occasion to carouse with anyone. I have to make contacts quickly before the heavy rains of winter begin. My nose will be to the grindstone all the way."

"Hah, derelict-duty papa can control the rain, yes? He consults the clouds and waves his finger to hold off heavy rain that floods the rivers and makes his return impossible, yes?"

Oh boy, I thought. She's done her homework; she'd probably questioned Gino and knows about the problems of crossing swollen rivers on an open ferry barge drawn by mules or bullocks with ropes and pulleys that can snap and send its passengers and cargo slewing down the river to dash to bits on rocks and debris in the swollen torrent. I'd seen the Yuba River raging and pounding everything in its path on my trip to the northern placers. Manon's concerns were all legitimate.

"I can't control the rains or the swelling of the river as you well know. That's why I have to go right now, so I can get back. The heavy rains normally hold off until late December and January. I plan to return in no more than ten days time," I said fibbing, as I had no idea how long I'd really need.

"Hah, in ten days time it will be December. So, if the heavy rains come early and stay late like in 1849, derelict-duty papa will be stuck in Sonora until Spring, yes? He'll miss Christmas with his family and spend it with roughnecks and fandango dancers, and if he's reckless, he'll leave his widow stuck with two babies to be raised by a replacement husband, yes?" She said with a malevolent smile.

Oh boy, the stakes were being raised high. My hand was a losing one from the start as Manon well knew. Time to eat a big helping of humble pie.

"Proud papa won't be reckless and risk losing everyone he loves and would defend with his life. He promises to return in ten days even if he doesn't complete his mission or get to either town. If anyone's going to spend winter on the other side of the Stanislaus River, it will be Gino. He's no good to us moping over Teri here, so if necessary, I'll have him stay and complete the mission alone. I will take no risks and turn back immediately in case the weather turns bad. You won't need a replacement husband. Our kids are going to grow up starting on papa's knees, then on his shoulders, and little Fanny will be on papa's arm for her first dance and down the aisle if she chooses to marry. Little Jules will learn to ride and shoot better than his papa and we'll see both of our kids graduate from both high school and college if they choose." By the time I got to the end of my spiel, I could see Manon's eyes tearing up. I put my arms out and she climbed into them willingly.

"You promise no more than ten days and you'll turn around and come the moment there are heavy rains, yes?"

"I promise." She kissed me tenderly. I had planned to tell her I would make a last will and testament leaving all my community property interest in our restaurant, ship and other business dealings to her and the kids, but it wasn't the moment. I'd have Hawthorne hold my holographic will in case something did happen to me.

California Gold Rush Journal
∞ PART 2 ∞

CHAPTER TWENTY-FOUR

San Francisco — November-December, 1851

Gino and I boarded the paddle-wheel steamer "Alcatraz" from the end of the Long Wharf on a chilly, windy morning threatening rain or worse. We'd left our gear on the Eliza and Georges helped us wheel our trunks and mail sacks to the loading dock on our steamer. We embarked on time as there weren't a lot of folks wanting to travel to Stockton in the face of winter. Manon provisioned us for the trip with fresh baguettes, pâtés, dry French and Italian sausages, dried fruits and nuts.

The wind blowing across San Pablo Bay was blustery and bone-chilling. Whitecaps blew spume at all the ship's windows as our steamer bucked the waves. Only those with cast-iron stomachs remained long at the ship's bar to quaff whiskey and beer chasers the locals call "boilermakers." Gino was not among them. I nursed a snifter of Calvados while bracing myself against the mahogany bar. Most of the serious drinkers made sport of the ship's motion to bet rounds of drink on whether they could time their volley of spit to land in the brass spittoons at intervals along the bar or watch it stain the sawdust on the floor.

The ship's rocking motion eased somewhat once we passed through the Carquinez Strait past Vallejo and Benicia and entered Suisun Bay. From there the small ship churned past the pulsing swift waters of the Sacramento River and continued into the Delta water system skirting small islands and avoiding tulle shallows. Our passage was marked by shrieking sea gulls trailing us for meal scraps from the galley and hordes of water fowl nesting and squabbling along the banks and on the small, uninhabited islets we dodged.

We veered south at the convergence of the Mokelumne and San Joaquin Rivers and docked in Stockton's bustling port well past time for an *apéritif*. Gino was still green about the gills but happy to quit the torturous rocking motion of our ship which kept him leaning over the ship's rail even when his stomach was empty.

Stockton was built on a neck of land formed by a bayou running into the San Joaquin River. Our carriage strained and sucked its way through the ankle deep mud tracks that passed for streets. Gino reserved rooms in a small, Italian run hotel-restaurant not far from the center of town. After stowing our trunks, we headed for the homey restaurant decorated with shelves of empty Italian wine bottles. The proprietor, Pietro Salvatore, a rotund, smallish man with red cheeks and nose and a big mustache, explained that restaurant patrons signed the bottles they ordered as a sign of good luck and guarantee of their safe return.

Signora Salvatore, his wife and the cook, proposed several possible veal dishes as they had just received a fresh supply of veal. I ordered *vitello ai funghi* as they had fresh mushrooms with the early rains. Gino settled for plain *risotto* in honor of his unsettled tummy. Gino ate sparingly and begged off to bed while I invited Salvatore to share a glass of Chianti and shoot the bull as his other diners had finished and retired. He accepted eagerly. I tried to explain our mission in halting Italian. He laughed and replied in heavily accented French.

"My assistant, Gino, is in charge of planning the trip to Sonora. But, as you can see, he's still queasy from the ferry trip. He said we could get close to Sonora by boat. What do you think?"

"I think you're better off joining a mule train and going by land, especially with all your heavy trunks. It may be a little slower, but it's a more reliable way to get to Knight's Ferry, cross the river and proceed to Sonora, especially with the unpredictable weather. The muleteers know the terrain and you're sure to get through. There's no guarantee you'll find suitable transport once a small boat can proceed no further." Salvatore motioned to his wife and addressed her in a rapid-fire Italian dialect I couldn't understand. She replied in their dialect.

"I ask my wife to send our stable boy to the inn where the muleteers stay. I think there's a train getting ready to travel soon. The *capo* will join us for some red wine and *biscotti*. We find out, *si?* I ask my wife to prepare a pitcher of wine from our native *Sardegna* as a special treat."

While we waited, Mrs. Salvatore brought us a plate of almond *biscotti* to nibble on. The wait was short. A burly man with flaming red hair, bloodshot eyes and dressed in soiled buckskins pushed his way through the door. He saluted my hosts in the same Sardinian dialect my hosts spoke. Salvatore introduced him to me as Rodrigo Ponzi. Mrs. Salvatore plunked down a third glass on the table and poured healthy portions of a frothy red wine the color of bulls' blood. Ponzi plucked two *biscotti* from the plate, popped them both in his mouth and as he crunched them with gusto, he drained his glass of wine and held it up for a refill.

Ponzi reminded me of our two Creole hunter-trapper

guides to the northern placers we'd hired in Marysville. When Georges and I met them in a drinking man's bar, they'd been drinking steadily all afternoon. Yet they ordered us up early and they were packed and ready to go before us. They'd hung several pottery jugs of whiskey from the pommels of their mules' wooden saddles. Their ability to function soberly and consume tremendous quantities of whiskey amazed me. Ponzi appeared to be made from the same mold.

As Ponzi spoke no French, Salvatore negotiated my needs in their native tongue. After several exchanges, Salvatore turned to me. "Rodrigo says he plans to leave for Sonora tomorrow morning early. He can secure six more mules to transport you and your trunks. He says it'll be cheaper than buying mules and reselling them in Sonora."

"How long will it take to get to Sonora?" I asked.

"He says with a 6 A.M. start, the train can get across the river at Knight's Ferry and arrive in Sonora the next afternoon. He says there's lodging all along the way."

"When are they returning to Stockton? I may need to return with them or another group in two or three days after I get to Sonora." Salvatore consulted Ponzi about my concerns.

"He says he can leave one of his mule drivers to escort you and a train of mules back to Stockton, but you'll have to pay the ferry charges for the animals as well as their rental for the extra days."

"How much are we talking about?"

"Rodrigo says Mr. Knight charges 20 cents a head for mules and 50 cents per rider on his ferry. You'll pay for everything on the way back plus lodging for his mule driver in Sonora and on the way back. He wants $90.00 to transport you, your assistant and your luggage to Sonora."

As time was of the essence, I readily agreed as we had no alternate plans. I was determined to keep my promise to Manon.

The weather was still an unknown. We shook hands on the deal and quaffed a round of grappa as the pitcher of Sardinian wine was empty. I thanked Salvatore for his help and asked for a morning wakeup call. Mrs. Salvatore promised there would be more *biscotti* to dunk in hot coffee in the morning.

Gino seemed relieved I had arranged ground transport and not another boat ride. We slogged along a muddy track for several hours before stopping to rest and eat at a roadhouse. The muleteers ate little and drank lots of beer to quench their thirst and wash away the mud splatter from the ride. We all smelled like our odoriferous mules—mule sweat mingled with mule piss and feces in the mud that their plodding sprayed on our boots and pant legs.

As the terrain was flat and barren, we made steady progress in the chilly weather. Ominous dark clouds threatened to unleash torrents of water on us, but held off until after our crossing of the Stanislaus River on Mr. Knight's ferry. He had teams of bullocks on both sides of the river to pull the heavy cables attached to his barge-like ferry similar to the flat-bottom river boats that ply the Mississippi River. Gino hung on to the railing attached to the small cabin for dear life. The mules brayed their displeasure at the rocking motion while the muleteers sat with backs to the tiny cabin and passed a jug of whiskey around.

While the river was not yet in flood stage, it flowed swiftly over the shallows of the ford and sprayed us with icy-cold water as it hit the side of the ferry. Had the threatening storm unleashed its fury on us during the crossing, it could have washed us into the torrent. Fortunately, we were the only passengers and were soon across. The storm broke half an hour further down the track. By the time we arrived at the nearest roadhouse inn, we were all soaked to the skin. Our muleteers wouldn't be caught dead in the practical ponchos Chileans and our two trapper guides wore during rain on my Yuba River trip.

The roaring fire in the large hearth of the roadhouse and a change into dry garments soon had us in good cheer. The pelting rain had rinsed off most of the road mud and animal smell. Our guides were soon tanking up on whiskey and ale and trying to coax the two buxom barmaids to sit on their laps to receive a coin down their bodice in exchange for a squeeze. Gino and I ate the hearty venison stew offered for our repast with red wine from our stash and retired early to our allotted spaces in the sleeping loft. I hoped to get some much needed sleep before our guides finished carousing and trying to entice the barmaids to service them for a price.

Next morning after an early breakfast of chicory flavored coffee and flapjacks, thick buckwheat crepes the Yankees eat smothered in molasses, we were on our mules' backs slogging slowly through the now inundated, slippery track. The sky was sullen and threatening more rain. The rolling flatlands had given way to rolling hills full of oak and pine. It was nearly dark when we saw the first cabin lights and dark when we finally arrived at our destination hungry, weary and sore from two days riding mules.

Derbec, now a regular customer at Manon's restaurant, counseled me to stay at the French Coffee House on Washington Street in the heart of the business district. In addition to lodgings and a full bar, the establishment affectionately known as the "El Dorado" offers a restaurant and *table d'hôte*—where patrons could mingle and eat a set menu at a common table.

I had no trouble securing adequate rooms for our stay in Sonora. The French Coffee House was too expensive for most miners wintering in town and most wealthy merchants or lucky miners preferred to winter in larger cities like Sacramento or San Francisco. In addition to the hotel and restaurant, the main attraction on the premises was a gambling room where a strikingly beautiful young woman in her late teens dealt monte and blackjack to rapt gamblers and shared her banter and smiles with onlookers and admirers. When Gino and I poked our noses into the card room on our tour of the premises, she looked up from the hand she was dealing, openly appraised the two of us and gave the handsome Gino a big, welcoming smile.

Oh boy, I thought. This is just what Gino needs to get over Teri. We opted to dine at the *table d'hôte* as it offered an opportunity to meet local French merchants and disseminate information about our mail delivery. I met Louis Veille, who was co-owner of the establishment, with Cleophas Le Coq.

Veille, a dapperly dressed Frenchman in his early fifties, who established the hotel-restaurant with his partner in 1850, made important suggestions about who I should see in town to accomplish my mission. After dinner, we sipped Calvados at the bar and traded stories about our lives in Paris and why we decided to seek our fortunes in the New World. Gino begged out of after dinner drinks and made a beeline for the card room.

"I noticed you have a very attractive and sociable young woman dealing cards in the gambling parlor. Is she a local girl?" I asked.

"Ah, you mean Mademoiselle Virginie. Yes, she's the daughter of early French settlers here. They came right after gold was discovered. She's a gold mine herself. The card room is packed every evening because of her. There are more admirers than players. She's only seventeen and she's already broken more hearts than most women can do in a lifetime. "

"I see why. She's got an hourglass figure, but doesn't flaunt it. She lets you admire her without having to stoop to wearing provocative dresses with plunging necklines like so many card dealers. Her face and skin have a natural glow of youth and her mop of black curls glistens and beckons. She seems to enjoy flirting with everyone, yet she portrays a wholesomeness you'd expect with your daughter or wife, but not your mistress." I also thought that with a room full of admirers and lovesick males,

Gino wasn't likely to get far with her despite the warm reception he'd received.

"Yes, she's all that and more. She's intelligent and knows how to deal cards and win. Can't tell you how many gamblers took her for granted as a young ingénue and wound up losing their poke. She's tough as nails at cards and has nerves of steel in high stakes games. I engaged her because she doesn't have to work for a wage and then sell her favors after work like so many barmaids and dealers in San Francisco and most mining camps. She's a free spirit. If she wants a man, she chooses him. She's not for sale."

Maybe Gino does have a chance, I thought. I'd rented separate rooms for us as the weather was extremely unsettled and I anticipated leaving Gino here to implement whatever agreements I could make in the next couple of days. He'd get back in his own good time. Meanwhile, he was free to romance Miss Virginie in his spare time if she'd have him. I thanked Louis Veille for his suggestions, bade him goodnight and retired to my heavenly comfortable bed and fell asleep the moment my head hit the down pillow.

"CITY OF STOCKTON," 1851.

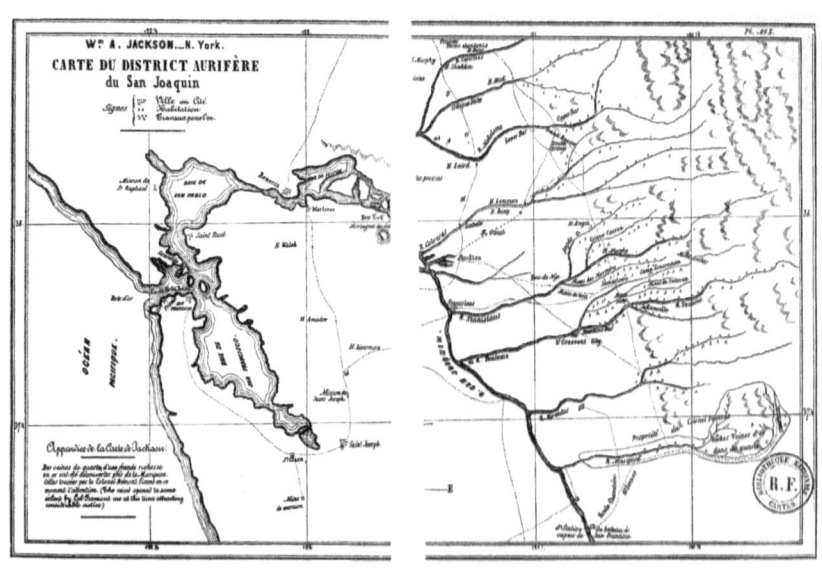

"MAP OF THE SOUTHERN PLACERS," 1851.

California Gold Rush Journal
✂ PART 2 ✂

CHAPTER TWENTY-FIVE

Sonora — December, 1851

N ext morning after a light breakfast of croissants lathered with local blackberry preserves and black coffee, I made my way down Washington Street toward the Plaza. Sonora was settled first by Mexicans who organized the commercial area around a central plaza as in Mexico and most of Latin America. Louis Veille counseled me to start with the general merchandise store owned by a former Parisian jeweler named Hughes Lyons and his partner Jules Buisson. They settled in Sonora in November 1850, and their store became the social hub of the French community. Buisson, at his own expense, sent a French messenger to San Francisco twice monthly, weather permitting, to gather newspapers and mail to be distributed to the French in Sonora and nearby mining camps as there was no post office in town.

Louis Veille proudly informed me that Sonora had over 100 mercantile establishments which included 35 hotels and restaurants, 8 butcher shops, 9 bakeries, 3 public bath houses, 2 express offices and 2 banking houses. As one of the banking

houses was managed by Michel de Satrustegui, a fellow coun-
tryman and Basque, he recommended I see him as he also
served as the French consular agent for the southern mines.

I was surprised at the number of French enterprises I en-
countered on my way to Hugues Lyons' store. Lyons' merchandise emporium was a grand affair that stocked mining and
agricultural tools, cooking utensils, pots and pans as well an
extensive selection of canned goods and preserves from New
York as well as some gourmet items from France. Prices were
roughly twice or more those in San Francisco. A large cast iron
stove faced the vast counter running the length of the store; two
round tables with six chairs circled the stove. The cozy arrangement encouraged patrons to relax, read the local newspaper, the
Sonora Herald, exchange news of a new gold strike, gossip or
read mail. Behind the cashier's box Lyons installed cubbyholes
for mail. As neither Lyons nor his partner was in the store at the
moment, the counter clerk suggested I return in late afternoon
when the partners were sure to be present. I left a note, my business card and the alphabetized list of letters we were carrying.

My next stop was The Alliance Hotel and Restaurant across
the plaza between the two sides of Washington Street. I ordered
a black coffee and invited the proprietor, Sophie Guillot, to join
me. She was a petite, dark-featured woman with hair swept into
a severe bun. She wore a simple muslin dress that emphasized
her still slim waist. I explained my business and gave her the
business card for our restaurant.

She raised her eyelashes in surprise. "Is it true that your
wife owns and runs your restaurant under her own name?"

"Yes, that's the major reason for coming to California. In
Paris she worked as an under-chef with no prospect of becoming a chef or owning her own restaurant. She has a lot of competition in San Francisco from established French restaurants,
all with male chefs, but she's holding her own, getting good

reviews and developing a loyal clientele."

Sophie Guillot nodded her understanding. "I'm glad to know I'm not the only woman to buck the tide of male ownership. Even here, successful women are expected to run parlor houses to please a male clientele or a rooming house to lodge miners, but not a restaurant. Alas, the discrimination and attitudes we hoped to escape coming here traveled with us on the same ships," she said with an air of bitterness.

"Where are you staying?" She asked.

"I'm staying at the French Coffee House. I wanted to take advantage of their *table d'hôte* to meet local French businessmen and get suggestions as to who to contact for my mission to deliver miners' mail for the French Consul in San Francisco. Louis Veille is very helpful. But I'd also like to eat at your restaurant. Do you think the bank manager Michel de Satrustegui would accept my invitation to dine with me here?"

Sophie Guillot laughed. "I don't see why not. Even though he's technically the acting French consul, he's more Basque than French at heart. It's good for his banking business as the French merchants feel obligated to patronize his bank. I use the American Adams & Co. for my money transactions. If he thinks you can promote his business, he'll eat anywhere to achieve that goal."

It was my turn to laugh. "I also bank with Adams & Co. Our twins were born here and are citizens by birth; my wife and I have applied and await our American passports. My wife will be pleased to learn that there's another woman restaurant owner in Sonora. Are there other independent women who own businesses here or nearby?"

"Other than brothels or boarding houses?"

"Yes."

"Well, not business owners. But I do know of some interesting, independent women who will make their mark here.

There's a woman who mines with her younger brother. She's quite a character. The moment she realized how impractical it was to mine river gravels with a pick and shovel in layers of petticoats, she decided to be practical and dress in male attire. She works her claim with her brother, Albert, and other French miners in canvas pants, muslin shirt, tall boots, slouch hat and colorful bandana. She dresses that way as well when they come to Sonora for supplies even though it's illegal for women to wear trousers."

"What's her name? She sounds like just the kind of woman my wife would love to meet. My wife dresses as an armed sailor boy when she wants to see places only men can go to."

"Well, the miners call her Marie or Madame Pantalon."

"Do you know her real name?"

"I think her real name is Marie Suize. She came here the same time as I did in 1850. She and her brother are from the duchy of Savoy near Switzerland. They work with a group of Savoyards up around the town of Jackson as far as I know."

"Is she wintering up there or by chance here in Sonora?"

"She winters with the rest of their group near their claims. Even if the river floods and it's impossible to work river gravels, miners can work the gulches which seem to produce good yields and are easier to work when water is abundant. They build log cabins on high ground and work in between storms. They stock non-perishable food, firewood and hunt for game. We won't see them until they have to provision in spring."

"I'll leave you my wife's business card. When you see her next, give it to her and tell her my wife would love to meet her when she comes to San Francisco. They have a lot in common."

I doubled back to our hotel to check on Gino and apprise him of our need to meet Hughes Lyons and Jules Buisson in the afternoon. Hopefully, we'd also be able to connect with the messenger they'd send to San Francisco.

Gino was dunking fresh croissants into black coffee in the breakfast room of the hotel. He looked ragged and lethargic. I hoped he wasn't out of sorts or moping from another rejection.

"So how did it go with the lovely Miss Virginie?"

"Alright, I guess," he replied not looking up.

"Alright as in she likes you? Or alright as in you're welcome to be another of her many admirers?"

"I don't know. I'm stumped when it comes to understanding women, especially here in California. She said she likes me and wants to get to know me. We had a drink at the bar after her shift. She asked a lot of questions about me and what I was planning to do with my life, what I do for you, what we're doing here and how long we plan to stay. She seemed real friendly and even flirted with me a bit, but when I suggested we go up to my room to talk where it would be more private, she laughed and said, 'I'm not that kind of girl.'"

"Women can like a guy without being ready to hop into bed just because the guy proposes it. Women expect to be courted and not taken for granted. Maybe you were rushing things too quickly." I was thinking of my conversation with Louis Veille and his comment that she could have any man she wanted and was not for sale.

"I wasn't trying to push myself on her. I wanted to be able to talk with her in private without the barman straining his ears to hear us and other patrons gawking."

"So, how did it end?"

"She said she had to get some rest and I could walk her to her house. When we got there, her mother opened the door and Virginie smiled and gave me a little peck on the cheek and said 'I'll see you tomorrow night.' Then she went inside." Gino said with disappointment in his voice and on his face.

"If you want my opinion, I think your first encounter went very well. She's got to know you; she likes you and plans to see you again. She knows you are very attracted to her, but she wants to go slow. She's young, only seventeen, and still lives at home. She has her pick of admirers, yet she chose you. You're the lucky guy and the rest have to be jealous as hell that you walk in for the first time, get the big smile and invited to have a drink and walk her home. Find out what days she's off. Invite her to dinner and to a dance hall or other amusement she'd like to go to. Show her you like to have fun with her, and if she wants to have a more intimate relationship, she'll let you know when the time is right," I said to encourage him.

Gino just shook his head in disbelief and took a deep breath. "Well, maybe you're right. She wants to call the shots and I guess I don't really have any choice, do I?" He said mostly to himself.

I brought him up to date on my morning and what we needed to do that afternoon. He needed to put his love life on hold until I completed my tasks and could head for home. He seemed to cheer up when I confirmed he would stay longer than me to follow through on our contacts.

After a light lunch, I made my way to the bank managed by the French consular agent. As Mr. de Satrustegui was tied up in meetings for most of the afternoon, I left my business card as well as that of Patrice Dillon and a note stating Consul Dillon had appointed me as a special agent to expedite French miners' mail to the southern diggings. I added that I would be dining at the Restaurant de l'Alliance this evening and invited him to join me at 8 P.M. if he was free. I figured the offer of a free meal and concerns about a mail problem and my role in it would be sufficient bait to join me for dinner, especially as thunder claps in the distance announced a new storm system approached.

After reserving for dinner with Sophie Guillot, I proceeded to the Union Store owned by Pierre Casimir Labetoure. Veille told me he'd be an interesting source of information as he was one of the first to set up his tent store that catered to Spanish speaking clients as well the French. He'd spent time in Louisiana and Texas before following the southern route to the gold fields. He had his finger in a number of local businesses where he often associated non-French partners in his business ventures to broaden his client base. According to Veille, he had interests in a bakery and dabbled in real estate.

The Union Store was another general mercantile store located at Washington and Church Streets; it also sold groceries. Labetoure wasn't present, but his partner, Guillaume Carrère, was behind the counter and chewing the fat with a couple of clients. They were busy speculating about the price of lots on the outskirts of town and whether the town would continue to grow sufficiently larger to make a profit on several parcels Labetoure had for sale. Rather than interrupt their animated discussion, I sat down to peruse the *Sonora Herald*.

I was surprised to see so many French and Spanish language classified ads. In addition to the merchants in Sonora, a Frenchman calling himself "The French Gardener" advertised his expansive vegetable garden for sale. He stated his land was "securely fenced" and located above the spring on the Matelot Gulch, one-half mile from the nearby mining town of Columbia. The buyer of his commercial enterprise would get a house "built entirely of shingles," two mules and a cart to haul the produce to market.

After the would-be real estate speculators departed, I chatted up the proprietor while placing a selection of tinned foods and crackers on the counter to serve as a survival pack on the trip home in case I got stuck by the rising river or bad weather. I explained my mission and handed him the printed list of miners we sought.

"I thought you might recognize some of the miners by name if they shop for supplies here."

Carrère ran his finger down the list on the first page. "I recognize a few, but most I know by sight and not name. You'd probably have better luck talking to Jules Buisson. He sends a messenger to pick up mail for all the French merchants here and some of the miners in the camps as well."

I had him tick off the names he recognized. I'd do the same with Jules Buisson. We'd try to eliminate duplication. But Carrère might have clients who didn't shop with Buisson. I'd learned in the northern placers that miners tended to be clannish and shopped only with certain merchants and not others. Sometimes it was due to personality differences, but often it was where the merchant hailed from and other subjective factors. I thanked Carrère for his time and did the same with several other merchants.

I'd told Gino to meet me at Buisson and Lyons at 4:30 that afternoon. As I had half an hour to kill and the thunder and lightning strikes were moving ever closer, I ducked into a saloon across the street from their emporium to wet my whistle, as the Yankees say.

Several loungers occupied barstools and were engaged in animated discussion about the two new girls, Camille and Louise, at Rose Cartier's parlor house, on the southwest corner of Church and Washington Streets. Madam Cartier charged an extra two dollars for their services as they were newly arrived. Another foursome played billiards and bet rounds of drinks and pinches of gold dust on each shot.

I ordered a Scotch whiskey and beer chaser from the burly, tattooed barkeep with a bushy beard and ruddy complexion. He seemed surprised and puzzled when I tendered a five dollar gold piece in payment. "Don't rightly have no way ta change 'dis 'ere coin. Clients pays drinks wid a pinch a gold dust," he said.

As I didn't carry a pocket gold scale or wish change in gold dust that is messy and often spiked with copper filings and other impurities, I rummaged through my pockets for some silver bits. I didn't know how much my drinks cost, but the barkeep seemed satisfied with the coins I produced and scooped them off the bar and into his vest pocket. I took my drinks to a vacant table where I could observe the billiard game and the patrons at the bar. I thought it unusual that the bartender should have exceptionally long fingernails.

As I watched the ritual of supplying drinks to patrons in their cups, I understood the bartender's ploy. As the price of a drink was a pinch of gold dust, he used his long fingernails to get much more than a pinch of gold dust when he dipped his thumb and forefinger into his patrons' poke. As with my silver bits, the extra dust would go into his poke at the end of his shift. My assistant, Georges, a connoisseur of bartenders' ploys, had explained the technique to me, but this was the first time I'd seen it employed openly. Georges claimed some barkeeps kept a candle lit under the bar so they could insert the soft wax drippings under their fingernail and get both a pinch and the gold dust that adhered to the wax. Georges assured me that there were many other ploys to mine a miner's poke. He'd pointed out that the barmaids, who weighed gold dust in the gambling palaces, managed to spill enough gold dust on the floor behind their work station, to earn a handsome tip when they swept it into a dustpan and dribbled it into their poke.

The drinkers at the bar hadn't paid any attention to my arrival and apparently hadn't pegged me for a Frenchman. After discussing the merits of the cocottes at Rose Cartier's bordello, they started telling jokes about the French Johnnies and "Frenchies" as they called us. The loudest of the group asked his mates, "A Frenchy who's about to be guillotined is asked what is his last wish? To learn English, was his reply." His mates laughed so hard, they were blue in the face. One actually fell off his stool. I polished off the remainder of my drinks and left the saloon in disgust.

California Gold Rush Journal
∽ PART 2 ∽

CHAPTER TWENTY-SIX
Sonora — December, 1851

I spotted Gino on his way to our rendez-vous and hailed him to join me. I was still smarting from being the butt of a stupid joke. I had heard Yankees refer to Mexican towns as "Greaservilles" and all Latin Americans and "Californios," settled here before the Gold Rush, as "Greasers," but the joke had hit home. No wonder the French miners at Mokelumne Hill hoisted their flag to snub the Irish who wanted to drive them off their claims. After I cooled down, I had to admit the sad truth: most French refused to learn English and didn't understand it when spoken and had no intention of settling in California; most hoped to get rich and take their earnings back to France.

Only Jules Buisson was in the emporium when we arrived as the first large raindrops pounded the street outside. Like other mercantile establishments in the town, a large pot-bellied wood stove was a center feature. Water in an iron pot and an enamel coffee pot shared the top of the stove. Patrons were free to serve themselves hot coffee in tin mugs or make tea. Jules Buisson greeted us with a vigorous handshake full of bonhomie. "So pleased to meet you," he bellowed in a deep, so-norous voice. "Have some hot coffee to warm you up," Buisson said as he stoked the woodstove from a pile of seasoned oak. His face was round and sensible. His protruding belly, promi-nent nose, affable smile and welcoming demeanor made us feel right at home, as fellow countrymen well met.

"Did you get a chance to review the list of miners we're looking for?" I asked.

"Oh yes, I'm so glad to see it. There's several miners down at French Bar on your list. They've been grumbling that I'm ignoring them and not picking up their mail in the city. Now we know it's with you. I hope you brought their mail," he said, luminous eyes pleading.

I laughed. "I wouldn't spend two days on a mule's back just to bring you a list. We've letters for every person on the list. We'll leave letters we know you and other merchants can either deliver or hold for pick up. Just tick off the names and give the list to my assistant, Gino, who'll stay in town until the lion's share of the letters are disseminated and accounted for. Hope-fully, you'll have a post office soon."

Buisson's turn to laugh. "The Postmaster General in Wash-ington could care less. With all the French, Mexican and Chil-ean miners around these parts, we're no priority despite the noise we made for service. California wants to tax us $20.00 a month and offers us no services. The American express com-panies and banks bring back mail for their clients as a favor when they return from delivering gold to San Francisco or Sac-ramento. I have to do the same for our people," he said pointing to the mail cubbyholes behind the sales counter.

"Who's the man you send to San Francisco to pick up let-ters and gather newspapers? I'd like to meet him if possible. He could stop by my office and pick up mail that we get from the French Consulate. The post office clerks can't read most of the foreign names or addresses. They just throw them in a pile and deliver them to the consulate for transmittal to my office. For them it's good riddance."

"Yeah, I figured something like that was going on. Unfortunately, Joseph is up at Angel's Camp picking up letters and delivering supplies. How long are you staying? I not sure with this big storm hitting us that he'll be able to get back anytime soon. He usually waits them out for a dry spell to cross the river."

"Be sure he meets my assistant, Gino. They need to coordinate deliveries and study the lists together. I have to return to San Francisco before the rains prevent me from crossing Knight's ford. Gino will stay as long as necessary. Perhaps they can return to San Francisco together so I can meet Joseph. I'll be sure to have more mail for him."

I left Gino to get acquainted with Buisson, note his distribution system and review our lists of letters together. The rain now pelted the town with increased ferocity. Fortunately, most of the commercial structures on Washington Street were two-storied with porticos to provide ground floor shelter from summer heat and winter rains. The steep roofs drained directly onto the street which was now awash. Even with my winter cloak and high boots, I would soon be soaked through just crossing the side streets. The increasing wind now brought the rain slashing down at a forty-five degree angle that would soon drench even the covered porches.

I made a bee-line to the boarding house where the muleteer to lead me back to Stockton stayed. He was in the stables at the rear of the boarding house feeding his animals.

"Jacques, I need to return to Stockton as soon as possible. This storm's liable to complicate crossing the Stanislaus River. When do you think it'll let up?"

"Dunno," he replied without looking up from filling feed buckets.

"Be ready first thing tomorrow morning to travel. I've got to get to Stockton before the river floods."

"Can't take the mules out in this storm," he said sullenly.

"Be ready. We leave as soon as the storm lets up," I commanded.

"Won't be an easy go. Tracks full of mud and water. Risks getting stuck in the open," he said morosely.

"We'll just have to take that chance, won't we? The longer we tarry, the worse it will get. So, we leave at first light tomorrow if the rain stops or is falling lightly."

I turned on my heel and left, not waiting for another crabby reply. He was naturally reluctant to leave the warmth and comfort of the town where he had no duties other than to feed and water the animals. I was alarmed at the torrents of water battering the streets. It reminded me of a sardonic lithograph published in a San Francisco newspaper in the Winter of 1849, which was republished each year at the height of the rainy season. The drawing depicted a miner being bucked off his sinking mule and landing on his butt with a splash. The caption read, "Streets not passable, not even jackassable."

I packed my bags so as to travel light in the hopes we'd make better time on the muddy tracks. All the trunks and mail would stay here. Hopefully, Gino would unburden us of most of the letters we'd brought. After leaving a box of cigars for Louis Veille as thanks for his useful insights and suggestions, I took advantage of a letup in the deluge to scamper over to the Alliance Hotel and Restaurant.

I installed myself in the gentlemen's smoking room, ordered a carafe of white wine, writing paper, pen and ink, the dinner menu and lit up a Havana cigar. I used the peace and quiet of this after dinner room to pen detailed instructions for Gino in my absence: who else to meet in addition to my brief contacts and to remember to offer to take mail back to San Francisco for posting.

Buisson advised me that they had problems in winter getting an adequate supply of stamps from Stockton. I brought five and ten cent stamps with me and left them with Gino. I'd told Buisson we'd leave any remaining with him to use. He figured it would take six to eight months for him to get the new denominations being printed in Washington. I assured him I had sufficient stocks of the five and ten cent first series in San Francisco and would see the mail brought to town by Joseph would be franked and posted.

After finishing Gino's instructions, I mulled over whether to draft another letter to Manon in case I ran into severe delays on my return.

I had entrusted a letter to her with the muleteer, Rodrigo Ponzi, to deliver to the innkeeper, Pietro Salvatore, for posting on his return, but who knew whether he'd honor or even remember that commission. I had unsettling visions of the letter fluttering in the mud of the trail or so stained with alcohol and grease as to be undecipherable.

Since I had time, I wrote again to confirm my safe arrival in Sonora, the completion of my business here, and tomorrow's date for the return journey. Having no means to send it, I stuffed it in my leather letter pouch and studied the restaurant menu. It was heavy on local meat—deer, wild pig, bear, turkey and duck but light on interesting sauces to complement the special flavors of wild meat. The terrines were imported rather than made in-house. The wine list was short and offered only French whites and reds in the ordinary and superior appellations—no *grand cru* wines we stocked for special occasions to offer the acting consul. There were some champagnes, but no well-known vintners. I deduced from Sophie Guillot's comments that the acting consul was not a frequent diner at her establishment.

Having finished my writing tasks, I returned the ink and unused sheaves of paper to the hotel reception desk. Some early

diners arrived during another lull in the storm. After Sophie
Guillot seated them and discussed the menu, she turned them
over to a waitress who bore a striking resemblance to Mademoiselle Virginie, the enticing card dealer at The French Coffee
House.

"Tell me, is your waitress related to the young woman who
deals cards at the El Dorado? The resemblance is striking," I
said to Sophie Guillot.

"Why yes, Pauline Collée is Virginie's younger sister," Sophie replied giving me a curious look.

"My assistant is quite struck with Virginie. Maybe if he's
turned down, he can cry on the sister's shoulder," I said trying
to make light of my inquiry.

Sophie Guillot laughed. "Not very likely. Pauline may be a year
younger, but she's nobody's fool. The family is very close knit. Virginie is the ambitious one. Pauline is more reserved and allowed
to work for me only until ten each evening and her mother fetches her when her shift is over. The money she earns is controlled
by her mother and older sister. They're saving it for schooling in
Sacramento. They're both good, serious girls. Their mother's very
strict with Pauline. She's being groomed to marry well."

"What about the older sister. She appeared quite open and
flirtatious when I saw her dealing cards. Admirers were drool-
ing in their beards in the brief time I observed her."

"Yes, she's outgoing and bound to break a lot of hearts
before she settles down. But she's strong as nails. She's deft at
cards. She has an unusual gift; she can remember every card
played from the deck she deals. So she can calculate the odds
for making twenty-one or what cards are left to win at monte.
It's uncanny. She can't lose for winning. When someone else at
the table wins, they tip her. When she wins, she puts her earnings away. She buys vacant lots in the outskirts of town with her
gains. If the town continues to grow and the placers hold out,

she'll be a rich woman one day."

More customers arrived. I took a seat near the bar with a view of the door and asked the burly barman to chill two bottles of the house's best champagne for my dinner and settled in to wait for the acting consul. I perused back issues of the *Sonora Herald* while I waited. I was pleased to note the number and variety of French merchants and tradesmen in the established mining camps who advertised their services and wares. From the crudely printed county map on the wall, one could see that Sonora was like the main axle of a wagon wheel. From Sonora, the mining camps radiated outward like spokes of a wheel in all directions.

I didn't have long to wait. A cloaked figure pushed the door open and rushed inside shedding water like a dog shaking its fur. The expensive cloak was made of camlet, a soft wool and silk fabric. Shed of his dripping cloak and hood, the tallish, fair-skinned man with sandy-colored hair adjusted his cravat, gave a little tug to the sleeves of his double-breasted frock coat and looked around. Spying me, the only person in the bar area, he marched directly to my table and extended his hand. "Mr. Dubois, I presume."

I gave him a little laugh. "The one and only. Glad you could join me on such short notice," I said shaking hands. "An *apéritif* before we go in for dinner?"

"Sure, what do you recommend?" Michel de Satrustegui replied.

I waved for the bartender to bring a bottle of champagne. "I'm afraid the wine list here doesn't compare to my wife's restaurant in San Francisco, so I took the liberty of ordering the best champagne they offer," I said handing him our business card for Chez Manon. "You must try our restaurant when next in San Francisco."

"I'd love to. As you've deduced, fare here in the mining towns is limited. One can get a hearty meal but nothing to match the many good restaurants in Paris or Bordeaux."

"Well, I think you'll find things have changed this year in San Francisco. We now have several top French restaurants that offer excellent viands and many dishes not available in France. Have you tried our local abalone?" I said sure that he hadn't.

The acting consul looked surprised. "No, what's that?"

"Ah, you must let us know when you're coming to San Francisco, so we can special order and prepare it for you. It's the king of all shellfish and melts like nutty butter in your mouth with an exquisite taste. Its oval, spiral shell is larger than the largest scallops, and its interior is lined with mother-of-pearl. We pan fry it and serve it like a steak with my wife's special sauce."

I could see his eyes gleaming and a satisfying smile as he imagined such a delicacy. "Of course, we have local lobster, fresh crayfish, squid, sea urchins as well as all the wild game you are accustomed to here," I said building rapport. A Frenchman is never far from thoughts of *la grande bouffe*, the fabulous cuisine of his native country and the incomparable wines that go with each the imaginative creations of our top chefs. I could read the nostalgia in his eyes.

The dinner offerings, as expected, were wholesome but lacking the sauces a connoisseur is used to. I ordered a duck *foie gras* to start and followed with *bécasse à la broche,* as the small woodcock is a seasonal bird we don't often get in San Francisco. After my pep talk on the merits of Chez Manon, the acting consul followed my lead and ordered the same. I instructed our waiter, an obsequious chap with a French Canadian accent, to instruct the cook not to over-roast the delicate birds on the spit. We wanted them tender and juicy to savor the flesh of this magnificent bird. I was disappointed Pauline Collée was not serving us.

The waiter gave me a sour look. The menu suggested a mustard-based sauce which would overpower the delicate taste of the bird's meat. I instructed the waiter to tell the cook we didn't want the sauce.

"Have the cook baste our birds using a mixture of the birds' fat, olive oil, coarse ground pepper and lemon juice and save the drippings for our sauce." The waiter rolled his eyes to say "give us a break."

The acting consul smirked at the waiter, pleased I'd put him in his place and delighted I knew the proper way to prepare our birds. The wine list was a problem as there were no wines that really complemented this entrée. I would have liked a good Burgundy wine, but there were only Bordeaux red wines on the list. When our waiter retreated into the kitchen, I signaled Sophie Guillot to come to our table.

She acted as if we had not spoken about the acting consul earlier. "What can I do to serve you? Oh, what a pleasure, Mr. de Satrustegui to have you as a guest tonight."

"The pleasure is all mine, I'm sure," he replied diplomatically. "We've just ordered the woodcocks as our main dish. I was wondering if you might have a Beaujolais or Burgundy wine not on the wine list that we could order to complement the succulence of the birds which I've asked be basted in an olive oil/lemon juice sauce as my wife does?"

She masked her alarm but snuck a peek at the door to the kitchen. "Let me see what I can come up with. I'll be right back," she replied hurriedly and made a bee-line to the kitchen.

The consul laughed. "Do you always intimidate the waiters and owners to get what you want," he said amusingly.

"We're used to pleasing our clientele and offering top notch fare. One can't expect that in the boondocks, but it never hurts to demand the best they can provide. Some of the best meals I've eaten outside of San Francisco have been in French mining camps, like French Corral on the Yuba River. There they used fresh ingredients and with their knowledge how to cook and with appreciative diners, they produced fabulous dishes. I think part of the problem in towns like yours the cooks cater to a mixed clientele who don't really know the difference."

"Yes, I think you've hit the nail on the head."

Sophie Guillot finally exited the kitchen and approached our table. "Please pardon the delay. Michel, your waiter, apparently was confused about your sauce requests and the cook as well. I certainly understand you don't want the birds overcooked and I will personally make your sauce. I do have a bottle or two of vintage Gigondas not on the wine list. Will that do?" She asked apologetically

"Yes, that's preferable to your Bordeaux Superior for this dish." I decided not to point out the wine offered was still a bit on the heavy side for our woodcocks and would have been more suitable for a cheese plate, but it was still a major improvement over the wine list.

"I don't think your waiter was confused," the acting consul piped in. "I think he was being impudent. Perhaps you could ask your lovely waitress to serve our table and assign the waiter to another table?"

"Yes, of course, as you wish," she bowed deeply and went to speak with Miss Collée, then scuttled back to the kitchen.

The acting consul had a self-satisfied look on his face as he watched her retreat. He'd got his pound of flesh. I decided to change the subject and get us back on track regarding our business affairs. I explained my arrangement with the San Francisco Consulate and our problems with the post office in San Francisco and their inability or unwillingness to spend time on French mail. I gave him my business card for my notary and detective business as well in the hopes he might refer clients. He assured me he would help in any way he could to facilitate mail delivery, but was non-committal regarding business referrals.

The little woodcocks were cooked to perfection and the wine passable. Had he been more encouraging about my work,

I would have invited him for after dinner drinks at the bar. Instead, I paid for our dinner and excused myself as I needed to make an early start in the morning if weather allowed. On my return to my hotel, I drafted a thank you note to Sophie Guillot thanking her for a lovely meal and apologizing for the acting consul's arrogant and rude behavior.

"STREET SCENES IN SAN FRANCISCO –
WIND AND MUD," 1850-51.

California Gold Rush Journal
∽ PART 2 ∽

CHAPTER TWENTY-SEVEN
Sonora-Stockton — December, 1851

My sleep was troubled by the incessant pounding of the rain and howling wind against the groaning shutters of my bedroom windows and dreams full of river crossing mishaps. It was a relief to see light timidly peeking through gaps in the shutter fastenings and hardware. I jumped up and threw open a shutter. The wind had calmed and the rain was misty. Water still raced down the street and at times spilled over the floor of shop porticos on the low side of the street.

With heart pounding, I hastily donned my traveling outfit and descended to the breakfast area. The night watchman, Jake, seemed surprised to see anyone stirring at this hour when one should be comfortably cozy in bed. I could smell burnt coffee fumes emanating from a porcelain coffee pot placed on the woodstove.

"Mind if I help myself to a cup of java?" I said pointing to the pot and a row of tin cups.

"Help yourself. 'Tis a bit strong now I reckon, but that's how I keeps meself awake. God awful storm if ya' ask me."

I poured a cup of thick, viscous coffee that now resembled pungent syrup. "I'm up early because I need to get across the river before it floods. Do you think the storm's blown itself out?" I asked nervously.

"Dunno. Could be a lull or could be the tail end of one storm followed by another. Hard to tell. Often we'll see a whole series of storms one after another, but not usually this early in the season. Even without more rain, it'd be a tough slog. Hope yer not plannin' ta try it by horse or buggy. Don't imagine they'd make it in the muck an' you'd never get them ferried across. Best go by mule an' hope ya don't git caught in a bad blow like last night."

Not reassuring words to say the least. If it was the start of an early, severe winter like in '49, I'd be stuck on the mountain side of the Stanislaus River and not get home until Spring unless I could get to Mariposa and chance another river crossing further south and make it to San Jose. My promise to Manon weighed on my mind. She'd be worried sick if I didn't return as promised and there'd be no means to get word to her I was safe. She'd think the worst.

Even in my high boots, it was a challenge not to slip in the swift flowing mud to cross streets. As expected, my reluctant guide, Jacques, was not up tending to our mules or readying for an early start. There was a light on the ground floor of his rooming house, so I pounded on the door. It took a good 3 minutes of pounding before the door opened a crack, and a grisly face half-hidden by a slouch hat grumbled, "What yer want creatin' such a ruckus and disturbin' peaceful sleep?"

"My muleteer, Jacques, was supposed to be up at first light and have prepared our mule train for travel. Where the hell is he?"

"You mean the Frenchie what be'n loungin' around here since his boss left? Har, I reckon he's sawin' logs wid the rest of 'em. Nobody in their right mind plannin' any travel today."

"If the owner of this establishment expects to be paid for the Frenchie's room and board and that of the mules', you'd best get him down here on the double. If I leave without him, you'll get stiffed for his and the mules keep all winter. You've got five minutes to rouse his lazy ass and get him down here," I said pushing my way into the dining room, pulling out my watch and starting the countdown.

The threat of lost money and prospect of being held responsible got the desired result. The old miner with a noticeable limp put down his cup of coffee and hobbled to the door leading to the stairs and slowly mounted them step by step, clutching the wooden rail and dragging his bum leg behind.

I poured myself a cup of coffee and dunked a stale roll into the dark liquid while I waited. Jacques made his sullen appearance ten minutes later.

"You better grab a cup of coffee and a roll quick and get the mules ready to go. Rain's let up and we leave town in twenty minutes," I consulted my pocket watch for a show of seriousness.

"Can't travel in this kind of weather. Storm's gonna pick up again an' we'll be stuck out in the open. Plain foolhardy tryin' to travel in all this water and mud," he said bitterly.

"The old timer I spoke with at first light, said there'd be a lull between last night's storm and the next one. We have to take advantage of that calm to get to and across Knight's ford before the next storm hits," I said in a commanding tone. It was all blarney of course as I intentionally misrepresented what I'd been told.

"Ain't gonna risk my life, my job and the mules doin' somethin' that's plain crazy. No siree," he stated defiantly.

"Fine, you can stay here, but you'll have to pay your keep and the mules' out your own pocket. My agreement with your boss was to pay your keep only until we left town and you led the mules back to Stockton. I'm leaving in twenty minutes with or without you. Put a saddle on the sturdiest mule and a pack saddle on another if you're not coming. I'll be back in fifteen minutes. I've got to talk to another guide who's willing to lead me," I said in a matter of fact tone, put my watch away, slurped the last of my coffee, and walked out the door without waiting for a response.

Hoping my bluff would work, I headed for a nearby French bakery to stock up on fresh bread for the trip. I opted for a large, still warm loaf of black bread and pastries stuffed with a mixture of minced walnuts and honey instead of the fresh baguettes and croissants, whose tempting aroma filled the small shop. If I got stuck on the track, they'd be more substantial than soft bread and croissants. I stuffed my purchases in my rucksack, picked up my meager travel packs and a hemp-braided pottery jug of cognac from my hotel and trudged my way to the stables behind the muleteer's boarding house.

I was pleased to see my threat to leave Jacques high and dry without resources in Sonora worked. The six mules were saddled and munching oats out of buckets. I secured my packs on a pack saddle and the jug of cognac to the pommel without addressing the still sullen Jacques. I paid the bill for Jacques' room and board and the keep for the animals.

Fortunately, the track out of town toward the river took us gradually downhill toward flatter ground. We avoided the rivulets of water that still coursed down the slope. Their bellies full, the mules plodded carefully through the mud and standing water. The sky was dark and threatening, but the rain while cold, was still misty.

We slogged slowly along over rises and down wooded vales until the topography became fairly flat and the trees and shrubs stunted. We lost some time finding shallows to ford rivulets and gullies that still coursed with rain water. I opted not to stop at an inn for lunch. I cut thick pieces of bread from my loaf of bread and slices of hard cheese from my pack with my Bowie knife and shared them with my unhappy and still morose guide. In early afternoon, we arrived at the inn where we'd spent the night after the ferry crossing on the way to Sonora.

Jacques assumed we'd put up for the night and started to lead our mules to the inn's stables. "Take 10 minutes to feed them. We're going to get to Knight's ferry before dark so we can get across," I stated authoritatively.

"We'll never make the ferry before dark. Don't even know if the river is crossable or the ferryman willing to cross it. This is insane!" He railed.

"If we don't or can't get across, we can always return to the inn."

"That's even more crazy. It'll be dark. Look at the sky. It'll start to drench us any moment. We've come as far as it's safe to go today," he pleaded. No doubt the thoughts of the warm fire, nourishment, drink and the inn's frisky barmaids were foremost on his mind.

He was right of course; thunder rumbled ever closer. I was sure the next storm was ready to break. However, I was desperate to get across the river if at all possible. Another big blow so soon after the last one might mean we'd be stuck on this side of the river.

"I'm going to chance it. Another big storm will set us back more if we're not across the river. Feed the animals. We leave in ten minutes," I commanded in my "do it or else" voice. While he sulked and fed the mules, I procured several faggots whose ends had been dipped in thick pine pitch that we could light to see the track in the dark.

Anticipating we'd get soaked on this next stretch of track well before we arrived at Knight's ferry landing, I pulled a heavy Chilean poncho from my pack and donned it instead of my hooded rain cloak. I learned from my Creole trapper guides in my trip through the northern placers that it's the best protection from the elements. Jacques looked at me in distain. I'd have the last laugh when he got soaked to the skin.

We made better time than I anticipated. A feeble light still peeked through the ominous clouds when I spotted the distant lights of Mr. Knight's cabins. My heart sank when we arrived at the landing. Mr. Knight's ferry-raft was beached and firmly secured by ropes and metal chains to thick trees much further up the embankment. The river roared and surged past the landing carrying with it broken tree limbs and even roots and stumps of trees ravaged by the storm and now turbulent waters. It was apparent, if Knight's ferry-raft were struck by the flotsam and jetsam of trees while trying to cross the raging river, it would capsize and drown its occupants.

I was about to turn around and return to the inn, when a stocky man in buckskin coveralls exited a small log cabin high on the embankment and hailed us. "If you aim to git across afore night, better give me a hand and be quick about it," he said.

I looked at him astonished. "How do you mean for us to cross?" I asked perplexed.

"Mr. Knight's on the other side with his missus who's cookin' in his cabin. It'll take all three of us to make the crossin' but we got ta hurry. Follow me," he replied.

We dismounted and followed him further down the landing to where an iron cable fastened to a large tree stretched high across the raging torrent. A small wooden platform was attached to the cable by chains at the four corners that in turn were attached to pulleys hung on the cable traversing the river. "Take your rucksacks and baggage and tie them securely to the rungs on the floor of the ferry so the weight is distributed evenly," he demanded. "I'll stable your mules. We'll see if they can cross tomorrow. All depends on the storm."

While he stabled our mules in a shelter near the cabin he'd

emerged from, we hastened to fasten our meager possessions as instructed. When he returned, I asked naively "Where are the bullocks?"

He laughed heartily 'til he was teary-eyed, "We're the bullocks," he chortled good-naturedly. "Climb aboard the ferry and stand firm in the middle. Watch me pull and then pull this here line the way I do and when I do, so we're all three pullin' together. Put gloves on if you have 'em," he said taking the lead position on the platform.

The line we were to pull was attached to the two, double pulleys. I spread my legs the way the ferryman did and indicated Jacques should stand and pull in the middle. It was an ingenious contraption. We pulled the platform loaded with us and our bags hand-over-hand well above the raging river full of detritus.

As the cables were well-oiled, it took only three or four minutes to arrive at the landing on the Stockton side of the river. "Take yer bags and drop 'em in the bunkhouse," the ferryman said pointing to a small cabin near the main cabin high on the embankment. "We'll see about your mules in the mornin'. If'n I can't get 'em across, Mr. Knight will rent you mules to get to the next inn where they'll have mules for rent all the way to Stockton. Juss' knock on Knight's door when you're ready and Mrs. Knight'll give you some victuals to eat." That said, he hopped back aboard the wire-ferry and pulled himself expertly back across the river.

The bunk house was Spartan but clean. Two series of six bunks each were separated by a partition. The arrangement would allow women a small bit of privacy from strange men. As we were the only guests that evening, I let Jacques select his bunk, then picked one as far from him as possible. The bunks, one over the other, were stuffed with a bedding of straw and provided a blanket for warmth. There was no woodstove and the outhouse was a few steps down the slope.

Knight's cabin was spacious and welcoming. A large hearth dominated one whole side and a long trestle table with hand-hewed oak planks atop the sturdy trestle legs ran the length of the room in front of the hearth. The glistening patina on the planks attested to their frequent use. Mrs. Knight responded to our knock and bade us to take seats in front of the roaring fire. She was a sturdy, hearty woman in her late forties. She wore a practical, high-collar muslin dress with a lace collar and a minimum of petticoats with a white apron over her bodice and skirt. Her auburn hair, now sprinkled with gray, was pulled into a bun held by a large tortoise-shell comb. Her hazel eyes still sparkled.

"You boys got across just in time," she said sympathetically as thunder claps echoed close-by and streaks of lightning dancing in front of the one small window in the lee of the wind that now gusted and unleashed pounding rain that briefly affected the smoke drawing from the chimney by sending a puff of smoke into the cabin. "Looks like we're in for a big blow," she stated matter-of-factly. She handed us each a porcelain cup from pegs hanging by the hearth. "Help yourselves to a cup of warm grog," she said pointing to a ladle handle protruding from a small metal pot hanging on irons to the right of the chimney. "Supper'll be ready when my husband finishes his accounts." He was bent over a desk illuminated by a whale oil lamp with his back to us.

Jacques and I took turns ladling healthy dollops of grog into our cups. The warm mixture of rum and water hit the spot and produced a warm glow all the way down to my stomach. Jacques emptied his cup of grog in two quick goes, while I savored mine by sipping the strong concoction slowly to feel the warmth spread throughout my body slowly.

Mr. Knight closed his account ledgers and joined us in front of the fire to which he added a log. He extended a hand to each of us. His grip was like iron. He was tall and ruddy-faced.

He helped himself to a big cup of grog bypassing the ladle by dipping his cup directly in the brew and letting the drippings excite the fire.

The storm hit full stride outside; the wind howled and drove the rain fiercely against the house seeking weakness in the chinking between the logs. "Have another spot of grog before we eat," he said pointing to the mulling pot. "Lucky she didn't break while you were crossing. We don't do ferrying in the rain. Too dangerous. Peter, on the other side, has got a good sense of timing. Haven't lost any passengers yet, but this winter may be a big challenge. They say it's gonna be like '49."

"What about our mules?" I asked.

"Well, that's another matter. They can be quite stubborn and difficult on the ferry rig you crossed on, especially with the sight and noise of the river. Have to take them one-by-one and tie them down on the floor rungs so they can't move and upset the balance. If the storm doesn't blow itself out, they'll have to stay on the other side. The next group of mule drivers supplying Sonora or the camps can leave their mules on this side and transport their wares with your mules."

"But our mules were rented. We need to get them back," I said concerned.

Knight just chuckled. "Not to worry. A mule's just a mule. As long as he's healthy, and can carry his load, we exchange them back and forth in winter. As soon as Peter verifies they're fit and healthy, I'll give you a credit chit for your mules and saddles. You'll pick up similar mules at the next station where you'll stop."

"And the stables in Stockton will accept these exchanged mules just like that?" I said doubt written all over my face.

"Do it all the time, especially in winter when we can't use the big ferry. It's not practical to ferry mules in this weather. Mules going to or from Stockton are pretty much the same. The system allows us to keep supplies moving to the mines."

"Okay, I'll trust your word on the matter."

Mrs. Knight set the table so we were all seated in front of the fire. She served us big helpings of venison pie on pewter plates and refilled our cups with grog. It was warm and delicious, a nice change from venison stew. As that was the main dish, we all had second helpings. For dessert, she offered us ladles of vanilla custard she'd made.

I was so delighted with the tasty, home-cooked meal that I donned my poncho and braved the elements to fetch my knapsack and jug of cognac. The Knights were thrilled to try the stuffed pastries I'd bought in Sonora. As it was still early evening, I offered Mr. Knight a cigar which he took but didn't smoke. Instead he filled his clay pipe and we sat around the fire drinking cognac in tin cups and shooting the breeze about winter life in the mining camps until my hosts indicated by yawning that we should all tuck in for the night.

Mrs. Knight fixed us a hearty breakfast of fried bacon and fresh eggs from her chicken coop. After settling our bill, we took Mr. Knight's mules and left ours on the other side of the river. The storm that raged through the night now produced only light rain. The track was muddy but passable. Even Jacques stopped complaining and muttering to himself. We were both eager to get to Stockton before dark and the comforts of a town.

We exchanged mules at the next inn and paused only to lunch hurriedly on rabbit stew. By late afternoon, the skies were again turning sullen and menacing. Lightning flashed and thunder crashed increasingly closer. We both spurred our mules harder. Darkness fell quickly and the rain increased. I lit two faggots and passed one to Jacques in the lead. We could see the lights of Stockton in the distance, but it was still quite a way off.

Two more hours trudging in the rain brought us to the outskirts of Stockton. Fortunately for me, Pietro Salvatore's inn was on the east side of town, closest to our arrival. I wasn't sorry to part company with Jacques and the mules, who had to travel several more blocks to his lodging. He was soaked to the skin and complaining bitterly about the trip. I was secretly pleased he'd got his due.

California Gold Rush Journal
∾ PART 2 ∾

CHAPTER TWENTY-EIGHT
Sonora-Stockton — December, 1851

Pietro Salvatore greeted me with a warm smile even though it was late and only two guests lingered over the last dregs of their wine. I dropped my rucksack and shed the Chilean poncho that kept me relatively dry but now dripped rain water on the entryway. "Glad you're back safe and sound and out of the storm. Where's your assistant?" He queried.

"I left him to finish up our contacts and mail distribution in Sonora. I have to get back to our business in San Francisco. We're short-handed and my wife just delivered twins." I fished a good cigar out of my rucksack and handed it to him in celebration of the births as is traditional here.

"*Molto bene! Congratulatzioni. Due bambini!* Rosa," he hollered in the direction of the kitchen and added more excited words in his native Sardinian tongue I couldn't understand. His wife joined us from the kitchen, wiping her hands on her soiled cooking apron spattered with a delicious smelling tomato sauce that set my stomach growling.

She waited patiently until her husband stopped pumping my

hand to ask, "You eat supper on the road?" I nodded "no" and pleaded my cause with my eyes glued to her apron. "I make a nice *salsa pomadora* an' I make a pot of *pasta tre colore.* You like?"

Salvatore added, "It's a semolina pasta flavored with dried vegetables, an Italian specialty. We were just going to eat, so you join us, yes?"

The pasta and sauce sprinkled with freshly grated Parmesan cheese was fabulous. Salvatore used the occasion to open two bottles of Italian red wine to hear the tale of my adventures. Mrs. Salvatore laughed when her husband repeated my account of the tribulations of my lovesick assistant and the charms of Sonora's Mademoiselle Virginie. Mr. Salvatore was particularly interested in road conditions and our ferry crossing in light of the series of recent storms. The red wine finished, we moved on to *grappa* and our cigars when Mrs. Salvatore retired for the evening.

Somehow, I managed to stumble up the stairs to my bed without disturbing the loud snoring of other guests. I was surprised next morning to see I hadn't slept in my boots. My head pounded as we French say *comme un pivert sur l'arbre* — like a woodpecker drilling a tree for worms. Mrs. Salvatore's strong black coffee and almond torte helped revive me for the day's tasks — to book passage back to San Francisco on the first boat available and buy presents for my neglected wife and babies.

I rented a covered cab for the trip downtown so I could cart my baggage and keep it dry. The cabbie knew where to find merchants who sold the gifts I sought, so we went there first. The rain and wind picked up as we arrived at the wharves.

A river steamer was scheduled to leave in twenty minutes, but it took an hour and a half's wait before the captain and crew would agree to stoke the boilers and sail in the increasingly foul weather after being harangued by the company's manager with threats of being sacked on the spot. Needless to say, the combination of stormy weather and a sullen crew didn't augur well for a pleasant journey.

The small, side-paddle steamer struggled and groaned against river waves, cold, slicing rain and a crosswind. I was sure we'd founder trying to negotiate the narrow channels between the numerous islets we had to skirt. My heart was on my sleeve several times as our ship's bow popped out of the murky downpour on a collision course with an obstacle, only to slide by it perilously close.

Matters didn't get any better when we finally left the river Delta and entered San Pablo Bay. The wind screamed and the white-capped waves assaulted our poor boat broadside. I was sure we'd sink as Manon had predicted. I was as terrified as when we fought our way around Cape Horn on the Clipper ship, "Flying Cloud." Fortunately, I skipped lunch in favor of a few crackers and a handful of nuts to tide me over.

It was close to 10 P.M. when our gutsy steamer finally tied up for the night on the Long Wharf in San Francisco. No cabs were available, so I donned my poncho and paid a deckhand to deliver my luggage to our ship on the same wharf while I hot-footed it down the wharf in the pelting, stinging rain and made a bee-line for our restaurant. Georges opened the main door just a crack at my insistent pounding, then let me pass to the warm interior. He, Giselle and Nelly were closing and preparing to leave. The evenings' few guests had eaten early and quickly scooted for home according to Georges. It was a night when not even the large population of scavenger rats ventured forth in the tempest. Georges informed me Manon elected to stay with the twins upstairs and let Giselle host the few clients who braved the storm.

I bounded up the stairs to our apartment. Manon, seated in an Amish-made rocking chair, was breastfeeding little Fanny in front of the wood stove in the living room. Little Jules gurgled contentedly in his bassinet alongside his sister.

"Ah, so prodigal papa has finally come home and just an hour before his promise. So, how were the hussies in Sonora and Mariposa?" She said mockingly.

"No time for distractions except for Gino now that I'm gone. He's fallen for a young card dealer he met. We only made it to Sonora before the rains started in earnest. I left between major rain storms and was lucky to get ferried across the river before it flooded."

"Hah, so Manon was right. You did jeopardize the future of your wife and babies just to keep your postal contract by taking big risks with the weather, yes?"

"But not with Indians, bears and drunken miners you fantasized about. My concern for the weather was only whether the river would flood and prevent me returning until I could be ferried across. So, *voilà*, here I am as I promised, ready to help you with the kids." I stated calmly. No way was I going to tell her about the harrowing ferry trip or my fears the steamer would capsize.

"So, are you finally ready to make yourself useful?" She said coquettishly, her ire abated for the moment.

"Of course. That's why I took the first ferry running from Stockton." I was tempted to explain the departure delay and late arrival, but thought better of it. It would only emphasize the risk of foundering in the rough weather and turbulent waters and get her back on her high horse.

"Good. Jules just ate his fill. So, why don't you change his diaper while Fanny finishes," she said pointing to a pile of nappies and a side table with a pitcher and shallow basin. "Mix hot water on the stove with the cool water in the pitcher so it's lukewarm. See you clean him thoroughly then apply the talcum powder to his bottom," she stated authoritatively.

I was tempted to give her a sassy reply, but thought better of it. She'd had her hands full running her restaurant and caring for two newborns while I travelled—an unfair division of labor, at best. Baby Jules gurgled happily. I pulled a small, silver cup from my pocket and passed it slowly in front of his visage. His grasping fingers sought to snatch it while his blue eyes tracked its movement. When I let him have it, I was surprised at his strong grip. He popped it immediately in his mouth. With him thus occupied, I picked him up and laid him out on the table with his diapers. Manon had left a large piece of oilcloth for the operation and I opened his swaddling garments.

What a perfect, although messy, little body—long torso, cherubic cheeks, shock of coarse black hair, chubby legs and a contented smile to melt your heart as he sucked my gift. I could feel Manon's eyes watching my every move as I changed his diaper, washed him and pinned up his clean diaper and lifted him in my arms to rock him gently to and fro. I was rewarded with contented coos and drool on my traveling costume.

"Since you've got the knack of it, Fanny could use a change before being put to bed," Manon said with an impish smile, holding out my daughter to me. I handed off Jules to her and repeated the operation. Little Fanny had only soiled her diaper and not pooped, so it went faster. She eagerly grasped the silver rattle I tendered her and shoved it quickly in her mouth while giving me a radiant smile. I marveled at her delicate fingers and toes, round cheeks and silky black hair. She smelled fresh and new when I lifted her in my arms and rocked her as with Jules.

Manon stuffed both infants in miniature sleeping attire and by the time both were burped and tucked in for the night, each was asleep.

"How long will our little angels sleep before their next feeding?" I asked out of curiosity.

"Prodigal papa will find out soon enough?" Manon replied with a mischievous smile.

"Prodigal papa could use some sustenance now he has

important tasks ahead for the night. If they wake up hungry, I'll bring them to you in bed if you like," I said sweetly.

"Your Manon would like that," she said smiling in kind. "What sort of gift did you get for Manon? Silver earrings? A cameo? A good luck charm?" She said coquettishly removing the pins from her raven tresses and letting them tumble down her shoulder and back before tossing her head for effect and letting them settle down her back.

"My beautiful wife will find out just as soon as she brings a tray of *saucisson* and cheese for her starving husband," I said saucily.

Manon returned with a platter of sliced salami and fresh goat cheese and a basket full of cut pieces of baguette. "Prodigal papa would like to join his long-suffering wife with a glass of red wine while he stuffs his belly, yes? Manon will bring some wine after she changes into more comfortable attire."

When she returned with a bottle and two glasses she was barefoot and had exchanged her milk-stained feeding blouse for the simple, diaphanous shift she'd donned to lure me to bed in Valparaiso after weeks in the horrible bunk beds in our Clipper cabin. She treated me to a pirouette backlit by the table lamps that showcased her now narrow waist, ample figure, luxurious head of black curls, and slender ankles.

"You like what you see, Big Boy?" I nodded my approval trying not to let my visage betray my lecherous thoughts. "So, I hope prodigal papa didn't forget to buy a little bauble for his hardworking wife, yes?" She said pouring two full glasses of a hearty French Burgundy and handing me one.

"Put down your glass and come stand in front of me," I said sweetly. "Now close your eyes and hold out your right hand and I will give you your present." I could tell she was cheating, squinting to see what I would produce from my pocket. I kept my surprise wrapped in a linen handkerchief until I got the clasp fastened around her delicate wrist. *"Eh, voilà,* I said with a flourish as I pulled the cloth away and let the heavy weight of the bracelet tug her wrist down.

Manon's black eyes grew big as saucers as she grasped the beauty of my gift. "Oh *Chéri,* they are so beautiful. They must have cost a fortune! It's so heavy!" She exclaimed gleefully. She held the gold bracelet with little gold nuggets attached like charms up to the nearest whale oil lamp and let the light play over the beautiful and unique forms of the nuggets. She was like a little girl getting her first doll that she'd pleaded for upon first seeing it in a shop window.

I picked up my glass of wine and nodded for her to do the same. "For my precious wife, only the best our new country can offer." I raised my glass and we toasted each other.

Manon motioned for me to sit in the large rocking chair where she'd nursed our twins, then climbed on my lap to give me a big welcome home greeting by searching for my mouth while she hugged my neck and pushed her warm, firm, lavender-scented body into mine. After a long, lingering kiss, she looked deeply into my eyes. "So Big Boy, your wife's bed has been cold and uninviting for ten days. What do you intend to do about it?" She said teasingly while gripping me even tighter.

I tried to get up with her in my arms, but the sudden motion sent the rocking chair first forward, then backward. Manon squealed and we both burst into laughter. Manon put a finger over her mouth to indicate we needed to be quieter; we didn't want to wake up our babes and spoil the moment. Once out of the rocker, she let me pick her up and carry her to our bed where she'd turned down the covers and lit a candle in advance. All thoughts of sipping red wine and finishing my simple dinner were dismissed.

While it was too soon after birthing to make new babies, we still reveled in each other's bodies as inventive lovers are wont to do until we were sated and fell exhausted into blissful sleep.

The full-throated cry of a hungry baby pierced its way first into my dream, then to slowly realized awareness that I had to get up and fetch my child. Manon was curled around my back and buttocks and gave me a good poke to remind me of my promise. After re-lighting lamps in the cold apartment, I realized we had not stoked the woodstoves in our rush to bed.

I grabbed an oil lamp and stumbled into the second bedroom we used as a nursery. Baby Fanny had her mouth open to improve upon her earlier wail, but paused when she spied me. Baby Jules was awake and eyeing me as well. When I picked up Fanny, he hollered his displeasure in a high-pitched howl.

Manon had an amused smile on her face as I delivered Fanny to her arms. "Do I bring Jules at the same time?" I asked, still slightly groggy and disoriented by my new responsibilities. "No, he gets fed after his sister. You pick him up and distract him until I call you to take Fanny and change her diaper." Oh boy, I had a lot to learn about being a father and helpmate, and not just a doting dad. No wonder Manon had been upset and felt betrayed when I took off for Sonora so soon after their births. One child would be a handful, but twins were more than double the work and responsibility, especially when one was alone.

I gave Jules Fanny's silver rattle to play with and put him in the bassinet near the woodstove where he could see me and I could tickle him from time to time while restarting fire in the stove. The clock on a side table indicated it was 6:30 A.M. The wind hadn't slackened and the incessant staccato of rain on the roof and against our bay window overlooking the street was unnerving. I took a good 45 minutes to get both infants fed and in clean diapers.

I naively thought once fed, our infants would go back to sleep and we could resume our slumber. Wrong of course. Both infants wanted to be entertained. Manon indicated she had done my part for ten days and now it was my turn. She turned over in bed to resume her sleep. Check-mate. I closed the door to our bedroom, put each infant near the now warming stove and prepared a pot of coffee to help me do my duty.

California Gold Rush Journal
⊂⊘ PART 2 ⊘⊃

CHAPTER TWENTY-NINE
San Francisco — December, 1851 – February 1852

I realized my ambitious plans to operate a full-time notary and detective agency had to be put on hold for the time being. Manon needed my help with the restaurant and our twins. She had been burning the candle at both ends and we were still short-handed with Gino stuck in Sonora and probably in no hurry to leave if he was making headway with Miss Virginie.

Even though business turned slow during the recent storms, we were fully booked through the end of December and most of January as folks scheduled family and business celebrations for the holidays. Manon needed to host her guests in the restaurant through this important period. With our private dining room in the back, we could handle private parties of 16-20 persons. However, it required more staff. Rose, our apprentice cook, had been serving tables with Nelly while Georges ran the bar and served wine as sommelier. With nightly full houses, we needed Rose in the kitchen.

Our disgruntled chef, Henri, complained loudly he was over-worked and his two apprentices insufficient to handle all the needed prep work. Now that he considered himself a "top chef," he felt his job was to sip wine, supervise the kitchen and take the accolades at the end of the evening while his apprentices did the actual cooking. Our two apprentices were making great strides towards becoming chefs in their own right, but couldn't handle the holiday workload on their own if we sacked Henri. Manon taught them cooking skills when Henri wasn't present, but we needed everyone working overtime to get through the holiday season as we were booked solidly for lunch as well as dinner.

Nelly had become an excellent food server, but she was needed to babysit the twins while Manon ran the restaurant. Manon asked both Giselle and Teri if they could work the evening shift as waitresses, but Teri demurred. Business was up on our wharf wine bar and food stall, and she was being pursued by a number of interesting men. Fortunately, Rose's brother, Jacques Boucher, was not the jealous type like Gino. Giselle readily agreed to help out evenings as she still refused to get involved with the many men who offered themselves to her.

Nelly couldn't care for our twins and serve tables at the same time. She worked as hostess and cashier when Manon fed the twins. I suggested we hire a wet nurse to feed and babysit them. Manon would have none of it. She also opposed hiring a temporary food server unless referred by someone we knew and trusted. I realized it was up to me to either find another food server who would fit with our close-knit staff or become the babysitter so Nellie could serve food. Manon hinted I should attack the pile of accumulated bills and do other paperwork in our apartment so our babies "could see more of their papa."

I wanted to spend quality time with our twins, but not as a babysitter. So, I hotfooted over to Pierre-Louis' new digs to seek his advice and see how he was getting along with his new bride. He and the new Mrs. Lerouge, the former Mrs. Gemmer, rented a ground level flat in a quiet area in the upper Broadway and away from the central business district now he was retired and she was running their household.

His wife, Mathilde, met me at the door with a big smile. As I had encouraged and not opposed their marriage, she had turned friendly to both Manon and me. "Come in. Glad to see you've returned safely from the wilds. Sorry you missed our celebratory dinner at the restaurant. Manon was very gracious, but my Pierre did miss you," she said. "Pierre's in the parlor reading. Would you like a coffee?"

"That would be lovely," I replied noting the inexpensive engagement ring she'd bought with her own funds had been shelved in favor of a large, gaudy ruby cabochon ring tucked safely behind a large gold wedding band. She'd replaced her nurse's costume with a fashionable dress with numerous pet- ticoats that emphasized her still trim waist and full bust as she pointed me to the parlor and bustled off to make us coffee.

I was pleased to see Pierre-Louis sitting comfortably in a large wingback chair in front of a cheery fire in the hearth. He put the newspaper he was reading on the pile near his chair and motioned me to the second wingback which I surmised was Mathilde's. As she was not present, I asked, "How are you finding married life?"

"Couldn't be better. I thought I'd miss the gossip and ban- ter of clients at the restaurant, but I don't. Mathilde fetches the newspapers and French reviews when she shops in the morn- ing. She's quite industrious and attentive to our welfare," he said tenderly and convincingly."

"Manon and I are so happy it's worked out well. How are the legs doing?"

"Well, it's still a struggle, but Mathilde sees that I walk every day with my canes, of course." I noted that he had lost belly fat, so she still kept him on a strict diet.

"Manon says you don't get to lunch at the restaurant much. Is the prepared food Georges delivers adequate?"

"Oh, yes. More than adequate; it's delicious, but Mathilde likes to do her own cooking most of the time. She's not one for the rich creamy sauces you and I both like in our cooking." I was going to probe what they did with the food we delivered, but thought better of it as Mathilde arrived with a coffee service on a silver tray. I would suggest to Mathilde that she might like to pick up meat and fish from our kitchen to prepare it to her own taste.

"Mathilde, I'd like your advice and help if possible. We're short-handed at the restaurant for the holiday season with Georges' wife needed to tend to our twins while Manon runs the dinner service," I said while she served coffee in delicate cups and saucers with a floral décor she must have brought to San Francisco. She gave me a quizzical, surprised look. "I thought you might know someone trustworthy who'd be able to babysit our twins every evening."

"Do you mean a wet nurse to feed them as well?"

"No, just child care. Manon will continue to nurse them. She feels it's especially important given she'll be so occupied with the restaurant during the busy holiday season."

"So, it'd just be short-term?"

"Not necessarily. It would have to be full-time as Manon supervises food deliveries, sets menus and instructs our two apprentice cooks in the afternoon and serves as hostess and cashier for the dinner service. I thought you might know someone suitable who's good with infants."

"Hum, I do know a couple of women who worked as nurses and housekeepers who want work, but they have small babies of their own to care for. Would Manon be open to a housekeeper or child minder who brought her own baby to work?"

"As long as she's of good character, I don't think it would be a problem. Might even be an advantage to have a full-fledged nursery, especially when they're old enough to talk and play with each other. Why don't you have the two you can recommend see Manon at the restaurant between two and four in the afternoon. She'll interview them and show them the premises. We'd provide lunch as part of the deal," I added on the spur of the moment. Better not to have to worry about meal preparation and have more time to entertain and instruct the babies.

"Yes. I will. I can see Manon needs help and there are so few legitimate jobs for women in this city," Mathilde said with emotion. Boatloads of married and single women looking for jobs and husbands kept arriving weekly. Other than the sex trade, there were few employment opportunities for women wanting to earn their own keep.

When Mathilde removed the coffee service, I turned my attention to Pierre-Louis. "What's been happening while I was in Sonora? Things still calm with respect to the Ducks and the détente between the civil authorities and the Committee?"

"Yes, interesting enough, not only are the Ducks content to return to Australia, but many of the failed miners here are joining them. Apparently, the word of the big gold strikes in Australia in 1850 has panned out. Some of the first to rush from here to Sydney and Melbourne have already returned to grouse they'd had to work beside convicts and ruffians. They've been complaining it was too hot to work claims in the infernal desert heat and the limited water is too unclean to drink."

"I can understand they missed the cool, fresh waters of the Sierra Nevada. Dry placer mining is tough, gritty work. Even here, only the Mexicans are willing to do it. They got used to it in the desert conditions in the mines in Sonora, Mexico," I added.

"I was just reading another account where an unhappy Yankee complained mosquitoes as big as wasps plagued the diggings, they had to eat kangaroo meat and a mate was hauled off by a crocodile when they camped by a river to wash their dirt. But the major complaints were that the government imposed a seven and a half dollar monthly miner's tax on Californians and wages are only half what they could earn here."

I guffawed at Pierre-Louis account. The spectacle of the miner's buddy providing a meal to a hungry croc struck me as risible.

"Poor Yankees are getting a taste of what it's like to be discriminated against. Hightailing it back to California where opportunities aren't so bad after all. Serves them right to get a dose of their own medicine," I said unsympathetically.

"So, how were things in the southern mines you visited?" Pierre-Louis asked. He relished the chance to supplement his reading with first hand reports.

"I never made it farther than Sonora. The rains started in earnest and I was afraid the Stanislaus River would flood and make the ferry crossing impossible. Lots of French merchants and businesses there, so I had to leave my assistant to finalize our mail deliveries. Manon needs me here to help with our affairs, as you know."

"Well, I'm glad you're back and your business is good. We missed you at our marriage gala at the restaurant. I'm content to have all that behind me. Never thought I'd be so content to be retired," he said with a sigh.

I considered giving him a couple cigars and a shot of cognac from my pocket flask to celebrate the arrival of our twins, but thought better of it. It would only rattle Mathilde's cage and create friction over my now welcome visits. "Well, after the desperate plight I found you in at the hospital, it's really good to see fortune has smiled on you. When you're more able to negotiate the streets, drop by the restaurant for lunch and a good chat over a bottle of wine."

He gave me a whimsical look and weak smile that said "those

were the days." I dropped by the kitchen on my way out to suggest Mathilde might prefer to pick up fresh meat and fish from the restaurant rather than have prepared dishes delivered. "Yes, thank you, I'd like that," she replied sweetly as she let me out.

As I was near the Italian quarter, I decided to visit Luigi Salterini to see if he had suggestions for another restaurant server to assist our staff. His new *trattoria* featured large brick kiln ovens his nephew insisted on. They now offered *pizza al taglio*, a menu of pizzas with several different toppings that could be purchased by the slice as well as whole. Several clients were seated munching slices of pizza and drinking red wine. One could order wine by the glass or in quarter, half, and liter carafes. The nephew, no doubt, had insisted on its new name— *Trattoria Napoletana*.

Luigi spied me and waved me over to a table by the bar with a big grin. "You looka like you needa glass of wine my friend. How 'bout you try some gooda pizza? Antonio justa make nice sausage pizza. Let's see how 'Frenchies,' lika new American food," he said tongue-in-cheek mimicking an American accent. We both laughed at his comic antics.

Antonio, Gino's cousin who'd worked for us briefly, arrived with a liter carafe of Italian red wine and a metal pan with what looked like a flat, crusty bread smeared with tomato sauce, melted cheese, peppered olive oil and chunks of homemade sausage. He set the piping-hot pan on the table and used a special tool, like we use to cut bunches of grapes from the vine, to score the flat bread into six pieces. Using a spatula, he plopped pieces onto small plates before Luigi and me and poured our wine. Before he could finish, the workers at another table hollered, "Hey, Antonio let us taste that one too. Smells good." They said pointing to the pan on our table.

As there were only table knives and no forks on the table, I sipped my wine and waited to see how Luigi proposed to eat his slice. The laborers who'd asked for more picked up their slices in their hands and stuffed the short ends into their mouth. Luigi watched my concern and laughed. "You're in Little Italy, my friend, not in a three star French restaurant. We Italians eat pizza with our hands. Try it. See if you like it."

I picked up the hot triangle of pastry-like flat bread and gingerly took a bite. "Wow," I exclaimed. The hot cheese hit the top of my palate and tongue at the same time, burning both. I gulped red wine to cool it down. Luigi laughed. "You need to get used to hot food. You French smother everything in cream sauces. We Italians come from a hot country and like our simple dishes peppered and hot. You see how those guys over there do it," he said pointing to the table where the three were now attacking the rest of Antonio's pizza he'd served us. "They eat with gusto. That's the way to eat Italian pizza," he stated proudly as he stuffed his slice into his mouth.

"So. It looks like Antonio's idea is working out, yes?"

"Better than I could ever imagine. The young people love the taste and variety. We're doing three times better than before. Lunch time all the tables are full and the same in the evening after work. We still make pasta dishes and a couple of meat dishes. But, think about it. No spoilage. We use flour, fresh tomatoes in season and tomato preserves and paste. We buy a local mozzarella cheese made by Italians, and we use vegetables and shell fish in season or dried—olives, mushrooms, peppers, anchovies, clams and our homemade sausage and salamis. So simple and tasty, yet cheap to make. Eat up, Antonio will be serving pizzas with different toppings soon for the lunch crowd," he said pointing to my slice.

As it had cooled, I had to agree it was a tasty snack. I could see how it might catch on with workmen on limited budgets and in a hurry.

"So, my friend, what brings the proud father of twins to

Little Italy?" Luigi asked as I handed him a cigar and he refilled our glasses.

"I had to leave Gino in Sonora to finish our work there. With the series of storms, no telling when he'll be able to return. The rivers will be impossible to cross. He helped Manon serve tables and now we're short-handed and fully booked for the next two months. I thought you or Antonio might know an experienced waiter you could recommend."

Luigi motioned Antonio to join us. He explained my need in rapid-fire Italian. Antonio addressed me, "My friend Mario might be able to help for a while. He and his sister, Antonia, worked in their uncle's bar in Bergamo. They made and served sandwiches and a daily hot dish and soup. I told Mario we may need him here if business keeps growing. He wants to learn to make pizzas."

"What about his sister. Is she here with her brother?"

"The whole family's here. Arrived three weeks ago."

"How old is the sister? Do you think she could handle waitressing for us?"

"She's twenty and could do the job, but she doesn't speak French."

"What about English? Has she picked up enough to carry on a simple conversation?" I queried.

"Don't know. We always speak Italian. Her mother says she studied English on the ship with other women."

"Why don't you arrange to have her and her brother visit Manon in the afternoon, if they'd like to work in a restaurant."

"Sure, they'd both be thrilled to have a job. There's so much competition and not much available in the Italian community with so many of us out of work after the fire. Even with the rebuilding, there aren't enough jobs to go around."

I had another glass of wine with Luigi and headed back to our restaurant to apprise Manon of my contacts and possible interviews.

California Gold Rush Journal
 PART 2

CHAPTER THIRTY

San Francisco — December, 1851 – March 1852

Manon threw me a wry smile when I told her of my prospects for a housekeeper and additional serving staff. "My, my, Papa has been busy this morning. Nice way to do recruitment business with glasses of wine, snacks and gossip, yes?" She said tutting me with her tongue. "And when does Manon get to interview these applicants?"

"Afternoons between two and four on days we don't serve lunch." I replied sweetly.

"Well, we'll see what comes of it. Meanwhile, long-absent Papa will babysit his progeny while Manon runs her restaurant this evening, yes?" I nodded my concurrence.

I grabbed a quick bowl of soup without drinking more wine before Manon could invent more conditions to keep me tied to home and hearth. The moment our apprentices arrived for their cooking lesson, I scooted out the door into the chilly, blustery afternoon that threatened more rain. I made my way to Attorney Hawthorne's small office.

I had tasked Georges with making a contact with a customs

or port authority official privy to the arrival of ships and their cargoes. He chatted up a low level customs official with the needed inside information about the arrival of Chilean sailing ships with cargos of wheat, dried fruits and wines from Valparaiso. The cargo of one ship included the large order of wines to restock Teri's ex-boyfriend's now rebuilt wine store. Georges traded an evening for two at our restaurant for the desired intelligence. The customs official was sparking a young tart who worked in a saloon and thought inviting her to our high-end, fancy French restaurant would land her in his bed. Manon was not pleased with the arrangement, but went along so we could intercept and seize Raoul's wine.

Attorney Hawthorne confirmed he'd received the necessary ship's paperwork and had set a hearing in Judge Roberts' court for the next morning. In consideration for the judge's kindness during our marriage ceremony in his court on short notice, Manon had invited the judge and his matronly spouse to a dinner on the house. It was now time to cull a favor in return. That's the way business is done in San Francisco. I had secured the order of attachment, but now the cargo was under custom's seal, we would need an order specifying the terms of our seizure of cargo for non-payment of debt to Teri. In fact, Raoul had stolen her money gained working for us, but a civil attachment case with a friendly judge was easier and quicker to win.

A Chilean woman suing a Chilean man with whom she had lived out of wedlock for theft or embezzlement, might not play well with an all male jury, especially if it were composed of Americans who considered all Chileans "greasers" and foreign scum. The proceeding in Judge Roberts' civil court would be decided by the judge without jury. "Has he responded officially to Teri's demands?"

"Not that I know of. He asked the court clerk could he represent himself in the matter and the clerk gave him the necessary papers to appear *pro se.* So it's unlikely he'll hire an attorney at the last minute if he files the papers to appear in his own behalf. Even if he changed his mind, a newly hired attorney would not be up to speed with the facts of the case."

"Will you have the right to cross-examine him if he appears as his own attorney?" I asked concerned.

"Of course, if he gives testimony contradicting our claims, which he must to prevail, both the judge and I may cross-examine him."

"Will he have the right to cross-examine Teri and her version of the theft?" I asked thinking that we would need to prepare her to counter her ex's assertions, insinuations and probable lies.

"Yes, of course, since he'll be acting as his own attorney, he has that right as does any attorney in American law."

"Can he cross-examine her in Spanish?" Teri was still mad as hell at her ex-boyfriend, and I could see them hurling the worst insults at each other as each pulled the other's chain.

Hawthorne laughed. "No, the proceedings and testimony have to be in English. If an attorney wants to introduce witness testimony in another language, then he must file a motion with the court requesting an independent, impartial translator be present; and the judge would have to agree it's necessary. We'd have the right to contest the qualifications of any translator. However, since the ex-boyfriend is acting as his own attorney, he can't speak in Spanish and have it translated. That's why he's obligated to hire an American attorney if he wants to testify in Spanish."

It was my turn to laugh. "So, if Teri testifies in English, he'll have to cross-examine in English even if he doesn't speak it fluently, right?"

"You've got the picture. If he wants to lapse into Spanish, I'll object and the judge will rule in my favor. He'll be at risk to tick off the judge who generally doesn't like smartass litigants representing themselves when they don't know American law and procedure," Hawthorne said with a "we gotcha" smirk.

"Good, I'll share your wisdom with Teri and Manon. Why don't you visit our ship this afternoon, so you can coach her testimony in English. I'll have Georges relieve her at the wine bar, so you can meet with her on the deck."

"Sure, that's fine. I'll be there about 3 P.M.," he said consulting his watch on a chain he pulled from his vest. I knew he'd jump at the chance to prepare Teri's testimony at the ship so he'd have an excuse to visit Giselle at work. She'd been trying nicely to cool his ardor and refusing his suggestions of romantic activities they could share together.

After my visit to Hawthorne's office, I doubled back to our restaurant to apprise Georges he'd need to sub for Teri while Hawthorne and Teri consulted. Manon informed me sweetly that I'd be the barman for the rest of the lunch service and reminded me again of my fatherly duties later that evening.

Teri's case was calendared for 10 A.M. the next morning. On instruction from Hawthorne, Teri was dressed very demurely in a loose-fitting muslin dress with petticoats which did its best to hide her ample figure and charms. She'd hidden her gorgeous blonde tresses in a maiden's bonnet borrowed from Giselle. The judge's clerk snickered at her appearance. He'd signed the judge's initial order on my promise he'd get to see a fiery, feisty, red-hot Chilean vixen when the case came to trial. He'd got a good look at the way she filled out her red tango dress with slits up both sides when she served as witness to our marriage.

We had to wait while a loan shark's attorney badgered a hapless real estate speculator in order to secure a default judgment and possession of the property in the case.

Judge Roberts allowed Hawthorne and Raoul Mendosa to make opening statements to outline the facts of the case and arguments for and against granting our requested judgment of attachment and levy. Hawthorne argued that after the fire of May 3-4, 1851 that burned Mendosa's store and wine stock, Mendosa faced bankruptcy when squatters occupied his lot and learned he could not get a loan to rebuild due to irregularities in his title to the land. Desperate to bring a quiet title action so he could rebuild and evict the squatters, he took all of Teri's earnings and savings, an amount exceeding $650, without her permission, then ceased his association with her. When asked to return her money, he refused and brushed off her demands claiming she had given him the money so he could save his business. In exchange, she would get her job back at his wine store when it was rebuilt and restocked.

Mendosa argued in broken English Teri offered him the money without his having to ask for it so he could restart his business and she could have her job back as sales clerk. She would be free to resume her job once his wine was released from the attachment order.

I watched Teri's reaction to Raoul's self-serving lies. She was fuming under her bonnet. If eyes could pierce skin, Raoul was as good as roasted on a skewer over hot coals. I whispered to Hawthorne to put me on the stand first to set the stage for Teri's testimony and give her time to cool down and compose herself.

"Your Honor, we call Pierre Dubois as our first witness."

"Mr. Dubois, please tell the Court what is your association with the plaintiff in this matter."

"I am her present employer and landlord. She runs a wine bar on the Long Wharf in conjunction with the food canteen owned by me and my wife. She also works when needed in my wife's restaurant, Chez Manon, on Dupont Street. She's been an employee and tenant aboard our ship, the Eliza, since May 4,

1851, the day of the fire."

"Did she confide to you the circumstances surrounding the loss of her savings?" Hawthorne had advised me this question was potentially hearsay until her testimony, but Mendosa or the judge would have to object and neither did.

"Yes, she came to me extremely upset the moment she realized her savings were missing. The money was savings from working for us. She told me Mr. Mendosa must have taken her money that morning as he left our ship and never returned. When she tried to confront him to demand he return her money, he just laughed and called her 'a stupid bitch.' She told me he had taken up with a Chilean woman who ran a bagnio servicing sailors on lower Broadway near the wharves."

Mendosa became agitated and indignant at my characterization of his new mistress and benefactor. His handsome face became livid and contorted with rage. He stood up from his table, pointed to me and shouted, "*Hijo de puta!*" Judge Roberts banged his gavel. "Any more disruptions or insults in this courtroom and I'll hold you in contempt of court and have the Sheriff haul you to jail to cool down your temper," the judge warned.

I snuck a look at Teri. She was trying to suppress a grin at Raoul's calling me a son of a whore and drawing the judge's ire. I hoped she realized Raoul was on the ropes. He'd admitted in his opening statement that he had taken the money from Teri, so the only issues we had to prove were that he'd taken her money without her consent and not repaid it.

"Did you verify Miss Rios' story?" Hawthorne asked.

"Yes, I checked Mr. Mendosa's lot and there were in fact squatters doing business on it. I verified Mr. Mendosa's new residence at Señora Batista's bagnio on lower Broadway. My wife had to loan Miss Rios money until her next payday. I helped Miss Rios search her cabin to confirm her money had been purloined. It had been there the night before and was now gone." Mendosa was still highly agitated and probably frustrated as well. I purposely used the word purloined instead of stolen as I was sure Mr. Mendosa, with his limited English vocabulary, would not know its meaning or be able to object. His left foot now tapped the floor furiously. "I even checked to ascertain Mr. Mendosa's lot could not be built upon until its clouded title was resolved by a legal proceeding." I had set the stage for Hawthorne to put Teri on the stand to confirm my account by asking simple, leading questions.

"Cross-examination, Mr. Mendosa?" The judge asked.

Mendosa got out of his chair and approached me shaking his finger menacingly. "You're lying, you son of a dog!" He shouted.

"Objection, your Honor. Not a question and no foundation," chimed Hawthorne.

"Granted. Mr. Mendosa you must ask questions on cross-examination and they have to be relevant to the case and relate to what Mr. Dubois has just testified," the judge admonished.

"It's not questions. He's just lying. Don't I have a right to say that?" Mendosa stated heatedly.

"That's not the function of cross-examination. If you believe Mr. Dubois is not telling his account accurately, you must probe his testimony and gain admissions by asking him questions," the judge said with exasperation.

Mendosa looked at me with malice and asked, "You're lying aren't you?"

"No, I've sworn an oath to tell the truth and that's what you heard me testify to. You'll have your opportunity to tell your side of the story as a witness," I stated calmly.

"Your Honor, may I call my final witness?" Hawthorne asked trying not to gloat.

"Yes, you may." Addressing Mendosa, he said, "Perhaps now you realize the folly of trying to be your own lawyer. You put yourself at a disadvantage by not knowing legal procedure and how to conduct a case," the judge said more kindly for the record while his court clerk smirked.

"Why didn't you appoint a lawyer for me then?" Mendosa remonstrated angrily.

"Because this is a civil matter. Attorneys are appointed only in criminal matters according to our Constitution and then only if you are charged with a serious crime and can't afford an attorney," the judge replied and motioned Hawthorne to proceed.

"I call the plaintiff, Miss Rios." Teri took her seat in the witness chair I just vacated.

"Now, Miss Rios, did Mr. Mendosa ask you for your life savings and explain what he planned to use them for?"

"No, he never asked or explained anything. He waited for me to go to work and when I returned, my money was gone along with his clothes and personal effects."

"Did you ask for Mr. Dubois' help in getting your life savings back as you heard him testify in court today?"

"Yes," Teri answered demurely as Hawthorne had prepared her to do.

"No further questions your Honor," Hawthorne piped cheerily.

The whole prepared scene of leading questions had Mendosa on his feet and shouting, *"Puta de perro.* You want to destroy my business. You're in bed and cahoots with all these *Gringos.* You double-crossing bitch," Mendosa's diatribe was cut short by Judge Roberts pounding his gavel furiously.

"Do you wish to testify and give your account in this matter?" The judge asked in a stern voice leaving no doubt he'd cite Mendosa for contempt of court if he continued his diatribe. Mendosa reluctantly took a seat in the witness chair.

"Like I say before, she loan me the money to get my business back. She want to have her job back. I tell her she get her money when I get store built and get wine to sell. Now she want to ruin my business 'cause I have new girlfriend," he stated trying to control his anger and avoid Teri's menacing stare.

"Cross-exam Mr. Hawthorne?"

"No your Honor. I'd like to call Miss Rios briefly as a rebuttal witness, if I may."

"Proceed,"

"Miss Rios do you make more money working for the Dubois' than you made working for Mr. Mendosa?"

"Yes, I make more than two times what I make in his store," she said pointing at Mendosa with a venomous look.

"Is it true you are now a partner with the Dubois' in their wine bar and food stand on the wharf and share in partnership profits from the business?"

"Yes, an' I never agree to work for that macho snake again. He lies!"

"Thank you Miss Rios. You may step down. That's all, your Honor. We rest our case."

"Any rebuttal, Mr. Mendosa? The judge queried.

Mendosa just sat in his chair pounding his boot on the floor and sputtering inaudible words to himself in Spanish as his face flushed darker shades of crimson.

"Fine, then the hearing is closed. Give me five minutes and I'll announce my judgment in the case." The judge then summoned his clerk who was salivating at Mendosa's discomfort and eyeing Teri with lust. After conferring with the judge, the clerk slipped out of the courtroom. Three minutes later he returned in the company of two, burly, armed court bailiffs who took up positions behind Mendosa's table.

Judge Roberts resumed his seat overlooking both counsel tables and after studying papers on his desk, started to speak, "Judgment is awarded the petitioner in the amount of $685.00 owed her in principal sum by the respondent plus additional amounts of $275.00 in interest on that sum and $685.00 in punitive damages for the wrongful taking of the original sum. Costs and attorneys fees in the amount of $750.00 are awarded petitioner's attorney. Petitioner's demand to levy the entire judgment including attorneys' fees on respondent's shipment of Chilean wine in the hold of the Chilean ship, "Esperanza," at anchor in the bay under customs bond is approved. Petitioner may seize wine from the shipment in an amount equal to the judgment based on the purchase price of the wine as it appears on the ship's manifest. Respondent shall bear the cost of customs duty on the seized amount."

As the judge started to sign the appropriate orders Hawthorne had prepared and submitted in advance, Mendoza jumped out of his seat, pulled a two-shot Derringer pistol from inside his vest, pointed it at Teri and fired just as the nearest bailiff knocked his arm upward. I instinctively hit the deck at the sight of the pistol while Hawthorne, his face drained white, and Teri froze in place. As I looked up from the floor, the bailiffs were hustling Mendosa out the door and on the way to jail. The Derringer was on the floor within reach. I picked it up and handed it to the judge who would tag it for evidence. The only damage I could see from the shots were two holes in the bear's rump on the California State Flag hanging on the far wall.

California Gold Rush Journal
∽ PART 2 ∾

CHAPTER THIRTY-ONE
San Francisco — December, 1851 – March 1852

Afte we recovered from the melee in the court, I invited the judge, his wife, Teri and Hawthorne to join our table for dinner the coming weekend. I decided with Teri to visit the "Esperanza" to select and remove wine that afternoon before Raoul's new benefactor could secure his release from jail on a bribe or bail. Jailors were notorious for accepting bribes, especially the prospect of being entertained and indulged for free by the coterie of "señoritas" at Señora Batista's bagnio.

Armed with Judge Roberts' orders and accompanied by a court bailiff and a sheriff's marshal to serve the court papers and execute the levy, I hired the largest lighter available to row us to the "Esperanza," which rested at anchor under custom's seal not far from the Long Wharf and our own ship.

Our boarding party was met by Captain Rodrigo Gomez, a tall, fair-skinned man in spit and polish uniform who mistakenly assumed we were customs clearance officials. "Welcome aboard. So happy to see you," the captain said in halting English while pumping our hands.

Teri quickly disabused him of the notion we were welcome customs officials prepared to clear his cargo so he could reload for the return to Valparaiso. The Sheriff's marshal handed him copies of Judge Roberts' orders to the now thoroughly confused captain. He stared at the papers in bewilderment. The court bailiff summarized the judge's order in English which Teri translated emphatically and demanded we be led immediately to where Raoul's wine was stored in the hold.

The captain stared at the many court seals stamped on the official papers and gave a resigned sigh. He ordered a ship's officer and several crew members to lead us into the hold. Most of Mendosa's wine was in casks, but some of the better wine was aged and bottled and ready for immediate sale in his store. We selected all the cases of bottled wine which included rich cabernet sauvignons, merlots, chardonnays and even several cases of champagne from the best Chilean vintners. As Teri was familiar with the wines, she cherry-picked all the best bottled wines and barrels. It took three trips on the rented lighter to transfer our new wine to the hold of the Eliza.

Teri ordered a case of Chilean champagne and aged cabernet sauvignon sent to our restaurant for our celebratory weekend dinner. Manon and I agreed earlier to buy the Chilean wines from Teri at cost, store them on the Eliza and sell them in our wine bar. With the judge's award of punitive damages, Teri would now have a significant amount to add to her nest egg. She'd agreed to run the wine bar for a minimum three years as part of the partnership agreement. At the end of that period, she planned to lease a shop in town and operate her own bodega selling groceries and wine.

Upon my return to our restaurant in late afternoon, Manon sat me down with a small carafe of red wine and bowl of bouillabaisse.

Between gulps of wine and slurps of soup, I recounted our

court adventure. We'd had no time for lunch in our rush to secure Mendosa's wine and I was famished. When I got to the bit about Mendosa's shooting his Derringer, Manon registered shock.

"*C'est pas vrai! Le salaud.* Teri won't be safe once he gets out of jail," Manon exclaimed furiously.

"Unfortunately, it's true if the bastard gets out of jail. I've invited Judge Roberts to dinner this Saturday with his wife so we can celebrate Teri's revenge and discuss how to ensure he goes to prison for a long time for attempted murder in the judge's court. The judge will see he's convicted and hopefully, he can be deported to Chile to serve his term. I'm going to explore with Hawthorne and the judge whether Teri can bring a civil action against Mendosa for assault or other action to get a big judgment she can levy on his property. He won't be able to run a wine shop in jail. Teri wants to have her own store eventually, so what better reward for Teri, than to get Raoul's store for herself? It would be 'poetic justice' as the Yankees say."

"My Big Boy is full of clever ideas. Do you think it could happen?"

"Why not? It all depends on what Judge Roberts says. If a civil case could be engineered into his courtroom and he's amenable to try it without a jury, Teri would have a big advantage. Raoul has to persuade his protector to hire an attorney and defend Teri's suit. It may be worth her while to recover her investment in his store even if she drops him as a loser."

"She will be furious with both Raoul and Teri, non?"

"Yes, but she's a business woman. We'd have to persuade her to cut her losses; convince her he and his store are a lost cause."

"An' how you propose to do that Big Boy? Hire some scoundrels to harass her whores? Threaten to burn down her bagnio?" Manon sounded intrigued.

"No, no threats or harassment from us. We go to the Executive Committee of the Committee of Vigilance and persuade them to investigate her bagnio and close it if she doesn't back off. Remember, they were investigating the leading brothels at the same time they outfoxed the Sheriff and Governor to retrieve their prisoners. I'm sure some of her "señoritas" have been sold to her by pimps and would be happy to turn the tables on their madam. We invite Ah Toy and her protector on the Committee to a private dinner and explore options. Ah Toy might be pleased to put a competitor out of business. We stir the hornet's nest enough, she'll be tempted to back off to safeguard her profitable business; we'd have nothing to lose."

"My Big Boy Papa has such delightfully wicked ideas! Manon likes." I was rewarded with a big, sloppy kiss that left bouillabaisse sauce smeared on both our faces and had us laughing until we nearly choked.

"Manon also has a surprise," she said seductively. Oh boy, I thought not another set of twins on the way. We'd started making love again and however hard we tried to be careful, we had been carried away on a couple of occasions recently. "You know the woman from the mining camp near Sonora you told me about? The one who dresses like a man and works alongside them in the river? Well, she and her brother are in town. I invite them to dinner Saturday, too."

"You mean you saw them? The woman they call 'Marie Pantalon?'"

"No, she sent a message to the restaurant with your business card saying she'd love to join us for dinner Saturday, if it's okay. I had Rose deliver a message to her hotel to join us Saturday at 8 P.M. Looks like we gonna need a big table for all our guests, non? The restaurant is fully booked, so we gonna have to squeeze tables to make more room."

"Do you think we should cancel the judge and Hawthorne and have the celebration another evening?"

"No, more fun this way. We make a big table next to the

entryway. Manon will make a special menu; she gonna call it 'Victory Menu,' and everybody's gonna be happy when we serve Teri's champagne to all our guests, yes?"

"You're the boss. Sounds like we're going to have a memorable evening, but what about the twins? I'm supposed to baby-sit them."

"Hah, Big Boy is worried, yes? If Manon can juggle two full-time jobs — running her restaurant and motherhood — she's surely not gonna leave poor Papa changing diapers and bouncing babies on his knee when he has to persuade Judge Roberts to lock up Raoul and throw away the key, non?" I gave her my best little boy sheepish look. "Manon has hired a new house-keeper and babysitter while you and Teri were busy skewering Raoul and pinching his best wines," Manon said eyes twinkling and mischievous.

"That was quick. Who is she and how do you know she's to be trusted with our little ones?"

"Because she's more like your Manon than any other woman I meet here so far. She came to this country to escape lack of opportunity for women in France, male control and family pressure. Her employer in Paris raped her and then when she gets pregnant, he arranges to marry her to one of his clerks by bribing him with a small dowry and a threat to discharge him if he doesn't marry her. She says no, I won't marry the rapist's employee who I don't love or want in my bed or to raise my child, so the patron can wash his hands of her. The patron paid her parents 'hush money' to go along with his plan. She still refused even though her parents threaten to disown her and chuck her out on the street unless she does what papa says. So, she finds the patron's hush money and runs away. She buys a ticket for San Francisco with the money."

"You mean she came over alone and pregnant with no one to protect her?" I said stupefied at such a story.

"Yes, she even had to agree to work on the ship cleaning up vomit and emptying night soil buckets when she was nauseous from her own pregnancy. Her baby boy was born two days after our twins in a room she shared with four other women. She needs a job badly, but she has pride and has refused offers to work in the sex trade even though she's very pretty. She wants to establish a nursery school where she can help mothers like herself, take in kids with working mothers and school them. I told her we can do that together. We start with her boy and our twins. An' when the three are walking, we find a nearby location and expand with other kids. I tell her my clever husband will find a suitable location, yes?" Manon's big black eyes glistened with emotion.

Oh boy, I thought Manon's crusade to empower women in the New World had just taken on a new sphere of interest. After experiencing Mendosa's failed attempts to intimidate and subjugate Teri, then kill her when he couldn't succeed, I realized Manon was right. More and more single mothers were arriving weekly. The newspapers estimated that twice as many women would arrive in 1852 as in 1851. Most of them would be French and German women and there were extremely limited options for child care. Not all would be able to marry successfully for some time and would want employment opportunities outside the sex trade. Why not be on the ground floor to meet this new need? The need to care for our twins was a case in point. Combining childcare with a nursery education was already a needed business that would only grow and expand with the changing, more permanent population. "Now that I think about it, I think your plan is a wonderful one," I said sincerely.

Manon threw her arms around my neck and rewarded me with another big, sloppy kiss. "Yum, yum, papa tastes good," she said coming back for an encore. "Manon is happy to have a husband who listens to his wife and understands when she knows best what we should do."

"What's the name of our new housekeeper and when does she start work?" I whispered in her ear as we both wiped our faces with napkins.

Manon was about to reply when there was knock on the door and a very pretty young woman with a radiant smile popped in as Manon and I were still in our lingering embrace and ready to erase the last traces of bouillabaisse from my mouth.

"Oh, sorry to interrupt. The twins are hollering to be fed," she said with an enigmatic smile at the scene she'd interrupted.

Manon laughed as the woman's cheeks flushed a lively pink.

"*Chéri* meet our new housekeeper, Monique Boudin. Monique, meet my husband, Pierre." We shook hands as Monique regarded me boldly with curious, beautiful lavender-hued eyes. She was of medium height, in her early twenties with an angelic, heart-shaped face with dimples. She wore a China crepe scarf to control thick, masses of raven-black hair. The bodice of her muslin dress was stained with seeped breast milk and the apron over her skirt smelled of talc and baby oil.

"*Chéri*, why don't you two get acquainted while I feed the twins and check on Stephen, Monique's little boy," Manon said sweetly. To Monique she said, "Pierre and I have been discussing your idea to establish a full-time nursery and school when our three little ones start to walk."

As there was still fish soup in the pot and wine in the carafe, I motioned Monique to take a seat. "I was just finishing a late lunch. There's still plenty of bouillabaisse and wine. Won't you join me for a bowl and glass of wine?"

"Oh yes, I'd love to. It smells heavenly." She took her seat and poured herself a half glass of wine while I fetched another spoon and bowl, a loaf of multi-grain bread and cheese board with a local goat cheese. I ladled most of the remaining soup into her bowl and cut hunks of thick bread for us both. I poured myself a glass of red wine and smeared a big gob of the now viscous cheese on my bread.

"Manon told me a bit of your ordeal to get here on your own. You're a brave and admirable woman to seek your future here. Your idea of a nursery-school is exciting and in my estimation will be a much needed new institution with more and more families and prospective brides arriving weekly. When the projected five thousand French arrive in spring on ships sponsored by the Lottery of the Golden Ingots, there'll be an ever increased need for all sorts of French schools, but most of them will be too poor to pay for schooling or child-care until they get established." I said while watching her spoon her soup ever more quickly. It was probably her first decent meal since quitting France. I ladled the remaining soup into her bowl. She smiled gratefully saying, "Thank you, it's delicious; your wife's a talented cook."

"Now that we've expelled and deported our arsonists and merchants are building fire resistant buildings wherever possible, some of the more wealthy merchants and city moguls are calling for more money for permanent institutions and city improvements—better firefighting equipment, digging of artificial reservoirs and water wells at short intervals to quench fires quickly, neighborhood schools, health clinics and hospitals, and streets of macadam instead of our repugnant, wooden-planked streets and sidewalks fouled by manure, raw garbage and sewage."

"There are many proposals afloat to organize benevolent societies to bankroll these projects, but the city reacts by raising taxes on businesses like ours. I just received a tax notification that our restaurant would have to pay the city two-thirds of the cost of replacing the soiled and disgusting plank sidewalk and street in front of our restaurant. Alas, any nursery school we establish will receive no municipal support, especially as it will benefit French kids. I'm interested to hear your ideas on how we might organize and a run a self-supporting nursery school."

Monique nodded, then swabbed her bowl with bread, smeared a large gob of cheese on the remaining morsel and took a small sip of wine before responding, "I had a chance to think about it a lot on the long, tedious, ship voyage. From what I've seen in the short time I've been here, most French don't make any effort to learn English; it was the same on the ship. I want my son to learn English so he can compete with the dominant English speaking establishment that runs the city. Manon shares this goal. Even Georges' wife, Nelly, expressed interest in my proposal," she paused to swallow a hunk of bread and cheese and wash it down with red wine.

"The nursery school should be bilingual. We teach French and English to our charges. We start them on the secondary language as soon as they are enrolled. We make fun games and read them nursery rhymes in both languages and they'll sing kids' songs in both languages."

"You'd start the language training that early, why?"

"Because that's how I learned to speak the German dialect at three years old. My grandmother took care of me often, and even though she spoke French and the German dialect, she spoke to me only in the German dialect, so I learned to speak it fluently over the years. I got my job in Paris with a wine firm that imported wines from the Mosel and the Black Forest area wineries in the south of Germany because I spoke and wrote the language and the boss didn't."

"And you think it will work with kids here outside a family setting?"

"Of course, kids learn from each other. Even many well-heeled Yankees send their kids to Paris to learn the language and culture. That's what Nelly said her parents did with her and she met many others in Paris, who'd been sent for the same reasons. As for your concern about financing, the school shouldn't be limited to French or Latin language kids. We want

English speaking kids from the affluent, nouveau-riche Americans who're building their mansions on Telegraph Hill and the higher reaches of the city with the best views." She paused take a sip of wine and I filled her glass.

"What better way is there for our French kids to learn English, and American kids to learn French than from kids doing fun activities and playing together. They'll learn from the other kids in order to communicate and be understood. I and other instructors and monitors just facilitate a natural process of child activity and curiosity."

"Very interesting, and you're sure well-to-do American families will pay to have their infants and kids learn French this way?"

"Yes, but it will probably won't be the rich who can afford private governesses and tutors; it'll be the nouveau riche and social climbers from modest backgrounds who want to give their kids an aura of refinement and class. That's why French women work in the gambling palaces and American men proposition every French woman who walks on the street. French language, culture and women, even of low social status in Paris, are perceived as debonair, sexy and chic."

"Won't you need instructors who are qualified to teach English as well to attract the clientele you described?"

"Yes, of course, that's what interests Nelly. She's starting to become fluent in French and is superbly qualified to teach English at all levels. She wants to be part of the project. We'll need to publish a promotional pamphlet detailing the curriculum, bilingual objectives and the qualifications of teachers and minders. Nelly and her well-to-do background and private school education in the East Coast will be essential to convince Americans to pay to enroll their kids."

"So, we promote an aura of exclusivity?"

"Precisely, and we do it before anyone else gets the idea,"

Monique said convincingly.

"Well, I'm sold," I said as Manon pushed her way through the doors and Monique took her leave to resume her duties upstairs.

"So, *Chéri*, what do you think of Monique and her plans?"

"I think she'll make a terrific business partner in a bilingual pre-school. She's intelligent, logical and persuasive; she's got a good business plan that dovetails with our needs for our kids and the fact she's very attractive will aid in selling the concept to the newly rich American daddies and their wives. As she said, 'French chic' works wonders in San Francisco."

"Good, I knew you would like her, especially the big violet eyes, yes?" Manon said provocatively.

"I personally prefer big black eyes," I said tongue-in-cheek. What's her living situation? She'll be working late and will need an escort home." "Yes, I thought we could rent her our cabin on the Eliza since we now live upstairs. That way Georges can escort Nelly, Giselle, and Monique with her baby back to the ship once we close the restaurant, yes?"

"The way she gobbled down your bouillabaisse and her bread and cheese argues for providing room and board as part of her employment with us. She can take her meals with Georges and the women. She loves your cooking."

Manon smiled broadly at my suggestion. "I will tell her. She will be relieved to have a private, safe place to live and work."

"By the way, how did you find her? Through Pierre-Louis' wife?"

"Non, I ask Dr. Benoit for a nursing mother like me in case my milk fails. He talked to the midwife who delivered Stephen and recommended Monique to me. I wanted more than just a housekeeper."

I laughed. "My Smart Cookie sure got a lot more than a housekeeper and nursemaid. *Chapeau!* Hats off to my clever wife."

California Gold Rush Journal
∽ PART 2 ∾

CHAPTER THIRTY-TWO
San Francisco — December, 1851 – March 1852

We were all excited in anticipation of Teri's celebratory dinner. Manon supervised the preparation of our repast. While the restaurant would serve reserved guests our set menu that night of *terrine de canard truffée, les écrevisses à la nage, la côte de boeuf à la béarnaise avec pommes frites et la tarte aux pommes* (duck terrine with truffles, local crayfish cooked in white wine lightly spiced with sweet dill, tender filet mignon steak with thin French fries to soak up the sauce *béarnaise,* and apple tart for dessert).

For our special celebration, she prepared *la truffe en feuilletage, l'ormeau sauce au beurre, le caneton aux choux, et les crêpes au cognac* (truffles in a light, buttery pastry shell, abalone steaks with a drawn butter sauce, young duck cooked with cabbage in port wine and cognac and served with potatoes soufflé, and crepes soaked in cognac for dessert). Manon showed our two apprentices how to make our special dinner while Henri cooked the set menu.

Manon announced to arriving diners that we were hosting

a small celebration dinner with friends this evening and invited them to share complimentary champagne. As soon as reserved guests arrived at 8 P.M. and were seated, Georges poured them champagne while Giselle and Nelly served plates of terrine and baskets of late-baked baguettes. Manon had invited Marie Suize, now known as Marie Pantalon, at 8 P.M. and our other guests for 8:30 P.M., so she'd have a chance to visit with Marie before the others arrived.

Marie Suize and her brother's arrival at 8 P.M. on the dot created quite a stir among the seated diners. Marie doffed her rough wool winter cape and miner's slouch hat and hung them on one of several clothes trees by the entryway. She was a small, wiry woman in her late twenties or early thirties with short, rough-sheared hair the color of dark oak streaked with silver. She was dressed in miner's attire — heavy buckskin trousers stuffed in knee-length boots, red calico shirt and red-checkered neck scarf. She'd ignored our notice for guests to remove any firearms and check them with Georges at the bar; she'd buckled a holster housing a large Colt six-shot pistol and about twenty rounds of ammunition loosely around her narrow waist like a gunslinger. Her face was sun-weathered and she greeted us with bright, hazel-green eyes. She carried a large hat box under one arm.

Her brother, Albert, was a swarthy twenty-one year old with blue eyes, broad shoulders, and still baby-faced despite his bulging muscles and deep suntan. He was dressed just like his older sister and also carried a large box. Manon led them to our table and poured them Chilean champagne in special flutes, long cylindrical French champagne glasses. Manon and I joined them in a toast while Giselle temporarily took over Manon's hostess functions.

"Thank you both for inviting us to your special restaurant. It's a unexpected treat we could only dream about up in Jackson. We rarely go into Sonora except for supplies and are used to simple miner's fare—venison or rabbit stew, rice, beans, lentils, potatoes and strong, black coffee," Marie said.

"What brings you to San Francisco?" Manon said. "According to Pierre, the merchants in Sonora were certain you'd stay in winter quarters near your diggings in order to use the extra water to wash gullies for gold and to prospect future claims?"

"Two things really," Marie replied looking at her brother who lifted his glass for a refill. "Albert is home sick and I thought a visit to San Francisco would be a good change. Also, we've been quite successful mining this last season. I'm not happy with the bank's handling our money and affairs in Sonora and thought your husband could help me find a banker here and perhaps advise me on investments. I'm determined to invest my gold in California land and businesses. Albert will eventually return to France, so he wants to check out options and bank here as well. If our money is in San Francisco, we can't be tempted to spend or gamble it locally."

"So you plan to stay permanently in California?" Manon said pleased.

"Oh yes, there's nothing for me in France, neither in Paris or Savoy. I watched Mother struggle to feed and care for ten kids. With crop failures, sickness and ever hungry mouths to feed, my mother worked herself to the bone in our fields. The only future there for girls like me was to clean houses, work in the fields for a bowl of soup, marry like my mother and wind up saddled with kids and struggle all my life to feed my family. In Paris, the only work available for country girls was to sew for a pittance, work as a maid, factory girl or prostitute. Albert, not being the eldest son, couldn't inherit our land under French law, so when he heard about the riches in California, I decided to accompany him." Marie paused to finish her flute of champagne. "Hmm, what a treat, it's only the second time in my life I've drunk champagne."

"What determined you to mine the rivers rather than seek employment in San Francisco?" Manon queried.

"Frankly, the opportunities for women here in 1850 were no better than in Paris except perhaps I could earn more. Because I was French and there were so few women in the town, men assumed I was a prostitute. I couldn't walk down the street even in my long dress to my ankles and bonnet without men accosting me and demanding, *'voulez-vous coucher avec moi?'* The more persistent ones would grab my arm and thrust a fist full of banknotes or small sack of gold dust in my face and become indignant when I refused to have sex with them. Most single French women worked as card dealers, dancers, musicians and waitresses or hostesses in revealing dresses in the gambling palaces and most could be had for sex at a steep price after work. Other than the sex trade, the only jobs available for women here were to serve men—washing, cooking or selling liquor." Marie paused and I refilled her champagne glass. She took several sips before continuing.

"Fortunately, I had Albert with me most of the time and he protected me from actual physical abuse. We decided to get to the mines as soon as possible. After listening to accounts of failed miners working as laborers on the wharves to earn passage home, we pooled our meager savings from my work as a maid in a rooming house and Albert as a stevedore and outfitted ourselves for the rigors of living in the harsh conditions of the mining camps we'd learned about. We left San Francisco for Stockton and on to Sonora. Albert learned from working on the wharves that a group of fellow Savoyards had a camp near Jackson and were mining stream banks not far from Mokelumne. We found their camp and they were enthralled to see me. They assumed I'd cook for the camp, wash and mend their clothes and be their camp maid."

Manon laughed and clapped her hands with glee, "And you

told them they had the wrong woman, right?"

"You betcha, I let them know in no uncertain terms I was no one's maid or cook. I came to mine gold and make my fortune just like them alongside my brother."

"How did they react to that?" I asked.

"Like typical spoiled, self-centered males, they made a ruckus complaining women didn't do mining; that it was too difficult physically for a woman and in any case, it was unladylike. I pointed out that I had seen wives working rockers while their husbands fed them with river gravels; that I'd seen Indian squaws with papooses on their back panning for gold, and entire Mexican families including wives and daughters working river gravels on the way to their camp."

"How did they react to that?" I asked.

"They sulked, claiming it wasn't right. Next day I tried to dig river gravels in my dress and shoes and only succeeded in ruining my shoes and getting my petticoats soaked. That evening I cut my hair and donned the men's costume — baggy pants, flannel shirt, high boots, slouch hat and neck bandana — and worked beside my brother dressed like a man. They told me it was against the law for a woman to wear a man's clothes, that I would be fined. I said 'phooey! If I can do a man's work, I can wear a man's clothes.' As they were fellow countrymen, I had little fear they'd denounce or expose me. We were all taking several dollars a day in gold, so they soon ignored me though never accepted me 'as one of the boys.'"

"Did that ever change?" Manon asked

"Not for a long time. The harsh conditions took their toll on most of us. We were often cold and had to eat moldy food in the inclement weather; we lacked fresh food and especially fresh vegetables and fruits. Our camps were filthy and our latrines fouled. Many took sick with grippes, scurvy and even cholera from the latrine seepage polluting our drinking and cooking water. I bartered tools, trinkets and knives with the local Miwok Indians in exchange for tubers, wild legumes and trout which I boiled into a medicinal broth to help cure the most sick and keep my brother and me well. The miner's diet of beans, salt pork, flour, potatoes and rancid cooking oil and grease is both monotonous and unhealthy." Marie paused to drain her glass of champagne before continuing.

"But we were taking so much gold out of our concessions that we couldn't be bothered to hunt or take time to go to town for fresh supplies. Later as other women appeared, exhausted with husbands and families from crossing the vast American plains, we were doing so well, I could hire the newcomers to work for me for $6.00 day. Their wives helped them at times, but only I wore pants. So, eventually the miners from home, and even the newly arrived ones, accepted me as a good, but eccentric character. Some started calling me, "Marie Pantalon," and others, "Madame Pantalon."

"What about the French working the hill above Moke-lumne? Are they still doing well?" I asked.

"Lordy, yes. They're still taking millions out of French Hill. The areas nearby are also rich in gold. It's fairly easy mining as it's not embedded in quartz veins. There's a lot of really big nuggets still being found in the old river channel," Marie said as our other guests arrived.

Manon's menu was a rousing success at our table. Neither Judge Roberts and his wife nor Marie and her brother had ever tasted the delicate, nutty, buttery flavored abalone steaks our apprentices pan fried to perfection. Before the dessert service, Marie made an announcement, "This is the best meal I've ever eaten. I want to honor my gracious hosts with some special gifts from our neck of the woods." That said, she opened her large hatbox and pulled out several woven baskets and present-ed them to Manon. Her brother opened his box and handed over several wooden and bone implements.

"These are all the work of our local Miwok Indians that the miners call "Digger Indians," Marie stated. I thought you'd like to see quality of cooking baskets and utensils our Indians use. These are the same Indians most uneducated and uncouth miners call 'savages' and 'unclean heathens,'" she said handing Manon a large Indian basket decorated with a crisscross lozenge design. "This is a typical Miwok cooking basket."

"How do they cook with a basket?" Manon asked. "Won't the cooking fire burn the basket?"

Marie laughed. "It could if they're not diligent. They use rounded, granite river stones of various sizes as cooking stones. These they place directly in the fire pit until they are white-hot. They remove the stones with these tools," Marie picked up two objects from her brother's box. "This looped string stick and wooden fire tongs are used to lift the cooking stones and place them in cooking baskets filled with water. The stones heat the water and the cook stirs constantly with this paddle stick," she said picking up hardwood paddle-shaped implement very similar to what we French use to stir soups we cook. "They cook four acorn staples this way— a gruel soup, a mush-like porridge, and two mixtures they thicken to make a thin biscuit and acorn bread they remove from the baskets and cook in earthen ovens. They also cook edible plants and legumes this way."

We were all so fascinated with the objects that Manon waved off Rose who had a platter of crepes for dessert. Marie handed Manon two smaller baskets made in the same way — coiled ropes tied so tightly, they were waterproof. Each basket was decorated with a different geometrical design. One basket was a dipper basket for water and the other a sifter basket. "I could only bring a selection of the smaller baskets and tools. The Miwoks make many other beautiful baskets—baskets for winnowing acorn meal, for seed beating, burden baskets for carrying goods, and gathering baskets," Marie said.

"How did you acquire these and learn so much about their culture?" Judge Roberts' wife asked.

"The Miwok way of life has been disastrously affected by the arrival of so many miners who have overrun and destroyed much of their traditional hunting and fishing grounds. The Miwok rely on the mule deer, longhorn antelope and dwarf elk for survival in winter, which like this year can be very harsh. Their game was plentiful before the miners arrived with their rifles and shotguns. The Indians used snares, woven traps and collective herding and beating to surround the game and direct them to openings where they could kill them easily. That's all changed as miners rely on specialist hunters to kill most of the game and the rivers are so polluted with silt and detritus from mining that fish cannot spawn in their usual gravel beds. In short, many Miwok are starving and forced to beg for food and eat their undernourished guard dogs. I trade food to the women for baskets and tools like these," Marie said pointing to the baskets and tools she and her brother brought as gifts.

"Why do they call them 'Digger Indians?'" Judge Roberts asked as Rose set up the small table and charcoal brassier to do the flambé of cognac for the crepes. Manon excused herself to attend to her other guests and ensure their menu and evening was satisfactory.

"The Miwok use a three to four foot long digging stick to dig bulbs and tubers in the sun-baked ground during summer. The stick is made from mahogany and the tip hardened by fire. It's more efficient than a steel spade as you don't have to remove as much dirt."

"The accounts we read in the local papers claim these Indians are lazy, uncouth savages who go naked, put bones in their noses and steal from miners at every opportunity. Isn't this the case?" Judge Roberts asked pointedly.

"They are certainly not lazy," Marie retorted. "Their life even before the arrival of the miners was hard, especially for the women who do most of the work — child rearing, basket making and food gathering. The men hunted big game for the meat they need to survive during winter. Their caches of acorns are not sufficient for survival without meat in winter. Yet the miners shoot most of the big game and edible fowl. Miners who don't know or respect Miwok culture pass judgment on physical attributes they see as heathen."

"Can you give us some examples?" the judge queried.

"Sure, the men wear only a simple breech clout of buckskin over their genitals and the women the same with the addition of a grass skirt or apron from the waist to the knees and the children go naked until about ten years old. This is summer attire to adapt to the extreme heat in the valleys and foothills. In winter, they wear blankets and dressed deer, bear, puma and coyote skins and live in winter lodges. The poorest ones have to wear rabbit skins and you see some today dressed in several layers of miner's clothes."

"Why miner's clothes?" The judge queried.

"Most miners don't wash themselves or their clothes. When they're too filthy to wear to a fandango dance or weekend gambling tent or bordello, they just throw them away and buy new ones. The Indians pick up these clothes and any other discarded items; they wash them and wear them in cold weather." Marie paused long enough to give the judge a severe look.

"You asked why the Indians are stigmatized and deemed as low as the Chinese, they call 'Celestials' or 'John, the Chinaman.' It's mostly due to ignorance; the miners make no effort to learn the ways of the Miwok or other California Indians. They judge them savages because their women don't cover their breasts, and they pierce their noses and all wear tattoos and body paint on ceremonial occasions. They ignore the fact these peoples have lived here peaceably with their customs for thousands of years; they respect the land and the animals they must kill to survive; they don't believe land should be 'owned' as the miners, who think by claiming it, it is theirs as a matter of right along with its gold which has no value to Indians. So, desire for riches and property dictate the belief that the only good Indian is a dead one, unless you covet his wife or daughter as a slave or sex object," Marie said heatedly.

Oh boy, I thought. This could get quickly out of hand and ruin our celebration even though I agreed with everything Marie said as it was the same treatment I saw of the displaced Maidu and Modoc Indians in my trip to the northern placer mines. I knew Judge Roberts was not above baiting Marie to make her even angrier. I was sure the judge had never seen a real Indian, but had seen plenty of Chinese who almost all officials held in low esteem. I signaled Rose who waited patiently by the kitchen door to start the dessert service and flambé the crepes. I invited Judge Roberts to join me for a tumbler of Calvados and a cigar at the bar while Rose entertained our guests with the dessert. I needed to speak privately with him on Teri's behalf as I'd promised Manon I would do.

When we returned to the table to enjoy our dessert, Manon had returned and steered the conversation to appreciation of fine wines and cooking and her tale of how she was able to procure the abalone and other specialties. Manon, sensing Marie's ire, invited her to join us for dinner on Sunday when our table would have no other guests. During dessert and after-dinner drinks, Teri regaled us with her version of the trial and subduing of Raoul Mendosa. Marie Pantalon's wry smile at the account of the ex-boyfriend's demise seemed to put her in a better mood.

"DIGGER INDIANS IN NATIVE TO
WESTERN ATTIRE," 1851.

California Gold Rush Journal
∽ PART 2 ∾

CHAPTER THIRTY-THREE
San Francisco – January – June, 1852

We were extremely pleased with our restaurant's performance, success and profits through and beyond the holiday season. Manon's menus were distinctive and seductive to all gourmands. Her restaurant was deemed a must visit by all visitors to San Francisco who could afford to indulge themselves and more importantly, Manon developed a significant repeat business among both French and American residents. More and more, locals reserved our private dining room for festive occasions, private parties and business reunions.

Our success corresponded with the overall regeneration of the city after the two disastrous fires of 1851. The brick manufacturers in Happy Valley flourished as did the city's sawmills, iron foundries, steam-engine works and boat building yards. More and more immigrants with construction skills forsook fortune hunting in the mountain streams for the steady, well-paying jobs the ever expanding city provided.

Huge steam-powered excavators nick-named "Paddy" were

heard throughout the city pushing sand dunes into the bay to create highly sought after, shoreline lots. The Paddies also excavated lots to create cellars for the new more fire resistant brick and stone structures built to replace all-wooden structures. As a result, the large sand hills of First, Second and Bush Streets were rapidly disappearing.

Newspaper columnists exclaimed tongue-in-cheek that gold was to be had even by mining San Francisco's sand dunes. Gold was found in quartz quarried from Telegraph Hill, in earth excavated along Broadway and from the new fire wells excavated on Stockton Street. While the most likely explanation was that careless merchants and miners seeking to hide their gold had stashed caches underground, the "gold in the city" theme helped excite the imagination. Some folks went so far as to dig up their back yards. Most found earlier buried trash full of oyster shells, animal bones, empty bottles and broken pottery.

Despite a serious outbreak of cholera in 1851, little was done to make the streets, businesses and habitations more sanitary. Streets were still covered with smelly, black, squishy mud. No attempt was made to control the fouling of street by carriage, omnibus and cab's horses or carters' mules. People discarded rubbish in dunghills, open rubbish dumps, where the city's large rat population fought for tidbits of garbage, and household sweepings were routinely swept into the streets. As most city folk drew drinking and cooking water from wells, it was no wonder that given the porous nature of the city's sandy soil, some became fouled by the proliferation of rats and garbage.

While the demise of the Sydney Ducks reduced arson attacks, political corruption persisted. There were more petty crimes and most were not prosecuted. Most miners, merchants and residents ventured out cautiously and well-armed. Women needed escorts to all but the most fashionable areas of the business district. With more people with greater wealth, the city featured more boutiques offering the latest Parisian fashions and the most successful courtesans parading them on the streets. Trade and profits were up over 1851. More and more mansions appeared on the heights of Broadway, California, Sacramento and Washington Streets. And, of course, there were more and diverse places for dissipation and amusement.

Many successful miners and businessmen, who returned to the East Coast after making their pile of gold or profits, actually returned to San Francisco. They missed the marvelous climate, the newness of everything, and the range of amusements was not the same in the more conservative East Coast towns and cities. Here one could see and bet on contests between a bull and a bear, yell and bet at Mexican cockfights, gamble around the clock, enjoy the pleasures of upscale parlor houses offering the services of exotic women from all over the globe and venture into Little China to join the dissipated addicts in the many opium parlors or buy the services of underage slave girls in the Chinese parlor houses and cribs that flourished as a result of highly increased numbers of Chinese immigrants.

The increase in wealth and willingness to spend it on expensive clothes, amusements, wine and foods aided our restaurant business enormously. While newcomers sought to jump on the band wagon and cater to gourmands willing to order the most expensive wines and liqueurs, Chez Manon had the advantage of being established. The smiling face of its beautiful owner and hostess with the charming French accent, as well as its attractive food servers, only added to its desirability and exclusivity. We were booked solid a month in advance and Manon always kept a special table in reserve to accommodate a late arrival of note.

The sharp increase in the price of staples, especially sugar, flour and rice, after the two disastrous fires of 1851 was now abated for all but the Chinese who with marked increase in arrivals and dependence on a rice diet, could not keep up with demand for rice. Casual perusal of the shipping news revealed the arrival of almost twice the number of foreign vessels over the same period in 1851. As many brought immigrants from France, I was curious to know how many were associated with the now notorious Golden Ingot Lottery drawing held in Paris on November 16, 1851. There were reports that the new emperor, Louis Napoleon Bonaparte, used the subscription to enrich his friends and deport his enemies and the low life of Paris to our unwelcome shores. I invited Etienne Derbec to lunch to get his take on what had transpired. He now wrote his own small newspaper, *L'Echo du Pacifique*, which was published in the French section of the San Francisco *Picayune*. His savvy political contacts in France were the best I knew of.

Derbec readily accepted my luncheon invitation. He loved rich food and good wines and his publishing enterprise was not successful enough for him to afford to dine with the nouveau riche of our city. Manon ordered our apprentices to pan fry an abalone for our main course after starters and a lobster bisque soup. Once Derbec stuffed himself and ooohed and aahed over the delicious offerings, I poured him more wine and got down to business.

"Is it true that Emperor Bonaparte rigged the Lottery of the Golden Ingots to favor himself and his cronies?" I put the question directly.

"Of course," Derbec replied. "The coffers of state were empty. It was a clever plan to rid himself of his enemies—the socialists and republicans he'd wooed to become president of the republic as well as many of the riffraff and low life of Paris he could stuff into ships with the promise of riches and new opportunities in California while he enriched himself."

"Wasn't the lottery heralded as fully secure? I read that the drawing was held on a Sunday in the Circus in the Champs

Elysées with over 40,000 persons in attendance. They had young boys pull the numbered balls from wire cages. The platform and apparatus for the balls were inspected by numerous high government officials who deemed the drawing secure from fraud. With so many witnesses in attendance, how could it possibly be rigged?"

Derbec laughed and lit the cigar I offered him. "It was a cleverly conceived scheme. All was in order when the officials inspected the numbered balls in the wire cages. Having young boys draw the winning numbers and changing places each time the cage was spun was also canny. It was all for show. The crime already committed." Derbec paused to drain his wine glass and extend it for a refill.

"How so?" I asked

"Simple. The official who received the numbered ball plucked from the cage by the youth simply switched the ball drawn for the one he palmed in his hand. In one of the cages eight correctly numbered balls were placed plus two with the same number. Missing was the number common to all the thousand of false tickets the organizers had printed and sold."

"False tickets?" I gagged. "You mean they sold thousands of tickets to the poor who had no chance win even the smallest prize?"

Derbec smiled conspiratorially and nodded yes. "In some cases they sold tickets with the same fraudulent number hundreds of times over. All the money from these tickets went directly into the pockets of the new emperor's friends and supporters."

"The bastard!" I exclaimed. "Create and advertise the illusion of rags to riches, so they would risk not eating to buy a lottery ticket," I said furious at the duplicity of the scheme. "I suppose the main prize of the 400,000 franc bar of gold went to the emperor's cronies as well?"

"Of course, all the major prizes went to his friends. The scheme co-opted his enemies because they, too, hoped to win a gold bar or one of the 214 prizes. With the promise to raise money via the lottery to transport the poor to a new life in gold-rich California, how could his critics oppose something to benefit the poor and unemployed?"

"Did one have to buy a lottery ticket to be eligible for transport to California?"

"No, they had to sign up for the free passage. Many poor French were selected to come, but it was apparent with the departure of the first ship the first batch of lottery emigrants was a mixed bag. There are some poor families, but Louis Napoleon's secret police rounded up prostitutes, their pimps, trouble makers, political opponents and prisoners to fill the ships. He declared he would rule as emperor just three weeks after the drawing."

"You mean they are already arriving?" I asked surprised.

"Yes, that part of the scheme is working as planned. Except for some of the forced political émigrés and pimps, they're poor as church mice. Free passage did not include a stipend, living expenses or a grubstake to get to the mines. Most of them are still on the ship anchored in the bay awaiting help from the French Consulate."

Oh boy, I thought. Here we go again. Just as with the fraudulent mining societies, emigrants were arriving penniless and destitute. The pimps and prostitutes would do alright in the seedier bars and fandango parlors near the wharves on lower Broadway where womanless men and sailors prowled and paid for sexual services. There'd be more mail to process and little remuneration for it from either the consulate or the family of the impoverished arrivals. We had to prepare ourselves for the wave of crime that would come with the arrival of more criminals, malcontents and hooligans.

No doubt, the city officials would pass on the increased

expense of these new arrivals to the city's merchants. As the "Ingots," as they were called, were French, the burden of increased taxes would fall on merchants like us. We'd already suffered from corrupt city officials dining lavishly at our restaurant and refusing to pay the bill. "Just send tonight's bill to the city treasurer and they'll pay you. Our meeting here was city business." We'd heard this line more than once and were helpless to do anything about this extortion. Corrupt city officials deemed it their right to free meals and liqueurs from restaurants, the services of a parlor house courtesan from time to time and anything else their position of power could command. In exchange, they might do us a favor in the future, if it suited their interests down the line.

I let Derbec finish the wine and his cigar before excusing myself.

His news was so depressing, I opted to climb the stairs to play with our twins rather than return to work.

California Gold Rush Journal
⌘ PART 2 ⌘

CHAPTER THIRTY-FOUR
San Francisco — March-December, 1852

We were alarmed by the hefty property tax increase the city tax collector slipped under the restaurant door. In the few months since we'd bought the business, the city sought to double our property tax as well as our business license tax. Others, too, cried foul. The newspapers were full of letters from angry businessmen and merchants. One furious individual worked out that the average tax — direct and indirect— per 30,000 residents was $45.00 per person. Our tax increase was on top of the two-thirds assessment to replace the plank sidewalk and street in front of our restaurant.

City officials were scheming to buy the newly rebuilt Jenny Lind Theatre on the Plaza and convert it into a city hall to replace the one that burned in June of 1851. One newspaper under a banner headline "The Jenny Lind Swindle," pointed out that the city was currently paying $40,000 year in rent after the fire for the structure which was inadequate to house the city's offices and courts. Now they proposed to buy the theatre for $200,000 and strip it to its outer walls and redo the interior as offices and courtrooms for another $100,000. We were asked as merchant taxpayers to help pay for litigation to block the purchase and remodeling. We declined. We were sure the city would get what it wanted and their supporters on the California Supreme Court would rubber stamp the city's position if a trial court decision were appealed. The city did need a new city hall and we were sure those who opposed it openly would be retaliated against by special taxes or other legal means.

As predicted, crime did increase with the arrival of the "Ingots" from France. Most families and fortune seekers were helped to mining areas in the southern placers by the French Consulate. There they could join other French miners like Marie Suize. I recounted to Consul Dillon how Marie and her fellow Savoyards were so successful in their diggings near Mokelumne that they were hiring new arrivals at $6.00 day to work their concessions and claims. The criminal element that arrived on the lottery ships wasted no time settling into seedy areas formerly occupied by the Sydney Ducks and other miscreants. Fortunately for us, they preyed on new arrivals and sailors in the wharf areas at the bottom of Broadway and not near us.

Gino finally returned from his sojourn in Sonora. "How did it go with your suit of the fair Virginie?" I asked.

"Terrible. We like each other and had some fun together, but the price for having her was to marry her and settle in Sonora," he said crestfallen.

"Sounds like a decent proposition. Why'd you turn it down?" I said thinking of how I'd agreed to marry Manon when she made it the price to keep her. I hadn't hesitated even though she hadn't yet revealed she was pregnant when I committed.

"I'm not ready to settle down in a small mining town and start a family. I still don't know what I want to do for the future. I'm torn because I'm crazy about her. But I'm not ready for a sales job, kids and winter in a hick town," Gino said with downcast eyes.

I laughed. "Then it's for the best. Once the initial romance wears off, there needs to be more than just physical attraction to make a good marriage. Boatloads of new women are arriving monthly. You'll soon have lots of women to choose from and all the amusements San Francisco can offer in winter," I said to cheer him up. "Meanwhile there's plenty of work to do here. Manon needs you to wait tables until she can hire another food server."

"What about Nelly? I thought she and Giselle were serving the tables."

"They still are, but Nelly's going to open a new business with our new housekeeper, Monique Boudin. Now that the twins and Monique's boy are crawling and soon walking, they are outgrowing our apartment. We need to find a suitable house on a large lot where they can offer day care and an outside play area for the three kids and other children whose parents want them well cared for during the day and taught both English and French. With 5,000 more French on the way as a result of an emigration lottery in France, there'll be an immediate need for instruction and child care for mothers who need to work in the city."

"What about Rose, she was also serving food?"

"Rose and Joséphine have progressed to the point where they are accomplished cooks and are needed full-time in the kitchen. Manon plans to promote them to chef very soon and give each a chef's toque."

Gino looked shocked. "What about Henri? Won't he be furious?" Gino asked with concern.

"Manon will give Henri notice and two months wages. Since the apprentices have blossomed as cooks under Manon's tutelage, Henri has let them do all the cooking while he sips wine and waits to be called out by our guests for accolades. It's unfair to reward his laziness when the two women do all the work and deserve praise for it."

Gino looked stunned. "Won't there be repercussions to

sacking Henri? Won't he make trouble?"

"He may try, but won't get far when word gets out that he can't hold his own in the kitchen because he tipples while working. It'll be up to him. He can go quietly and have a recommendation for the work he's done, or he can make a fuss and ensure he's unemployable as a cook."

Gino shrugged as if to say "tough luck Henri." "So how long will I have to work in the restaurant?"

"Only until Manon hires and trains a new employee. Rose knows someone who may fit the bill, so it may happen quite soon."

"I hope so. My luck with serving women has got me down. I've had it with trying to hook a steady girlfriend. I'll just play the field until I know what I want to do. What's the new housekeeper like? Is she pretty?"

I laughed. "She's more than pretty. Monique's beautiful. Her raven-black hair, heart-shaped face and lavender-hued eyes could melt most men's hearts. But she's no good for you unless you want a serious woman and ready-made family. Like Manon, she's made her way here on her own toil and grit and plans to make something of herself."

"It figures," Gino mumbled to himself.

"What's the situation in Sonora? Were you able to deliver most of the letters?" I asked to change the subject back to our business. Gino tends to get maudlin when he mopes over his love life.

"Things went pretty well. You were right about miners frequenting favorite merchants, often where they could buy on credit or who had some connection to their home towns, and ignoring the others. By the time I made the rounds of all the merchants, I could check off almost all of the names on our list and leave letters to be picked up."

"Good. Were you able to connect with Buisson's mailman, Joseph?"

"Yes, he made it back from Volcano in a lull between storms.

He was very helpful in knowing which miners were in the various camps. He will visit your office when next in San Francisco."

I sent lovesick Gino off to inquire about house rentals listed with real estate brokers while I scanned classified ads for a suitable rental for our nursery school project. While I muttered over the paucity of available houses and horrendous prices of even modest bungalows unsuitable to our enterprise, the door to the restaurant opened with a bang and Nelly and Monique burst in flush-faced in their bonnets. Nelly exclaimed nearly out of breath, "We've found the perfect location!" Monique nodded her head vigorously in assent.

"Whoa, slow down and calm yourselves. Sit down so we can talk. Have you discussed your find with Manon?"

"No, not yet," Monique squeaked.

"Good, then go fetch her from upstairs so we can hear your good news together." Monique raced out the door and Nelly threw herself down into a chair, flung off her bonnet and poured herself a glass of water from the carafe on the table. Manon and Monique rushed into the restaurant before Nelly finished her glass.

"So, what's this exciting news that can't wait a second longer?" Manon said in a voice full of curiosity. Nelly pointed to Monique to reply as she gagged on her water.

"We rented a cab with Georges and made a tour of the city checking out houses for sale and their locations. It became clear right away that downtown locations were both too expensive and impractical."

"How so, impractical?" Manon queried.

"Too difficult for parents to drop off and pick up their kids with carts rumbling by all day and tradesmen hawking their wares. Also, it's too noisy and distracting in the center of town. We realized we should seek a quiet environment to teach languages, and where kids can play and nap when needed."

"So, what did you find?" I asked impatiently.

"We found the perfect location at the top of California Street," Monique asserted firmly.

"The top of California Street is still mostly sand dunes and very steep," I countered.

"Yes, but it's the perfect location for us. Lots for sale there are large and it's the area where the successful merchants and miners are building their mansions. They'll be the ones able to pay our fees to send their kids to our bilingual nursery school," Monique said excitedly while Nelly's head bobbed her assent.

"You said lots," Manon queried. "Are you suggesting we buy a lot and build from scratch?"

"Yes, actually, we should buy two lots so we can expand when needed. Nelly and I envision both a nursery school to start and grammar school when the first batch of kids is ready for formal education. We start small and expand as needed. The key is to secure enough land in the right location while it's available and affordable. Once the streets nearby are full of mansions, prices will soar. There are no suitable buildings to house our nursery in any case. Even if we bought an existing building elsewhere, we'd have to remodel extensively. We don't need a school with two levels as most houses are built; we should build at one level only so little kids aren't going up and down stairs where they can fall. Building a structure suitable to our needs will be cheaper in the long run and we expand only when needed. It will be so convenient for mothers to drop off their children in a residential area close to their homes and far away from the dangerous downtown areas," Monique argued passionately.

Manon gave me that look with raised eyebrows that signaled she was impressed with Monique's thought provoking plan. It would be my job to negotiate the deal. It made a lot of sense to start slow and buy the land. The initial capital outlay would be affordable. If the project didn't work out, the lots would increase in value and be a good investment and we would be able to resell at a profit. Manon complimented Monique and Nelly on their diligent research and promised Gino and I would get to work on it.

I had to admit the notion of starting an exclusive private school would dovetail with our restaurant interests. We'd be proprietors of two exclusive enterprises which both catered to the upper crust of society. We'd gain new clients for both enterprises and they'd have the means to pay for school services not available anywhere else. We'd be part of an expanding, booming economy.

The latter half of 1852 brought unexpected benefits and more potentially disastrous events. The City once again suffered a near disastrous fire in early November. It started on the corner of Merchant and Kearny Streets and destroyed 32 wood buildings including the Union Hotel. The brick and metal buildings weathered the fire and as a result, two insurance companies agreed to provide fire insurance for the more fire resistant structures. The issue of insurance posed a problem for us. It would be cheaper and more interesting to build the nursery school using seasoned redwood from the Mendocino coast than using bricks and steel. With redwood, we'd be without fire insurance, which was expensive, but almost all fires to date occurred in the congested business and commercial districts.

The months of November and December brought a number of terrible disasters to the state. Lake Merced in San Francisco dropped 30 feet as a result of an earthquake which opened a channel to the sea where it drained. A furious December gale accompanied by excessive rains destroyed many low lying wooden houses, ships at anchor and wooden wharves in the city and broke a levee protecting the low lying commercial and business district of Sacramento, which already been hit by a great fire in November that destroyed 55 square blocks of the town, and displaced over 7,000 people. All of Sacramento was inundated and most provisions for the city and destined to supply the southern mining districts perished. As a result, prices of basic foods and commodities jumped to outrageous levels and threatened hunger and disease to miners holed up for the winter in their mining camps.

We were blessed to suffer no losses from these disasters and contributed to the relief effort for Sacramento. As with previous fires and losses, the criminal element became bolder and the profiteers gouged their clients. One bit of good news was the establishment of telegraph service between the major cities and towns in California.

In light of the terrible gale on December 17th, we decided to celebrate our good fortune by closing our restaurant Christmas Eve and Christmas Day and do dinner for us and our staff. It was quite a change to see the restaurant taken over by three crawling babies, soon to be toddlers. Manon had commandeered several abalones and local lobsters which Rose and Joséphine cooked to perfection. They were tickled pink to be out from under the thumb of Henri, who'd opted to take 60 days severance pay and a Christmas bonus rather than raise a ruckus. He probably thought he'd be a prize catch at one of our competitors' restaurants.

Rose's brother, Jacques, had agreed to stay in San Francisco and help with the planning and groundbreaking for our new nursery school instead of heading to Sacramento where distressed merchants were paying bonuses to skilled carpenters and other builders in an effort to get businesses up and running before Spring after the double blow of fires and floods. Jacques put us in touch with an architect and now we had drawings and blueprints for the building project.

We were all excited at our prospects for 1853. Rose and

Joséphine had earned their toques and along with Manon were planning to go head-to-head with the competition for the recognition as the best French restaurant in the city. Nelly and Monique couldn't get their new school up and running fast enough. Nelly was especially excited as she was pregnant and would add another babe to the enrolling class. She was busy working on lesson plans for the school.

Teri and Giselle looked forward to the New Year as well. Business was booming on the wharf and their nest eggs were growing. At the end of their three year commitment, they'd have enough money to start their own business if they chose.

Gino had begged out of joining us with the excuse he had to help his uncle and cousin in Little Italy. We knew he couldn't face celebrating with us with Jacques Boucher and Teri present after Jacques had replaced him in Teri's affections. Georges was excited to be a papa and that his marriage was a happy one. He loved being our barman.

Manon and I, too, were excited by our prospects for the coming year. Manon had her restaurant and was her own boss. I was receiving correspondence from France with lots of requests for help finding missing relatives and my contacts from my trip to the mines were bearing fruit for my role as notary and detective. Our twins were growing out of their clothes faster than we could buy them. They were robust and a continual source of fun and amusement. They were the future of this city and we wanted to make it a safe and exciting place to grow up.

1853 was just around the corner and we all looked forward to engaging the challenges that lay ahead.

End of Part Two
of Pierre Dubois' Journal

December 31, 1852

California Gold Rush Journal
∽ PART 2 ∾

AUTHOR'S NOTE

T he decision to follow the trials and tribulations of the characters introduced in the first volume of this trilogy from 1851 through 1856 was prompted by the positive response from so many readers of the first volume. I have also responded to their questions at length in the questions for book club discussion and the companion interview which follow this short note.

While most of the characters in this second volume of the trilogy are completely fictional, all the characters we meet in Sonora, California are based on actual French merchants and persons residing in Sonora in 1851. I am indebted to Mary Grace Paquette and her diligent research published by The Tuolumne County Historical Society in Sonora, California entitled *Then Came The French — The History of the French in Tuolumne County California.* She provided much of the detail for Pierre Dubois' contacts, persons and meetings in the chapters set in Sonora.

As with the first volume, my French translator, Suzanne Maseo has assisted me greatly with her suggestions for notable

French characters like Marie Suize (aka Marie Pantalon) to be included. Her lively and entertaining translation of this second volume will appear later. I am also indebted to Joe Miller for his careful reading and critique of the last draft.

California Gold Rush Journal
∽ PART 2 ∽

BIBLIOGRAPHY

Allende, Isabel, *Daughter of Fortune*, Harper Collins, 1999.

Ashbury, Herbert, *The Barbary Coast*, Alfred A. Knopf, Inc, 1933.

Bancroft, H.H., *History of California*, Vols. 1-7, San Francisco, The History Co., 1884-1890.

Barrett, Samuel A, and Gifford, Edward, W., *Indian Life of Yosemite Region-Miwok Material Culture*, Yosemite Association, Yosemite National Park, California, 1933

Beilharz, Edwin A. and Lopez, Carlos, U., *We Were 49ers — Chilean Accounts of the California Gold Rush*, Ward Ritchie Press, 1976.

Borthwick, J.D., *Three Years in California, 1857*. Reprint, Oakland, CA, Biobooks, 1948.

Brock, Leo, *To Harness The Wind*, Naval Institute Press, Annapolis, MD, 2003.

Butruille, Susan. G., *Women's Voices From The Mother Lode*, Tamarack Books, Inc., 1996.

Calhoon, F. D., *Coolies, Kanakas and Cousin Jacks*, Cal-Con Publishers, Sacramento, Ca, 1986.

Clappe, Louise, *The Shirley Letters from the California Mines 1851-1852*, New York, Alfred A. Knopf, 1949.

Clark, Arthur, H., *The Clipper Ship Era*, G.P. Putnam's Sons, New York & London, 1910.

Coburn, Jesse, L., *Letters of Gold-California Postal History Through 1869*, The U.S. Philatelic Classics Society, Inc. and The Philatelic Foundation, Inc., 1984.

Dana, R. H., Jr, *Two Years Before The Mast*, P. F. Collier & Son, New York, 1909.

De Russailh, Alfred Bernard, *Journal de Voyage Californie — 1850-52*, Aubier Montagne, Paris, 1980.

Dumas, Alexandre, *Le Grand Dictionnaire de cuisine — 1*, Gibiers & Volailles, Edit-France, 1994.

Fohlen, Claude, *La Vie Quotidienne Au Far West (1860-1870)*, Librairie Hachette, 1974.

Foucrier, Annick, *Le Reve Californien. Migrants Francais sur Ia cote du Pacifique (XVIII-XIX siecles)*, Belin, Paris, 1999.

Guming, Deanna Paoli, *The Italians of San Francisco — 1850-1930*, Center For Migration Studies (in English and Italian), New York, 1978.

Holliday, J. S., *Rush For Riches — Gold Fever and the Making of California*, Oakland Museum of California & University of California Press, 1999.

Heizer, Robert F. & Almquist, Alan F., *The Other Californians — Prejudice and Discrimination under Spain, Mexico and the United States to 1920*, University of California Press, 1971.

Kemble, Edward, C., *A History of California Newspapers — 1846-1858*, Edited by Helen Harding Bretnor, The Talisman Press, 1962.

La Reyniere, 100 *Merveilles de Ia Cuisine Francaise*, Seuil, 1975.

Le Bris, Michel, *Quand la Californie était française*, Éditions Le Pré aux clercs, 1999.

Lydon, Sandy, *Chinese Gold — The Chinese in the Monterey Bay*

Region, The Capitola Book Company, Capitola, California, 1985.

Marryat, Frank, *Mountains and Molehills*, Longman, Brown, Green and Longman, London, 1855.

McMullen, Jerry, *Paddle Wheel Days in California*, Palo Alto, Stanford University Press, 1944.

Monaghan, Jay, *Chile, Peru and the California Gold Rush of 1849*, Berkeley, University of California Press, 1973.

Nasatir, A.P., *A French Journalist in the California Gold Rush — The Letters of Etienne Derbec*, The Talisman Press, 1964.

Nasatir, A. P., *French Activities in California*, Stanford University Press, 1945.

Paquette, Mary Grace, *Then Came The French — The History of the French in Tuolumne County California*, Tuolumne County Historical Society, 1996.

Paul, Rodman Wilson, *Mining Frontiers of the Far West, 1848-1880*, Holt, Rinehart & Winston, 1963.

Pryor, Alton, *Those Wild & Lusty Gold Camps*, Stagecoach Publishing, 2006.

Soule, Frank, John H. Gihon and Albert Nisbet, *The Annals of San Francisco*, New York, D. Appelton & Co., 1855.

Stewart, George, R., *Committee of Vigilance — Revolution in San Francisco, 1851*, Ballantine Books, Inc, 1971.

Weston, Otheto, *Mother Lode Album*, Stanford University Press, 1948.

Windler, Adolphus, *The California Gold Rush Diary of a German Sailor*, Edited by W. T. Jackson, Howell North Books, 1969.

White, Stewart Edward, *The Story of California*, Halcyon House, 1940.

ABOUT THE AUTHOR

KEN SALTER is a professor emeritus in Communication Studies at San Jose State University, San Jose, CA, where he taught critical thinking and persuasive writing and directed pre-legal studies. He is also an international attorney specialized in international real estate and mining. He directed a placer gold mining company for 15 years based in Mexico and Chile. He is author of several books about famous legal trials, including the *Trial of Dan White*, who killed San Francisco Supervisor Harvey Milk and Mayor George Moscone. He and his French wife live in Berkeley, CA and in the Auvergne, France. See his web site at: www.salterken.com.

California Gold Rush Journal
◌❡ PART 2 ❡◌

READER'S GROUP GUIDE

After the disastrous fires of May 3-4 and June 22, 1851 destroyed both the commercial center of San Francisco and much of China Town, City Hall, the courts, and Sydney Town, the lair of the Sydney Ducks, the business and professional community looked to the Committee of Vigilance to restore order, arrest and punish the arsonists and their criminal associates preying on the merchant and business community.

TOPICS AND QUESTIONS FOR DISCUSSIONS

1. Were San Franciscans "justified" in resorting to vigilante justice in the belief the civil and law enforcement authorities were corrupt and ineffectual?
2. What factors, if any, justify the Committee of Vigilance to hang "English Jim?"
3. Once Whittaker and McKenzie are "rescued" by the authorities, is there justification for the Committee of Vigilance to storm the jail and seize the prisoners in the Sheriff's custody? First from the ship transporting them

to Sheriff Hayes? Then, from the assault on the jail and hanging them before the civil authorities could demand them back?

4. Whose actions risked the possibility of "civil war" in San Francisco more — the governor, sheriff, police or the Committee of Vigilance?

S. Is Manon justified to hire two women apprentice cooks with the intent to teach them become chefs in order to replace Henri Royat? Were two months wages and a Christmas bonus adequate compensation for sacking Royat?

6. How does Manon seek to empower women? Discuss the following women:
    a. Teri Rios
    b. Giselle Gaillard
    c. Rose Boucher
    d. Joséphine Arras
    e. Monique Boudin

7. Was Manon justified in inviting the famous Chinese courtesan, Ah Toy, to her restaurant's grand opening knowing it would prove embarrassing to several male invitees?

8. Is Pierre Dubois' scheme to solicit 5 francs (worth $1.00) from relatives of French miners in California ethical? Should Sophie Benson aid him in this endeavor?

9. Are Pierre Dubois and Attorney Hawthorne justified in manipulating the civil trial of Raoul Mendosa in favor of Teri Rios? In seizing his best wines? In attempting to enlist Judge Roberts in a scheme to seize Mendosa's wine store?

10. Most European, Latin American countries and States in the USA including California had laws penalizing women who wore men's trousers or impersonated men. Was Marie Suize, aka, "Marie Pantalon" justified in dressing in a miner's costume and openly carrying a Colt six shooter and Bowie knife in her belt?

11. Were the miners in the Sonora area justified in occupying the Digger Indians' traditional hunting and fishing grounds after the Mariposa Indian War of 1850?

12. Evaluate the claim by Yankee and English speaking immigrant miners that they had a better right than non-English speaking miners to claim and exploit the richest gold bearing claims because the foreign miners planned to make their fortune and return with it to their homeland.

13. Was the $20.00 month miner's tax on foreign miners discriminatory or justified?

14. Was the treatment of Digger Indians and the Chinese overtly discriminatory and unjustified?

15. Evaluate Louis Napoleon's scheme to use the Lottery of the Golden Ingots to send 5,000 indigent French to California.

16. What should the civil authorities in San Francisco have done, if anything, with the following groups of "Ingots" arrivals: Deport them? Arrest them? Reform them? Leave them alone?

     a. Political dissidents including republicans, socialists, communists and anarchists?
     b. Convicted criminals?
     c. Prostitutes and pimps?
     d. Jezebels and con-artists?

17. With the ratio of single men to women still approximately 100-1 in 1851, was the California legislature justified in granting women immigrants the right to inherit directly, control their earnings and own businesses without supervision or control by their husband or father contrary to the norm in Europe and the rest of the United States?

     a. Was this policy calculated to appeal to "gold diggers?" The "sale" of eligible daughters?
     b. Was the policy successful even if women still had no right to vote in the 19th Century?

California Gold Rush Journal
∞ PART 2 ∞

AN INTERVIEW WITH KEN SALTER

Q: *Why did you choose to tell the history of the California Gold Rush through the experiences of French immigrants instead of Americans?*

A: There were many factors and considerations. French women were among the earliest to arrive and compared to Chilean and Chinese women, French women were considered "chic" and more desirable even if they had been lowly "street walkers" in Paris. Paris was the capital of world fashion and dictated what women must wear to be fashionable. Owners of the major gambling palaces were quick to appreciate the attraction of French women — their seductive dress and charming accents. By employing them as baristas, musicians, and hostesses to attract lonely miners to the gambling tables, the gambling palaces were guaranteed a roaring business. Also, French food, wine and liqueurs, like French couture and fashion, were considered the best in the world in this epoch. And lastly, as the majority of French and other Latin language speakers didn't speak much English, they were considered "outsiders" by the English speaking miners. This led to inevitable clashes between these groups over rights to mine. By following the saga of French immigrants, one can explore and highlight the social and cultural differences between the various groups as well as their attitudes and biases.

Q: *What prompted you to choose French protagonists rather than Italians, Spanish or South Americans or other European groups?*

A: Well, I studied French and Spanish in high school and was awarded a scholarship as the top foreign language student on graduation. I continued to study French language and literature at U.C. Berkeley and never lost my fluency as I continued to read French literature even after graduation from law school at Berkeley and embarking on a dual career as college professor and international lawyer. It's prophetic that my high school French teacher from Strasbourg predicted one day I would have a deep connection with the French and probably live and work in France; these were her final words to me just before she returned to France after retirement. Lo and behold, I met my talented French wife in France and we have always lived together in both California and France.

Q: *What piqued your interest in the California Gold Rush?*

A: A friend took me bottle digging in an 1850's trash dump in the Bay Area and one of the first of many major finds was a small pharmacy bottle and rouge or unguent pot embossed with the name "Druggists / San Francisco / B. Lefevre & Companie." I realized as I examined the porcelain pot with the tantalizing black transfer label that I had found a real and exciting piece of California history. I was determined to learn more of the origins of the artifact collection I was assembling. Together with my wife, we researched the French presence and collected the maps, books, letters, bottles, artifacts and ephemera that documented their lives during the Gold Rush.

Q: *Was there one special bottle or artifact that determined you to write your trilogy on the Gold Rush?*

A: It was really cumulative. We amassed such a large collection over many years that we determined to donate it for posterity to a French museum dedicated to portraying the history of the French in the New World. We gave our collection to Le Musée du Nouveau Monde in La Rochelle, France as they had fabulous artifacts documenting French Canada, the spice islands of Guadeloupe and Martinique and the trappers and slave traders of the 18th C., but few items on the French in California. Our donation is on permanent display in the museum including the one bottle that did spike considerable interest and intrigue. Among the hundreds of champagne bottles I've dug over the years, there was only one with an applied seal. It came out of an 1852 dump of mostly French material near the shoreline. The seal applied to the bottle was an embossed royal coat of arms. After much research, I was able to determine the coat of arms was none other than that of King Louis Philippe of France who was deposed in the riots of 1848. I reasoned that the champagne bottle was probably from the stock in the French consulate in Monterey or San Francisco. Was it drunk to celebrate or mourn the overthrow of the King?

Q: *Why write historical fiction instead of a history of the French in the California Gold Rush?*

A: To be honest, I've read so many history books and narratives full of wonderful historical accounts, but most often written in dry, professorial prose that turns off all but the most ardent fans of the period. By telling the historical story through fictional characters using dialogue, I believe an author can bring the history to life in a more interesting way and appeal to and interest a much broader audience to this exciting period.

Q: *That brings me to my final questions. How did you arrive at the characters of Pierre Dubois and Manon Rousseau? Were they based on actual persons during the Gold Rush?*

A: No, they are really composites of various personalities I have observed.

Q: *It seems that in Part II, Manon plays a more significant role than in Part I. Is that intentional?*

A: Yes, and that is due in large part to reader interest and feedback. While male readers seemed fascinated with Manon's sexy looks, spunkiness and cooking abilities, women readers responded more favorably to her, as well as Teri and Giselle's, quest for independence and demand to be treated as equals with males in a male-dominated environment. California's novel legislation granting women property rights to tempt them to marry and settle in California offers a unique opportunity to tell an important but little known consequence of the California Gold Rush.

Q: *Will you continue to develop this theme in Part III?*

A: That will depend on the feedback to Part II. I can tell you, however, you'll meet some of San Francisco's most interesting and famous visitors and settlers who left their mark on the City and State. We'll meet the notorious Lola Montez, who charmed princes, became the mistress of the King of Bavaria and wowed audiences with her famous "Spider Dance." We'll also make the acquaintance of Mammy Pleasance — the famous African-American cook and abolitionist; M. Boudin, the French baker who invented San Francisco's famous sour dough French bread; M. Ghiardelli, the Italian chocolate maker; Levi Strauss, the Bavarian tailor who invented jeans, the staple of the miners' costume which endures to this day, as well as a host of other memorable characters — some savory and some not.

www.ingramcontent.com/pod-product-compliance
Lightning Source LLC
Chambersburg PA
CBHW031947130726
47904CB00012B/289